Sourcebooks, Inc.

All rights reserved. No part of this book may be reproduced in any
form or by any electronic or mechanical means including
information storage and retrieval systems—except in the case of
brief quotations embodied in critical articles or reviews—without
permission in writing from its publisher, Sourcebooks, Inc.

The characters and events portrayed in this book are fictitious or
are used fictitiously. Any similarity to real persons, living or dead, is
purely coincidental and not intended by the author.

Published by Sourcebooks Casablanca, an imprint of Sourcebooks, Inc.
P.O. Box 4410, Naperville, Illinois 60567-4410
(630) 961-3900
Fax: (630) 961-2168
www.sourcebooks.com

First Season copyright © 1983 by Jane LeCompte
Bride to Be copyright © 1999 by Jane LeCompte
Cover and internal design © 2015 by Sourcebooks, Inc.
Cover art by Paul Stinson

Sourcebooks and the colophon are registered trademarks of Sourcebooks, Inc.

All rights reserved. No part of this book may be reproduced in any form or by any electronic or mechanical means including information storage and retrieval systems—except in the case of brief quotations embodied in critical articles or reviews—without permission in writing from its publisher, Sourcebooks, Inc.

The characters and events portrayed in this book are fictitious or are used fictitiously. Any similarity to real persons, living or dead, is purely coincidental and not intended by the author.

Published by Sourcebooks Casablanca, an imprint of Sourcebooks, Inc.
P.O. Box 4410, Naperville, Illinois 60567-4410
(630) 961-3900
Fax: (630) 961-2168
www.sourcebooks.com

First Season originally published in 1984 by Signet, a division of The New American Library, Inc., New York.

Bride to Be originally published in 1999 by Bantam Books, a division of Random House, Inc., New York.

Printed and bound in the United States of America.
RRD 10 9 8 7 6 5 4 3 2

Contents

First Season

Finch, Fenton

One

"WELL, I DON'T LIKE IT HERE," SAID NICHOLAS Wyndham, looking around the elegantly furnished blue drawing room with a jaundiced eye. There was nothing obviously offensive in the delicately molded white ceiling, the thick Turkey carpet, or the fashionable French tables and sofas, but his brother, Sir William, the elder by a year, seemed to concur. He grimaced sympathetically and shrugged. "We must do something!"

"But, Nicky, what could we possibly do?" William's deep blue eyes widened.

Nicholas sighed. He and his brother looked much alike, resembling their mother in soft brown hair, pale coloring, and fine bone structure. And William was a splendid fellow for a tramp through the woods or a wild gallop, neck or nothing, behind the local hounds. But Nicky often felt that their father's heir lacked some quality that he himself possessed in abundance. "Scores of things!" he retorted, drumming his slender fingers on his knee and considering.

Sir William Wyndham, very conscious of his responsibility as head of the family, sat straighter in the blue velvet armchair and shook his head. "Now, Nicky, don't begin one of your high flights."

His brother snorted. "You've been pleased enough with some of them. What about Mr. Winston?"

William grinned. Mr. Winston, a late and unlamented tutor in the Wyndham household, had left it precipitously. "That was Susan, not you."

"It was my idea to set her on him."

"Yes, but…"

"Well, I admit that Susan is enough for anyone."

As the brothers pondered this truism, in perfect agreement, the subject of it came hurtling through the double doors that led to the hall, leaving them standing open behind her. "Here you are!" She stood, hands on hips, green eyes smoldering. "I suppose you thought I shouldn't find you here?"

They eyed her warily. Susan Wyndham, the youngest of the family, had inherited a mass of flaming red hair from her paternal forebears and an irresistible temper from sources unknown. Her brothers had long since learned to respect her opinions. "We thought you were busy upstairs," ventured Nick.

"You didn't! How could I be, in this beastly place? I hate it here." Coming farther into the room, she subsided into the armchair opposite William with a flurry of white muslin skirts.

"All of us do," agreed William, putting his chin in his hand.

"Well, we should go back home, then," replied his sister. "Let us speak to Mama at once." She made as if to rise.

William laughed shortly, and Nicholas said, "Mama is out. And, besides, she likes it. I heard her say so."

Susan's auburn brows came together, and her full lower lip began to protrude. Both brothers braced themselves. But before she could gather voice for an initial blast, there was a soft sound from the doorway and then a scraping noise from behind the sofa where Nicholas sat. "Daisy?" wondered Susan.

"Oh no." William sprang up and shut the doors. "Is he scratching the table? Nicky, look and see."

Reluctantly, Nicholas peered over the sofa back, directly into the yellow eyes of an immense ginger tomcat, who had sunk his front claws into the scrolled leg of a Louis Seize table. Holding the boy's gaze, the cat bent slowly forward and fastened his teeth on the same object. Nicholas shuddered and drew back. "Yes."

"Get him!" William ran around the sofa.

"Daisy!" shrieked Susan, leaping to the rescue. The cat streaked under the couch, coming out directly under Nicky's feet and causing him to jerk them up convulsively.

"Come on," shouted William. "We'll corner him."

His brother swallowed and rose, squaring his shoulders. "I'm coming." He moved forward like a soldier going into battle.

"No," cried Susan. She ran over and scooped the animal into her arms, his oversized body drooping on all sides. "Leave her alone!"

William sighed again. "Him, Susan. I keep telling you. I can't understand why you had to drag that horrid creature off the streets. You might have had a kitten of your own if you'd asked, and not some wretched alley cat."

"She was starving," replied Susan with finality, caressing Daisy's flat head. The cat purred but continued to stare at the Wyndham brothers with malicious glee.

William gazed at the gigantic animal skeptically, but merely shrugged. Nicholas shuddered again and turned away.

"Daisy can help us," added Susan, lugging him back to the armchair and settling him across her lap.

"Help us what?" asked William.

"Get home again." Susan's dimples showed. "Cook doesn't like her."

"None of the servants do," agreed Nick, in a tone that suggested he was wholeheartedly of their opinion.

"Yes." Susan smiled again.

"That don't signify." William was superior. "They'll simply get rid of the cat. They wouldn't…"

His sister's green eyes flashed, and she drew herself up. "I should like to see them try!"

"Yes, but, Susan—"

"This isn't getting us anywhere," interrupted Nick. "We have to decide what we're going to do. I can't bear it much longer." He glanced at Daisy.

"Nor I," agreed Susan. "London is the dreariest place I've ever been."

"Well, I can't see what we…" began William, but at that moment the drawing-room doors opened again to reveal two ladies in modish evening dress.

"Whatever am I to do with her, Anabel?" the elder was saying. "She…" They saw the Wyndhams.

"What are you doing downstairs at this hour?" exclaimed the other woman. "Why aren't you getting into bed?"

"We were just talking, Mama," replied Sir William Wyndham, full of the maturity of his ten years. "I was about to take the children up."

His brother's lip curled.

"I don't want to go to bed," protested Susan, six. "Nor does Daisy." She held up the cat's head so that her mother and grandmother could see it over the chair arm. "*She's* not the least sleepy."

Both women looked pained. "I daresay not," answered Lady Anabel Wyndham. "But you must go up." She sent a footman in the hall to fetch Nurse, who arrived a few moments later in a confusion of starched white and protests that she had been searching for the children throughout the upper floors. "That is no doubt why they came down here," responded their mother, shepherding the three toward the stairs.

"Will you come up and say good night?" begged nine-year-old Nicholas.

"In a little while, if you get into bed."

Susan grimaced, but they went.

"Really, Anabel," said Lady Sybil Goring when they had the drawing room to themselves. "Shouldn't the boys be in school? They aren't a very good influence on Susan, apparently."

Anabel laughed. "I assure you it is quite the other way about, Mother. But you're right, they should go. I have been trying to bring myself to send them for a year." She shook her head.

"I'm sure they've been a great comfort. But, Anabel, it has been three years since Ralph died."

"I know." She looked down again and sighed. "It doesn't seem so long."

Her mother watched her with pity and some impatience. She had married Anabel off very young to a most eligible baronet, and she had thought her well and happily settled until the untimely death of Sir Ralph Wyndham three years before. At that tragedy, she had understood and respected her daughter's grief, allowing her every indulgence in her power and taking care not to manage her life, as she had been greatly tempted to do. Lady Goring's powerful common sense quite often led her to intervene in her friends' and family's decisions. But now she thought it was time Anabel shook off her despondence and began again. She was, after all, not yet thirty, and she did not look the least like the mother of three growing children. Indeed, with her soft brown ringlets, large, expressive blue eyes, and delicately made frame, Anabel could have passed for a girl of twenty. Only her mother knew that her fragility was deceptive: Anabel might look as if a strong wind would carry her away, but she had great reserves of strength.

Accordingly, Sybil had swept her daughter up to London for the season, over her protests, and she was determined that its gaieties should dispel the last clouds of bereavement. Her only concern was the children, whom Anabel had insisted upon bringing. They seemed out of spirits in town, and their unhappiness was the one thing that might spur Anabel to open rebellion. "I was wrong to let your father convince me to marry you without a come-out," she murmured. She did not realize that she had spoken aloud until Anabel looked up, smiled, and shook her head.

"I didn't mind, Mama."

"That is because you knew no better. You had no taste of town life, and you still have not. You don't know what you missed."

"I know what I gained." Anabel smiled reminiscently.

Her mother ignored her. "But we shall make up for that now. You shall go to all the balls and entertainments just as if it were your debut, only you will enjoy them a great deal more because you have the freedom of a married woman." As soon as she said this, she wished she hadn't, but Anabel merely shook her head again.

"I am too old for a debut."

"Wait until you have gone about a bit before you decide."

"This ball tonight…"

"Oh, it is not a ball. A trial before the season really begins, nothing more. You must not go by it."

"Mama." Anabel smiled. "Content yourself with managing Georgina. I shall stay in the background."

"Nonsense," snapped Lady Goring, but this brought back her earlier grievance. "Anabel, what am I to do about Georgina? I'm sure when I told your uncle that I would bring her out I was happy to help. He hasn't been up from the country since Clara died, fifteen years ago. But now that I have seen her…" She made a helpless gesture.

"What precisely is wrong with her?" asked Anabel, who had not yet met her much younger cousin. "She arrived this afternoon?"

"While you were shopping."

"Is she coming down to dinner?"

"I suppose so. I mean, I should count on it." She laughed bitterly.

"Mama..."

A footman opened the double doors to admit a girl of seventeen or eighteen to the drawing room, and Anabel saw at once what her mother had meant. Georgina Goring possessed an altogether too ample abundance of flesh. Her frame went well beyond youthful plumpness, and as if to call attention to the unfortunate flaw in her appearance, she entered eating a large cream-filled chocolate.

"Georgina, dear," murmured Lady Goring in a faint voice.

"Hullo," replied Georgina around the candy. "Is it dinnertime?"

Anabel bit her lower lip.

"Nearly, dear. This is your cousin Anabel. My daughter, you know."

"Hullo," said Georgina again. "Are you coming out this season too?"

Her smile broadened. "In a manner of speaking."

Georgina nodded. "You will do better than I. It is all so stupid. I don't see why I need bother." She took a twist of silver paper from the pocket of her pink muslin gown, extracted another chocolate, and ate it.

Lady Goring made a stifled noise. "You won't care for any dinner, will you, Georgina, if you keep eating sweets."

"Oh, yes, I shall."

Anabel looked from one to the other. Perhaps this visit to town would be more amusing than she had expected. When her mother had first insisted that she come to London, she had refused. For three years her life had revolved around her children, and before that she had become accustomed to living in the country. She had neighbors to rely on for company and aid, and she knew her family loved the outdoors. But her mother had overborne her objections, holding out the lures of excitement and change. Anabel had been tempted, she knew, and she had also realized that her children needed her less and less with each passing year. The boys should go to school, and Susan was nothing if not independent. She had consented half reluctantly, but now her lively sense of the absurd was aroused by the contest of wills she saw shaping before her, and she felt the first stirrings of gratitude. She had been feeling a bit old and weary lately. Perhaps her mother was right.

She glanced from the older woman to Georgina again. She knew her mother's strength of purpose only too well, but something in Georgina's expression suggested that Lady Goring might have met her match. The girl seemed both stubborn and not particularly concerned with Lady Goring's opinion. Surveying her, Anabel realized that she was not really unattractive. Though undoubtedly fleshy, she had fine pale blond hair and gray eyes with thick dark lashes. Her hands were lovely. Turning, Anabel met her mother's gaze, and her lips twitched. It was compounded of chagrin and a dawning fanatical determination.

"Dinner is served, madam," said the butler from the doorway. Georgina followed him eagerly into the hall.

"You see?" said Lady Goring in a low voice.

"She is a little plump. From the way you were talking, I expected a hunchback at least."

"A *little*? Anabel!"

"Well, Mama…"

"You may think it a good joke, but I have promised to bring the girl out and find her a husband, if possible, of course. Her fortune is only moderate; I had hoped she would be pretty. If only the current fashions were more flattering to…but these waists, and no lacing at all." She shook her head. "Chocolates! How can she?"

Anabel started toward the door. Georgina would be wondering what had become of them.

Her mother's chin came up as she turned to follow. "I have two weeks before the season officially begins," she finished. "I'm sure a great deal can be accomplished in that time. She must come with us tonight, but it is a mere hop. Hardly anyone will be there."

"Perhaps we needn't go, then," replied Anabel mischievously as they walked down the corridor.

"Anabel! Don't you begin now, or I shall certainly go distracted."

"You, Mama?"

"Indeed I shall. If anyone had told me that I should sponsor the first seasons of a thirty-year-old woman and an absolutely…massive schoolgirl, I should unhesitatingly have pronounced them mad."

Anabel began to laugh. "Not *quite* thirty, Mama."

"How can you be so unfeeling?" Lady Goring met her daughter's dancing eyes and started to smile. Linking arms with her, she strode into the dining room, where Georgina was already seated and looking impatient. "Amuse yourself while you may," she concluded. "I shall triumph in the end—wait and see."

Two

It was fortunate, thought Anabel as the three of them descended from the carriage at the front door of the Rivingtons' festively lit town house, that this ball was not one of the great events of the season. Neither Georgina nor Lady Goring was in the best of tempers after wrangling throughout dinner over what the girl should or should not eat. Indeed, Anabel herself had started to feel the strain of the contest of wills before she thought to remind her mother of the time. Georgina had not spoken once during the short journey, and Lady Goring's comments, though general, had retained an acerbic tone. Anabel was very glad to give her wrap to a footman and climb the stairs to greet her hostess. She would avoid her family until the entertainment put them in better frame, she decided.

The ballroom was more crowded than she had expected, and the hum of talk and glitter of evening dress abruptly reminded Anabel that she loved parties. She had scarcely attended one since her husband died, at first because she was in mourning and then because she had somehow gotten out of the habit. Now she felt a rising excitement. London parties must be quite different from the dinners and small assemblies of the country. She had told her mother that she hadn't minded missing her long-ago debut, but she remembered now that this wasn't entirely true. She had pined a little for the balls and routs and Venetian breakfasts until she became so contented with Ralph and the children.

"Lady Wyndham," said a voice behind her. "I didn't know you were in town."

Anabel turned and greeted a woman she had met some time ago at a house party. "Mrs. Brandon, how pleasant to see you again." She would have an easier time now than she would have had at eighteen, she realized. There were one or two familiar faces in the room.

When they had exchanged commonplace news, Mrs. Brandon added, "You must come and meet my daughter. It is her first appearance in society, and she is naturally a bit uneasy. She will be so happy to see an acquaintance."

Glancing around, Anabel saw that her mother and Georgina were lingering near the door, the former scanning the crowd and the latter looking remarkably sulky. "I should be delighted," she replied, and allowed herself to be led to the other side of the broad chamber.

It was evident at once that Julia Brandon had no memory of meeting her and that she was by no means pleased to see either of them. A tall, Junoesque brunette, as Mrs. Brandon must have been before putting on flesh, Julia was talking to a gentleman when they came up, and her irritation at the interruption was almost as clear as her mother's anxiety. Anabel surveyed him with interest and some amusement. What about the man inspired such disparate emotions in mother and daughter?

Part of the answer was obvious immediately. He was extremely handsome. Julia Brandon's height had made her companion's less evident from a distance. Now, looking up, Anabel felt dwarfed. The two women outstripped her own moderate inches, but the man was taller still, and he held himself with a consummate assurance. His hair and coloring were dark, and he was blessed with the fine shoulders and well-molded legs to set off the high Corinthian mode he affected. Though Anabel had never lived in town, even she could recognize the elegance of his dark blue coat and fawn pantaloons, the one chaste

fob dangling at the front of a severely unostentatious
waistcoat. Here was an example of the nonpareils she
had only heard of. Anabel was suddenly acutely aware of
the outmoded cut of her evening dress. Her mother had
assured her that it was fine enough for this early ball, but
she wished now that some of the London gowns she had
ordered had arrived to replace her old blue satin.

Raising her eyes, she looked into the man's face. The
high cheekbones, broad forehead, and dark arched brows
matched the rest of his appearance. His mouth looked
haughty, she thought. And then she met his gaze.

Anabel felt a shock run through her, from her throat
to the pit of her stomach, leaving her shaken and absolutely astonished.

The man's eyes were a curious pale green, and they
reflected a masterful and complex personality. That
was clear at a glance. But why should they affect her
so strongly?

Mrs. Brandon had murmured her daughter's name
and Anabel's. Now she added, "Sir Charles Norbury,"
in a voice thick with disapproval and concern. She had
moved close to Julia's side, and her stance made it clear
that nothing would move her until she could coax the
girl away.

Anabel saw in Norbury's eyes an appreciation of
the situation that matched her own. A silent current of
amusement passed between them. "Wyndham," he said.
"I knew a Julian Wyndham at Oxford."

"My husband's cousin," replied Anabel.

"Ah." There was a subtle shift in his gaze.

"My dear Lady Wyndham," exclaimed Mrs. Brandon.
"I did not even mention your sad loss. I beg your pardon.
It was such a shock, Sir Ralph going off that way. Julia
was much affected, weren't you, dear?"

Julia, whose entire attention remained on Norbury,
didn't appear to hear.

"You are very kind," replied Anabel. "It has been three years now, and so we are over it, as much as we ever shall be." Mrs. Brandon nodded sympathetically, and Anabel was a little surprised to realize that this now-familiar platitude was quite true. In the country, with her family and surrounded by objects that recalled Ralph, she had not really felt the fading of grief. Here it was clearer.

"Oh, Julia, there is Maria Kingsley, and her daughter, I believe. Come, we must speak to them." She took Julia's arm and urged her away. "You will excuse us?"

Their murmured responses, and Julia's frown, were swept aside in Mrs. Brandon's determined retreat. Anabel wondered again why she was so eager to get away.

"My fault, I'm afraid," said Sir Charles Norbury.

"I beg your pardon?"

"The abrupt departure. I'm not considered a proper companion for young girls just out of the schoolroom." He smiled, teeth startlingly white against his dark skin. "Thank God."

Anabel couldn't help smiling back, though she was startled by his apparent reading of her thoughts and by his remarks.

"Why not?" she couldn't resist asking.

He laughed a little. "I'll leave it to others to malign my character, I think. Will you dance?"

The ball had opened in a rather disorganized way as they talked, and now a new set was forming. Anabel, intrigued, nodded and put a hand on his arm. She was a little disconcerted to find that it was a waltz.

"You haven't been up to London before," said Norbury when they were circling the floor together.

"No. We always preferred the country." It seemed to Anabel that he was disturbingly close. She had waltzed at local assemblies countless times, but somehow this was different. Norbury's arm about her waist and firm clasp of her hand seemed to make it a new experience, and she felt foolishly younger than her years.

"Really?" He treated it as a joke, and Anabel was too preoccupied with her own odd sensations to correct him. "But you must have spent at least one season here. Perhaps we even met? Yes, I must have danced with you. My taste has always been impeccable." He smiled down at her, his light green eyes glinting.

"No. I married out of the schoolroom." She felt it a clumsy reply, and was again amazed at herself. What was making her so inept? Ralph had always called her a wit.

"That accounts for it, then." Sir Charles was still smiling.

"For what?"

"You are quite the youngest and loveliest widow I have ever encountered, Lady Wyndham."

"Widow," she echoed distastefully. "How I hate that word. It makes one think of…"

"Precisely. But you confound all the clichés delightfully."

Anabel had never met anyone who anticipated her in this way. It had always been she who surprised and amused her circle, her conversation that set the standard. She was slightly stung at being interrupted, but even more she was interested and challenged. "And you? Do you *not* go to Jackson's, and Manton's Gallery, and White's, and the Daffy Club?"

"Not?" There was an arrested look, and a shade of puzzlement, in his eyes.

"Clichés." She left him to work it out, which he soon did, throwing back his head in a laugh so genuine and wholehearted that several nearby couples turned to look.

"A leveler, Lady Wyndham! Or perhaps I should say a telling comment, not wishing to betray my lamentable lack of originality. How dare you hide in the country all this time when you might have enlivened the desert of society with such home thrusts?"

"Ungallant, sir. Not *all* this time," she answered, looking demure.

He didn't laugh again, but the spark of delight remained in his eyes. "I most humbly beg your pardon." He guided her in a sudden turn, his arm tensing around her, and Anabel drew in her breath. This was the most stimulating conversation she could remember.

"You *are* here for the season, I hope," he added. "Have you taken a house?"

"No, I am staying with my mother, Lady Goring."

"Ah. Yes, we are acquainted. I hope you will allow me to call upon you there?"

Anabel inclined her head.

"In fact, as this is your first extended visit to London, perhaps you would allow me to show you some of our landmarks. The park at the fashionable hour is well worth seeing. Will you go driving with me tomorrow?"

"In a high-perch phaeton?" she asked.

He laughed again. "In anything you like, my dear Lady Wyndham. A Roman chariot, a stagecoach complete with yard of tin."

She smiled speculatively up at him, then shook her head. "I should like to ride in a phaeton."

"Letting me off so easily?"

"Oh, no. I shouldn't like being stared at in a stagecoach on Rotten Row."

"But that is the chief object in London—being stared at."

"In a particular way. Not with ridicule."

"Indeed. But many do not see the distinction." The music ended, and Sir Charles looked disappointed. "Tomorrow, then?"

Anabel nodded, and they drew apart with the end of the set. She felt both glad and sorry that it was over. It had been exhilarating but also a little overwhelming. She looked around for her mother and discovered her standing in the doorway that led to the refreshment room. Norbury offered his arm. "May I get you something?"

They walked across to Lady Goring, who greeted them with raised eyebrows and turned to join their progress. "I have hardly seen anyone," she replied to Anabel's question. "I have spent most of the evening in here." She sounded so irritated that Anabel and Norbury exchanged a glance. But Anabel had a suspicion of the cause, confirmed when she saw Georgina standing close to the buffet table, alone.

They joined her, and Anabel made introductions. Neither Sir Charles nor Georgina appeared enthusiastic about meeting.

"Georgina, darling," said Lady Goring. "You really must come into the ballroom. Everyone is still dancing." Her voice was oversweet, and her eyes rested on the plate of lobster patties and meringues in Georgina's hand.

Georgina shrugged and took a bite of meringue.

Anabel struggled with a smile. She looked at Norbury to see if he shared her amusement, but he was eyeing Georgina with a mixture of weariness and disgust. His mouth had turned down, and his lowered lids eloquently expressed contempt. Anabel felt uneasy about what he might say.

"Georgina," said Lady Goring again, sharply. "This is a ball, not a dinner party. No one else is—"

Anabel felt she had to intervene. "How are the meringues?" she asked, then grimaced. That was hardly the question to ease the situation.

Georgina looked at her. "All right."

This effectively halted the conversation. Lady Goring had become aware of her audience. Sir Charles looked bored. "If you will excuse me," he said, "I see Allingham." With a careless nod, he walked away.

"You had an ample dinner only two hours ago," Lady Goring said to Georgina more quietly. "I wonder you can eat anything."

"I am excessively fond of meringues," responded the girl defiantly, taking another bite.

"Excessively indeed." Lady Goring was uncharacteristically cutting.

Anabel couldn't bear any more. "Mama, I think Mrs. Rivington was looking for you. She wanted to ask you something."

"Me? What could she possibly…"

"I don't know. Perhaps you should go and see."

Her mother eyed her suspiciously, then sighed. "Very well, Anabel, I shall go. But I must say first that I am not pleased by your choice of a partner."

"My…"

"Norbury, my dear. I didn't know you had met him."

"I was introduced here."

"I see. Well, it is too bad, but I suppose you can avoid him in future."

"Why?"

Casting a meaningful glance at Georgina, Lady Goring turned to go. "We will discuss it later."

Anabel frowned at her back. Really, her mother was becoming more managing rather than less so with age. She had been almost unkind to Georgina, and now she evidently thought to dictate her own friendships. She would have to realize that Anabel was no longer a schoolroom miss. She turned back to Georgina, who was finishing a meringue. Their eyes met.

"You don't have to stay here with me," said Georgina. "I am quite happy alone."

Nonplussed, Anabel watched her pick up another confection.

"I prefer it, actually," added the other.

"At a ball?" Anabel could not help but ask.

Georgina shrugged. "I don't care for balls. I hate crowds of people."

"But…the season."

"I shall hate it. I knew I would. I never wanted to come to London, but Papa insisted. We were quite happy at home together, and then last year he suddenly began to talk of London and of writing my aunt. He wouldn't listen to me at all."

Anabel noticed incipient tears in the girl's eyes. "I'm sure he thought it would be best for you."

"How could he? He knows I loathed the assemblies and evening parties he made me go to at home. *He* hates them too. He never goes out. We are just alike, Papa and I." The tears threatened to overflow, and she blinked them back furiously.

"What do you do at home?" asked Anabel gently.

"We read. We both love books. And we have very good dinners. Our cook is French. And no one tells me that I should look better in my ball gown if I did not eat my dinner. And no one is forced to dance with me when he does not wish to." Georgina sniffed and ate another meringue.

"Perhaps your father was thinking of the future," offered Anabel. She was feeling a great deal of sympathy for her cousin and wanted to comfort her.

"I am his only heir," replied Georgina bluntly. "I will have the house and an adequate income. He has told me."

"Well…but you should have a family of your own and…"

"Why? I don't want one." The girl sounded both defiant and unhappy.

Anabel did not know just what to say to her. On the one hand, her mother was right. If Georgina would do something about her appearance, she would no doubt have a pleasanter time in London. But she realized now that what she had taken for sullen stubbornness in Georgina was in reality a mask for bewilderment and hurt. Perhaps some young man had been rude to her this evening, and certainly Lady Goring's criticisms had wounded her. She was striking back by refusing to change, and she had some justification. Anabel did not know what she could do for her, but kindness was surely better than further humiliation. "What sort of books do you like?" she asked.

Georgina's gray eyes brightened a little. "Novels. Do you read them?"

"I have little time for reading, I'm afraid. I seem to be always busy with the children."

She nodded, accepting this. "Are you glad you came to London?" she asked. "You like it here, don't you?"

"Well, yes. I do enjoy parties." Anabel felt almost apologetic.

"You are pretty. Everyone likes you."

She laughed. "Hardly."

Georgina shrugged again. "That man you were dancing with does, and he didn't even want to look at me."

So she had noticed Norbury's reaction. Anabel had hoped she had not. She tried to think of some reassuring answer.

"It's all right. I don't care. I am perfectly happy the way I am." Georgina picked up another meringue.

But Anabel, watching her, knew that it wasn't true, and she wondered again what she could do for her touchy young cousin. The girl couldn't be pushed; that was clear. Was there some more subtle means of aid? No thoughts occurred to Anabel, and the musicians were striking up another waltz in the ballroom, drawing her irresistibly away. Dancing again had been wonderful.

"Go ahead," said Georgina.

Anabel hesitated, then turned toward the music. She would think about her cousin tomorrow.

Three

ANABEL ENJOYED HERSELF HUGELY AT THE BALL, AND AS
a consequence slept luxuriously late the following morning, waking barely in time to dress for her appointment
with Sir Charles Norbury. Thus, she was not downstairs
to receive a morning caller who asked for her with some
impatience. Indeed, no one was about, and the footman
left the gentleman in the drawing room to go in search
of Lady Goring.

The man paced the elegant room in long, swift strides,
obviously preoccupied. Once, thinking he heard a sound,
he stopped and turned quickly. But no one was there. He
was dressed in well-tailored traveling clothes, though not
in the height of fashion, and there was something very
appealing in his ruddy blond complexion and alert blue
eyes. He was just above medium height and just past
thirty years of age, and his handsome face fell naturally
into lines that suggested laughter.

Still pacing, this time he did not hear the faint noise
from the doorway. But it was followed almost immediately by a shriek that brought him swinging around.

"Uncle Christopher!" A diminutive figure hurled itself
across the carpet and onto his chest, nearly knocking the
breath out of him. "You're back, you're back!"

"Hello, Susan," he replied, hugging her like a man
accustomed to such assaults. "I am. I arrived this morning."

"How did you know where we were?" Susan had
drawn back a little and was pulling him toward the sofa,
where she settled herself on his knee.

"I saw it in the newspaper."

The child's green eyes went wide. "Are we in the newspaper?"

"Your mother is. It says she attended a ball last night." His tone in imparting this information was ambiguous.

"Oh. That." Susan's interest vanished. "I am so glad to see you, Uncle Christopher. You must take us all home at once."

Christopher Hanford eyed the small girl meditatively. He was not really her uncle. The Wyndhams and the Hanfords had been neighbors in Hertfordshire for generations, and he had grown up with Ralph Wyndham and remained his closest friend even after the latter's marriage. Upon his untimely death, Hanford had naturally become the mainstay of Wyndham's bereft young family, and all of the children called him "uncle." Anabel, too, relied on him. He had always been happy to oblige. But in the last six months or so he had gradually realized that his happiness was not simply that of a faithful friend. The Wyndhams had less and less need of him as the grief for Ralph faded and Anabel learned about running an estate and managing alone. Yet he called as often and found himself resenting the change. Finally the truth had struck him. He had, in the past three years, fallen deeply in love with his charming neighbor, and he could no longer be content without her.

This knowledge had unsettled him, chiefly because Anabel herself showed no signs of returning his regard. She was always glad to see him and treated him with the relaxed informality of long-standing friendship; she seemed delighted by his love for her children. But on the few occasions when he had tried to express more profound feelings, she had not understood, or perhaps, as he sometimes thought, she had pretended not to, thinking he would see that she could offer him nothing more. This conclusion had so cast him down that he embarked on a sudden voyage abroad, resolving to stay away until he had conquered his unrequited passion. He told the Wyndhams only that he was leaving, and he did not write. But this accomplished no more than to keep him wondering how they were through the entire trip. Last week he had given it up and turned homeward, determined to confront Anabel and find out his chances. But almost the first thing that greeted him in England was the announcement that she had brought her family to town. He was irrationally angry that she should have taken this step without consulting him, and uneasy about its consequences.

"Have you seen her?" asked Susan, tugging at his lapel to get his attention. "Uncle Christopher!"

"What? Seen whom?"

"Daisy. My cat. I'm looking for her. She comes down here all the time, and the servants get angry."

"I haven't seen her, Susan. I'm sorry."

Susan shrugged and smiled angelically up at him. Not for the first time, Hanford marveled at the strange combination of seraphic face and hellish temper.

The drawing-room door opened again, and Nicholas peered around it. When he saw Hanford, he looked first astonished, then delighted. "William!" he called over his shoulder. "Here." Then he in his turn ran forward and embraced the man, to be followed quickly by the elder male Wyndham. "How good that you are back," said Nicholas when their greetings were over. "You can speak to Mama."

Hanford smiled at his assurance. "About what?"

"Going home, of course. I daresay she will be more willing to go now that you will be there."

"What makes you think so?" he replied rather sharply.

"Oh, things were dreadfully flat after you went. We all said so."

"Your mother too?"

This time Nicholas glanced up at his eagerness, slightly puzzled. "Oh, yes. Will you tell her? We dislike London so." William and Susan nodded vigorously.

"We shall see." He felt a rising hope. Was it possible that Anabel had come to London because she missed his company?

The footman opened the door and ushered Lady Goring in. Hanford put Susan aside and rose to greet her. But before either could speak, a large mass of ginger fur streaked past her ladyship's feet, almost oversetting her, and buried itself in one of the blue velvet draperies. It was hotly pursued by another footman, who arrested his headlong rush barely in time to avoid his employer. He came to attention, breathing hard and pulling at his coat to adjust it, just outside the room.

"Whatever is the…" began Lady Goring, then stopped and sighed. "The cat again, I suppose."

"Yes, ma'am," answered the footman. "He got into the kitchen, and Cook says—"

"Susan, you promised me you would keep that animal upstairs," interrupted the other, not wanting to hear what Cook had said. She could easily imagine it.

"I *did*, Grandmama. Only, Miss Tate said I had to do my lessons, and so I—"

"I know you want to keep him, Susan. But he is really not the sort of pet for you to…"

Seeing Susan's ominously reddening face, Hanford ventured, "I believe he is climbing the curtain."

He was. William and the footman ran to the window, followed more slowly by Nicholas. The cat's progress was evident only from a moving agitation of the cloth, but he was already above the reach of the brawny footman. "A chair," suggested Hanford, and one was quickly shifted. Daisy was retrieved with an ominous rip and a flurry of claws and teeth. Susan ran to cradle him.

"Go downstairs and have Mrs. Beecham tie up your

hand at once, James," said Lady Goring in a long-suffering voice. The footman, hands behind his back to hide the bleeding, hurried away. "Susan!"

"Daisy was just frightened. She didn't know what they were going to do to her, did you, Daisy?"

The giant cat focused a derisive yellow eye on the group.

"If he cannot be kept upstairs, Susan…"

"I will. I will, Grandmama. I promise!"

Lady Goring sighed. "We will try it once more. But only once, Susan. Do you understand me?"

"Yes, Grandmama." She gripped Daisy more tightly, his tail, legs, and belly hanging over her small arms. The cat surveyed his audience complacently.

Lady Goring stepped forward, holding out her hand. "I beg your pardon for this uproar. I am Anabel's mother, and though we have not met, I have heard a great deal about you. I am delighted to make your acquaintance at last."

Hanford bowed slightly as he took her hand. "And I yours." His bright blue eyes were still dancing at the scene he had just witnessed, and Lady Goring found herself smiling.

"Shall we sit down?"

They had hardly done so when the unwounded footman came in again, announcing, "Sir Charles Norbury," and ushering that gentleman into the room.

There was an immediate alteration in the atmosphere. The tall, very fashionable figure who strode to the middle of the carpet and looked down at them was in marked contrast to the inhabitants of the household. Lady Goring was well dressed, but common sense rather than changing modes always governed her choices. Christopher Hanford was a countryman, and his clothes, although good, had no pretensions to elegance. In his many-caped driving coat and gleaming Hessian boots,

Norbury seemed to epitomize the town buck, and his sardonic expression as he scanned each of them merely increased this impression. "Good day, Lady Goring," he said. "I hope I do not…intrude?"

Hanford disliked him at once, for no discernible reason. And Lady Goring's reply was not warm. She implied, without actually asking, a question about his visit.

"I am here to fetch Lady Wyndham for a drive in the park," he said. "Did she not mention it to you?" His slight smile and one raised brow were very handsome, and extremely annoying to his adult listeners. Hanford's dislike was confirmed, and joined by suspicion. Lady Goring frowned. Their visitor appeared amused.

"I want to go, too," stated Susan, putting Daisy down on the floor. "Mama said we might go to the park, but Nurse never wants to take us."

Norbury eyed her with distaste, and Lady Goring recalled her duties as hostess with a certain relish. "You haven't met my grandchildren, Sir Charles," she said cordially. She gave their names. William and Nicholas made very creditable bows, but Susan merely moved closer to the man and stared up at him with a fixity that earned her a haughty look. "And forgive me, Mr. Hanford, I ought to have mentioned you first. Mr. Hanford is a neighbor of my daughter's in Hertfordshire."

"I see." Sir Charles was obviously impatient. "I fear I cannot keep my horses standing too long, Lady Goring. If Lady Wyndham might be informed of my arrival…"

"Oh, John has gone to tell her. I daresay she will be right down." She seated herself and indicated with a gesture that the gentlemen should follow suit.

Daisy had been scouting the perimeters of the room since being set free, and now he looked out from under the sofa, drawn by the high shine of Norbury's boots. Nicholas, under whose legs the cat emerged, drew them quickly up. Daisy stepped out, head extended, and sniffed delicately. The sound attracted Sir Charles's attention, and the sight of Daisy brought a twist to his lips. Some instinct made the cat raise its head and meet the man's pale green gaze. In an instant the streetwise creature had retreated out of sight.

"You have been traveling abroad, Mr. Hanford?" said Lady Goring.

"Yes. I've only just returned."

"How did you find the Continent now that the war is over? Much changed?"

"Well, I had never visited it before, so I am not the person to say. But it is certainly interesting."

Norbury's face showed contempt at this commonplace, and Hanford, who had replied at random as he tried to work out what he would say to Anabel when she appeared, felt a strong desire to hit him.

"My husband and I visited Paris on our wedding journey," said Lady Goring. "We always meant to return, but the war came, and then Gerald's death, and we never managed it. Paris is a wonderful city."

Hanford agreed. Sir Charles hardly tried to conceal his impatience.

William and Nicholas had effaced themselves since the second caller arrived, feeling that their presence was now unwelcome, at least to him. But Susan was unhampered by such scruples. She had wandered to the window and now she approached Norbury's chair. "Is that your carriage outside?"

"Yes."

"I've never seen one like that. What is it called?"

He looked annoyed. "A high-perch phaeton." His voice was clipped.

"Why is it so tall?"

Alarmed by Sir Charles's languid annoyance, Lady Goring and Christopher Hanford spoke at the same moment.

"That is the fashion," she said.

"You can see a great distance from the seat," he said.

They glanced at each other, smiled slightly, and apologized. Norbury looked pained.

"But…" Susan was never easily diverted.

"I am so sorry I am late," exclaimed a breathless voice from the doorway, and Anabel hurried in, looking charming in a white sprig muslin gown, with tiny blue flowers and long tucked sleeves, and a chip straw hat. She carried a dark blue pelisse over her arm.

The gentlemen stood, Norbury stepping forward.

"Christopher!"

"Hullo, Anabel."

"When did you get back?"

"Just this morning." She had come forward and offered her hand, and he took it and squeezed it warmly. The way her face had lit when she saw him had speeded his pulse.

"However did you find us so soon?"

"You were in all the society papers."

"I?" She seemed both astonished and a little pleased.

"Yes, indeed. 'The charming Lady Wyndham.'" His eyes teased her.

"Oh my."

"I beg your pardon," put in Sir Charles, "but I really cannot leave my horses standing much longer."

Anabel turned quickly. "Indeed, it is my fault. I am sorry." She looked back at Hanford, biting her lip. "We must go."

He said nothing. He refused to tell her it was all right.

"Are you staying in town long, Christopher?"

"A few days." He had planned to go straight home, but her presence changed that.

"Good. I will see you later, then. Good-bye Mama, children."

"I want to go with you," said Susan. "You promised I could see the park."

"Nurse will take you this afternoon, dear."

"I want to go now!"

Seeing Norbury's face and knowing her daughter, Anabel cravenly fled with a hurried "Another time, love." Lady Goring, watching the youngest Wyndham's imperiousness turn to outrage, braced herself. William and Nicholas waited with identical grimaces.

"The park is very dull at this time of day," said Christopher Hanford. "I know a better place. Have you heard of Astley's Amphitheatre?"

"Where they have the wild beasts?" asked William.

"That's it. Why don't we have a look at it today?"

The boys leaped up and began to pelt him with questions, their exuberance revived. Hanford kept one eye on Susan. At first it seemed that she would cling to her grievance. But when William's hope that there might be lions was confirmed, she gave in and joined the group. Lady Goring, amazed and grateful, watched the exchange with a smile, then saw them all off in a hansom cab. As Hanford was bidding her good-bye she said, "I hope we shall have an opportunity to talk again, in better circumstances. Will you come to dinner one night?"

"I should be delighted."

"Tomorrow? We are at home."

He agreed and, as the children were clamoring to go, stepped up into the carriage. Lady Goring saw them off before turning back into the front hall, a meditative look on her face.

Four

CHRISTOPHER HANFORD WAS SO PUNCTUAL FOR HIS dinner appointment the following evening that he arrived before either Lady Goring or Anabel had come downstairs. As the footman took him to the drawing room to await them, Hanford felt unexpectedly awkward. He had purchased several new coats in Paris, having been assured by one of the best tailors that they became him and were in the very latest mode. He wore one tonight, but he had an uneasy suspicion that he could not compete with Sir Charles Norbury in this area. He looked like a sensible, well-bred gentleman, one whose family had been prominent in the county for centuries, but he was no Corinthian, and he never would be. Walking through the door the footman held open for him, Hanford again told himself that it was very common for ladies to be taken driving in town. It meant nothing in particular. Anabel could not be well acquainted with Norbury after such a short stay; perhaps she had merely gone out of politeness or the desire for variety. But he found his arguments unconvincing. The image of the polished Norbury had lingered painfully in his thoughts through the night, and his expression as he crossed the Turkey carpet toward the fireplace was wry and concerned.

"Oh!" said a female voice. There was a scuffling sound and then a cascade of small objects over the sofa front.

"I beg your pardon," said Hanford, moving around it. "The footman did not tell me there was anyone here."

Georgina Goring scrambled up. She had been reclining on the sofa, wholly engrossed in a book and fortified with a box of chocolate creams. The story was so enthralling that she had not heard the door open, and not until Hanford's footsteps were quite close had she noticed him. Startled, she had jumped, overturning the confections and raining them in confusion on the rug. Her heart was pounding because she had at first thought the intruder was Lady Goring, and braced herself for a scold. Discovering her mistake, she felt both embarrassed and irritated at facing a stranger and a male. "You crept up on me," she accused.

Hanford eyed the very plump pale girl with some amusement. The scene told him a great deal. "Indeed, I did not mean to. The servant did not say you were here."

"He didn't know," admitted Georgina. She had formed the habit of slipping about the house, so that Lady Goring would have difficulty in finding her and preventing her pleasures.

Hanford knelt and began to pick up the scattered chocolates. He handed her the book that had fallen facedown on the floor. "*The Monk's Curse*," he read. "Is that a novel?"

"Yes." She snatched it from him.

"Are you fond of novels?" He deftly returned the last candies to their paper holders and put on the box's cover.

"Yes." Georgina rose, taking this also from him and clutching both to her. She was a trifle disheveled, and her gray eyes sparkled defensively.

"So is my sister. She is continually telling me to read one or another, but I fear I am not a great reader. What do *you* like about them?"

The girl surveyed him suspiciously but could find no trace of mockery in his face. She thawed a little. "The stories are so exciting. I always feel as if I were hurtling down a long, dark tunnel with no notion of what is to come next."

Hanford was surprised. The girl looked dull, but she

was obviously not. "Do you? It sounds too terrifying for me." He smiled at her to show that he was joking.

Georgina gazed at him with wonder and dawning interest. No gentleman but her father had ever bothered to be kind to her before. And this was a very attractive gentleman.

"I am Christopher Hanford, by the way."

"Oh no!"

He raised his eyebrows, still smiling.

"I beg your pardon. But you are coming to dinner."

"I am."

"I mean, you are here for dinner, and I have not changed. I did not hear the bell. My aunt will be angry with me. I must go at once before she comes down." But even as she hurried toward the door, still awkwardly grasping her possessions, it opened and Lady Goring came in, impressive in silver-gray satin.

"Georgina, what are you doing?" Her ladyship's sharp gaze took in the morning dress, the book, the box of chocolates, and her lips turned down.

"I was just going to change!" The girl almost ran past her and out of the room.

Lady Goring sighed heavily, then moved toward Hanford. "Good evening. I see you have met my niece."

"Yes. A very intelligent girl. I fear I startled her when I came in."

"No doubt she thought it was me. Sit down, please." They sat. "Georgina and I do not agree on a number of things." She noticed a lone chocolate, which had rolled under an armchair, and bent to pick it up. "Why will the wretched girl persist in eating candy? I am losing all patience with her! Can she not see that…" Remembering her company, she stopped.

"I daresay chocolates are what she has learned to love," replied Hanford, feeling some obscure kinship with Georgina Goring.

Lady Goring stared at him, and he felt a little sorry for his comment. "Anabel has told me that you are an extremely perceptive counselor. You have helped her with the children more than once, I know. It is for Georgina's own sake that I wish her to keep away from chocolates and the like. She will be much happier in London if she does."

He nodded. "It probably seems a criticism, however."

"What am I to do?" wailed his hostess. "I cannot manage Georgina, and here is Anabel mad after a notorious rake. I had no idea when I asked her to visit that—"

"Norbury?" he snapped.

Once again aware that she had said too much, Lady Goring bit her lip. "I don't know what it is about you, but I am letting slip things I would not say to anyone else. Yes, Norbury is not the sort of man any mother would approve."

"And she is 'mad after him'?"

Something in his tone made Lady Goring look up sharply. What she saw in Hanford's face narrowed her eyes. "I exaggerate. Anabel is merely intrigued."

"As yet." Her words had filled him with a disappointment so sharp that he had difficulty breathing normally. It would be unbearable if he were to lose Anabel in this way, to such a man.

"I daresay it is a passing whim. She was never exposed to town life, and she is finding it interesting."

"Interesting!" The tone was so bitter that Lady Goring's suspicion turned to certainty. She cataloged Hanford with care. From what she had seen, he was just the man for her daughter.

The door opened again, and Anabel came in. She was wearing a soft blue evening dress tonight that emphasized the size and color of her eyes. Her brown hair was dressed in a knot at the top of her head, with curls falling over her ears, where tiny sapphires sparkled. She came forward holding out her hand with undisguised pleasure. "Christopher. How good to see you again. You were away such an age."

He took it, feeling his throat tighten, and bowed slightly. "It seemed long to be away from my friends," he agreed.

"Oh, I'm sure you were having far too fine a time to think of us." She laughed. "Was it splendid?" She gazed up at him, her eyes shining with open happiness and affection. It really *was* wonderful to see him again, she realized. She had missed him more than she knew.

The others, watching her closely, felt varying degrees of satisfaction. Lady Goring was confirmed in her resolve, and Hanford felt stirrings of hope, though the image of Sir Charles Norbury lingered in the back of his mind. "My journey was pleasant, but I did indeed think of you. In fact, I have some things for the children I would like to bring."

"Presents. You spoil them so, Christopher." Anabel spoke teasingly, knowing that it wasn't true. He had been an unimpeachable substitute father since Ralph's death. They smiled at each other warmly over this old joke.

The group settled on the sofa and armchairs. "Are the children in bed?" asked Hanford. "I hoped to see them again."

"Yes." Anabel threw a mischievous glance at her mother, who grimaced. "They had an active day, and we sent them off early."

"Active!" Lady Goring's tone spoke volumes, and Anabel laughed.

"You invited them, Mama."

"Yes, dear, and I love them all. But I had forgotten how wearing young children can be. I am happy to have them here and also happy when it is time for them to go to bed." Her comical grimace made them all laugh, and Georgina Goring entered the room to general merriment.

The footman was right behind her, announcing dinner, and they went into the dining room in very good humor.

It was the most enjoyable meal Anabel could remember in London. Her mother and Georgina did not quarrel at all. Once, it appeared they might begin, but Christopher somehow smoothed over the contretemps and turned the conversation with an amusing anecdote. They talked of the Continent, Lady Goring reminiscing movingly, and then, surprisingly, of novels. Georgina became almost animated. By the time they went back to the drawing room for coffee, Hanford seemed as much an old family friend to the Gorings as to Anabel. Lady Goring was amazed by the ease with which he adapted to them, and very much bucked up by his charm and endearing smile. Anabel seemed to glow in his presence as her mother had not seen her do in years. As for Georgina, she simply thought Christopher Hanford the most wonderful man she had ever met, perhaps surpassing even her beloved father.

When they had drunk their coffee and the footman had come in twice to put fresh logs on the fire, Lady Goring rose to her feet. "Georgina," she said, "I have something to show you in my room."

The girl looked surprised, then concerned. "Just now?"

"Yes, dear, come along." Lady Goring tried to convey with a look her desire to let Anabel and Hanford have a little private talk, but Georgina was oblivious.

"Can we not do it tomorrow?" Georgina had been having a wonderful time; she did not want it to end.

"No, dear." The older woman moved toward the door, beckoning.

Georgina's brow puckered resentfully.

"Come along."

She looked for support, but the others were talking. Sullen again, she rose and followed her aunt slowly from the room.

Anabel looked up in surprise when the door shut. "Where are they going?"

Hanford, who had seen and been humorously grateful for Lady Goring's maneuvers, shrugged.

"Well, it is fortunate. We can have a comfortable talk." Anabel smiled at him, and his heart turned over.

"Yes. You are enjoying London?"

"I am. I did not think I would at first, but I am beginning to realize that I had shut myself away too much."

This sounded ominous. "What made you decide to come up for the season?"

She smiled again. "Mama. Need you ask? I was feeling very flat at home, and she leaped at the chance."

"Flat?"

"Yes. I do not know how it is, but this summer seemed horridly dull."

Hanford hoped again. He had been away for the whole summer. "The children must be enjoying themselves. There are so many new things to see."

"They enjoyed Astley's," she answered with a grimace. "I must thank you again for taking them there. I hadn't thought of it, nor did Mama, of course. They have not been overly pleased with London until now. Your promises of future treats altered their view somewhat."

"My father first brought me to town when I was about Nick's age and showed me all the sights. I remember the trip vividly to this day."

Anabel held out a hand and, when he took it, squeezed his. "Thank you, Christopher. I can always count on you. I don't know what we have done to deserve such a friend."

He almost spoke then. He had opened his mouth to tell her what she had done when Anabel continued, "I was too taken up with my own pleasure to provide for theirs. Have you ridden in the park at the fashionable hour, Christopher? I have never seen such a spectacle."

The image of Norbury rose before him. He dropped her hand and sat back. "I'm told it is amazing."

"So many human types. And Sir Charles knew them all, of course, and could tell me their histories. I don't know when I have laughed so much."

"You like this Norbury?" He hadn't meant to mention him, but the question slipped out.

"I have never met anyone like him. He is…" Anabel tried to formulate an opinion while Christopher watched her narrowly. She had had a fine time on their drive the previous day. It had been a bit strained at first. Sir Charles had seemed annoyed, perhaps at having been kept waiting. But when they had begun talking, Anabel had again felt that nervous excitement he had aroused when they met. Sir Charles was certainly intelligent as well as handsome. His sketches of fashionable London had been hilarious, and it was obvious to Anabel that he was held in high esteem. Many people had greeted them, and others had looked and commented. She had been very conscious of her position beside one of the most elegant men in town. "…interesting," she finished, a bit lamely.

"I see."

She looked up, surprised at the dryness of his tone. "You do not like him?"

"I? I have hardly spoken one word to him."

"I know, but…Mama has the absurd notion that he is not… Oh, never mind, Christopher. As if I could not take care of myself by this time." Anabel laughed, her glance encouraging him to join her. But Hanford, convinced that she was far from able to take care of herself, remained serious, his lips turned down. After a moment Anabel's smile faded. She was puzzled. Christopher had always been the first to savor a good joke. Surveying him, she saw worry in his face. His bright blue eyes were shadowed. What was wrong? Knowing his love of the country, she thought that he might be missing his home. "When do you return to Hertfordshire?" she asked. "You will find everything much the same there, though Mrs. Petty has managed to wrest the Poor Committee from old Mrs. Duncan at last."

This made him smile a little. "Has she indeed? But I am not certain I shall go down at once."

"Really? Why not?"

"I am thinking of staying in town for part of the season." His eyes gauged her reaction to this.

"You, Christopher? I cannot imagine you here."

This stung. "Some would have said that of you only a few months ago."

Anabel smiled. "That's true. But do you mean to join the season and make the rounds of parties and all that? You dislike parties so."

"No doubt the London festivities are more amusing than those in the country." His tone was a little clipped. He was angry at the implied comparison with Sir Charles, who was perfectly at home in town.

Anabel eyed him curiously. "Well, I can only marvel at this change. I have heard you swear you would never be caught in London during the season."

"Perhaps I have changed my mind." He was very annoyed with her now. Could any woman really be so blind? *She* was here, so he would stay, however much he disliked parties. Surely the connection was obvious?

Light seemed to dawn on Anabel. "I have it! How foolish I was not to see it at once."

He looked at her.

"You have decided to marry at last, and you have come to town to find a wife." She laughed up at him.

This was too much. He merely stared at the floor, lips set.

"*Is* that it, Christopher?" She sounded both surprised and not completely pleased. "I was only funning." His continuing silence daunted her. Could this really be his reason? She had never pictured Christopher marrying, though of course nothing would be more natural, she realized. He ought to marry. But when she tried to imagine it, to think what sort of woman would be best, Anabel felt a sudden, unaccountable rush of annoyance. She tried to explain it to herself. Christopher might have informed her of his plans. They were, after all, old friends. And how would the children feel at the intrusion of a stranger into their familiar circle? They would not understand, particularly when Christopher began to desert them for his own prospective family. He might have prepared her for this, so that she could prepare them. But it was all of a piece. He had gone abroad with hardly more than a word, and now he meant to alter their old, comfortable relationship in the same way. It was really unkind. Her surge of emotion satisfactorily explained, Anabel raised her head and met his eyes, her softer blue ones hot.

Hanford, who had been watching her expression shift, was cautiously elated. She had not at all liked the notion of his marrying, he saw. Well then, perhaps he would let her consider it further. She might even discover that her feelings for him were not simple friendship and that she herself wished to fill the position of his wife. Accordingly, he merely shrugged in response to her questioning look.

Anabel was outraged. She had confidently expected a laughing denial and she felt cheated and deceived. Christopher had never said one word about marriage through the years of their friendship. Clearly, she was not really in his confidence; he had no respect for her opinion at all. Anabel rose. "It is late."

"I beg your pardon. I shall take my leave of you, then." Hanford had some trouble controlling a smile. He was very pleased with her reaction.

Chin high, she held out her hand. "I daresay we shall see you at some of the season's events."

"No doubt," he agreed amiably.

"I hope you do not find them tedious after all."

"Anabel, I think that extremely unlikely." Now he did smile, and she, interpreting it as anticipation of the courting ritual, pulled away her hand and stepped back. Hanford left the room with a jaunty salute and a lingering smile.

Five

As a result of this conversation, Christopher
Hanford paid a rather early morning call the following day, to a small but very elegant town house in
Regent Street. Mrs. Amelia Lanforth appeared astonished
when he followed the butler into her drawing room.
"Christopher? Are you still in London? I was sure you
would be safely in Hertfordshire by this time, tramping
about your muddy fields."

"I have decided to stay in town for a while, Amelia."

She gaped at him. The two were remarkably alike,
both just above medium size with ruddy blond hair and
bright blue eyes, but Mrs. Lanforth's tresses were fashionably curled à la Méduse, and her pink muslin morning
gown had obviously come from one of the most skillful
London modistes. "Is something wrong?"

"No."

"It must be. You needn't spare me, Christopher. Is
it Aunt Seraphina? She wasn't at all well the last time I
called, but—"

"Nothing is wrong. Can I not spend a few weeks in
town without arousing this astonishment?"

She looked at him again. "No, you cannot. You have
not voluntarily visited London for more than two nights
since you were twelve years old, Christopher. Come to
that, you have never called on me more than once in a
visit since we settled here. And you have repeatedly told
me how silly I was to enjoy town life. *What* is wrong?"

Hanford gazed down at his sister with a wry smile.

She was, of course, perfectly right. And if he wanted her help, he was going to have to provide some explanations. He and Amelia had disagreed on a number of things during their lives. From a very early age he had devoted himself to the estate and country amusements, whereas she had counted the moments until her London debut. She had reveled in her first season and married a man who habitually came up for that period, returning home only for occasional holidays and to be with their mother for the births of Amelia's two children. After the older Hanfords died, she ceased these visits, and she and Christopher now saw each other only a day or two each year, when he was in town. Yet strong bonds of affection remained between them despite this separation. Their disagreements had never been acrimonious; indeed, they almost enjoyed arguing their divergent points of view. Christopher had no doubt his sister would do as he asked, after she had twitted him over his change of heart. His expression became more wry. "I want to be a man of fashion, Amelia. Will you oversee the transformation?"

Her mouth dropped open. "You're bamming me!"

"Word of honor."

"But…but…"

Her amazement was so comical that he laughed.

"Christopher! You have nothing but contempt for 'men of fashion,' even poor Lanforth, who is far from a pink of the *ton*. What has suddenly changed your mind?" Before he could reply, her blue eyes sharpened. "A woman, I suppose."

He looked down.

"I had received the impression that you were interested only in your neighbor, Lady…oh. She is in London this season, is she not?"

"Have you met her at last?"

"No, but I remember hearing that Lady Goring has

her daughter with her. This is your reason, then?" Her eyes had started to dance.

Sheepishly Hanford admitted it. "She is much taken with town ways and..."

"And town beaux, I suppose. Oh, Christopher, I could not have hoped for such a perfect revenge if I had planned it for years. You see where your country stubbornness has brought you." She was laughing almost too hard to speak.

"To throw myself on your tender mercies," he agreed. "I am in your hands, Amelia. Will you help me?"

"I wouldn't miss it for anything." She thought of something. "But you must do as I say, Christopher. No contemptuous sputterings."

He sighed but nodded.

"What fun I shall have!" She walked slowly around him, as if making notes.

"I have rather given Anabel the impression that I am hunting for a wife," he added.

"As you are. Oh, you mean among the debs?" Amelia's delighted smile returned. "How devious of you, Christopher. This may be easier than I thought. You have the instincts of a tulip already." As he grimaced she continued. "First, you must get rid of that coat. You should never wear olive drab, with your coloring. It is cut well enough, but..."

"I bought this coat in Paris," he protested.

"And I said it was well enough. But the color is all wrong. You should always wear blue, or buff or black, but never olive."

"But it was—"

"Christopher! You promised you would do as I say."

Their very similar eyes met. "Very well," he muttered.

"Good." Amelia smiled. "We must get you a new haircut, of course. And your cravat will never do. Oh,

Christopher, we shall have such fun!" She clapped her hands gleefully. Her brother grimaced again. "Are you still at Claridge's? I will send someone for your things." Seeing him start to speak, she added, "You must stay here, naturally. It is one thing to claim you will give me too much trouble on a one-night visit to town—which is ridiculous, as I have always told you. But if we are to carry through your plan, you cannot be so far off. You can have the blue bedchamber. It's all ready."

Hanford watched her animated features as she set forth an arduous program of shopping for the next several days. He had rarely seen his sister so pleased. It made him glad he had sought her help, though he knew he would not enjoy much of it. If anyone could prepare him to compete with Norbury, it was Amelia, and he was determined to do everything in his power to win in this unforeseen contest.

❧

The first major event of the season was the Duchess of Rutland's ball the following week. Amelia had no trouble securing an invitation for her brother, and she hounded his tailors so mercilessly that he was completely reoutfitted in plenty of time. As he came into the drawing room that evening both Lanforths turned to look at him, Amelia with a professional's critical eye and her husband, George, with a combination of fellow feeling and curiosity. He, too, had been a victim of his brother-in-law's mockery of the *ton*. Christopher felt ridiculous. His new clothes seemed outlandishly exaggerated, despite his sister's assurances that both cut and fabric were very plain. His hair, cut and brushed into a Brutus by a fellow he had found intolerable, seemed stiff and strange. And he was almost frightened of the valet Amelia had made him hire to care for his new finery. "Here I am," he declared, stopping beside them. "Complete with cap and bells."

"You look splendid," encouraged George. "Top of the trees."

"You have left off your quizzing glass," objected Amelia. "I told you, it is to hang—"

"I *could* not," he interrupted. "I have tried my best to be docile, Amelia, but I simply could not."

Meeting his gaze, she smiled a little. "Oh, very well. You *do* look splendid, Christopher. Even I did not imagine that you could look so polished." She eyed his black evening coat and knee breeches, his snowy cravat tied in an Osbaldeston, his silver-shot waistcoat. "Indeed, I would hardly have known you for my country-squire brother."

"I hardly know myself," he replied ruefully. "I glance into a mirror and start to nod to the overdressed stranger."

"Nonsense. You are not the least overdressed. Shall we go in to dinner? We do not want to be late."

"Do we not?" murmured Christopher. But he took her proffered arm and led her into the dining room.

Only a few streets away, the ladies of the Goring household were putting the finishing touches on ball gowns and toilettes before also sitting down to dinner. Anabel, surveying her reflection in a full-length glass, was very pleased with the effect of the ball gown that had arrived yesterday from her dressmaker. It was of deep blue satin with an overskirt of creamy Mechlin lace. The bodice and short puffed sleeves were also overlaid with lace, and it was belted with a matching blue velvet ribbon. She had got out the sapphire pendant Ralph had bought her in Paris, with its companion earrings, and her soft brown hair had been done in a cloud of curls. The overall impression was of exquisite fragility, and she smiled a little before going along to the nursery, as she had promised to show the children her gown.

Georgina's feelings were far different. She, too, had a new dress, of fine pink muslin trimmed with knots of darker pink ribbons. But her silhouette was anything but fragile, and as Lady Goring's maid applied the hot curling tongs to her pale blond hair, she frowned at her pudgy features in the dressing-table mirror. Everyone would laugh, Georgina thought. It was silly to fuss over her hair and to buy new gowns. She would be miserable at the ball, as always. She wished that she dared get out her box of chocolates in front of the maid. Dinner was late tonight, and she was hungry.

When Lady Goring, splendidly dressed in purple satin and amethysts, met her two charges in the drawing room some minutes later, her thoughts echoed theirs. She reveled in her daughter's beauty and despaired at Georgina's bulk. But she said merely, "We must hurry. What have you been doing, Anabel? You are late."

"The children kept me, admiring my lace." Anabel smiled. "Susan wants a gown exactly like this one for her birthday in September."

"And doubtless she will get it," answered her mother dryly. "I shudder to think what that child will be like at her come-out if she is demanding quite unsuitable dresses at the age of six."

"Susan will be a belle, of course. She is already pretty enough."

"And capricious enough," countered Lady Goring. "Come in to dinner."

❧

The line of carriages beneath the glittering windows of the Rutland town house stretched far down the street as each halted briefly to deposit its elegantly dressed passengers, then moved on to make way for the next. The Goring party arrived in good time and, after greeting their hosts on the landing, made their way up to the half-filled ballroom. "Look at the flowers!" exclaimed Anabel at once.

"Very beautiful," responded her mother, surveying the great garlands of pink roses and greenery that festooned the walls. A trellis had been erected in one corner, and it looked remarkably natural.

"I have never seen so many roses in my life. Isn't it wonderful, Georgina?"

The younger girl nodded, but her eyes were on the other guests. Several were looking in their direction, probably talking of who they were and how dreadful she looked.

"I wish I had worn pink, as you did," added Anabel in an effort to cheer her.

Georgina merely looked disgusted.

"There is Jane Danvers," said Lady Goring. "Let us go and join her."

The room filled rapidly, and in a very short time the duchess gave the signal to begin the dancing. Anabel was asked at once, but Lady Goring had to summon a partner for Georgina, who accepted him with as little grace as he had showed at the command. When the first set ended, she escaped to the supper room, ignoring all frowns cast her way and hiding when Lady Goring came to search for her. Anabel, glowing from the country-dance, was delighted when the orchestra struck up a waltz, and more so when Sir Charles Norbury came up to claim her hand. She hadn't seen him arrive.

They moved onto the floor as the music began, and Norbury pulled her into a quick turn, making her very aware of the strength of his arm around her waist and the closeness of his body to hers. She felt small beside him, irresistibly guided by his whim. It was a new sensation, and uncertainty mixed with pleasure as they moved around the ballroom. Sir Charles remained an enigma to her. The men in her life had been very different— her father, a genial, uncomplicated creature extremely fond of his only daughter; Ralph, a bluff and hearty squire, pleased to have found such a wife; Christopher, a reliable, amusing friend. Norbury was none of these things, except perhaps amusing. In his polished looks, his assured, almost arrogant manner, and in the feeling of trembling excitement he engendered in her, he was unique in Anabel's life. She found him fascinating.

Norbury's thoughts were similar as they turned in the waltz and chatted. He had never encountered a woman precisely like Anabel. Most of those he knew had been schooled for years in the rituals of the *haut ton*, and the one or two countrywomen he had met had shown none of Anabel's easy understanding or quick wit. She was a curious mixture of naïveté and wisdom, and very pretty besides. He had had serious reservations about continuing his acquaintance with her when he discovered the existence of three tiresome children and their attendants. But Anabel's charm on their drive together had slowly disarmed his doubts. He enjoyed her company, he realized, more than that of any other female he could name, including his current inamorata. This was an odd circumstance, and one he wished to explore.

"Isn't that the lady you pointed out to me in the park?" asked Anabel then.

"Which?"

"There, in the puce satin. Did you not say that she has four daughters out at once?"

"I did indeed. The Marsden ensemble, each uglier than the next. There they are, sitting in a row on that blue sofa."

"Where? Oh."

"Remarkably like a row of gargoyles on a cathedral porch, aren't they? Just as avaricious and terrifying."

"How can you?" But she couldn't help but laugh. There *was* something grotesque in the Marsden sisters' expressions.

"Easily. I have endured too many pretensions and

too much fustian to be impressed by my fellow man any longer. Most of the people here, Lady Wyndham, are masterpieces of falsity and pettiness."

"Well, at least they are good at it, then."

"I beg your pardon?"

"If they are masterpieces, they must do it very well. That's something." She smiled up at him.

Sir Charles laughed. "Indeed, we certainly have the best of everything in London—the most single-minded greed, the greatest hypocrisy, the most refined cruelty."

"You are very severe."

"I have learned to be, watching this spectacle through the years." He gestured around them.

Anabel looked thoughtful. "I suppose you are very fond of Byron's poetry?"

"What?" Sir Charles was startled.

"Are you not? I said so only because that sounded very like some of it I have read." She didn't smile this time, but her eyes danced.

Her partner was speechless for several moments, then he laughed again. "You are astonishing," he said. "I don't believe anyone has ever spoken to me so."

"I suppose they are afraid of you."

"Afraid?"

"Knowing your low opinion of mankind. I am quite terrified myself. What will you say of me during the next set?"

He gazed down at her, shaking his head. "Nothing! I should not dare, for fear your wit would grow even sharper. Where, my dear Lady Wyndham, did you learn it?"

She shrugged, smiling again, and their eyes held as he spun her in a final turn to the conclusion of the music. Bowing over her hand, he said, "I believe they have shortened the length of the sets tonight. I never knew one to go so fast. Will you honor me again later?"

"Perhaps. If you ask me."

"You sound as if you do not think I will."

"I have been hearing a great deal about your reputation, Sir Charles. It seems that a woman mustn't set her heart on your promises."

"Ah. That depends on the woman." Another acquaintance had come up to ask Anabel for the set just forming, and Norbury stepped back. "I will see you later."

Anabel merely smiled, moving off on her new partner's arm. Norbury, watching her go, was surprised by the strength of emotion she had aroused in him in one short dance. She really was extraordinary.

From the doorway, another pair of eyes also followed her. Christopher Hanford had arrived in time to see Anabel dancing with Norbury, and apparently enjoying herself very much, and to observe their parting. It made him frown.

"That must be Anabel," murmured his sister. "She is very pretty, but what is she doing with Norbury? He is…" Christopher's frown had deepened at the name, and Amelia saw it. "Oh. I begin to understand. But, my word, Christopher—Norbury! A new coat is one thing; rivaling a noted Corinthian is quite another."

"No doubt," he said between clenched jaws.

His sister looked sidelong at him, then out over the ballroom. "Well, you cannot dance with her now. Come, I will present you to some of my friends."

She did so, including a number of the season's most charming debutantes. Hanford planned to flirt mildly with any who would respond, to see what Anabel made of that. But he found the girls very tiresome, and even before the set had ended, he was bored and irritated.

He looked around the room, his eyes lingering on Anabel before passing on. Lady Goring was surrounded by a group of her friends; he would greet her later. The few others he knew were dancing. His gaze came to the archway leading into the supper room, moved on, paused, and returned, recognizing a solid figure half visible there. "I am going to speak to someone, Amelia," he said.

"Who?"

"Anabel's cousin, Miss Goring. She is over there."

"That very *large* girl? But, Christopher, you mustn't be seen with a creature like that. Everyone will think you—"

"I may have put on the clothes of a popinjay, Amelia, but I refuse to take on their manner as well. Miss Goring is an intelligent girl, unlike those you have presented to me, and she is obviously having a very unpleasant time. It is simple kindness to speak to her."

Amelia acknowledged the truth of this with a sigh. Her brother would never change, and what was more, she was not sure she wanted him to.

Christopher grinned. "She is extremely fond of novels, Amelia. I imagine you have a great deal in common."

"I shall ask her to tea," replied his sister firmly. "But, Christopher…are you going to *dance* with her?"

He hadn't thought of it, but her tone made him rebellious. "Why, yes."

Georgina had disappeared when he turned to walk across the floor, but he found her inside the supper room, holding an ample plate of delicacies from the buffet and watching the entrance uneasily. When she saw him, she looked surprised, then cautiously pleased.

"Good evening, Miss Goring," he said. "I thought I saw you come this way."

Georgina's smile faded, and she lowered the plate a little while keeping a firm grip on it.

"Would you do me the honor of dancing this next set?" he continued.

The girl's mouth dropped open a little, and she stared at him.

"You do remember me? Christopher Hanford? I

dined at Lady Goring's last week." Her stupefaction made him wonder if he had misjudged her intelligence.

"Yes. Yes, of course." Georgina was overcome. No gentleman had ever voluntarily asked her to dance in her life.

"Shall we?" He offered his arm.

Thrusting the plate aside without even looking at the table, Georgina took it, and they walked into the ballroom together. A country-dance was just forming.

"Thank God it is not a quadrille," said Hanford. "I should quite disgrace you if it were."

"The steps are so complicated," agreed Georgina shyly. "I have never learned them properly."

Hanford smiled down at her as they took their places, and Georgina's heart turned over. A whole new world seemed to open out before her.

Conversation was difficult as they moved through the figures, and Hanford simply maintained his pleasant smile. Georgina smiled tremulously back throughout. He let his gaze wander about the room, discovering Anabel dancing on the other side and Amelia not far away. He would approach Anabel for the next waltz, he decided.

But Norbury was before him, and led Anabel onto the floor. A wave of anger so strong it made his hands clench sent Hanford to the prettiest deb his sister had presented to him. He secured her company for the waltz and concentrated all his faculties on amusing her, keeping the girl laughing throughout the set and the supper interval, which followed. He did not look at Anabel or at anyone else, distrusting his control if he had to watch her with Norbury. Thus, he saw neither her surprised glances nor Georgina Goring's woebegone expression.

When the dancing began again, he solicited another of the season's belles and then another. He ignored the Goring party and scarcely spoke to his sister, single-mindedly bent on showing Anabel that he, too, was attractive to the *haut ton*.

He succeeded very well. When he cared to exert it, Christopher Hanford had a quiet charm and humorous warmth that few women could resist. One girl after another came away from a dance thinking he was well worth cultivating, and determined to tell her mother to invite him at the first opportunity.

Anabel was also dancing during this time, but her eyes often strayed from her partner to follow Hanford. Sir Charles had left the ball for another gathering after supper, begging her pardon for the prior engagement, and as she had noticed Christopher's arrival some time before, she did not really mind. She was eager to talk with him and compare impressions of London. Too, he was looking more elegant than she had ever seen him, and she longed to tell him so and rally him about the change. She had consulted her mother about procuring invitations for Christopher, since he had decided to stay in town, and was prepared to surprise him with a number of them. She could not understand why he did not approach her. At first she had been merely puzzled, but as the ball continued and he devoted himself to one lovely eighteen-year-old after another, her bewilderment shifted to hurt, then anger.

The last dance of the evening was a waltz. Hanford, who had been carefully calculating his movements, joined Anabel at precisely the proper time to secure her hand for it. They walked onto the floor in silence, her chin high, and swung smoothly into step together. They had danced with each other many times, at private balls at home and at country assemblies, and they moved in perfect harmony. But Anabel's expression remained sulky, and Christopher, still angry at her for giving Norbury two waltzes, did not try to alter it.

"You have a new haircut," she said at last.

"Yes. My sister has taken me in hand."

"Your... Oh, of course. I had forgotten she lives in London." Anabel felt an irrational chagrin. Christopher's sister would shepherd him through the intricacies of the season. He would need none of her feeble help.

"I must present you to her."

"That would be pleasant."

They had never been so carefully polite to each other before, and both felt and regretted the change. Abruptly Hanford relented. "You may tell me I look ridiculous if you like. I certainly feel it in these borrowed plumes."

"But you don't." Anabel looked squarely at him for the first time since his approach. "You look wonderful, Christopher. Very handsome indeed. As many would agree, from what I have seen tonight."

So she had noticed his dancing, he thought, his spirit lightening a little.

"I suppose your sister is gratified that you are ready to settle on a wife?"

"Oh yes. She pushed all the debs on me."

"It is lucky you have such a zealous sponsor." Anabel's tone was sour, though she didn't hear it herself. Hanford smiled. "It was prodigious kind of you to include Georgina among your partners."

At this evidence that she had followed his progress closely, Hanford was even further cheered. "Miss Goring is an amiable girl."

It really *had* been kind, Anabel thought. Christopher remained the generous, selfless man he had always been. He deserved a flawless wife. Anabel, acknowledging this, wondered why she could not be happy about the prospect.

"Have you enjoyed the ball?" he asked.

"Oh yes. It is much more grand than any I had seen before."

"Indeed. I suppose we shall both be surprised by a number of things in London before we return home again."

Anabel frowned up at him, trying to interpret this remark, but he whirled her suddenly around and forced her to turn her attention to her feet.

Six

ANABEL WOKE THE FOLLOWING MORNING CONSCIOUS of a feeling of lassitude. Her memories of the ball were less exhilarating than she had expected. A pall seemed to hang over them. And as she washed and dressed and walked downstairs to breakfast, she felt tired and slightly headachy. What was wrong with her? she wondered. Surely any woman should be satisfied with a night like the last. She had danced every dance and been complimented on her looks several times. She had had the success of a young girl rather than the sedate entertainment of a widow, and she had enjoyed it very much. Never in her life had she been the focus of such varied and favorable attentions. Yet now she felt restless and irritable for no cause. It was extremely odd.

Her mother was already seated in the breakfast room with her morning letters and a boiled egg. As Anabel slipped into her chair Lady Goring looked up and said, "Your cousin Amory is very pleased with Vienna. And they will have a fourth child in the spring."

Anabel nodded, not deeply interested in this news of her diplomatic cousin today. She poured herself a cup of tea and drank half of it quickly.

Lady Goring had opened another letter. "Julia Richards is a grandmother again," she said. "That must be the sixth...no, the seventh time. They are certainly a prolific family."

Anabel remained silent.

"Are you all right, dear? You look rather tired."

"I am, a little. I suppose I am not accustomed to late nights."

"You should have slept this morning. Your eyes are quite heavy."

"I'll be fine." A servant had brought hot toast, and Anabel took some and began to eat.

Lady Goring read her mail. The ticking of the clock on the mantelpiece was the only sound in the room for some time. Finally she put down the last envelope and refilled her teacup. "I wonder where Georgina… Oh, there you are, dear. Did you sleep well?"

Georgina Goring, who had just entered the room, nodded as if abstracted. She was carrying a flat silver-paper box and a reticule clutched to her chest. Instead of going to her chair, she walked directly up to Lady Goring. "I want to give you these," she said breathlessly.

"What are they, dear?"

"Chocolates," she replied, putting the box down quickly, as if afraid she might not be able to do it. "And this is the pocket money my father gave me." She placed the reticule beside the box. "I want you to keep it for me, to use when we are shopping or…or something."

Lady Goring looked puzzled. "But, Georgina, you can manage your own allowance. I—"

"If you have it, I can't buy more chocolates," gasped the girl. She was finding the conversation very difficult, but she was determined to carry through.

"Can't…" Lady Goring's puzzled frown slowly shifted to surprise, then to amazed delight. "My dear Georgina, do you mean that you are taking my advice at last? How splendid! You will be very glad in the end, I promise you."

"Yes." Georgina did not sound very certain. She turned and started to leave the room.

"Where are you going?"

"To my room. I shall be upstairs if you want me."

"But you haven't had any breakfast. Sit down and let me ring for fresh tea."

Georgina gazed longingly at the table, with its toast racks and pots of jam, then at the sideboard, where chafing dishes held eggs and bacon, and a cold ham beckoned enticingly. She swallowed, her face anguished, then shook her head. "I...I'm not hungry."

"Not... Nonsense, of course you are hungry. It is very wise of you to give up sweets, Georgina, but you cannot stop eating altogether. Come and have a little. That is all you need do, you know, simply eat a little at each meal rather than...." Lady Goring let the sentence trail off, not wanting in any way to mar this miracle.

"That is harder than having nothing," wailed Georgina.

"Nonsense," replied her hostess again. "Come, sit down."

Slowly she did so. Anabel, who had been watching this exchange with some amusement, greeted her. Lady Goring beamed as she hurried to make up a frugal plate for her niece. Grimacing, Georgina began to eat.

Anabel could not resist probing a little for the cause of this change. "Did you enjoy the ball last night, Georgina?" she asked.

The girl seemed to find the question difficult. Finally she said, "Yes," in a tone that implied the negative as well.

"I saw you dancing with Mr. Hanford. I thought he looked very well in his new evening clothes."

Georgina's gray eyes abruptly shone. "Mr. Hanford is the most *wonderful* gentleman I have ever met!"

Lady Goring glanced meaningfully at her daughter, conveying a mutual understanding of Georgina's motives while hiding her own curiosity as to how Anabel would take this schoolgirl crush. She was certain of Christopher Hanford's feelings, but she was by no means privy to Anabel's.

Anabel was struggling with a violent, unreasoning annoyance. It was just like Christopher to encourage

such a ridiculous passion, without being the least aware
of doing so, of course. He was so kind to everyone. But
he should realize that here in town things were quite
different. Girls were not the daughters of old friends who
could correctly interpret his behavior for their offspring.
And the season naturally raised certain expectations. Its
most exclusive assembly was known as the "marriage
mart," after all. He was liable to find himself in a very
awkward situation. Perhaps she should speak to him.

It was then that she remembered Christopher was in
town to find a wife, and last night he had danced with
every pretty ninnyhammer at the ball. He didn't require
her advice. Far from it! But perhaps Georgina did.
Looking across at her, Anabel frowned a little. Georgina
had not begun eating again; she was gazing at the wall
with a rapt expression. "He is certainly very kind,"
said Anabel. "I have rarely known a man so mindful of
others' feelings."

"Oh, yes," agreed Georgina.

"Indeed, it is so marked that it is sometimes misin-
terpreted." Anabel, her attention focused on Georgina,
did not see her mother's satisfaction at this remark. "On
several occasions I have seen people make more of it than
he meant."

The girl nodded. "I can see how that would happen.
One must go beyond trivialities and discover true
motives." She contemplated this a moment. "He danced
with all those girls last night because they were pretty
and amusing," she went on. "He thinks I am intelligent,
however. And if I were also pretty…" She pushed away
her plate and stood up. "I think I will go walking in the
park this morning, aunt."

Lady Goring, who had been suppressing a smile, blinked.
She had repeatedly urged Georgina to take exercise.
"Splendid, my dear. Take your maid with you."

Nodding, the girl went out.

"Well!" said her aunt, gazing at Anabel expectantly. "What do you think of that."

Anabel also rose. Georgina's reasoning had shaken her. Christopher had called her intelligent, and if the girl's looks did improve under her new regimen, might he not possibly find the wife he desired in her? "Oh, it is all ridiculous!" she snapped, refusing to think about the implications of her feelings.

Lady Goring's eyes danced. "Well, I don't care why it is happening. I am only glad that Georgina has decided to do as I asked. I had nearly given up in despair." Savoring Anabel's mulish expression, she added, "Georgina will be a very pretty girl indeed if she slims, don't you think?"

"Doubtless." Anabel's tone was curt. "I shall be in my room if you want me, Mama." She swept out, leaving Lady Goring free to allow her pleased smile to spread across her face.

Striding quickly up the stairs, Anabel was oblivious to everything but her own ill temper. Everyone was being so stupid. Why couldn't Christopher behave as he always had? It was not that she begrudged him a season in London, she told herself, but he was almost certain to fall into a scrape. She was only thinking of him.

Immersed in her excuses, Anabel did not notice two small faces peering through the stair rails on the top landing. She moved off below them toward her bedchamber, frowning, and they watched her go.

"Mama looks angry," said Susan in a low voice. "Isn't she coming up to see us before lessons? She always did at home."

"I don't know," answered Nicholas. "I suppose not."

"Is Uncle Christopher taking us to the play today? He promised he would."

Her brother sighed. This was not the first time, nor the twentieth, that Susan had asked this question. "He did not set a day. I'm sure he will do so when he has the time."

Susan stood, gripping the rails with her fists. "I hate it here!"

Nick nodded heavily. "Come along to the schoolroom. We must find William and have a council."

William was already there, sitting at the battered schoolroom table and scowling at an open book. He looked up when they came in. "I can't do this, Nick," he said. "Each time I work it out, I get a different answer. You must help me again."

"In a moment," replied his brother absently. "Just now we must decide something."

"What?" The older male Wyndham turned in his chair.

The others joined him at the ancient table. The schoolroom was a large, wide-windowed chamber near the top of the house, filled with cast-off furniture from downstairs and the discarded toys and books of generations of Gorings. It was a comfortable, unpretentious place, but it was not their schoolroom and their mother was seldom in it, so the Wyndhams disliked it.

"We must make up our minds what we are going to do," declared Nicholas, putting his elbows on the tabletop and his chin in his hand.

"Are you still thinking of that?" William was resigned.

"I want to go home!" insisted Susan, her green eyes glinting and her red hair brilliant in the shaft of sunlight from the window.

"I know, Susan, but we cannot," explained her elder brother.

"We might," objected Nicholas, "if we could just think of a plan."

"A plan," scoffed William.

"Try!" Nick's plea was so intense that all three frowned in thought, Susan's small face screwed up comically.

"You could pretend to be ill," William said to Nicholas then.

Nick, who had been considered sickly as a very small boy and strongly resented reminders of his weakness, answered, "Or you could fall into a truly dreadful scrape."

William scowled. He was prone to scrapes, often the result of his slower wits in carrying out one of his brother's plans. Susan looked interested.

"Or Susan could throw a particularly nasty temper tantrum," added Nick. "But I do not think any of those things would serve. Mama might simply send us home and remain here herself."

This prospect was so awful that they gazed at one another solemnly for a long moment. Then Susan jumped as if kicked. "Oh!"

"What?" said her brothers simultaneously.

She pointed toward the windows. Outside, on the narrow ledge, stalked Daisy, his bulk seeming much too wide for his perch. He was not looking at them but rather at a hapless sparrow twittering a few feet ahead.

"She'll fall!" shrieked Susan, leaping up and running to the window. "And if anyone sees her outside my room, she will be sent away. William! Nicholas! Do something!" Her screams frightened the bird, which flew away.

Daisy paused, disgusted, his eyes turning to glare at his small mistress. He seemed quite comfortable on the window ledge.

"Don't be frightened, Daisy," said Susan. "We will get you down." She whirled to gaze at her brothers.

They rose reluctantly, particularly Nicholas. William carried his chair over to the window and climbed onto it to reach the catch. Then he threw up the sash and reached for the cat. Daisy backed away with a hiss.

"Daisy, come here!" commanded Susan. She started to scramble up beside William. The chair wobbled.

"Look out!" Nick cried.

With a shout from William, the chair toppled backward, flinging him heavily to the floor, with Susan kicking and protesting on top of him. Nick ran to see if they were all right. As he bent to help them up Daisy stuck his nose across the windowsill, took in the situation, and leaped solidly onto Nick's bent back, claws fully extended. They dug through the boy's coat and shirt to his skin and jerked him upright with a howl. Daisy jumped to the floor and ran under a convenient bookshelf.

"Devil take that cat!" cried Nick, with great satisfaction in at last having an opportunity to use an expression picked up from a stable boy. He snatched up the book William had been using and looked for Daisy, but the cat was well beyond his reach by this time.

"Nick!" screamed Susan. He put down the book.

William was on his feet, brushing the dust from his coat and looking intensely annoyed. "Of all the stupid—"

"I have it!" cried Nicholas. "It came to me just now." He noticed the others' blank stares with impatience. "The plan."

William pressed an elbow and winced. "Oh no."

"It's a good one. Listen, what do we dislike most about London?"

"No fields. We hardly ever get out," responded William.

"Too many people telling us what to do," said Susan at the same time.

"Yes, yes. But that is not what we hate *most*." Nicholas paused for effect.

"Mama is always occupied or out," supplied Susan.

Her brother frowned at this anticipation of his words but nodded. "We were accustomed to seeing her every day, for hours. Now we never do. And she is always thinking of something else."

"We know *that*," said William.

"Well, let us do the same to her. Then she will see how unpleasant it is here."

"What do you mean?" They frowned at him.

"We must be too busy to see *her*. We must pretend

that we have no time for visits and that we are interested in other things."

"But we are not!" exclaimed Susan. "There is nothing to be interested in here." She indicated the room with disgust.

"I know, Susan, but if we act as if there is, Mama will miss us just as we miss her, and she will take us home again, where we can all be comfortable."

"She will?"

William looked doubtful. "I don't know, Nicky. This sounds like one of your harebrained schemes. Mama hardly notices what we do lately. She won't care."

"She doesn't notice because we are just as we always were. If we changed, she would wonder soon enough. I only worry that Susan will forget and spoil the whole plan."

"I can do anything you can do," protested his sister at once. But she looked confused. "What am I to do?"

"Just pretend you do not care whether Mama comes to us or not, and that you have a great many more interesting things to do when she does."

Susan's full lower lip protruded. "That will be very hard."

"It will, Nick," agreed William. "I don't know if *I* can do it. Without Mama…"

"We shall have each other," insisted Nicholas. "And we must always remember that playing our parts will get us home again and make things as they used to be." He looked from one to the other. "Will you try?"

William and Susan had learned to trust Nick's intelligence. After a moment they nodded.

"Good, here is what we must—"

The door opened, and a tall, spare young woman entered. "You are all here. Splendid. We can begin at once."

Nicholas closed his mouth, and the three children shuffled into their chairs around the table. In the country their mother had supervised their lessons each morning, but here in London Lady Goring had insisted on a governess. Miss Tate was neither unkind nor unamusing, but she was still a stranger, and her substitution for Lady Wyndham made the children slow to warm to her. They did their lessons and generally obeyed her commands but did not offer confidences or affection as yet.

As they fetched books and pencils Nicholas signaled the others with jerks of his head and grimaces that they would finish their conference after studies. He was extremely pleased with himself, certain that his idea would work within a fortnight. As always, the exercise of his intelligence exhilarated him, and he even managed to slip William the answer to the problem that had been plaguing him without Miss Tate seeing.

Seven

THE FIRST FEW WEEKS OF THE SEASON PASSED QUICKLY.
Neither Anabel nor Christopher had ever experienced
such a whirl of social activity, and Georgina was almost
dazed by the constant round. To Lady Goring's amazement and gratification, her niece maintained her resolve
to avoid chocolates and other sweets, and the effects
soon became apparent. Georgina's face looked more
slender within just a few days, and her figure slowly followed suit. The image that emerged was quite engaging,
and Lady Goring was certain that she would be very
pretty indeed if she continued. Georgina herself, astonished at the reflection her mirror showed her, became
even more Spartan in her self-discipline and often had
to be urged to eat.

Anabel watched the process with a mixture of amused
encouragement and chagrin, for though she was happy
that Georgina should feel more comfortable in town,
she always felt an irrational annoyance when she saw the
girl with Christopher. Her adoration was so patent, and
yet he did nothing to discourage it. Anabel felt someone
ought to speak to him, but for some reason she hesitated
to do so herself.

For one thing, she was too busy. They went out nearly
every night, and as the days passed, Anabel became more
certain of seeing Sir Charles Norbury at each event they
attended. At first she had met him only intermittently,
and she heard that he was known for ignoring invitations
he judged boring. His presence at a party was considered

a great coup. But as time went on, he turned up at more and more of the gatherings and practically devoted himself to her. People began to gossip about it, and Anabel knew she should withdraw, but Norbury continued to fascinate her. His polished manners, sardonic opinions of the world of fashion, and aura of barely controlled passions attracted her despite whatever firm resolves she made. When he approached her, she forgot the staring crowds in the heady new game of flirtation. And when some brief flash in Norbury's pale green eyes suggested that it was more than a game, Anabel felt a tremor of excitement and half-apprehensive anticipation.

Watching this spectacle, Christopher Hanford grew progressively more dour, though it was obvious only to those most interested in the outcome. He flirted with the debs, danced, and drank champagne among the *haut ton*, but his gaze was most often fixed on the woman he was *not* partnering, and he moved like an automaton through society's rituals, scarcely aware of what he said or did. He was losing Anabel, he knew, and nothing else mattered to him. His sister rarely looked at him without a frown now, and Lady Goring was filled with annoyance and concern for both him and her daughter. Yet nothing either said appeared to make a particle of difference.

In this charged atmosphere the children's scheme fell rather flat. They exerted themselves mightily to carry out Nicholas's orders, but their mother hardly seemed to notice the withdrawal. Once or twice, when she visited them in the nursery, she wondered that they did not greet her more enthusiastically, but Anabel's mind was too occupied with her own situation to concentrate on anything else. Nicholas was much downcast by the failure, and Susan and William were indignant.

By the beginning of Georgina's second month in London, Lady Goring was feeling so pleased with her that she determined to give a ball for her charge. There had been no such entertainment at the Goring house for nearly a year, and she felt in the mood to give one. If she could have discovered some excuse for *not* asking Sir Charles Norbury, she would have been perfectly content.

She could not, however, and when the gilt-edged invitation cards went out, one was addressed to him. They received a flattering number of acceptances, considering the rather impromptu nature of the ball, and Lady Goring threw herself into the preparations, with occasional help from Georgina. She was so busy that she scarcely noticed Anabel's lack of participation or her frequent absences during the day. And, indeed, Anabel's mind was in such turmoil that she would not have been of much use. Norbury's attentions had become so marked, so unmistakable, that she knew she could expect a declaration soon. Even the gossips had altered their tone. Norbury was notorious for his intense, and short-lived, flirtations, and he customarily conducted them with willing young matrons, who could not threaten him with marriage. At first Anabel's widowhood had seemed to put her in the same class, but when Norbury's campaign continued and even intensified, the *ton* began to look more closely. What they saw suggested to more than one gossip that Sir Charles's famous immunity to serious attachments had at last given way. This was ten times more interesting than his flirtations, and the talk redoubled, with gentlemen placing bets at their clubs on the timing of the announcement in the *Morning Post*.

Anabel found this public scrutiny of her private affairs highly unsettling. She began to feel reluctant to enter crowded drawing rooms, and the knowledge that she could expect an offer, without any certainty as to when, strung her nerves too tight. Worst of all, she was not completely sure how she felt about Norbury. It seemed very soon to make a decision, though she knew many women made such a choice after even shorter acquaintance. Nonetheless, she felt hurried. There seemed too many elements to consider; they all rose up to badger and confuse her. When she was with Sir Charles, the thrill of his presence dispelled her doubts, but when he was gone, she again wondered. It was a new experience; Anabel had accepted Ralph Wyndham on her parents' recommendation, never thinking of refusing. She had had no practice in the games of courtship.

On the night of the ball, Lady Goring, Anabel, and Georgina met early in the drawing room to receive a few dinner guests before the main entertainment. They had had new dresses made up for the occasion, and each in her own way looked splendid.

Lady Goring had chosen an emerald silk whose brilliance and sheen were merely enhanced by the very simple cut. She wore emeralds and diamonds, and had fastened a spray of them in her hair.

Anabel wore a warm peach satin embroidered around the hem and sleeve with ivory blossoms. Ivory ribbons fluttered at the high waist, and one of the cameos her grandmother had brought back from Paris years ago was fastened close about her throat. She looked cool and untouchable as a Dresden shepherdess, but inside she was seething with expectation and uncertainty.

Georgina's appearance was the most remarkable. In the weeks since her revelation she had shed a surprising amount of her bulk. She was still far from sylphlike, but the fashion of the day was charitable toward a slight thickening of the waist and hip. In a gown of floating white muslin, with sleeves cut to the elbow and a generous flounce about the hem, she made a very creditable show. And her face was by now almost beautiful. As its fullness declined, the finely sculpted bones became evident, and her thickly lashed gray eyes seemed larger and more expressive. Tonight a becoming color stained her cheeks, and her pale hair had been dressed by Lady

Goring's maid into a helmet of curls. Georgina was trembling with excitement.

"Well," said Lady Goring, sinking onto the sofa. "I believe we are actually ready at last. I cannot think of a single thing left to do. If you had asked me last week, I would have vowed this moment would never come!"

"The ballroom is wonderful," breathed Georgina.

"It does look well, doesn't it?" answered her aunt complacently. "I must say, I think it was a good idea to use the ivy. Don't you, Anabel?"

Her daughter started. "What? I beg your pardon, Mama?"

Lady Goring frowned at her, hesitated, then shook her head. She was beginning to think that her husband had been right when he married Anabel off without a come-out.

There were sounds of arrival in the front hall below, and in a moment a footman was announcing Christopher Hanford and his sister and brother-in-law. Lady Goring greeted them warmly, Georgina with tremulous smiles and Anabel abstractedly. Hanford frowned and turned to the younger girl. "You are looking very pretty tonight, Georgina," he said.

She swallowed, trying to dislodge the lump in her throat. "Th-thank you."

"I hope you are saving a dance for me." He was gazing sidelong at Anabel as he spoke; she didn't seem aware of anyone.

"Oh yes!"

The fervency of her answer transfixed him. Surveying Georgina more closely, Hanford made a discovery. The girl was deep in the throes of calf love, and he himself was the object! He almost groaned aloud. He wanted to concentrate all his faculties on Anabel, and here was this schoolgirl with worship shining in her eyes. It wasn't fair.

Meeting her unwavering gaze again, he sighed, then

smiled. Calf love was one of the most dreadful experiences in life, as he well remembered. He had to do what he could to ease her through and out of it.

More dinner guests were ushered in, and after a few minutes they went in to dinner. Norbury had not been included in this party—Lady Goring had been determined on that, at least, and Anabel had not objected. There were two old friends of hers, carefully chosen parents of offspring about Georgina's age, and their sons and daughters. Georgina was seated between two of the former, to ensure her partners for some of the dances, and Anabel was cunningly placed beside Hanford. Georgina at first resented this exile, but when the young men seemed inclined to admire her, she unbent and, to her own astonishment, found things to say that made them both laugh.

"We haven't talked much recently," said Hanford over the first course. "It seems odd, after the way we used to do so in the country." He was ready to use whatever weapons he could now—to give up flirting, to return to his old coats—if that would win Anabel away from the hated Norbury.

"Yes," she agreed. "It is very different here, of course."

"Very. How are the children? They seemed a trifle out of sorts when I saw them last week."

"When did you see them? They didn't mention it to me." Anabel was astonished. The children always described their outings to her in great detail.

"We went riding. I thought they would like it, as they are accustomed to get out at home. We found a fine pony for Susan at the livery."

"How kind of you." Anabel's reply was a bit faint. She was wondering why she had not thought of providing the children with mounts. They adored riding. And why had they not told her? Suddenly anxious, she frowned down at her plate.

Hanford saw it with pleasure. Perhaps he could still reach her. "I promised we should go again on Friday. Will you come with us?"

She nodded. "I should like to."

"Good." He left the matter there, satisfied that the hints he had thrown out would stay with her, and the conversation drifted to more general topics.

They didn't linger at table. By nine the party had moved to the ballroom, and Lady Goring was greeting the first new arrivals under the archway. The room soon filled, and Georgina was called upon to play the part she had been dreading—opening the dancing with a young man presented to her by Lady Goring. She was quaking when the music struck up, but as they moved through the steps and her partner made it clear that he did not feel the task a penance, she felt better. By the end of the set she was even smiling at him and talking in a voice that was nearly normal.

Anabel had not joined the first set. Still vaguely worried, she had slipped upstairs to look at the children. She had bade them good night earlier, after showing them her ball gown, but she needed to see them again to reassure herself of their well-being after Hanford's surprising revelations. Susan was fast asleep, curled in a tight ball and clutching a tattered rag doll that she claimed only at night. She looked angelic, and Anabel smiled at the deceptiveness of sleep as she tucked the blanket closer around her neck. No one would guess her daughter's strong will from this picture. The boys were in bed but not yet quite asleep. They blinked up at her candle when she came in and asked what was wrong. "Nothing. I just came up to say good night." She bent to kiss each of them, her throat tightening at their hugs and the fresh child smell of their skin. She missed them, she suddenly realized. They had seen much more of one another at home. "I am going riding with you and Uncle Christopher on Friday," she whispered.

"You are!" They bounced up, eyes shining.

"Yes. But you must lie down now. It is late."

It took her a while to get them settled and, indeed, she lingered a little, feeling very happy. But at last they were quiet, falling into sleep, and she took up her candlestick and slipped out again. The music from the ballroom filtered up the stairs, and she moved down them slowly, her blue eyes soft with memory.

"There you are," said someone from the hall below. "They said you had gone upstairs."

She looked down to find Sir Charles Norbury gazing up at her. A tingling shock ran through her body, and the candle trembled a little, dripping wax.

"You have missed the first waltz," he added, meeting her at the bottom of the staircase and taking the candlestick from her hand. He snuffed the flame between forefinger and thumb and set it aside. "And I came early especially to engage you for it."

"I wanted to look in on the children." As always, his presence overwhelmed her. He seemed to tower over her, yet his pale green eyes felt close and compelling. She found it hard to breathe.

"It is a country-dance now, unfortunately. Mayn't we wait outside here for the next and hope?" He smiled and reached for her hand to lead her across to a small empty anteroom.

Anabel knew she should say no, but her voice seemed to have died, and she went with him silently and allowed him to escort her to a sofa and sit beside her, his arm thrown along its back.

"You look exquisite tonight," he said softly. "The loveliest woman at the ball."

This outrageous compliment revived her. "What a plumper. There are dozens of prettier ones."

"No."

"Flatterer." She smiled, but when she met his eyes, they were very serious.

"No," he said again. "To me you are the most beautiful." He held her gaze for a moment, then slowly bent forward and took possession of her lips, his arm tightening around her shoulders.

Anabel's slight trembling increased, and her mind dissolved in confusion. She should pull away, part of it cried; this was terribly fast, and someone might come in at any moment. But another part urged her on, fascinated by Sir Charles's attractions and filled with curiosity.

His kiss was very expert, and nothing at all like her deceased husband's, Anabel's only standard of comparison. His lips seemed to draw all strength out of her, leaving her limp and pliant, yet she felt disconnected from the expected sensual pleasure. He knew how to draw response from her body, clearly, but her heart and mind remained in turmoil.

Norbury, on the contrary, was in the grip of feelings stronger than any he had ever experienced, and for him the kiss confirmed a decision. This was the woman he wanted. Never had his passions been suffused with such emotion. Beyond thinking, he moved his free hand to Anabel's knee and slid it upward caressingly, savoring the curve of her waist under the thin satin dress and cupping his fingers around her breast. She drew her breath in sharply.

A scuff of footsteps in the hall, followed by a scrap of conversation and a laugh, jerked Anabel upright. She pulled away from him only just in time to avoid being caught by two couples coming into the room. But it was obvious in the way that the newcomers stopped, smiled, and apologized that their appearance gave them away. Anabel rose and hurried from the room, Norbury behind her. Her cheeks were flaming, and she felt that she could not possibly face the crowd in the ballroom.

Sir Charles caught her arm and turned her to face him. "I beg your pardon. That was entirely my fault, and I apologize. I would not worry you or expose you to embarrassment for the world."

"It...it doesn't matter," replied Anabel, her voice a little choked.

"On the contrary. Lady Wyndham...Anabel, you must know that I have something to ask..." A laughing couple came out of the ballroom and stood nearby, the lady fanning herself and complaining of the heat. Norbury scowled. "We cannot talk here. If you..." Looking at her face, he realized that this was no time to suggest they withdraw. "May I call on you at eleven tomorrow morning?" he finished.

Anabel couldn't think of anything but escaping from prying eyes. "Yes, of course."

Sir Charles bowed his head, then offered his arm. "They are playing a waltz at last. We can slip in among the dancers without attracting undue notice."

Nodding, she took his arm. They moved to the archway, and Norbury guided her deftly among the circling couples. Even the ones nearest hardly glanced at them. Anabel sighed with relief and relaxed a little in his arms.

"All will be well," he murmured.

But all was not well for several people in the ballroom who had been on the watch for Anabel. Christopher Hanford, dancing with Georgina, was barely able to control the hot surge of rage at the sight, and his fist closed convulsively, nearly crushing the girl's hand. "What is the matter?" she exclaimed.

"Nothing, nothing." He had been trying his best to be at once kind and unencouraging to Georgina, but now he had no thought to spare for her. His face fell into hard lines, and he kept his eyes on Anabel.

Georgina, scanning his features anxiously, searched her meager experience for the proper words. This had been the most wonderful evening of her life. Several young men had asked her to dance without being prompted, and now she was in the arms of the gentleman she most admired. She had been approved to waltz by Almack's patronesses only tonight, and this was the first time she had tried that stimulating dance. Everything had been perfect until a moment ago. What should she say? She wanted very much to comfort Hanford, to both share and erase the trouble she saw in his face, but she didn't know how. Biting her lower lip, she followed his lead and worried.

The other two who had seen Anabel come in had moved toward each other soon after. Lady Goring and Amelia Lanforth had met recently, and despite the difference in their ages, they had discovered much in common. A series of meaningful looks at an evening party two nights before had assured them that they shared certain hopes for Anabel and Christopher. They had said nothing aloud, but tonight's developments dissolved their reserve.

"He is going to offer for her," said Amelia in a low voice when they had left a group of friends. "I can hardly believe it."

Lady Goring did not have to ask whom she meant. Her daughter's face when she returned to the ballroom, and Norbury's, had told her a great deal. "I wish I had never made her come to London," she repined.

"You think she'll accept him?" Amelia's eyes shifted to her brother. He was staring at Anabel in the most transparent way, she saw.

"I fear it, though I can't say for certain."

"Christopher will be so unhappy."

Lady Goring merely shook her head. "Norbury is a great catch, but not the sort of man I would want for my daughter."

"He seems to care for her," replied Amelia, trying

to be comforting. When the other did not answer, she added, "I suppose there is nothing we can do?"

"I have tried talking to her, more than once. She won't listen."

"Ah." They watched the set end and the couples break apart. Hanford escorted Georgina to them and turned away without a word, almost stalking across the floor to Anabel. They watched him stop before her, speak, and then lead her away despite an involuntary restraining gesture from Norbury. Both men were frowning. Norbury stood alone for a moment, but he soon recognized that their exchange had drawn notice. He set his lips and walked out of the room.

Christopher, taking Anabel's hand as the music started again, was silently grim. She did not see it at first, still too wrapped up in her own concerns. But as the dance went on and he did not speak, she finally looked up, encountering an angry gaze. "What's wrong?"

"Wrong?"

She had never heard him use such a cold, angry tone. And she had never seen his face so haughty and withdrawn. This was not her old reliable friend Christopher but some daunting, fashionable stranger. Had the whole world gone mad?

"Perhaps I am disappointed to see you become one of the *on-dits* of the town," he added between his teeth, "if you wish to make a fool of yourself in public, I cannot, of course…"

This was too much, after her embarrassing return to the ballroom. How could he imagine she had done it on purpose? "It is none of your affair what I do!" she snapped.

He had to wait a moment before answering. He was so angry that he was afraid he would shout. "Perhaps not," he managed finally, "though some would say that years of friendship gave me a claim. However, as you do not acknowledge that, and since you appear to have no respect for my opinions, I—"

"Please say no more!" Anabel's brain was whirling. In nearly ten years she and Christopher had had no such disagreements. She had always believed that they had wholly congenial tempers and ideas. And even if he disapproved of her conduct tonight, not realizing that it had been unintentional, she did not understand why he should attack her so viciously. Could he not see how it hurt her? Indeed, it hurt so much that she was having trouble keeping time to the dance. That strangers might think her imprudent had been upsetting; that Christopher should was somehow many times worse. It seemed to Anabel that everything in her life was going awry.

They finished the set in silence. Hanford's mouth was thin and unforgiving, and Anabel kept her perpetually tearing eyes on the floor. She was miserable, and had never been more grateful than when the music ended and she could retreat upstairs to the room set aside for the ladies.

Christopher left the ball without speaking to anyone. He couldn't bear any more talking, and his heart sank when he thought of the future. Anabel was slipping away from him, and he was helpless to do anything about it.

Eight

SIR CHARLES WAS EXACTLY ON TIME THE FOLLOWING morning. Anabel received him in the library rather than the drawing room because her mother's reaction to the impending visit had been so carefully unemotional that Anabel decided it would be better if they did not meet. She had put on a white muslin gown delicately striped with a blue that matched her eyes and dressed her soft brown hair in curls, but she did not feel she looked her best. She had not slept well after the ball. Consciousness of the approaching decision and worry over Christopher and the children had kept her tossing on her pillow for hours.

Anabel had never endured such uncertainty. The large problems of life had always been settled by someone else. Her father had decreed her marriage, then Ralph had taken his place. When Ralph died, she had naturally turned to Christopher for help with the arrangements and all business matters. Anabel had run her house and cared for her children, but she had never really determined the course of her life. Now, with her mother noncommittal and Christopher incomprehensibly cold and withdrawn, she had to, and the knowledge made her uneasy.

Norbury looked splendid in a coat of olive-green superfine and buff pantaloons. His Hessian boots gleamed as he followed the footman into the room, and his waistcoat was a model of fashion and propriety. As she held out her hand to him Anabel thought how handsome he was. He was the most impressive figure she had ever been intimate with.

"I hope you have recovered from last night," he said with a smile.

Her heart beat faster. "Yes." She didn't feel able to tell him she felt tired and heavy-eyed.

"Shall we sit down?"

"Oh. Of course." Moving to the sofa before the fireplace, she did so. Norbury sat close beside her.

"I can think of nothing else, so I will come directly to the point," he went on. His green eyes were very serious. "I believe you know what I wish to say to you. I have fallen in love with you and hope you will be my wife."

Anabel trembled a little. Though she had expected the question, still, to hear it was exciting. She looked up and met his steady gaze. The gossips had been eager to tell her of Norbury's past flirtations; her own mother had made it clear that he was a man of wide experience and impervious heart. He had examined scores of debutantes with a jaundiced eye and sampled the charms of a series of stunning older women, but he had never offered his hand. Anabel was by no means unaware of her unique position. His proposal would cause a sensation. She would be envied and honored for her conquest. It was terribly flattering to be the choice of such a man. His wealth and position were nothing to it.

And the man himself was an added inducement. As always in his presence, Anabel felt fascinated and attracted. Sir Charles radiated confidence. Something in the set of his head, the way he moved and looked at her, made her vibrate with an unidentifiable tension. The memory of his touch made her feel slightly faint. He overwhelmed her.

"You must say something, you know," he said.

The command made her look down again. What did she want? she wondered. She didn't really know. Her wants had always been supplied to her almost before they were formulated. She had wanted what she had been expected to desire and accepted others' giving of it. Her father, Ralph, Christopher, had seemed certain of what was right, and she had left matters to them. She was accustomed to that. Now, for the first time, she was being asked to choose for herself—and her choice did not have to be the safe one. Meeting Norbury's eyes again, and feeling that quivering thrill, she slowly nodded. "Yes."

He smiled and took her hand, letting out his breath. "You made me quite uneasy for a moment. I didn't realize how difficult it could be to wait for a word." He kissed her hand. "I shall do my utmost to be an exemplary husband, Anabel. As I am sure you have been told, my record is not a good one. But that is past. Having met you, I am yours alone."

Anabel said nothing. She was feeling confused. Having made her decision, she ought to be happy, she thought, but she felt only relief that it was over and she need worry no longer.

"Why so silent?" he teased, putting his arm along the sofa back around her shoulders. "You have not even assured me you return my flattering sentiments, you know."

Gazing at him, Anabel could see that his light tone masked sincerity. He wanted her to say she loved him. She opened her mouth to do so—she must or she would not have accepted him—and stopped. It suddenly seemed to her that she didn't know what the word meant. Or, more to the point, she didn't know in this case. She loved her mother and had loved her father; she adored her children. But for her husband she had always felt a kind of warm, ironic affection different from both of these feelings and very different from those Sir Charles elicited. If she had loved Ralph...but had she? Perhaps not; perhaps what she felt now was really love—this trembling excitement and uncertainty. "I...I do." She faltered, her voice sounding false in her own ears.

Norbury did not seem to hear it. He smiled and drew her closer. "I had begun to fear that this moment would never come, that I would never find a woman with whom I could spend my life. You are very precious to me, Anabel." Bending, he kissed her. Once again Anabel felt that melting sensation in all her bones. His practiced hands knew just how to move, and she felt as if she were being carried away by an irresistible tide. She was powerless, motiveless; all her senses swam.

It was some time before Norbury pulled away. His breathing had quickened, and his green eyes were clouded with desire. He held her away from him and laughed shakily. "Enough of that, I'm afraid. I can't answer for myself otherwise. You fill my veins with fire, Anabel."

She blushed a little, half flattered, half confused. No one had ever said such things to her before.

He took a deep breath and straightened. "When shall the wedding be? Soon."

"I…" She hadn't thought further than the proposal.

"Next month? There is no reason for us to wait."

"But I must tell my mother, my family."

He smiled. "That will hardly take a month. Let us set it for a month from today."

He was so eager that she found it hard to resist him. But she wasn't ready to go this far. "We can decide that later, can we not? There is so much to do."

Norbury frowned, then shrugged. "Very well. I'll send the announcement to the *Morning Post* today, and you can begin your vast preparations." He smiled again. "You must come down to Kent and meet my mother. She doesn't get to London now. She will be delighted. Shall I tell her next week?"

"I…" Anabel felt overwhelmed by all these sudden plans.

"We don't want to leave it too long."

"I suppose I can."

"Splendid. I'll write her today."

She made an effort to contribute something. "You must become better acquainted with my children also. Shall we go out together?"

Norbury's smile faded a bit. In his infatuation with Anabel, he had tried to forget that she was burdened with a family. He didn't want to think of her as another man's wife or as the mother of any but his children. "Of course."

She caught the change in his tone and looked up anxiously. "I'm sure you will love them when you know them."

"No doubt."

"When shall we go? Monday, perhaps?"

"I had thought of starting for Kent Monday."

"Oh. Well, before that, then." She frowned. "They are right here, after all. You needn't go anywhere."

Seeing her growing concern, he nodded. "I can be free for a while on Saturday morning."

It seemed a grudging acceptance, and Anabel's frown remained.

"Where would they like to go, do you think?" he added. "I know very little about children."

"They love the park. We could go walking."

He nearly grimaced, but her expression made him suppress it. There would be plenty of time to deal with the children later. "I will see what I can arrange."

She smiled, relieved, though he had set no time.

"And now I should go, I suppose." He rose. "We shall be very busy for the next few weeks."

She got up and walked with him to the library door. There he paused and pulled her into his arms again, molding the length of her body to his. Anabel put her arms around him, feeling the movement of hard muscle in his back. "I can scarcely wait so long," he murmured before bending to kiss her again.

Only his embrace held her upright as his hands caressed her shoulders and back. She was again swept away by a tide of intense sensation. Her brain whirled with it, and when he drew away again, she found it hard to breathe.

"I shall see you tonight," he said, smiling. "And the announcement will be published tomorrow." He went into the front hall, and she followed him shakily.

When he was gone, Anabel returned to the library for a few moments to regain her composure. She must go upstairs and tell her mother and the children, she knew, but not just yet. She wanted to explore her own feelings first. She should be happy, she thought, but she wasn't. She was breathless and confused, and wished she had someone to talk with about the events of the day. Her mother would be unsympathetic, and there was no other woman in London to whom she could turn. She thought suddenly of Christopher. How comforting it would be to ask his advice and receive his usual sane, sensible counsel. The thought of Christopher was like a rock in the swirling chaos of her emotions. He would know what was right. But as soon as she thought it, she shook her head. She couldn't go to him about this. Even had they been on their former easy footing, it wouldn't be proper. And now that Christopher was so changed, it was out of the question.

Abruptly Anabel felt terribly dispirited. Her life had been so simple once; now it seemed unmanageably complex. And for the first time she had no one to turn to for help. This, naturally, led her thoughts to Sir Charles. He was the logical source of aid after this morning. But somehow she could not imagine going to him with her problems. He was not that sort of person. And he was too much a part of her uncertainty to understand or judge it.

Sighing, Anabel rose and started upstairs. She had to

speak to her mother. The announcement would come out tomorrow, and she must be told well before then.

Lady Goring was sitting with Georgina in the drawing room, looking over some new dress patterns. But she looked up when Anabel came in, her expression concerned. "I have good news, Mama," said Anabel.

Her mother's face went rigid. "Yes, dear?"

"Sir Charles Norbury and I are going to be married."

Lady Goring nodded, as if taking an expected blow, and said, "I see. And are you very sure, Anabel, that this is what you want?"

Her own doubts receded before opposition. "Of course, Mama. I should not have accepted otherwise."

"Yes. Well, I wish you happy, dear." Lady Goring rose and embraced her daughter, smiling with an effort.

"Sir Charles Norbury?" put in Georgina, who had been sitting very still, eyes wide, since Anabel made her announcement. "How can you?"

"What do you mean?" asked Anabel, annoyed.

The girl blushed furiously. "I beg your pardon. I didn't realize I had spoken aloud."

"Sir Charles is a very charming man."

"Oh, yes. Of course. I mean, I hardly know him, and I am sure he is much kinder with *you*. I don't...that is, I never..." She paused, struggling to amend her slip. "He frightens me, that's all."

"Frightens you?" In her defensive anger, Anabel was contemptuous. "That's ridiculous!"

Georgina nodded humbly. "I daresay it is only because I am so unfamiliar with society. He just seems so grand and...*above* everyone. If I should have to speak to him, I should be terrified of receiving a dreadful setdown."

Lady Goring looked as if she agreed, but she said nothing.

"Nonsense," replied Anabel, with an uncomfortable feeling that there was something in what Georgina said.

Charles did not particularly enjoy talking to her. "And you *will* speak to him. Often. He will be here a great deal now."

"Oh." Georgina looked apprehensive, then brightened. "But he will wish to be with you, of course."

Anabel's frown led her mother to intervene. "We must have him to dinner soon, to meet the whole family. Will you discover a good day, Anabel?"

"Yes."

"I suppose we must have your great-aunts. It is too bad your papa is so far off, Georgina."

The girl seemed doubtful about this, but she said nothing.

"I will be going to Kent to visit the Norburys next week," added Anabel.

"Ah. Old Lady Norbury is quite formidable, I understand." Lady Goring had been observing her daughter carefully, and her eyes were now brighter with cautious hope. Anabel did not show the bubbling happiness a love match usually engendered. Indeed, she looked positively petulant. Perhaps there was still a chance.

"I must go up and tell the children," was her daughter's only reply. As Anabel turned and left the room Lady Goring exchanged a glance with Georgina. Then she opened the pattern book once again.

On the stairs, Anabel felt immediate relief. Mama might really have more sympathy with her, she thought. One could not expect Georgina to understand anything, but Mama should try to enter into her feelings. She was no green girl attaching herself to a fortune hunter, after all. Charles was eminently eligible, a great catch in fact. It would be very good to reach the nursery. Her children had been her greatest source of happiness and comfort for years now.

The young Wyndhams were at their lessons when Anabel came in. In the past her arrival would have been the excuse for immediate abandonment of books and a great flurry of welcome and exuberant embraces. Today, however, the boys merely looked up and said hello. Susan leaped from her low chair, then seemed to think of something and sat down again. The governess raised her eyebrows. She didn't approve of parents who interrupted the lesson period.

"Excuse me, Miss Tate," said Anabel, smiling apologetically. "I'm sorry to take time from school work, but I have something rather important to discuss with the children."

The governess inclined her head and rose, leaving the nursery with a distinct air of disapproval. Anabel grinned conspiratorially at the children, but Nick and William were still bent over their books, and Susan quickly suppressed her impish response. Anabel felt disproportionately aggrieved. Did no one in her family care a rap for her feelings? What was wrong with the children? They had never been like this. Chagrin made her abrupt. "I have something to tell you, children," she said. "Some good news."

Susan looked eager. "We are going home?"

Anabel's annoyance increased. "No. I have told you over and over that we shall spend several months in London."

Susan, whose idea of the length of a month was hazy, pouted.

"I am going to be married," continued Anabel. "You will have a new papa."

All three of them stared at her, stunned.

Anabel moved uncomfortably under their gaze, feeling she hadn't handled the revelation particularly well. "He is Sir Charles Norbury. You met him in the drawing room one day. Remember?"

There was another shocked silence, then Susan burst out, "I *hate* him!"

"Susan!"

"I do! And so does Daisy!"

"Nonsense. You have hardly spoken two words to him. You will like him very well when you know him better."

Susan's small mouth set in an obstinate line. "Shan't!"

Exasperated, Anabel turned to her sons. "Have you nothing to say?"

Nicholas still looked stunned, but William, conscious of his responsibilities as the oldest, made an effort to pull himself together. "We...we wish you very happy, Mama."

"You will be happy, too." Anabel felt goaded. "You have always wished for someone to take you hunting and teach you to shoot."

"Uncle Christopher is going to do that!" blurted Nick, then flushed. "I mean, he *was*."

Anabel nearly snapped back at him, but she restrained herself. This was wholly unexpected news to the children, she realized, and they could hardly be blamed for their reaction. When they had had time to take it in, they would no doubt feel better about the change. Though some part of her remained unconvinced by this argument, she said, "We shall be very happy together. You will see. Sir Charles is coming to dinner very soon, and you will all be allowed to dine downstairs to meet him. He is very charming." Nagging doubt tried to surface again, and she suppressed it.

"He's a blighter," answered Susan, using a word whose power she knew by Nurse's horror when she had first uttered it.

But Anabel simply laughed. "Mind your tongue, Susan. Where did you hear such an expression?" Looking from one to another pair of wide, reproachful eyes, she hesitated. "Everything will be all right. You'll see."

They continued to gaze at her.

"We shall be a whole family again," added Anabel, less strongly. And when their expressions did not change, she was overcome by a kind of cowardice. "I must let you get back to your lessons. We are going riding tomorrow, don't forget." With a falsely bright smile, she left them.

When the door had closed, there was a short pause, then William burst out, "This is all your fault, Nick!"

"Mine?" His brother stared at him as if he had lost his mind.

"Yes! If you had never made us start this foolish scheme of avoiding Mama, she—"

"She would have done exactly as she has done. *We* have nothing to do with it." Nick's tone was bitter.

"Perhaps she was lonely without us, and…"

"Did she *seem* lonely?"

William was forced to shake his head.

"I tell you, we didn't matter a whit," insisted Nicholas, his delicate face flushed with hurt and anger. He was valiantly suppressing tears. "No one cares for us anymore."

William set his jaw to keep it from trembling.

"Well, I *won't*," exclaimed Susan, stamping her small foot, her green eyes blazing with rage.

"Won't what?" responded her brothers simultaneously.

"I won't marry that…that awful man. He doesn't like us."

"You can't tell whether—"

"I can so! I saw how he looked at me, at all of us. He doesn't like us at all."

Thinking back to their one meeting with Sir Charles, the boys frowned. There was something in what Susan said. They had all sensed that Norbury was not interested in them. "Well, you are not the one who is marrying him," replied Nicholas pessimistically. "Mama is, and there is nothing we can do about it."

"Is there not?" His sister's eyes blazed.

"Susan, what are you thinking of?" The boys exchanged an apprehensive glance.

The little girl gazed at them with irate contempt. "I shall—"

Her answer was cut off by the reappearance of the governess, who, knowing nothing of what had passed, was calmly determined to return to lessons. William and Nicholas obeyed resignedly, but Susan continued to glower at her book for the rest of the morning.

Nine

WHEN CHRISTOPHER HANFORD CAME DOWN TO breakfast the next morning, his sister was already sitting at the table, poring over the freshly arrived edition of the *Morning Post*. She was so engrossed that she did not hear his approach, but when he pulled out a chair and sat opposite, she started violently and swept the newspaper onto the floor with a convulsive gesture, gazing at him with wide, apprehensive eyes.

"Did I startle you? I'm sorry," he said. He lifted the lid off a silver dish. "Muffins!"

His sister made no effort to retrieve the paper. She continued to stare, then, recovering herself, looked hastily at her plate. But her fork remained forgotten beside it.

"I'm going riding with the Wyndhams today," added Christopher, helping himself to tea. "*All* of them." He looked very cheerful at the thought. "We used to ride together often at home."

Amelia made a small stifled noise.

"It's not so pleasant in London, of course—no space for a real gallop. But I daresay we shall have a fine time nonetheless." He buttered a hot muffin liberally, glancing up. "Is something wrong, Amelia? You look pale."

"No, no. I'm perfectly well."

He nodded and bit into the muffin. "Have you finished with the newspaper? I should like to see it if you have."

"No! I mean..." She looked down at the crumpled pages on the carpet. She could hardly claim she was reading. "It...it is sadly dull today."

Her brother eyed her quizzically.

Amelia frowned. She did not want him to see the announcement. It would make him so unhappy. Yet he would have to know sometime. And if Anabel Wyndham mentioned her engagement while they were riding today, and he found out then... With a sigh she bent and reached for the paper, handing it to him. It was already folded to the relevant page, and Amelia watched as he spread it out on the table, sipping his tea, and began to scan the announcements. She couldn't look away.

At first Hanford read with a slight smile. The reported doings of society always amused him. But when his eyes reached the middle of the second column, his face suddenly froze. He leaned forward, read again, and looked up at his sister, stricken.

Amelia met his blue eyes with sympathy, then with surprise at what she saw there. She had expected chagrin, disappointment, perhaps anger. She had been ready to comfort and condole. But she had always thought of her brother as a self-sufficient and imperturbable person, not bothered by depths of feeling. Even as a child he had always seemed untouched by emotion, and Amelia, five years younger, had often been annoyed by his bland competence. Now she realized that she had been wrong. The anguish in Christopher's eyes was unmistakable. All of his calm authority was gone. He even looked different—the set of his shoulders and lines in his face had shifted so that he seemed almost a stranger. "I'm so sorry, Christopher," she murmured. "I know you..."

"I have lost her, Amelia," he said. He gazed at her with a bewildered hurt she had never thought to see. "What shall I do?"

Amelia bit her lower lip. She had always been the one who asked advice. Many people relied on Christopher so, she knew. It was disconcerting to have the tables turned and see her invincible brother at a loss. But after a moment's uncertainty she straightened, determined to help him in the way he had helped her so often. "It is only an engagement, Christopher. Engagements are broken every day."

"Not by Anabel. She is not that sort." He bent his head and rested it on his palm. The shock of seeing Anabel's name publicly linked to Norbury's had not worn off.

"She is dazzled by Norbury's manner," suggested Amelia, hoping she was right. "It will wear thin, you will see."

"When she is married to him?" he retorted bitterly. "When it is too late? That is worse still."

His sister grimaced. She thought this scenario only too likely, but she did not wish to increase his unhappiness. "Perhaps before. You must not give up, Christopher. Anabel will see—"

"See?" He laughed harshly. "In nearly four years she has *seen* nothing. I have tried in every way I know to show her my love, and she has taken it as a matter of course, as mere friendship! Good old Christopher! Reliable Christopher! And the moment she meets a posturing, arrogant Londoner, she..." He threw himself back in his chair and expelled a despairing sigh. "She doesn't care for me, Amelia. It's obvious."

"She does. She is always so glad to see you."

"As a friend, yes. As someone who will help her out of scrapes and tidy up her tangles. But not as a man to love." He put a hand to his eyes again, furiously dashing away a hint of moisture there. "Perhaps I should just go home. I don't belong in town."

"Oh, Christopher!" She rose and went around the table to embrace him. "It is not so hopeless. You are exaggerating. I don't think Anabel knows *what* she feels. And I don't think you should give up so easily."

Hanford put his hand over hers on his shoulder and patted it. "You are trying to be kind, I know, Amelia. But perhaps I would be better off out of this."

She hesitated, wondering if he were right, then shook her head. In his country house, alone, he would only lose himself in his miseries. "No, you must stay, and wait. I have a feeling something will happen."

He smiled slightly. "A feeling? Am I to risk my happiness on so thin a support?"

"My feelings very often turn out true," she insisted, drawing back a little to look at him.

Christopher gazed up at her. "But I do not know if I can bear it, watching her with him, seeing the whole *ton* acknowledge their engagement. She will expect me to be glad for her. I…" His voice broke, and he stopped, clearing his throat.

His anguished expression struck Amelia to the heart. "Oh, my dear," she said, embracing him again. "I am so sorry!"

They remained thus for a long moment, then Christopher straightened and she stepped back. He was staring at the wall as if it told him something. "I wonder what the children said when she told them?" He turned to Amelia. "Norbury doesn't care for them."

"He wouldn't."

Hanford set his jaw. "Perhaps you are right. Perhaps I should stay for a while. It will be damnably difficult, but I suppose I can manage it. If she should change her mind…" A muscle jumped in his cheek. "But I shan't hope for that. I shall just make certain that they are *all* happy with the change, and then I shall go home."

Amelia wondered if he were deceiving himself about his motive, but she said nothing to alter his decision. She had her own ideas about Anabel's attachment, ideas that were difficult to state and impossible to prove, and she thought it likely that there would be further developments before any wedding took place.

"I have to get ready to go out," her brother added. "How can I take them riding after *this*?" He struck the newspaper with the back of his hand. "I feel like shaking her."

"It might do her a great deal of good," replied Amelia.

Christopher smiled, shaking his head. "I will have to devote myself to the children to keep my temper."

That would be a very wise thing to do, agreed Amelia, but not aloud. She watched her brother walk out of the room, then abandoned her half-finished breakfast to hurry to the morning room and write a note.

The Wyndham family was ready and eager when Christopher arrived at their door an hour later. The children jumped up and down with impatience at the sight of the hired horses he and a groom had brought from the livery, and Anabel held out her hand with a smile. He hardly knew how he answered, but somehow they mounted and set off, one of Lady Goring's grooms joining the other behind them.

"We are fortunate to have such a fine day," said Anabel. The sun was shining, and a soft breeze was refreshing without being cold.

"Yes," he agreed. He was finding it difficult to look at her, and talking was out of the question. He wanted to rail, to accuse, but he had no right. Luckily Susan dropped back beside them, her pony diminutive beside Hanford's roan.

"I want to see where *you* live," she demanded of him.

He smiled down at her determined little face. The sun made Susan's red hair brilliant, and her green eyes sparkled. "I thought you wanted to go to the park."

"Yes. Afterward."

He laughed. "Well, we can ride past the house, I suppose. It is not far out of the way. But we are *not* going in."

Susan nodded, satisfied. Hanford called to the two boys, who had ridden a little ahead, and the party turned right at the next street, riding past the Lanforth town house. Susan gazed around her with intense interest and eyed the facade as if memorizing it. Then, abruptly, she declared she was ready to go on. Her brothers sighed with relief; they had been afraid she would drag them to some other dull place. And the adults exchanged a smile. For a moment Christopher felt happy, then he remembered the engagement and urged his mount forward.

"You're quiet today," he said to William and Nicholas when he came up with them.

William shrugged. Nick said, "We're thinking. Have you heard that Mama is getting married?"

Feeling as if he had taken a blow to the chest, Hanford nodded.

"Well, we're wondering what we can do about it."

William snorted derisively.

"Do?" Hanford felt a bit guilty inquiring. He had no right to interfere, he knew, but he couldn't resist finding out the children's attitude toward the match.

"To stop her. She is to marry that Norbury, you know."

"Yes."

"We don't like him!"

"Don't be an idiot, Nick," put in William. "There's nothing we can do."

"Not if we don't even try!" replied his brother hotly.

Hanford's intense gratification at their remarks made him more uneasy. He should not be talking so to Anabel's children, yet it was hard to resist.

"Do *you* like him?" asked Nicholas with a frown.

"I?" Christopher was at a loss. "I…I scarcely know him."

"I didn't think so." The boy nodded, satisfied. "There's something wrong with him. Even Susan sees it."

"I didn't mean…" Hanford groped for words. He didn't want to lie, but neither could he in conscience encourage Nick.

"I shall think of something," was the younger Wyndham's only response.

They reached the gates of the park, and Anabel and Susan caught up with them so that they entered in a group. The children immediately kicked their mounts' flanks and trotted off at the fastest pace allowed in this fashionable enclosure. Christopher and Anabel watched them.

"It was so good of you to think of this," she said. "I don't know why I didn't myself. They love riding so."

"They're very good at it too."

"I hope so. They certainly don't take much care. I have scolded them about it over and over."

He gazed after the three bouncing children. There was no chance of a neck-or-nothing gallop here, but they were throwing themselves into their more sedate progress. William had a fine seat and good hands; Nick, though slightly less skilled, clearly made up for it in spirit, and Susan showed all the signs of a future belle of the hunt. She would be the kind of rider, Hanford thought, who drives the young men frantic in their efforts to keep up and surpass her. Few would manage the thing.

"Uncle Christopher!" called Nick. "Come on." He signaled vigorously.

Smiling, Hanford rode forward to join them. He noticed that they did not summon their mother. In another moment he was pulled into a lively game of follow-the-leader, each rider having to imitate the antics of the first. The children's attempts to find some new challenge made him laugh so that he almost forgot Anabel.

She was watching from nearby, smiling at first at the way they were all enjoying themselves, then, gradually, becoming pensive. None of them shouted to draw her attention to some particularly astonishing trick. They didn't ask for her approval or arbitration of a dispute.

They hardly looked in her direction. Her own children and her dearest friend gamboled there, and ignored her. In the past this would have been unimaginable. She would have laughed at anyone who suggested the possibility. But it was happening now. Slowly the sight of them grew oppressive. Had they forgotten she was here? Even Susan, squealing with delight as she played leader and forced the males into the most ridiculous contortions, did not turn wickedly sparkling green eyes for her approval. Anabel drooped a little in her saddle.

She knew the children were not pleased about her engagement, but now that she thought about it, she realized they had been rather aloof for some time. The close, easy relationship that had always existed in her family was breaking down. And Christopher—he must have seen the announcement in the *Morning Post*, but he had not even wished her happy. He had been cold lately too.

Anabel felt very isolated, sitting on her horse and watching the others cavort. It seemed to her suddenly that she had no one. Her old life was shutting her out, and the new one had not yet developed to take its place. Tears of self-pity started in her eyes. But before one could drop, she shook her head and kicked her horse's flanks. She was being ridiculous. "May I join the game?" she called in the gayest tone she could muster.

"We've just finished," answered Nick. "Susan won. We're going to ride down that avenue now and see what's on the other side of the park."

With that, they all started off, leaving Anabel to follow in their wake. Christopher felt another wave of guilt as he rode. He shouldn't encourage the children to show their displeasure so openly. But he hadn't actually urged them; he had simply gone along with their schemes. And since he agreed wholeheartedly with their reaction, he felt his behavior was sufficiently justified. He was no self-sacrificing martyr, to argue against his own interests.

All in all, the riding party could not be called a success. They explored the lanes of the park for another hour, the children chattering to one another and to Christopher but speaking to Anabel only when directly addressed. Hanford exchanged commonplaces with her, unable to mention the engagement, and she grew more and more silent and withdrawn as the morning progressed. Everyone seemed relieved when they turned toward home again.

They rode back on one of the more-traveled avenues of the park, by this time filling with members of the *haut ton*, and their pace slowed perforce. Christopher soon noticed that Anabel was attracting a great deal of attention. Elegantly dressed ladies in smart barouches whispered among themselves as they nodded greetings. Pinks on horseback eyed her with speculative appraisal. Here is the woman, their eyes all said, who won the unconquerable Norbury. What is so special about her? How did she manage it?

Anabel saw it too, and found her new notoriety dreadful. It had been bad enough when everyone was wondering if Norbury would propose; now the attention was redoubled, and she hated it. "Why are we dawdling like this?" she said, moving forward and almost colliding with a landaulet. The children looked mystified—all morning she had been urging them to slow down—but Christopher understood, and even his anger with her could not prevent sympathy.

"Yes, we should be getting back," he agreed, guiding them around the carriage and toward the gate.

The ride through the streets was generally silent. The children went on ahead, and Anabel was too occupied with her own thoughts to talk. When he left the Wyndhams at Lady Goring's house, Christopher was thoughtful. Perhaps Amelia had been right. There might be developments before the wedding took place. He would stay in town a while yet.

Anabel, walking up the steps and into the front hall, was wondering how she could excuse herself from going to the play tonight. They had planned the evening some time ago, and Georgina was very eager to see the melodrama, she knew. But could she not plead a headache and stay home alone? She dreaded facing the curious stares and whispered evaluations of the crowd in the playhouse.

In the event, she could not. Lady Goring was called to the bedside of one of the servants just after dinner, and the girl was ill enough that she felt she should stay with her until the doctor came. "I will join you later, if I can," she told Anabel and Georgina. "It is only some trifling thing, no doubt, but Nancy is terrified of the doctor, and I want to make sure she sees him."

"Perhaps we should all stay," ventured Anabel.

Georgina looked desolate.

"Nonsense. There is nothing for you to do. Go on and enjoy the play. I daresay I shall come in before the second act."

Meeting her cousin's eyes, Anabel could not refuse to go. Thus, the two of them set out together soon after, Georgina chattering about the play and Anabel morosely silent.

They entered their box in good time. Georgina had insisted they come well before the curtain. Anabel sat down and glanced quickly around, holding herself very straight. At least she could be confident about her appearance. She had put on a new gown of soft rose satin, which she had fallen in love with at the dressmaker's shop. The cloth seemed to shimmer with a dusting of muted silver, and she had had it cut with a scoop at the neck, tiny puffed sleeves, and a wide ruffle around the hem. It clung to the curves of her body with just the proper mixture of enticement and propriety, and looked lovely with a set of silver filigree that had belonged to Ralph's mother. None of the gapers could claim that she *looked* peaked or out of sorts, though she felt far from confident.

Georgina was gazing eagerly about the theater, smiling at people she knew and flushing with pleasure when some of the young men she had danced with saluted their box. The girl's happiness had been increasing with each new day of the season, as she received further proofs of her attractiveness and gained poise. "There are the Learningtons," she said. "Oh, I hope George will come by at the interval. I want to tell Sophie about the rout party on Thursday. She had the headache and missed it."

Anabel did not look up. Her interest in the Learningtons was minimal. She instead wished that the play would begin so that she could retreat into dimness. For it was obvious that their box was attracting attention. People indicated it to their friends with pointed glances, then bent to murmur comments to one another. It was worse than in the park.

At last the curtain rose. Georgina leaned forward and became absorbed, and Anabel relaxed a little, letting her rigid back and fixed smile slip. She fervently hoped that her mother would indeed join them, though she knew it was unlikely. But Lady Goring's sensible presence would be a great help tonight. She would not hesitate to face down anyone ill bred enough to stare. She would fix them with her lorgnette and raised eyebrows until they retreated in embarrassment. The picture amused Anabel and elicited a real smile, making her feel a little better. The *ton*'s avid interest would pass, she told herself; some new sensation would arise, and she would be forgotten. She need only endure.

Lady Goring did not arrive, and at the first interval several of Georgina's new friends stopped by the box to chat with her. Anabel gratefully retreated to the rear and left them to it, marveling at the change in her cousin since her first days in London. Who would connect that pallid, sullen girl with the laughing, almost slender one before her now? Georgina was not beautiful, but she was far from ugly. Her well-shaped face and fine gray eyes were transformed by expression. Happy, she was very engaging.

"Contemplating the merits of the play?" asked a voice near her ear.

Anabel started and turned to find Sir Charles beside her.

"You looked very thoughtful," he added, "and not well pleased. My opinion precisely."

She smiled. "I wasn't thinking about the play."

"No? What, then?" His eyes caressed her.

"Nothing. Georgina."

Norbury glanced briefly at the girl, then dismissed her. "Alas. You might have been thinking of me."

"I have been. I could hardly help it." This didn't sound just right, she realized at once. She hadn't meant to be tart.

Norbury wasn't offended, however. "There has been some reaction," he agreed. "Only natural. The *ton* has so little to occupy it."

"It's…rather unpleasant." It was good to have someone to share her discomfort.

"You don't find it amusing to set their silly tongues wagging?" He looked around the theater with a superior smile. Their tête-à-tête was the center of many eyes. "But we are practically social benefactors. They would be so deucedly dull without us."

Anabel tried to smile, but his joke seemed sadly flat tonight. "I don't seem to have the character for philanthropy."

"Nonsense." He laughed. With the air of a man turning from trivial to important things, he added, "I have arranged our visit to Kent. My mother is delighted; she is very eager to meet you. We go down on Wednesday."

"Oh." Anabel felt a bit annoyed at his assumption that

she could leave whenever he chose. "I believe we were engaged for dinner on Wednesday."

He waved this aside. "It is far more important that you become acquainted with my family."

She frowned and started to protest, but the interval was ending. People had returned to their seats, and the curtain was about to rise again.

"I will remain here with you," said Norbury with a smile. "There appears to be an empty chair." And in the dimness that followed the resumption of the play, his hand curled over hers in her lap. Anabel stirred a little, afraid the gossips would see. But the theater was too dark.

Throughout the second act, with Charles's fingers warm and suggestive around hers, she tried to analyze her feelings. The day had been far from satisfactory. She had been shaken first by her novel isolation from the children and Christopher, then by the half-malicious scrutiny of the ton. Now, with Charles at her side to support her, she ought to feel better, she thought. Love was supposed to overcome all sorts of ills; she was his acknowledged choice, the envy of many less fortunate women. Why, then, did she still feel dispirited and uneasy? Glancing over at Charles in the dim light, she traced the handsome contours of his face. He looked supremely confident and content. Perhaps it was just that she was unused to town life. The furor would decline, and surely the children would come round when they became accustomed to the idea of her marriage and knew Charles better. She must see to that.

When the second interval was announced, Anabel spoke first. "You must come to dinner with the children. Mama mentioned it. What about tomorrow night?"

Norbury's smile faded. "I have an engagement tomorrow."

"Oh. Sunday, then?" When he hesitated, she added,

"You must get to know them better. They are not…
wholly reconciled to the idea of my marrying again."

He frowned. "What has it to do with them?"

"Well, Charles…" She searched for words, astonished
by his reaction. "We will be one family, after all."

Hearing the doubt and amazement in her voice, he
shrugged. "Of course. You must make allowances for the
fact that I know nothing of children." He had released
her hand, but now he bent closer. "Though I hope to
learn a great deal very soon." His eyes were provocative,
and she could not mistake that look for interest in her
own children.

"You will come, then?" she replied a bit stiffly.

"Yes." He smiled, and she told herself that all would be
well when he and the children were better acquainted.

Norbury escorted them to their carriage at the end
of the play. They were repeatedly detained by other
members of the audience offering congratulations
and full of questions about their plans. Anabel left the
answers to him, though she was not always in agreement with them, because she could not face the innu-
merable pairs of avid eyes and falsely smiling mouths.
None of these people truly wished them happiness, she
felt; indeed, they would be much more interested in the
opposite. And they inquired only to have news to retail
to other, less-informed friends. There was no warmth
in their faces.

Norbury didn't seem to care. He took patent
pleasure in accepting their good wishes and dropping
carefully rationed bits of information to one or the
other. He was in his element, Anabel thought, without admitting the implications of their very different
responses to the situation.

As he handed her into her carriage he dropped a
light kiss on her wrist. "Shall I see you tomorrow at
the Atleys'?"

"No." Anabel felt she couldn't bear another such evening. "I must...help Mama."

This was weak, and he raised his eyebrows. "Help?"

"Yes." She pulled the carriage door, and he shut it. "We will meet at dinner on Sunday."

"Ah. Yes."

"Good night." She smiled and drew back. After a moment he stepped away and signaled the coachman to start. Anabel sighed with relief, very glad to see the end of this evening. She had been longing for the quiet of her bedchamber for hours.

But once there and in her dressing gown, she remained restless. The days ahead seemed full of difficult tasks and unwelcome events. For the first time since the season had started, she wished she was back home. There, she had never felt so alone or endured a day like this one. She had been surrounded by family and friends, secure in their undoubted affection. She had not been plagued by decisions and worry over whether she had decided correctly. Perhaps she should never have come to London.

Then, climbing into bed, she shook her head slightly and scolded herself for cowardice. Things could not remain always the same. The children were growing up alarmingly quickly, and in a few years she would have been alone in the country as well. It was time she took charge of her life, and she would become accustomed to the process eventually, she had no doubt. In any case, things always looked better in the morning.

Ten

ANABEL DID NOT SEE SIR CHARLES AGAIN UNTIL THE
evening set for dinner. Indeed, she did not go out on
Saturday, having had her fill of unwanted attention. Lady
Goring was once again available to chaperone Georgina,
and Anabel left them to attend a ball while she stayed
home with her thoughts. She spent the early evening in
the schoolroom with the children, trying to recapture
their old intimacy, and partly succeeding. They could
not resist her affectionate overtures. But a pall remained
over the family, and the younger Wyndhams showed a
notable lack of enthusiasm when told that Norbury was
coming to meet them.

He arrived punctually at six, and Anabel, who had
been on the watch, came downstairs as the footman let
him in. The atmosphere in the drawing room was stiff,
and she wanted to take him in herself.

"Good evening," he said, handing his hat and gloves
to the servant and offering her his arm. "Here I am, as
commanded. Do you know, I have never in my life
eaten my dinner at six. It will be a novel experience."

"The children always eat early," answered Anabel, a
little piqued by his mocking tone.

"Of course."

They walked up the stairs together.

"They…they are still becoming accustomed to the
idea of our marriage," she added in a rush. "You must
understand if they are…a bit…wary at first."

"Ah?" He raised one dark eyebrow, not helping her.

"It is difficult for children to adjust to new arrangements, you know. They like everything to stay as it was."

"Indeed? And I thought I had been told they were very flexible creatures. My mistake, I imagine."

Anabel frowned. No one was making it easy for her. She felt like a clumsy diplomat, trying to negotiate between warring states. Her mother had been elaborately bland about the evening, and Georgina didn't seem to understand how awkward it might be.

They entered the drawing room. "You know my mother, of course," said Anabel. "And I believe you have met my cousin, Georgina Goring." Norbury nodded. "And this is William." The children had been thoroughly coached. William came forward and made his bow. "Nicholas." The younger boy followed suit. "And the youngest, Susan." Susan curtsied, but her expression remained sullen.

"How do you do?" replied Norbury, smiling dutifully.

There was a short silence.

"Shall we sit down?" said Anabel, feeling desperate. She had not realized until this moment what divergent topics of conversation she used with Norbury, the children, and even her mother. None of them was interested in the others' favorite subjects. She could not imagine Charles discussing a new pony for Susan, or William's dogs, nor her mother enduring Norbury's gibes at society in silence. She had to say something, but she couldn't think of any neutral topic that would include them all.

"You boys are not at school?" inquired Sir Charles with a geniality that did not conceal his boredom.

William glanced quickly at his mother, then shook his head.

"Taking a holiday?"

"We don't go to school," responded Nicholas. "Mama teaches us. Or, she did. *Now* we have a governess."

"Really?" His eyebrow cocked again, Norbury turned

to Anabel. "Do you think that wise? Boys are usually better off at school."

The children glowered, and Anabel felt a spark of resentment. "I have considered sending them. They are very young yet."

"They look like well-grown lads to me." He attempted joviality again. "And I daresay they wish they were in school with other boys. Don't you?"

William and Nicholas simply scowled. Lady Goring watched the scene with interest, her expression bland but her eyes sparkling. Georgina was looking from one to another of the group with the dawning apprehension that something was wrong.

"Well, well," added Norbury, sensing opposition. "We can talk of that another time. Tell me, William, are you fond of hunting?"

Though riding out with the local hunt was one of William's passions, he shrugged.

"No? I would have pegged you as a bruising rider. What about Nicholas?"

Seeing his mother's pained expression, Nicholas relented and admitted they liked to hunt.

"I have a hunting box in Leicestershire," replied Norbury. "We had some splendid runs last season."

In any other circumstances the boys would have pelted him with eager questions about the Quorn, but Norbury's position in the family, and the fact that he made no move to invite them to hunt with him or even to suggest that they might at some future time, left them silent.

Sir Charles, annoyed at their unresponsiveness, turned to Susan. "And what do you like?" he asked. "I suppose you have a great many...dolls?"

His tone was condescending, and Susan, who had one much-beloved rag doll and a host of less important ones, pursed her small mouth and shook her head. "I hate dolls!"

Norbury raised his eyebrows again.

"I believe dinner must be ready," blurted Anabel, looking beseechingly at her mother.

Lady Goring had been letting events take their course with some satisfaction, but now she took pity on her daughter. "Yes, I think we might go in." Rising, she took Norbury's arm and started toward the dining room. "Did you notice Julia Buckingham's new town carriage at the ball last night, Sir Charles?" she asked. "That's the third this year, is it not? I hope Buckingham can stand the nonsense."

Norbury responded wittily, and the first half of the meal passed in similar remarks between the two. He repeatedly sought to bring Anabel into the conversation, but she was too conscious of the children, silent and ignored, eating their dinner without looking up from their plates. Georgina occasionally spoke to them, but tonight she elicited no more than monosyllables.

With the second course came another silence. Lady Goring had exhausted her fund of gossip, and in any case she wished to give her daughter another dose of reality. She addressed herself to a Chantilly cream. "This is very fine, isn't it, William?" she said.

William, who was fond of sweets, nodded enthusiastically.

"I forgot to ask. Did you have a good ride in the park on Friday? Were the horses from the livery suitable?"

"They were slugs," answered Nicholas. "But better than nothing. We had some first-class games with Uncle Christopher."

"Yes," seconded William heartily.

"We like Uncle Christopher better than *anybody*," offered Susan.

Her brothers seemed to feel that this was going too far. They fell silent again and concentrated on their plates.

"'Uncle' Christopher?" queried Norbury. "Ah. That

would be the fellow I met here one day. Hanford, wasn't it? One of your bucolic neighbors."

His tone made Anabel's cheeks redden slightly. But before she could reply, Georgina snapped, "He is a wonderful man!"

"Is he?" Norbury eyed her with cool amusement. "I must become better acquainted with him."

Georgina turned fiery red and looked down.

"He is a good friend and a close neighbor," said Anabel. "I don't know what I would have done without him when Ralph died."

"Indeed?" He looked less pleased.

"Shall we remove to the drawing room?" asked Lady Goring. She was happy to see Anabel learning some home truths about Norbury, but she had no intention of letting things get out of hand. "You must come with us, Sir Charles. We are a household of females and have no proper port."

They returned to the drawing room, and the children went to bed soon after, followed by Georgina. At this, the situation eased somewhat, and Anabel found conversation easier. But when Lady Goring excused herself a little later and Charles came to sit close beside her on the sofa, she was not in the mood for dalliance. "It didn't go particularly well," she said.

"What?" He seemed honestly puzzled.

"The dinner. I had hoped you and the children would…like one another."

"Like?" He frowned in perplexity. "I daresay we shall rub along quite well eventually. The boys must go off to school, of course; it is past time. And as for Susan"—he smiled provocatively at her—"I have not yet encountered the female I could not captivate." His arm tightened around her shoulders.

Thinking that he was unlikely to have encountered one like her daughter, Anabel sat very straight. "I am not sure I wish to send them to school. I put it off because I wanted them with me."

He shrugged, smiling. "There is no need to discuss it now. You will be making a great many changes. Pleasant ones, I hope." Bending his head, he kissed her.

Gradually Anabel relaxed against his arm, feeling again that languorous helplessness Charles always produced in her. His free hand wandered along her silk-clad body, and slowly she brought one arm up and about his neck. The kiss seemed to go on forever. Anabel's annoyance and objections slipped from her mind; she felt reasonless, without volition.

When he drew back, he was breathing rapidly, his hand at rest on her hip. "Lovely Anabel," he murmured. "Do you know how I love you? There is no woman like you in the world."

She gazed into his pale green eyes, still tremulous from his caress. He cared about her. It was obvious. But what did *she* feel, beyond that pliant loss of will? She was less and less certain, and that fact was increasingly unsettling. "It's late," she said.

He laughed a little. "Don't you trust me? You can, you know. And that is more than could be said for almost any woman I have known. Do you feel your power?" He pulled her closer and kissed her again, then straightened and rose. "I will go, with great reluctance. We must set a wedding date, Anabel. Very soon."

"I...I haven't thought."

He laughed again. "Well, do so, my heart's darling. Think very hard." He took her hand and kissed the palm. "And dream of me." With a last flashing smile, he went out.

She looked at her hand for a moment, then let it fall and suddenly shivered. She didn't understand anything anymore, least of all herself. Events seemed to be rushing forward, out of control. She knew she had to do something, but what? She didn't even know what she wanted. She had thought she did; she had been dazzled by possibilities and new sensations. Now nothing was clear. Her brain seemed to whirl dizzyingly from one image to another, never pausing long enough for her to really see any. Her emotions were in turmoil. And no one could help her.

With a sigh, Anabel turned toward the stairs. She would have difficulty sleeping again tonight, she could tell. But it did no good to stand here and worry. Perhaps time would solve her problems for her.

The following day was very quiet in Lady Goring's household. Anabel did not go out. She prepared for her journey to Kent and spent a great deal of time sitting and thinking. In the afternoon she went up to the schoolroom to tell the children she would be away for a short time, and met the predictable unenthusiastic response. As she was coming down the stairs again she encountered Georgina, dressed for the street and accompanied by her maid. She looked excited. "Are you going out?" asked Anabel.

"Yes." The girl smiled. "I am invited to tea with Amelia Lanforth. It is so close that I am going to walk."

Anabel felt chagrin. Why was her cousin asked to the Lanforths and not she? She had known Christopher for years, certainly his sister might have included her in the invitation. They had chatted at several gatherings, and though they had never had an opportunity to become well acquainted, Anabel liked Mrs. Lanforth very much. She would have been happy to see her more intimately. Had Christopher's inexplicable new coldness spread to his sister? She frowned.

"I must go," added Georgina. "I don't want to be late." And with a sense of half-guilty relief, she skipped past and down to the hall. Georgina was finding Anabel puzzling lately. Her older cousin seemed either abstracted or overanimated, and the previous evening had been dreadful.

At the Lanforths, Georgina was taken directly up to the drawing room and greeted with a smile by Amelia. They had confirmed their mutual passion for novels during a visit Amelia had made to Lady Goring after the announcement of Anabel's engagement, and they both looked forward to a long, cozy chat comparing all their favorites.

They settled on the sofa and fortified themselves with cups of strong tea. But before they could really begin, the drawing-room door opened and Christopher came in. Georgina's eyes brightened, and her cup rattled slightly in its saucer.

"Christopher," said Amelia. "I thought you had gone out riding."

"Yes. But I returned early. The park is too crowded. Will you give me some tea?" He smiled also, but his voice and stance conveyed depression.

"Of course." She poured out another cup. "But I give you fair warning we mean to talk about novels. We have met just for that purpose, and you won't stop us."

Hanford's smile became more genuine. "Ah. Didn't I tell you, Miss Goring, that my sister's interest in them equaled your own?"

Georgina nodded, speechless with joy at his joining them.

"And do you have favorites in common?" he added.

"We haven't discovered that yet." Amelia smiled at the girl. "I am excessively attached to Mrs. Radcliffe."

"Oh, yes! I have never been so frightened as when the wicked duke..." They fell into an energetic exchange, and Christopher allowed their voices to fade into a background for his thoughts. Despite his resolutions, he was finding it extremely difficult to remain in London. He thought of nothing but Anabel, though he rarely saw her. And he had nothing to do. At home he would manage his estate and ride out every day. Here there were only parties which reminded him again of his loss. He didn't know how much longer he could endure it.

"Yes, I was reading it only last night before Sir Charles came to dinner," said Georgina.

Hanford looked up. "Norbury came to dinner yesterday?"

She turned to him. "Yes. Anabel wanted him to meet the children and…become friends." Her tone was so doubtful that both her listeners understood the attempt had not met with success. Christopher felt a rush of guilty joy.

"I suppose the children are not very pleased about the engagement," said Amelia. And as the others looked at her she added, "They rarely are in such cases. It is a great change."

Georgina, frowning over this novel viewpoint, slowly nodded, "I think you are right. I have never seen them so sullen as last night. Of course, Sir Charles did not help. He does not know how to talk to children."

This naive statement made Amelia smile and Christopher lean forward, unconsciously avid. Georgina noticed it, and compared his earlier despondence with the intense eagerness in his eyes now. A revelation swept over her, and she sat back abruptly, stricken.

"I admit I do not see how they will go on together," said Hanford. "Norbury is settled in London. He goes into the country only to visit or hunt. But I cannot imagine Anabel or the children staying here permanently."

"He…he means to send the boys to school," managed Georgina. Her throat seemed to be obstructed by a large lump.

"School. Well, it is time they went. But I should have thought Anabel would want to decide. Is she going to let him take over her life?" This last came out charged with emotion and, realizing it, Christopher shut his mouth and turned a little away.

Georgina scanned his profile and wondered at the confusion of emotions she felt. It hurt to discover that the man she so admired was in love with someone else; yet she could not help but see the logic of it. He had known Anabel for years, and her cousin was very lovely and charming. To her own surprise, she realized that her strongest response was pity. She wished she could do something to comfort Hanford and to change things so that he might be happy. She loved him, but... "I...I think Anabel was a little annoyed with him when he suggested it," she ventured.

Amelia, hearing the quaver in her voice, looked sharply at her. What she saw made her eyes soften and a slight smile curve her lips. Unconsciously she reached over and patted the girl's hand. When Georgina looked up, startled, she said, "More tea?" knowing that to acknowledge the girl's state would be unforgivable.

Georgina shook her head, turning back to Christopher.

"Annoyed? Was she really?" he could not resist asking.

"Yes. It was not at all a pleasant evening." She wanted desperately to cheer him.

"Ah."

"And I heard Lady Goring say that Sir Charles's mother is disagreeable. So perhaps when Anabel goes to Kent to visit her—"

"She is going out of town?"

"Yes. Tomorrow. But only for a day."

Hanford leaned his head on his hand briefly, then straightened. "I beg your pardon. I have remembered something I must do. Please excuse me." He left the room in three strides, the women silent behind him. Georgina anxiously watched the door close, and Amelia watched her.

"Will he be all right?" the girl asked finally.

Amelia shrugged.

"It is so… I didn't know… I would never have…"

"You did splendidly," Amelia assured her. "Your aunt—and your father, no doubt—would be proud of you. Indeed, I am."

Georgina frowned doubtfully at her, biting her lower lip. She felt exposed.

Amelia bent to pour more tea. "But you were telling me about a new book you have found. I must hear all about it. I have been searching for something fresh to read this age."

Georgina took a deep breath and tried to gather her thoughts. What book had she been talking about? She had no idea.

"Was it called *The Count's Revenge*?" prompted Amelia.

"Oh. Oh, yes." And with a massive effort she took up her description again.

In the library downstairs, Christopher sat alone, head bent. Anabel was going away; she had freely accepted another man, and she continued to ignore his feelings. He had never felt so low in his life as he did at that moment. All hope of happiness seemed gone. He would gladly have throttled Sir Charles Norbury, but he had no excuse to do so. The children's dislike was no motive. Anabel liked him—loved him!—and that tied his hands and racked his heart.

Eleven

ANABEL DEPARTED FOR THE VISIT TO NORBURY'S family at ten the following morning. She was not at all eager to make the journey, feeling that many things required her attention at home, but she had agreed to go and Charles seemed set on it. As they would spend only one night at his mother's and return the following afternoon, she made no objections when he arrived in his traveling carriage and handed her in.

The drive was about three hours, and during it Charles was once again the charming, sophisticated companion she had admired at *ton* parties. He did not make love to her; rather, he pointed out sights along their route, reminisced about his childhood trips on that road, and asked her opinion about various arrangements he had made. Before long she was feeling more in charity with him than she had for a while, and she laughed at his sallies unrestrainedly.

"You have told me nothing about your family," she said as they began the last stage of the journey. "I know I am to meet your mother. Will there be others as well?"

"I fear so. My marriage is such an astonishing development that every ambulatory Norbury has gathered to witness the miracle." He looked comical, and she laughed again.

"But who is that? You must prepare me."

"I dare not. You might simply jump out of the chaise and leave me to face them alone."

"Perhaps I shall if you keep me wondering what I am in for."

Norbury smiled. "Very well. Besides my mother, whom you will like very much, I think, there will be two uncles with their families. One is my late father's younger brother and the other my mother's older one. Enough?"

"Not at all. How many cousins?"

He groaned. "Three. But we are fortunate. There are three more who will not be present for one reason or another."

"You don't get on with them?"

"We cordially despise one another, and have since we were in short coats."

Anabel looked doubtful; this didn't sound like a happy family.

"Don't judge until you have met them," added Norbury.

After a moment she nodded. "Have you no brothers or sisters?"

"None. The explanation, according to one of my uncles, of all my character flaws. Overindulgence."

"You are making me dread this visit, Charles."

"You asked to be warned. You see I am being completely honest with you." He grinned. "It is unlike me."

"Well, I think you are teasing me. They are probably all very pleasant people."

He smiled. "You may decide for yourself. Here we are."

Anabel looked out the window. They had turned in at a massive stone gate and were trotting up an avenue lined with oaks. At the end, she could see a pillared portico of gray stone, windows glittering in the afternoon sun. Well-kept gardens extended around the sides to the back, and the place had an air of carefully controlled wealth. She turned back, to find Norbury gazing at her expectantly. "It is beautiful."

"Is it not? Your new home."

Inevitably this made Anabel think of the less grand but comfortable and familiar house she had left behind. It would be very hard to abandon it for this.

They pulled up to the front door with a flourish, and it opened before they could climb down. A liveried footman ushered them into the hall and took their wraps as another fetched the luggage and a third waited to escort them farther into the house. Anabel was startled by the number of servants. Seeing her expression, Norbury said, "My mother holds to the formalities of her girlhood. She will laugh about it, but she will not give them up. Come, let us go and see her."

"Shouldn't I go upstairs first?" She put a hand to her hair, wondering if the curls had been crushed by her hat.

"You look lovely." He smiled and took her hand, and Anabel allowed him to lead her up to the spacious drawing room on the first floor.

At first glance, it seemed remarkably full of people. Two sofas were occupied, and a number of gentlemen were leaning against the mantelpiece or turning the pages of newspapers. Anabel hesitated. Norbury squeezed her hand reassuringly, then guided her in, a hand on her elbow. They stopped before an imposing woman, clad in dark green, on one of the sofas, and he said, "Mama, this is Anabel. My mother."

"How do you do?" said Anabel, smiling and giving a sketch of a curtsy.

"My dear." It was plain where Sir Charles got his dark hair and pale green eyes. Indeed, he resembled his mother in most particulars. She, too, was tall and had a commanding presence, and although an ebony cane was propped on the cushion beside her, she sat very straight. But Anabel found her gaze 'cold, and it was not clear whether she was responding to her greeting or addressing her son.

"How are you feeling?" inquired the latter.

Lady Norbury made a dismissive gesture. "You must present Lady Wyndham to the others, Charles."

He grimaced slightly, and her stern face relaxed into a thin smile. "Anabel, this is my Aunt Alice Norbury and my Aunt Anne Bramton. Uncle Anthony Norbury and Uncle Gerald Bramton. And these idlers are my younger cousins. John Norbury." The dark young man lounging against the mantel raised a negligent hand. "Arthur Bramton." The pale stripling on the other side of the fireplace bowed. "And Cecily Bramton." A thin girl on the sofa opposite stood and curtsied awkwardly. "The older cousins have better things to do than come down to Kent. They are all married and parents of hopeful families of their own." He glanced maliciously at his Uncle Anthony as he said this, and that gentleman bridled. Anabel realized that that branch of the Norburys was heir to the property until Charles had children. She looked away.

The older generation seemed indistinguishable at first. Each murmured a greeting, and Anabel strove to fasten the correct labels to the faded blond Mrs. Bramton, the embittered-looking Mrs. Norbury, and the two stout men who belonged with them. She and Charles sat down, and silence fell.

"Did you have a pleasant journey?" asked Lady Norbury after a while.

Anabel waited a moment, but Charles said nothing. "Yes. It is not far, is it, and the day is so fine."

"Oh, you mustn't say it isn't far," answered young John Norbury in a jocular tone. "You will spoil Charles's excuse for not coming down more often."

"He comes very often," retorted Lady Norbury crushingly. From the surprised looks the others gave her, Anabel saw that this was a novel pronouncement. "You were a Goring, I believe?" added the hostess.

Anabel glanced at Charles, but he did not seem to find anything amiss with this question. "Yes."

"And you have children?"

"Three," she replied crisply.

"What are their ages?" Lady Norbury seemed wholly unconscious of any rudeness. She might have been asking about the weather.

"William is ten, Nicholas nine, and Susan six." She saw that her tone made the Bramton women wince.

"Ah. Two boys. They are in school, I suppose?"

"No, they are not. They are in London with me because I wished to have them there."

Lady Norbury looked up and met Anabel's eyes. Their gaze held for a moment, and Anabel realized that Charles's mother was by no means as pleased by his engagement as he had told her. In fact, she was not pleased at all. And since Charles had been certain she wished him to marry, it could only be that she did not approve of Anabel. Perhaps a widow with young children was not her idea of a proper bride for her son. Anabel's chin came up defiantly.

"No doubt you are tired after your drive," continued Lady Norbury. "I will have the housekeeper show you your room. I fear I do not get about as I used to. Dinner will be at seven. We keep country hours here. Arthur, will you ring?" He did so, and the silence remained unbroken until the summons was answered. Looking at Charles, Anabel saw that he was unaware of any awkwardness. He had strolled over to the hearth and was exchanging desultory remarks with his cousin John. As she followed the housekeeper from the room she heard Lady Norbury say, "I wish to speak to Charles. We will gather again for dinner." The others were moving toward the door as she left.

Upstairs, in a bedchamber that looked as if it had not been refurbished in a decade, Anabel sat down and thought over her welcome. It was certainly not what she had expected from Charles's glowing reports. His mother was far from the charming, witty creature he had described. She obviously ruled her family with an iron hand, and Charles with some subtler methods. And she disapproved of his choice of a wife. Would she tell him so now? Anabel wondered.

And how did she herself feel about this development? Part of her was annoyed and combative, ready to show Lady Norbury that she had no power over her and that she cared not a whit for her good opinion. Another part wished to go back to London at once and forget the whole matter. Still a third very softly suggested that perhaps her hostess was right.

Pushing this thought aside, Anabel rose to get out her evening dress. It would be a very long visit, she saw. She would speak to Charles and ask him to be more helpful. Once he realized how uncomfortable she felt, he could no doubt do a great deal to ease the situation.

❧

The house party met in the drawing room before dinner. Anabel had changed into a gown of rose pink silk, very severely cut, which she thought should placate Lady Norbury, but when she saw her hostess, forbidding in black satin trimmed with jet, she abandoned that hope. The older members of the family, clearly taking their cue from the hostess, were dour. But John Norbury smiled mischievously at her when she came in, and Arthur Bramton offered her a chair. She took it, wondering where Charles could be and how he could leave her to face this scene alone.

Silence fell. Anabel looked around. The aunts and uncles avoided her eye. Cecily looked frightened. Anabel tried to think of some commonplace remark to begin a conversation, but the atmosphere in the room seemed to press in on her brain, stifling thought.

"I trust you are recovered from your journey," said Lady Norbury at last.

"Yes, thank you."

"One must be more careful, past a certain age, not to wear oneself down."

Anabel's blue eyes widened, then her eyelids dropped. If her hostess thought she would take such gibes, she was mistaken. "Do you find it so?" she answered sweetly. "I myself am never tired."

John Norbury snickered. His formidable aunt silenced him with a glance, then turned back to Anabel with a glare of combined anger and surprise. More than one adversary had mistaken Anabel's fragile looks for timidity in the past. "You have a quick tongue."

"Thank you," answered Anabel perversely.

"You are very pleased with yourself, are you not?" Lady Norbury sounded goaded, and Anabel wondered what Charles had said to her during their tête-à-tête.

"Not overly pleased, I hope." It was very odd, she thought, the way no one else in the room spoke at all. They might have been wax figures. Were they really so firmly under Lady Norbury's thumb?

"Indeed?" The older woman sounded contemptuous.

To Anabel's vast relief, Charles came in. He smiled at her and at his mother, not seeming to see the others, and said, "I'm sorry to be late. My valet is a careless fellow."

The butler, who had been on the watch, announced dinner. Lady Norbury stood slowly and gazed at Charles.

He obediently offered his arm. The aunts and uncles paired up and hurried to follow. Cecily clutched her brother's arm when he would have approached Anabel, which left her to John Norbury.

"What do you think of this bedlam house?" he murmured as they walked toward the dining room.

She merely raised her eyebrows. She would not make the mistake of talking freely to any of these people.

"Right. Mum it is. But I'll give you a piece of advice. If you really want to marry Charles—can't see it myself, but you've accepted him—get him away from here and keep him away until the knot's tied. My aunt is poison."

Anabel looked at him curiously.

"Wondering why the heir apparent is so loose-tongued?" He laughed a little. "*I* don't want this place. I'd as soon live in a mausoleum." They had entered the dining room, and he escorted her to a chair between his father and his uncle before going to his own, farther down the table. Anabel slid into it quickly—the others were already settled, Charles beside his mother—and the meal began.

It was long, slow, and, to Anabel, excruciating. Her neighbors did not speak to her. The only conversation was at the head of the table, and a few murmurs on the opposite side, where the cousins alternated with the aunts. There were five courses, each consisting of far more dishes than she could sample, and the intervals between them seemed endless. At first Anabel was uneasy. She tried more than once to elicit some comment from the uncles. Then she felt inexpressibly weary and bored, and finally angry at the way she was being treated. Why didn't Charles say something? she wondered. But by the time the last course was offered round, her pique had given way to amusement. It was really ridiculous, this solemn party, the heavy silence, the furtive eyes of the people around her. Whatever they might feel, Lady Norbury had no hold on *her*, and she refused to allow her spirits to be depressed. The evening would end eventually, and tomorrow she would depart, never to visit here willingly again. The future implications of this decision she pushed aside.

At last Lady Norbury rose, signaling the ladies' departure. Taking her cane, she walked slowly along the table, spurning an aunt who offered assistance.

"Do not linger too long over your port," she told the gentlemen.

"Don't worry, Mama," replied Charles. "We shall join you soon."

The walk upstairs was slow. Everyone kept behind Lady Norbury, and she obviously found the climb very difficult. But she refused help again, sharply, and nothing more was said.

At the drawing-room doorway, Anabel excused herself and ran up another flight. She was determined to stay in her room until it seemed likely that the gentlemen would have come up. She could not face another period of icy silence, or another exchange with Charles's mother.

She calculated correctly. When she entered the drawing room again, the whole party was there. Defiantly she crossed to sit beside Charles on a sofa. He smiled at her and turned back to his mother. The others remained as before.

Anabel watched their interaction curiously. She had not considered it until now, but Charles's devotion to his mother was uncharacteristic. It did not seem to fit his Corinthian pose. She listened to their conversation.

If asked, she would have predicted that Lady Norbury complained about her ills, questioned her son's doings, and tried to dictate to him. She was mistaken. Lady Norbury was hardly talking at all. She was listening to her son repeat some triumph he had achieved—Anabel did not completely understand what; she had missed the beginning of the anecdote— and murmuring praise and admiration as he spoke. When he finished, she added that she had always known he was superior to any man in the country, let alone London, and Charles smiled slightly, as if he acknowledged a truth rather than a compliment.

This went on for half an hour, Anabel growing more and more amazed. She had never heard such a litany of self-congratulation. They did not discuss any other person or any events but those in which he had participated. It was as if the world existed only for Charles to shine in it. She watched his face. He seemed younger. The bored mask was gone, revealing an intense, eager personality that might have been very attractive had his attention ever wandered from himself. Shaken, Anabel rose and walked over to a window, parting the curtains to look out on the moonlit drive. Charles did not seem to notice, though Lady Norbury did. Anabel's mind felt peculiarly blank. She looked out but did not really see anything.

"My mother says Charles was indulged all out of reason," whispered a voice close beside her. Starting, she turned to find John Norbury at her side. "I heard her tell Papa so. My Aunt Norbury has insisted he was perfect since he was born."

Anabel moved away from the window to face the room.

"I suppose we can't talk about that, either. This place makes me nervous as a cat." He paused. "Do you like London?"

"Uh…yes, very much."

"*I* haven't been. But I shall, as soon as I come of age." He eyed his parents darkly.

Before Anabel could do more than wonder how to respond to this, Charles was helping his mother to her feet and looking around for her. "Mama retires early," he said. "I shall just take her up. I won't be a moment."

Anabel came forward to say good night. Lady Norbury acknowledged it with a nod, and the two went out.

It was as if a great weight had been lifted from the group. Mrs. Norbury leaned forward to speak to Mrs. Bramton, and the two uncles beat a hasty retreat, muttering about the smoking room. Arthur Bramton joined Anabel and John, and after a hesitant moment Cecily followed. "Whew," Arthur murmured. "That's over. These dinners are almost more than I can stand." Cecily cast a frightened glance at her mother, but the older women were paying no attention.

"How about a game of billiards?" suggested John. "All of us. We can trade off."

"Right." Arthur nodded. "Come, Cecily, I'll give you four strokes." They all looked at Anabel.

"I must wait for Charles."

"He'll come and find us," said John.

She was tempted, but she did not really want to play billiards. She wanted to talk to Norbury. "No, you go on."

John shrugged and led the others out. Anabel returned to the sofa, smiling to show that she would be happy to join in the aunts' conversation. But they were discussing some stranger's prolonged illness, and as they did not explain any of the particulars, she was soon lost.

It seemed hours before Charles reappeared. Lady Norbury had no doubt kept him as long as she could. But finally he came in, smiled at her, and held out a hand. "Come, there is something I want to show you."

She was happy to follow. He led her downstairs to a door opening on the back terrace; they walked across it and onto a gravel path bisecting the lawn. "I should get a shawl," said Anabel.

"It isn't cold. Come."

She took his arm, and they walked to a copse some way from the house. The path twisted among the trees and then emerged in front of a tiny white gazebo, the interior furnished with dark green cushions. Moonlight was pouring over the small clearing in which it sat, gilding everything with silver, and the air was very soft and still. "Come," said Charles again, and he led her up two steps and seated her on a cushion. "This has always been one of my favorite places."

"It is lovely."

He sat beside her and pulled her close within the circle of his arm. "You see? You don't need a shawl." His clasp tightening, he kissed her slowly.

But Anabel was too unsettled to respond. When he drew back, she moved a little away and said, "Charles, I must talk to you about something."

His hand caressed her shoulder. "What?"

"Has…has your mother said anything to you about me?"

"She thinks you charming." He started to pull her close again.

"But, Charles." She did not yield. "Did she say so?"

"I can tell what she thinks." He sounded impatient. "She is very happy for me, for us. There is nothing for you to worry over." And as if the issue were settled, he bent his head again, his free hand coming up to encircle her waist and mold her against him. His kiss was insistent and compelling. Anabel found her thoughts becoming less clear. Could she have imagined Lady Norbury's resistance? He must know his own mother better than she, after all. And did it matter?

But as Charles's expert lips and hands once more lulled her into a kind of blank surrender, a remote part of Anabel objected. She stiffened. She was nearly reclining on the cushions by this time, Charles bending over her. She struggled to sit up.

For a moment he prevented her. Then he seemed to recollect himself and drew back. "You are right, my love," he agreed. "We had best go in. This is a dangerous meeting place." He looked around the tiny space as if reviewing fond memories, but he stood, pulling her up against his side and moving toward the door. "We must decide on a wedding date, however, my darling. I am on my best behavior, but I am not superhuman." They walked outside and back along the path. "What about three weeks from tonight? We needn't make too great a fuss. That should give you time to prepare."

"I...I must think," she replied breathlessly, conscious of a strong desire to put off this decision.

He chuckled. "I am happy to know that I can so disrupt your thoughts. We will talk it over tomorrow." They had reached the terrace door again. "But tonight, one last farewell." Sweeping her into his arms, he kissed her passionately again.

Twelve

IN LONDON, THE FOLLOWING MORNING DAWNED bright and clear, but in the schoolroom at Lady Goring's house, storm signals appeared as soon as the children finished their breakfast. "I don't want to do lessons," Susan told her brothers. "I want to go riding first, as we do at home."

"We can't," responded William. "We haven't any horses, and we can't hire them ourselves."

"Why not?" Susan's little face was screwed into a mighty scowl.

"Well…" William turned to Nicholas.

"They wouldn't give them to us," the latter said. "And anyway, we wouldn't be allowed to ask. Perhaps Uncle Christopher will take us again soon."

"I hate it here!" declared Susan. "At home I can go riding whenever I like."

Though this was not strictly true, neither of the boys dared point this out to her.

"When is Mama coming home?" she added. "She has been gone forever."

"This afternoon," answered Nick. "She promised to sit with us at our dinner."

"Will she bring that man?"

"No." Then, realizing that he could not guarantee this, Nick amended, "I don't think she will."

"She has been visiting him," replied his sister accusingly.

"His family, yes."

"And when they are married, he will live with us all the time, will he not?"

Nicholas nodded wearily. He recognized Susan's mood. She was at her most intractable, and it was going to be a tiresome day.

"I don't like him!"

"We know that. Neither do we."

The governess came in then, and their conversation was cut off. But throughout the morning lessons Susan glowered, and William and Nicholas waited apprehensively for the explosion that always followed these sulks. After one blast of temper Susan would be all right again, they knew.

It did not come. Instead Susan grew quieter, and when they were dismissed for luncheon, she declared she was not hungry and was going to her room. The boys could only be grateful for her unusual restraint. They discussed it over bread and milk at the nursery table. "I expect she's up to something," said William. "She always is when she gets quiet."

Nick frowned. "But what?"

His brother shrugged, concentrating on his plate.

Before they finished, Nurse came in. "Where is Miss Susan?" she asked them.

"In her room. She said she wasn't hungry."

"She must eat her luncheon. Go and fetch her at once."

"But we're eating," objected Nick, not at all eager to confront his sister.

Nurse put her hands on her hips and glared, and both boys rose and went along the hall to Susan's room. "I expect she'll let loose now," sighed Nick. William nodded glumly.

Susan's bedchamber was empty, however. There was no sign that she had been there since rising. Exchanging a puzzled look, they went to the schoolroom. It was also untenanted. "Why would she go downstairs?" wondered William.

"Perhaps she changed her mind about eating and

went to ask Cook for something special," suggested his brother. They descended to the kitchen, but Susan had not been seen there. Frowning now, they hurriedly looked into the rooms on the other floors. Susan was nowhere in the house.

"I *told* you she was up to something," said William as they paused before her room again. "Where can she have gone?"

Nicholas was thinking hard. "Go and give Nurse some excuse," he said. "We must plan."

"What excuse?" answered William helplessly.

"Think of something!"

Shaking his head, he went, only to return in a moment with the news that Nurse wasn't there. "I think she went down for more milk. The pitcher was gone."

"Good." Nick pulled his brother into Susan's room and shut the door. "We must decide what we are going to do."

"About what?"

"Susan's run away."

"Run…! How do you know?"

"I checked the room while you were gone. She's taken her cloak and the net purse Mama gave her at Christmas. You know she keeps all her pocket money in it. And…" He paused for effect. "The cat's gone as well."

William snorted. "He's always gone somewhere."

"No. She's been very careful since he ate the leg of lamb in the kitchen. She made this bed for him and everything." He indicated a nest of old blankets in the corner. "She's gone."

"But…where?"

Nick shook his head. "Home, I expect. Remember her complaining this morning?"

"But she can't get home by herself!" William was aghast.

"Try convincing Susan of that."

Silently they thought of their sister's stubbornness. "Mama will be furious," said William. "We must tell someone, start a search."

"Ye-es." Nick was hesitant.

"Of course we must. Come on!" William started toward the door.

"Wait a moment."

He hesitated with one hand on the doorknob.

"I think we should go after her ourselves. That way, no one need know she has run away."

William gaped at him. "Have you run mad? We should never get her back here even if we found her."

"Why not?"

"Because she won't listen to us, bacon brain. She never does."

"I believe I can convince her."

William shook his head and started to turn the knob.

"Are we just to sit in this house, then, as we have been doing for weeks and weeks?" Nick's voice was exasperated. "What's happened to you, William? Have you turned cow-hearted?"

"This isn't one of your pranks, Nicholas! Susan is wandering about London alone. It's not a question of—"

"We could find her. We know how she thinks."

"I don't!"

"Oh, come, William. Let us at least *try*."

The older Wyndham hesitated, obviously torn between duty and the call of adventure. "I suppose we could look around for an hour or so, then come and fetch help if we had no luck."

"That's the ticket," agreed Nick, ready to accept even partial capitulation.

His brother frowned, then gave in. "Oh, very well." And a few minutes later, having gathered the necessary supplies, the two boys slipped unseen out the front door and into the street.

It was hardly half an hour after that that the bell rang to announce a caller. No footman or maid appeared in the hall, and after a pause the bell rang again. Georgina Goring was hurrying across the upper landing just then, and she hesitated, looking worried, then ran down the stairs and opened the wide front door a bit, peering out through the narrow aperture. "Oh, Mr. Hanford!" She pulled the door wider. "I'm sorry no one came. We are all rather upset. The children have disappeared." Seeing a movement behind him, she drew in her breath. "Susan! Do you have them, then? Thank God!"

Christopher was frowning. "Susan came to see me about an hour ago. Are the boys missing as well?"

"I did not come to see you!" declared Susan irately. "I was running away, and I thought you would help me." She pushed past them and into the hall. "Have William and Nicholas gone, too? If I had known, I would have waited for them."

Christopher exchanged a wry glance with Georgina. "They aren't here," she said. "Nurse discovered it a few minutes ago and fell into a fit of hysterics."

"Nurse did?" responded Susan with ghoulish glee. "She is silly."

Hanford shut the door and went down on one knee beside the little girl. "Susan, where have Nicholas and William gone? Running away is not going to solve anything. You must see that."

"It would," insisted Susan, "if you would help me. I do not see why you are being so stuffy. Mama can live with that man, and I will live with *you*." She gazed at him with a mixture of appeal and irritation.

His face showed pain for a moment, but he answered merely, "I fear that isn't possible, Susan." Georgina, watching him, bit her lower lip; she thought she had never known anyone so noble. "Now, where have they gone?" asked Hanford again.

"I don't know." She sounded uninterested. "They didn't tell *me* they were leaving. They don't tell me anything."

He took her shoulders and looked into her green eyes. "Is that true? Did you not plan to run away at the same time?"

"No! William mentioned it once, but Nicholas said it was wrong, and he agreed with him. They worry about everything!" She considered the matter. "I suppose they only went because *I* did, and they finally saw what a splendid idea it was."

Christopher stood. "I think she is telling the truth. She does not know where they are."

"What are we going to do?" said Georgina. "Anabel will be so worried."

"I believe I can guess their object."

She gazed at him in admiration. "What?"

"I imagine they have gone after Susan."

"Oh!" Georgina looked at the little girl with amazement.

Susan crowed with laughter. "They have! They have! How stupid boys are."

"I think I can find them," added Hanford, eyeing Susan with amusement and resignation. "I wager they've started for home, thinking that she went there."

"As if I would be so silly," exclaimed the child. "I know I cannot get so far alone." She glanced at Hanford with annoyance. "I thought *you* would take me."

"I am sorry I could not." He turned to Georgina. "I will leave Susan with you. And I shall hope to return with the boys before the day is out. Tell Anabel."

Georgina nodded. "She should be back at any moment."

His face clouded, remembering where she had gone, then he straightened and nodded. Georgina thought again how splendid he was and wondered how her cousin could reject him for Sir Charles Norbury.

"I am going with you," declared Susan.

"No. You must stay here and see your mother."

"I don't want to see her! I *shall* come. I shall!"

Christopher, impatient to be gone now that he had formed a plan, was unwilling to take the time to cajole her. "Very well. We should be no more than a few hours," he told Georgina. "Susan will be just as well with me. Indeed, she will be less trouble, I imagine. You can tell them where we have gone."

Georgina nodded earnestly.

"Don't worry." He smiled at her. "I'm sure they are all right, and I shall have them back very soon."

"You are so good to do this!" she could not help but say.

He raised his eyebrows. "The children are very dear to me." Susan grasped his hand and pulled it impatiently. "Yes, we are going. We will see you later today, Miss Goring."

"Good-bye."

When she closed the door behind them, Georgina leaned on it, her face dreamy with admiration. Anabel might be older and more experienced than she, but she was still very foolish. Anyone could see that Mr. Hanford was far finer than Sir Charles. If only he… But no, he loved Anabel; that was plain. How could she fail to see it? Or did she know? Was she simply letting him love her and enjoying the sensation, while she dallied with Norbury? Georgina frowned. She had seen such behavior here in London and found it shocking. Some members of the *haut ton* lived by a set of rules far removed from those her countrified father had instilled in her. She had not thought that Anabel was one—but Norbury? She frowned in doubt. It would be unbearable if Christopher Hanford were being so grievously hurt on a whim. Even as this idea made her scowl the bell rang again. Georgina started and turned to open the door.

Anabel swept in, looking irritable, followed by Sir Charles and a servant carrying her case. Georgina started to speak.

"My lady!" shrieked Nurse from the upper landing. "Oh, my lady, thank God you are home! The children are gone. They've disappeared!"

Anabel stared up at her in horror.

"They were just as usual when I got them up," she continued. "They had their lessons. But during luncheon I went down for more milk, and when I returned, they were gone. Oh, my lady, do you think they've been kidnapped?"

"Nonsense," drawled Sir Charles. "I daresay they have simply gone to the park or some such thing. Get hold of yourself, woman." He, too, seemed annoyed. Georgina glared at him, and Nurse bridled.

"Have you searched?" asked Anabel in a strangled voice.

"All the men are looking," Nurse replied. "Lady Goring was out, but I have sent after her. I would have gone myself, but—"

"It is all right, Anabel," began Georgina.

"Of course it is," interrupted Norbury. "You are all making a great fuss about nothing. I daresay they will come home directly, very pleased with the uproar they have caused."

"They do not go out alone in London," said Anabel. She gazed about the hall, distracted. "I must look for them. May I use your carriage?"

"A traveling chaise? You would be much better off—"

"I don't care what sort of carriage it is!"

He stiffened at her tone, "Very well. Of course."

"Anabel," called Georgina, but she was waved aside as they climbed up and urged the driver to start.

Thirteen

THAT AFTERNOON WAS PROBABLY THE WORST OF Anabel's life. She had been very glad to return home. Norbury had pressed her all through the journey to set a definite date for their wedding, and she had steadfastly resisted doing so. Some part of her wanted more time for that decision. The exchange had irritated them both. Norbury had been infuriated at this thwarting of his wishes; he was accustomed to capitulation. And Anabel had felt beleaguered. She was still very unused to directing her own life, and the effort of not only taking a position but holding to it in the face of strong opposition exhausted her.

In this mood she had discovered the loss of her children, and nearly fallen into a panic. Questions of her future with Charles evaporated. Never since their birth had she not known where her children were or with whom. The thought of them wandering alone and unprotected in London made her frantic.

Sir Charles offered her no aid. He rode with her as she directed the chaise through the park, oblivious to the stares of fashionable saunterers, and around the streets near the Goring house. But he sat back in a corner, arms folded, making his disapproval of her actions palpable. At first Anabel didn't notice, but as time passed and they found no clue, she turned to him in desperate need of reassurance. "Can you think of anywhere else we might look?" she asked.

"I think this whole exercise is futile," he replied.

"You cannot see anything from a moving carriage. We may have missed them repeatedly in the park. More than likely, they have turned up at home by now, happily unconscious of causing any anxiety."

"Do you truly think so?" She wanted to believe this.

"Yes." He was offended both by her stubbornness on the subject of their wedding and by her complete forgetfulness of him during the last two hours. He was convinced that the children would return, and her exaggerated concern inflamed his jealousy. She had not shown this much emotion for him.

"Perhaps we should go back and see." Anabel was torn. The afternoon was ending, and they hadn't found the children. Yet it was difficult to give up. They might be around the very next corner. She looked at Norbury, whose set face was turned away. He could be right. "Very well. Let us do that."

He gave the order to the driver, and they turned toward home. Unbending a little at her acquiescence to his suggestion, he said, "Have your children any close acquaintances in town? Perhaps they went visiting without telling anyone."

Anabel straightened abruptly. "Christopher! Why didn't I think of him at once?"

Norbury looked displeased.

"We must stop at his sister's house and inquire. It is on the way." Anabel felt revitalized. Christopher would know what to do even if he had not seen the children. The mere thought of him comforted her immensely. How could she have forgotten to consult him? She sat back, relaxing for almost the first time that day.

Norbury's sidelong glance was cold.

But at the Lanforth house they were told that Christopher had gone out of town. He had left so hurriedly that none of the servants had been informed of his purpose, and Amelia had been out all day and thus had not seen Susan or heard of the trouble. She was very sympathetic but could offer no help. Certain that he would return before evening, Hanford had not left her a note.

Unreasonably, Anabel felt deserted and betrayed. She was not thinking clearly and knew only that her mainstay had failed her. She allowed Norbury to direct the carriage home and to help her down when they reached her mother's house, but her mind was full of dreadful visions of what might befall unguarded children in the city streets.

Lady Goring met her at the front door, enfolding her in her arms. "Anabel, my dear. Are you all right?"

"Have they come home?"

"No. But all the servants are out searching. They cannot fail to find them very soon."

Slumping against her mother's shoulder, Anabel burst into tears. Lady Goring embraced her, stroking her hair and murmuring soothing phrases as all the tension and worry of the day poured forth.

Norbury, forgotten, stood stiffly beside the front door. He was not intimidated by female tears. He had seen many in his life. But he was accustomed to being the central figure in such scenes. He could soothe or spurn with equal skill when a woman's feelings for him gave way to sobs; he had had no experience, however, with outbursts from other causes. And he didn't much care for them. The intense emotion that seemed only natural when he himself was the object appeared hysterical and unnecessary here. To him children were rather like dogs. They went their uncharted ways and returned when hungry or weary. He had never felt any great attachment to either species. "My horses will take cold," he said. "Perhaps I should go home and change." Meeting Lady Goring's contemptuous look, he added, "I will return at once, of course, and remain with you until the children return."

Anabel did not surface, but Lady Goring dismissed him with a curt wave that might have offended him if he had not been so eager to depart. When he had gone, Lady Goring helped her daughter up the stairs to the drawing room and removed her bonnet. Her sobs lessened a little. "I will get you some water."

The room was dim. Darkness was falling, and there were no servants in the house to draw the curtains and light the candles. Anabel struggled for control and slowly managed to stop crying. She groped for a handkerchief and wiped her streaming eyes, sniffing.

Georgina rose from an armchair in the corner and approached. She had been sitting here in the dimness for some time, waiting for Anabel's return. Her cousin's crying had touched her deeply, and she had delayed only until it seemed that her news would be understood before rising to impart it. "Anabel," she said.

Anabel started violently and looked up, her eyes red and swollen. "Oh, Georgina. I didn't know you were here."

"I have been waiting to tell you—"

"You might have been out helping us search. But of course my children are not *your* responsibility." At some level Anabel knew this was utterly unfair, but Norbury's abandonment had cut her to the quick, and it seemed to her that no one cared for her or her plight. Christopher was gone, and the man she had agreed to marry was merely annoyed by her anguish. In her upset she turned on the nearest available object.

Georgina understood some of this. "I did not go because—"

"Oh, it doesn't signify," interrupted Anabel bitterly. "Why should you? My promised husband has gone off to change his coat. And my dearest friend has gone out of town without a word. Charles hardly knows the children, of course, and he means to return. But Christopher *might* have done something. How could he be so thoughtless?" This was even more unreasonable, she knew. Christopher could not have known that an emergency would arise. But Anabel was conscious only of a need for his stalwart presence; she was incapable of logical thought.

Georgina was outraged. Not only was the noble, unselfish Mr. Hanford being unjustly accused but Anabel actually dared to praise Sir Charles Norbury at his expense. It was more than unfair; it was intolerable. Georgina's pity for her cousin dissolved in righteous anger. As Lady Goring returned with a tray she threw back her head and strode from the room.

"Oh dear," sighed Anabel as her mother urged her to try to eat something. "I have offended Georgina. I didn't mean to say such ridiculous things. I don't know what is the matter with me."

"Of course you do. You are terribly upset. Georgina understands that." Anabel was Lady Goring's chief concern just now. She had no doubt Georgina would recover. "Do take just a little of this soup. It will make you feel better."

The evening passed without news. Some of the servants returned, having looked every place they could think of, and at nine one of Norbury's footmen arrived with a note saying that he would call in the morning. Lady Goring read this with a curled lip and did not even tell Anabel. She had not asked for Sir Charles and was clearly not thinking about him. Georgina came in a bit later, looking repentant and wanting to speak to Anabel, but Lady Goring insisted she go to bed, refusing to listen to a word. Georgina actually told her the truth, in a rather disjointed sentence, but her aunt's attention was so wholly taken up with her daughter that she did not really hear, merely replying, "Yes, dear, you can tell us all about it tomorrow. Now run along upstairs."

Slowly and reluctantly Georgina went. She felt very

uncertain, but she was not accustomed to forcing her opinions on other people, and Lady Goring stood in the place of a parent. She decided to wait in her bedchamber for a while and then try again to tell her story. Unfortunately she had no sooner lain down on her bed to wait than the emotional exhaustions of the day descended, and she fell deeply asleep.

Anabel and her mother remained in the drawing room, with no thought of retiring. Anabel's feelings ran the gamut from guilt and apprehension to sudden, wild hope when a passing carriage seemed to slow before their door. Finally, at eleven, she leaped to her feet, crying, "They have gone home, of course! They dislike London and have often asked to go. I must start out at once."

Lady Goring rose also, frowning. "Do you think so?" She did not really believe that the children would flee without a word.

"Yes, yes. That must be it. Will you order the carriage for me, Mama? I will just fetch my hat and cloak."

"But, Anabel, this does not sound like William or Nicholas. And I do not think they would allow Susan to lead them." Realizing that her daughter had not really heard her, she took her shoulders in a firm grip and met her wildly elated gaze. "Besides, Anabel, you cannot search for them in the darkness. We must wait for morning now."

"No!" She struggled free. "I must do something!"

"I understand how you feel, but it is no good wearing yourself out tonight. You might easily pass them in the dark."

Abruptly Anabel's eagerness collapsed. "Oh, Mama, what am I going to do?" She dropped onto the sofa again and put her head in her hands. "It is all my fault. I should never have gone away."

"Nonsense. If it comes to that, it is my fault. They

were lost from my house. But we won't waste time repining. First thing tomorrow, we shall begin an organized search. We can have the Bow Street Runners."

Her daughter looked up. "We will find them, won't we?"

"Of course! There is no question about that."

Trying to smile, Anabel held out her hand. Lady Goring took it and squeezed it reassuringly, hoping that she was indeed right. "Why not go up to bed?" she urged finally. "Nothing can be done just now."

"I couldn't sleep. You go on."

"No. I shall stay with you."

They lapsed into silence again. Midnight passed, and the sounds from the street outside gradually subsided. The ticking of the mantel clock became loud. Anabel seemed to feel it inside her head.

At last both women began to droop. Such a high pitch of anxiety could not be sustained indefinitely. Lady Goring's head gradually dropped onto the back of the armchair, and she dozed. Anabel, though she didn't sleep, curled into the corner of the sofa in a kind of stupor. Thus, when they heard the sound of carriage wheels approaching the house in the small hours of the morning, they both started up convulsively, jarred by the sudden noise in the predawn silence.

"It is nothing," said Anabel shakily, sinking back. "A carriage." But she strained to listen.

"It is slowing." Her mother went to the window. "I think...yes, it is stopping here, Anabel." The other was already at the drawing-room door, then running for the stairs.

They had the front door open before the vehicle was completely stopped. Anabel found it difficult to breathe as it pulled up and the door swung open. But when first William, then Nicholas emerged, she rushed forward and swept them into her arms, shaking with joy and relief.

The boys were sleepy. They accepted their mother's embraces in good part, but they also bore her backward toward the house and their beds. "Where have you been? Where did you go? Where is…" Anabel looked up at this moment and saw before her Christopher Hanford, cradling a drowsy Susan in his arms. She was struck speechless.

"Everyone come inside," ordered Lady Goring. She herded the boys before her and put a hand in the small of Anabel's back. They all went in and upstairs to the drawing room once more.

"I'm tired," complained William, stretching and yawning.

Lady Goring looked from Anabel to Hanford. "I will take you up to bed," she answered. "Here, Mr. Hanford, give me Susan."

"I will take her if you like."

"Nonsense. She is quite light. I can manage." Urging the boys before her again, she went out.

Silence fell. Anabel stared at Christopher as if she had never seen him before, and he waited, uncertain. Then, as if impelled by some external force, she ran forward and threw herself into his arms, burying her face in his shoulder.

Hanford was startled for a moment. In all the years they had known each other, he and Anabel had never embraced. Moreover, he could not understand her violent reaction to their return. He had left a clear message of his intentions. But these concerns were soon lost in sensation. For the first time Christopher held the woman he had loved for so long. Against hope, she had come to him. Throwing questions to the wind, he tightened his arms around her and, when she looked up, bent to fasten his lips passionately on hers.

Anabel was beyond surprise. When she had seen Christopher holding Susan, it had felt as if a lightning bolt went through her brain, dazzling her senses and paralyzing thought. She knew only that something had happened to her; she could not interpret it. Moving into Christopher's arms had seemed natural, and when she rested her head on his shoulder, she suddenly felt as if everything were all right again, after an endless agony. She had raised her head to say something like this, only to be overtaken by his kiss.

This was equally astonishing. She had never thought of kissing Christopher, but now his touch seemed to set her on fire. She had never felt anything like it. Her hands moved of their own volition to caress his upper arms, his shoulders, and to tighten about his neck. She felt his lean strength along the length of her body and was acutely aware of every contact. She felt no languor, as she had with Norbury; every part of her seemed newly alive and singing with energy.

At last, reluctantly, Hanford drew back. He had felt Anabel's response, and it had filled him with joy and redoubled ardor. But, inevitably, other concerns intruded. He could not wholly forget that she was promised to another man.

Anabel took two trembling breaths and moved away. She could not assimilate this change quickly after the day she had had. Her familiar world had turned upside down. "I…" She swallowed. "Where did you find them?"

"On the road home, as I suspected. They were indignant when they saw that Susan was with me."

"With you?" Anabel thought that perhaps her brain was not working properly. His words made no sense to her.

"Yes." He frowned. "Didn't Georgina tell you?"

"Georgina?" She was completely lost.

"She promised to…never mind. Susan came to my sister's house this afternoon…or yesterday it is now. She informed me that she was running away and I was to help her." He smiled slightly. "Naturally I brought her back, but by the time we arrived the boys had already departed in search of their sister. They concluded that she was going home and took that road. I guessed and followed in my traveling carriage, coming up with them some hours later." He shook his head. "They were very resourceful; they had convinced a carter to give them a ride. Susan insisted upon coming along when I would have left her here. But I told Georgina my plan." He stepped forward and took her icy hands in his warm ones. "Didn't she tell you?"

"No!" Anabel considered. "That is, she may have tried. I was very worried."

"Poor Anabel." He made as if to embrace her again, but she drew away.

"I... Thank you!"

He shrugged, dismissing her thanks, and waited. He would not force her into any declaration, but neither was he willing to help her avoid the issue. Her response to him had been unmistakable; she would have to say something.

For her part, Anabel did not know what to do. A great many things were coming clear to her, and others clamored for her attention. It was obvious that she had made a complete mull of things so far. She did not want to compound her mistakes. But when she looked into Christopher's eyes, she could think of nothing but him. "I...I'm exhausted," she said, gazing at the floor. "And I must see that the children are all right. Will you...will you come to call tomorrow, so that I may thank you properly?"

What did she mean by "properly"? he wondered. But he could only agree. She did look tired. "Of course." He hesitated, hoping she would speak again, then turned and went slowly out. Anabel collapsed on the sofa and sat very still, listening to the front door open and shut and the sound of his carriage driving away.

Fourteen

SHE DIDN'T GO UP TO THE CHILDREN. SHE REMAINED where she was, her body motionless but her mind racing. Everything that had happened to her in the last three months had suddenly taken on a new significance. It was as if with one small shift in her outlook, all those events had changed, so that she had to review each one and alter her ideas about it. Christopher had been the center of her life for some time, she saw now; it was only when he had left to go abroad that she had felt restless at home. Her feelings for him had been growing deeper and stronger for years. Why she had not seen it before she did not know. Perhaps the easy gradualness of the process had disguised it. They had been so in harmony and so content with each other that she had never before had occasion to draw back and examine the situation. She had taken him wholly for granted, not pausing to think how fortunate she was to have him always near.

And when he had gone, she was hurt and lonely, she saw now. But she had hidden the knowledge from herself and come up to London, like a fool. She had been no better than a green schoolgirl, awed by new sights and swept into a mistaken engagement. Sir Charles had dazzled her, but he had never touched her heart as Christopher did. Anabel bowed her head on the sofa arm and sighed. How could she have been so stupid? She had thought Sir Charles exciting; he had appealed to her vanity and her pride. But Christopher's kiss tonight had shown her the emptiness of that attraction. Christopher's touch had set her afire with longing; Charles merely induced surrender.

Anabel rose and walked about the room, frowning. She did not even see her mother look in at the door, watch her face for a moment, and then retreat. She was trying to understand her failure and to sort out her feelings so that she could think what to do.

The night was almost over. Outside, the sky was lightening with the first pale hues of dawn, and muted sounds from below indicated that the servants were stirring. But Anabel was aware of nothing but her own inner turmoil. Though exhausted by the emotions of the past day, she did not think of sleep.

When the sun had appeared over the horizon and the scent of breakfast was rising from the kitchen, she was suddenly distracted by the sound of running footsteps on the stairs, and in the next moment Georgina hurtled into the drawing room, still wearing the gown of the night before and looking wild-eyed and crumpled. "Oh, Anabel," she gasped. "I fell asleep. I meant to come back down in a few minutes and speak to you. I do beg your pardon. I was to tell you—"

"I know," she replied. "Christopher told me when he brought back the children."

"He *did*, then? I mean, of course I knew he would, but I wasn't certain when they would arrive."

Anabel merely nodded. She still felt far away.

"Mr. Hanford is wonderful!" exclaimed the girl. "He knew at once where they had gone, and I suppose he found them without the least trouble. How I wish I had been here when he came back."

Anabel looked at her, and she flushed, then raised her chin. "You admire him very much, don't you?" said Anabel.

"Yes." Georgina sounded defiant.

"Why did you not tell me at once what he was doing?"

"I tried! But no one would listen. And when you began abusing him, I…"

She trailed off, feeling guiltily conscious that she had no real excuse.

"Abusing Christopher? I?"

"Well, you were saying that he didn't care, and ranking him below Si—" She stopped herself before saying Norbury's name.

Anabel didn't recall her words, but she had no doubt Georgina was right. "Oh, Georgina—I was very worried. I didn't mean what I said."

"No." Georgina hung her head. "I know. I…I beg your pardon, Anabel. I was very stupid."

Her cousin sighed, gazing at the fireplace. "Not so much as I," she murmured.

"What?"

"Never mind, Georgina. It doesn't matter now. The children are safe, and all is well." At least with them, she added to herself.

Georgina eyed her, sensing a difference. "Did you sleep at all?"

"No, I couldn't."

"You should go up now and rest this morning."

Anabel shook her head; she was far too restless still. "The day is beginning. I can sleep tonight. Why don't we go down and have some breakfast? I believe it is ready." She suddenly realized that she was extremely hungry. "Did you have any dinner last night?"

"I… No." Georgina seemed surprised.

"Well, then." With an attempt at a smile, Anabel linked her arm with her cousin's.

"Should we change first?" asked the girl, looking from her own crumpled gown to Anabel's creased traveling dress.

"We can do so when we have eaten," declared the other, urging her forward, and they walked down to the breakfast parlor together.

Lady Goring found them there twenty minutes later, surrounded by the remains of a substantial breakfast. "Oh, Mama," said Anabel. "Did the children fall asleep at once? I must go up to them. I would have come last night, but…" She hesitated.

"They were asleep almost before I put them to bed, and they are still sleeping now. I asked Nurse on my way down." She looked from one to the other. "What of you?"

"I fell asleep in my gown," replied Georgina sheepishly. She rose. "I must go and change it."

Lady Goring looked at her daughter as Georgina went out. "And you, Anabel?"

"I had too much to think about."

"Indeed?" She surveyed her closely.

"Yes."

She did not explain, and Lady Goring did not press her, despite her curiosity about what had passed between her daughter and Hanford the previous night. It was obvious that *something* had, but she decided it would be best to wait and let it develop.

"I must change also," added Anabel, pushing back her chair. "I will look in on the children when I am dressed."

Lady Goring nodded and reached for the teapot.

But as Anabel was ascending the stairs the bell rang and a footman went to the door. She lingered on the landing, wondering if it could be Christopher so early. But the voice that drifted up to her was that of Sir Charles Norbury, calm and confident of his welcome. He had stepped inside and seen her before Anabel could move. "Ah. There you are," he added, striding quickly up to her. He glanced at her dress. "Are the children not back, then?"

"Yes. They are here." Her lips felt strange, almost stiff.

"As I foretold," he responded, taking her arm and guiding her into the drawing room. "I was right, you see."

This was too much. "My friend Christopher Hanford *brought* them back," she retorted, "after searching for them for most of the night!"

"Indeed?" Norbury's chiseled mouth turned down. "How very, er, enterprising of him. What led him to take this task upon himself?"

"*He* was worried about the children!" As you were not, her tone implied.

"The children, of course," he sneered. "How very touching."

Anabel gazed at him with new eyes. Had Norbury been sympathetic and understanding this morning, as he had not last night, her new viewpoint might have wavered. As it was, she wondered how she could have ever thought she wanted to marry him. Gazing at his fawn pantaloons, his superbly tailored blue coat, and his gleaming Hessians, worn with such assurance and so perfectly complementing his dark, hawklike face, she admitted to herself that his appearance certainly encouraged infatuation. Indeed, he had a power of personality that could overwhelm others' wills. But now that she had discovered her true feelings about Christopher, Norbury's spell was broken, and she knew she would not fall under it again.

Norbury noted the unaccustomed disapproval in her eyes. He was furious at this latest development. Not only had the children's ridiculous prank diverted Anabel from subjects infinitely more important, but now this Hanford was pushing himself forward and trying to ingratiate himself at Norbury's expense. Sir Charles was fully aware of Christopher's feelings for Anabel; the rivalry had added spice to his triumph, and Anabel's ignorance of the contest had been quite amusing. But he sensed a change now. He could not have pointed to the evidence, but a new tone in her voice told him that her opinion of Hanford, and of himself, was altered. Cooler-headed,

Norbury might have been conciliating, might even have pretended to admire Hanford's initiative in finding the children, and thus have won back some of Anabel's sympathy. But he was impatient and frustrated by her refusal to plan for the future. He had determined to marry—he wanted to marry—why was she thwarting him?

"I am surprised that the heroic Mr. Hanford is not here," he said contemptuously. "I should have expected him to dig in at the scene of his rescue."

Anabel had her lips pressed very tightly together. She was afraid to answer him for fear of what she might say; she knew it would be disjointed and overemotional. She needed to think carefully and prepare herself to confront him; he was certain to argue, and Anabel hated disputes. "The children are safe, that is all that matters," she answered. "Thank you for calling to inquire about them."

"Of course." He paused. "Shall we sit down?"

"I was just on my way upstairs." She indicated her crumpled gown with a gesture.

"I shan't stay long."

With a sigh, she sat. She was too tired to fight him just now.

"As your worry over the children is so happily set to rest," he continued, "perhaps we might return to another subject—that of our wedding date."

"And a much more important one?" she replied caustically.

"I did not say so." He raised one dark brow.

"Your tone implied it."

"Nonsense. You are imagining things. Now, I looked over the calendar last night, and I have chosen three days that would be suitable." He took a slip of paper from his coat pocket and held it out to her.

Anabel was furious. While she had been sleepless, terrified about her children, Charles had been studying calendars! She did not take the paper. "I have not slept all night," she said, rising. "I am exhausted. We can talk of this another time."

"Surely you can spare a moment." He rose to face her. "You seem remarkably uninterested in this subject. I should think it would be foremost in your mind."

Anabel opened her mouth to tell him that she would never marry him, but a great wave of fatigue engulfed her. It was all too much. She could not form a rational sentence. She shook her head.

Gazing at her, Norbury was forced to admit that she did look worn. Her pallor and drooping posture touched that emotion that had led him to offer for her in the beginning. In his way, he loved her, though this had not taught him to put others' concerns before his own gratification. Slowly he returned the paper to his pocket. "I suppose we can talk tomorrow. One more day will make little difference. You should go to bed."

Anabel merely nodded, grateful to be spared more reproaches.

"I will call in the morning again, and we can settle everything."

Yes, thought Anabel, that will be best. I will prepare myself and tell him then. She nodded again.

Norbury summoned a smile and came toward her. When his arms slipped around her, Anabel did not protest. She could not find the energy. He pulled her close and kissed her gently. Anabel tested her sensations; she felt nothing, not even that boneless surrender he had once evoked in her.

He sensed some change and tightened his hold, kissing her again, more passionately. Anabel remained passive for a moment, then drew back. She did not exactly push him away, but the effect was the same.

"What is the matter?" he demanded, touched on one of his vainest points.

"Nothing. I am tired."

"Indeed?" Her reaction made him angry again. Did she not realize that he had treated her with more consideration than he had any other woman in his history? He had suppressed his passions ruthlessly, and now she begrudged him even a kiss. He felt like shaking her or pushing her to the sofa and showing her precisely what she was rejecting. He was confident of his ability to change her stiffness to eager response.

The image pleased him, and he smiled a little, thinking of the future. If she remained so cool, it would be an even greater pleasure to subdue her. He imagined Anabel pleading for his caresses, and his smile widened.

She did not like his expression. Moving out of his arms, she walked toward the door. "I'm...I'm sorry. I am very tired," she repeated.

"Of course. I will take my leave." Following, he took her hand and held it lingeringly to his lips, his pale green eyes holding hers. Then he turned and left the room.

Anabel took a long breath, relieved. What had that strange look in his eyes meant? She had never seen it there before. Sighing, she rubbed her face. She *was* exhausted. Perhaps she should try to sleep after all. She moved toward the staircase and then paused, surprised to hear male voices from downstairs.

"Ah. The conquering hero," said Norbury in a scathing tone.

"Sir Charles." Anabel started. It was Christopher's voice.

"Come to enjoy Anabel's gratitude?" Norbury laughed a little. "It is something, I suppose, though I myself prefer more palpable pleasures." His voice implied a great deal. Anabel flushed.

"I have no doubt of it," answered Hanford, angry but controlled.

"I fear you will find the lady rather tired. In fact, I do not believe she is receiving callers."

"Then I am sure she will tell me so," answered Christopher. "As she has anytime these ten years."

"Ah, yes. You are an *old* friend. Your *comfortable* relationship is admirable. Anabel hardly thinks of you as a man, I believe." This was a clear insult, and Anabel could imagine Norbury's sardonic expression. She stepped forward to intervene.

"You know very little of what Anabel thinks," responded Christopher positively. He spoke without rancor, as if simply stating a truth, but the implications were as cutting as Norbury's. "And now, if you will pardon me. I do not wish to detain you."

There was a slight sound from the staircase, as if one man had jostled the other, a scuffle, then silence. Anabel hurried onto the landing, her heart pounding.

They were facing each other halfway down the staircase, Christopher one step above. Their chests rose and fell rapidly, and both were glaring.

"Christopher!" said Anabel.

The tension broke. Norbury, though he looked furious, bowed very slightly and continued on his way. Hanford ran lightly up to her, a smile replacing his scowl. He had waited for this moment all night, anxious to see how she would receive him. "How are you? Is all well?"

She led him into the drawing room, hearing the door close behind Norbury as they sat down. "Yes. The children are still asleep after their adventure."

"As you should be." He was scanning her face. "You *are* tired."

"Only a little." It was true that now Christopher was here, she felt much less exhausted.

Their eyes met and held. They did not notice the lengthening silence. Each saw everything he needed to know, and Christopher's hand moved irresistibly to take hers. "Anabel," he murmured at last.

She looked down. How could she have dreamed of

preferring Sir Charles to Christopher? she wondered. It seemed so obvious to her now that she had been in love with Christopher for years. And Norbury's polished elegance faded into insignificance beside his warm appeal. She looked sidelong at his ruddy hair and startlingly blue eyes, at the set of his shoulders in his blue coat and the curve of his leg in his yellow pantaloons. Everything about him spoke to her as Norbury could not, never had. Why had she not seen it? How could she have been so foolish?

"I cannot help but speak," said Christopher. "I vowed I would not, unless I had some sign from you. I love you, Anabel, with all my heart and soul."

She took a trembling breath.

"I know you are promised to Norbury." He waited, hoping she would interrupt. "I had thought…you have only to say one word, and I will be silent forever on this subject." He bent to see her face. "Do you say it, Anabel?"

"No." She struggled to speak more clearly. "I have made a dreadful mistake, Christopher. I…I don't know how I could have been so blind. I love you—I have for the *longest* time."

His heart pounding with elation, Hanford swept her into his arms. Again Anabel felt that leap of response and marveled at the difference. It was some time before they spoke again.

At last they drew apart and smiled tenderly at each other. Christopher settled Anabel's head against his shoulder. "What are you going to do?"

"Break off the engagement. I would have today, but I was so tired. Tomorrow I will speak to him."

He nodded. "I had almost despaired of being so happy."

"I am sorry, Christopher. I—"

He put a hand gently over her mouth, shaking his head. "We won't talk of that. It is over now."

She nodded, and he took his hand away. "I want to go home very soon. Are you ready to leave London?"

"Utterly. We can be married in our own parish church. Vicar Prentice will be delirious with joy."

Anabel turned to him, smiling. "Is that an offer, Mr. Hanford?"

He looked surprised. "Hadn't I offered already?"

"You had not."

"Good God!" Disentangling himself, he sank to one knee before her. "Anabel, would you do me the great honor of becoming my wife?"

She put a hand to her breast and opened her eyes very wide. "Mr. Hanford! I don't know what to say to you."

"The deuce you don't!" He rose and pulled her close again, speaking with his lips brushing hers. "Say yes."

"Yes," she murmured, and he kissed her slowly. Anabel drew her hands along his upper arms to his shoulders, filled with a great happiness. This was the way she should feel, she now knew, every fiber rejoicing in her love's touch. After long searching, she had finally discovered that truth.

Fifteen

WHEN CHRISTOPHER HAD GONE, PROMISING TO RETURN for dinner that evening, Anabel went upstairs to her bedchamber. She no longer felt like sleeping, and she bathed and put on a primrose sprig muslin gown with fluttering green ribbons. She wanted to sing as her maid brushed out her soft brown hair and dressed it in ringlets around her face. When she was dressed, she walked up to the school-room floor, listening for sounds of the children. They were up; she heard them in the nursery and turned that way, opening the door to find them at breakfast. William and Nicholas were eating with great concentration; Susan was slipping a forbidden treat to Daisy, who crouched on the floor beside her feet. They all, except Daisy, who was merely avid, looked happy. Anabel smiled, then sobered and walked into the room to stand over them, crossing her arms on her breast. Nurse, seeing her pose, retreated into the next room. William grimaced and put down his spoon. Nicholas, becoming aware of her presence late, froze, his spoon poised over his bowl. Susan looked up blithely. "Hello, Mama. Would you like some porridge?"

It taxed all Anabel's faculties not to laugh. She was feeling so happy that she could scarcely bear to scold the children. But they had been very naughty. "No, thank you, Susan," she replied, keeping her voice and expression stern. "I wish to talk to all of you."

The boys cringed.

"You know you have behaved very badly, and you will have to be punished."

"I only went to see Uncle Christopher," protested Susan. "We often do so at *home*." She sounded accusatory.

"Not alone. And not without telling me where you are going," answered Anabel. "And London is not home. You cannot wander about here as you can in our park."

"I *know*," replied the little girl with great feeling.

Anabel's lips twitched, and Nicholas saw it. "We are very sorry, Mama," he said at once. "We will never do it again. We just thought we could find Susan before anyone noticed and bring her back." He made a face at his sister. "We might have known we couldn't think as *she* does."

"No one *asked* you to look for me," retorted Susan. "I was perfectly fine."

"It does not matter what you thought," interrupted Anabel. "You all were at fault, and you all knew you were being naughty. For the next week you will have lessons in the afternoon as well as in the morning, and at the end of that time I will hear you recite what you have learned."

The children groaned. Even Nicholas, who loved books, was not overfond of lessons.

"You will go out only when accompanied by Miss Tate, for a walk in the park."

"But Uncle Christopher promised to take us riding again," protested William.

Anabel thrilled at the name, but she said, "I think you have caused enough trouble for Christopher. What if he had not come after you?"

"We would be home by now," muttered William, then subsided under his mother's frown.

"I want you to understand how serious the results of your misbehavior might have been," she concluded. "You were very fortunate; you could have been hurt or lost. London is very large, and not all parts are safe. Do you see what I mean?"

Slowly William nodded. Nicholas was quick to do so. Susan pouted for a moment. "*I* knew exactly where

Uncle Christopher's house was. I asked him before."
Under her mother's eye, she scowled, then shrugged.
"I'm sorry."

Anabel smiled. "Good. That is settled, then. And I
may give you some good news." All three looked up.
"We are going home soon, perhaps in two weeks."

Their faces brightened. "Truly, Mama?" said William.

"Truly. I think we have been in town long enough."

"Hurrah!" replied William, leaping up.

"Did you hear that, Daisy?" said Susan, bending
down. "We are going home. You will like it there."

But Nicholas was thoughtful. "Is that man coming
with us? Norbury?"

"No." Anabel hesitated. She shouldn't say anything
until all was settled, but she couldn't resist. "We won't
be seeing him anymore."

"Aren't you going to marry him?" asked Nick.

"No."

"But you said you were."

"I…changed my mind." Anabel felt slightly awkward.

"Hurrah!" shouted William again, jerking the back of
his brother's chair until he nearly dumped him on the
floor. "Everything will be as it was again."

Anabel debated whether to tell them about Christopher,
but decided she should wait until she had spoken to
Norbury. They would tell the children together, with no
fear this time of complaints.

Nick and Susan had risen now, and the three of them
were dancing around the room in a ring. Daisy, excited by
this movement, streaked in and out between their feet, his
claws scrabbling on the wooden floor. In one pass he managed to trip up both William and Nicholas, and the group
collapsed in a confused heap, panting. Anabel laughed down
at them, and they all grinned. "You had best finish your
breakfast," she said. "I expect Miss Tate is waiting for you in
the schoolroom."

There was another general groan, but they untangled themselves and returned to the table. "I will see you at dinner," finished Anabel, turning to go. "Uncle Christopher is coming, so you will dine downstairs with us." She shut the door to a general cheer.

"You see?" said Nick complacently when they were alone again. "I told you it would work." He took a large bite of porridge.

"What?" William, too, concentrated on his breakfast again.

"My plan, of course." The others stared at him. "Well, we are going home, are we not? And Mama is not to marry that Norbury."

"Yes, but your plan had nothing to do with it," answered his brother.

"What do you mean?"

"It's all because I ran away," said Susan, her small face smug. "You were too cowardly, but I knew Mama would listen then."

William snorted in disgust. "You are both ninnyhammers. It had nothing to do with either of you." He ignored the clamor of protest this brought down upon him and ate his breakfast.

"If you know so much," said Nick finally, "what did make Mama change her mind?"

William pondered, his spoon vertical in his fist. "I don't know *that*."

The others made derisive noises.

"But I do know that Mama was different today."

"Different?" echoed Susan.

"Yes. Something has happened. You could tell. I don't know what, but that is the reason we are going home, and I don't believe it had anything to do with us."

"Stuff!" replied Susan, bending to offer Daisy a bit of bread. But Nick looked thoughtful.

The day passed quietly for the Goring household,

seeming shorter because of the late start. Anabel stayed at home, sitting in the drawing room and pretending to write letters. She actually spent most of the afternoon simply rehearsing the events of the past few weeks and marveling over the outcome. Occasionally she worried about what she would say to Norbury, but since she did not have to face him until the morning, she usually put such thoughts aside. Christopher was much more often in her mind, and at these times a dreamy smile played about her mouth and she forgot everything but memories of what had passed between them.

Lady Goring and Georgina went out shopping late in the afternoon, returning only in time to change for their early dinner. Though Anabel had said nothing to her, Lady Goring was certain that there had been important developments. And the fact that Christopher Hanford was coming to dinner encouraged her greatly. She did not broach the subject, however, fearing to say something wrong and mar the delicate equilibrium she sensed. Mr. Hanford could be trusted to arrange things, she felt. She had been further impressed by his strength of character in the last few days.

Georgina was the first down that evening. She had changed quickly to escape the chatter of her maid, which was all of Mr. Hanford's heroism. Her emotions had been unsettled all day, since she had seen the serene happiness on Anabel's face, so unlike her previous hectic gaiety. Something had happened, she was certain, and it had made her own blunder last night insignificant. But she did not know what, and the mystery made her restless.

She knew that Christopher would never care for her. She had accepted it. But his fate was still very important to her; she thought of him a great deal of the time.

A movement caught her eye, and she started. She had been pacing the drawing-room carpet as she thought, and it was her own reflection in the glass that had attracted her attention. Moving closer, she surveyed it. This was not the Georgina Goring who had come to London. Her father would hardly recognize her. She had shed all of her plumpness by this time; the gray eyes that looked into the mirror seemed large, with unaccustomed depths. In her modish pink gown, with her blond hair dressed à la Diane by Lady Goring's maid, she seemed wholly changed. And it was only right, she thought, for she felt a completely different person, too. So much had happened to her since she came reluctantly up to town.

"Good evening, Miss Goring," said a male voice from the door.

She whirled to find Hanford there, smiling at her. "G-good evening," she stammered past a lump in her throat.

"You're looking very smart." He came forward, gestured toward the sofa, and they sat down.

"Th-thank you."

"I hope you have recovered from the alarms of last night?"

She nodded, then blurted out, "I am so sorry I didn't tell Anabel. I *tried*, but no one would listen to me. And then I fell asleep." She hung her head. This wasn't the strict truth, but she was not going to mention Anabel's criticisms of him.

"It doesn't matter. Things turned out well in the end." And I am grateful you did not speak, he added to himself. If Anabel had known the truth all along, she would not have been quite so happy to see me, and we might never have reached an understanding.

Watching his face, Georgina said, "Did they?" in a tentative voice.

Hanford met her eyes. He had done his best to be kind to this girl while showing her that his affections were firmly engaged elsewhere. He knew that her youthful infatuation with him was nothing more than that; it would fade soon. But he also remembered the painful throes of calf love. He felt no guilt, but there was pity in his gaze as he answered, "Very well. Anabel and I are going to be married, Miss Goring."

"Oh!" Georgina blinked. She had not expected anything so revolutionary. "What about Sir Charles? I mean…"

"That is at an end."

"Oh, good," responded the girl before she could think. She flushed bright red. "Er…that is…"

Hanford laughed. "*I* certainly think so."

"I never liked him somehow," confided Georgina.

"Neither did I," he replied feelingly.

They laughed together. "I wish you very happy. I know that you.… I noticed…" She faltered. Christopher's confidences had made her feel very grown up; yet she didn't know what to say to him. Her own confused feelings seemed to tie up her tongue. She was glad for them. Mr. Hanford had received his heart's desire, and Anabel would be much happier with him than with Norbury. But she also felt a lingering, wistful love for him herself. If it had been she he offered for… She thrust this thought aside. There had been no question of that.

"You are a remarkable girl, Miss Goring," added Christopher.

Looking up, she saw in his eyes knowledge of her feelings, and flushed again.

"You have true greatness of spirit, and someday you will be as happy as I am just now." He smiled, hoping to reduce her confusion.

Georgina couldn't think what to say.

"Your first season has been remarkably eventful so far," he continued in a lighter tone. "I wonder if you expected London to be so busy."

"I didn't." Taking his cue, Georgina spoke jokingly. "Indeed, I never imagined half the things I have done."

"I hope you have been enjoying yourself."

"Oh yes."

They both turned as a footman came in. He held a silver salver on which reposed a folded sheet of paper. "A note for you, Miss Georgina," he said. "The man is waiting for an answer."

"For me?" She tore it open. "Oh, Lydia Mainwaring is holding a waltzing party tomorrow and particularly wishes me to come. I must write her at once." She started out of the room, then remembered Hanford. "If you will excuse me a moment?" Her gray eyes were glowing.

"Of course. I shall be quite all right."

With a smile, Georgina went out. Hanford sat gazing at the opposite wall, a thoughtful smile on his face as well. Georgina would soon forget him, it was clear.

"Mr. Hanford." Lady Goring came in, and he rose to greet her. "How glad I am to find you here alone. I wanted to speak to you."

He raised inquiring eyebrows.

"*What* has happened? I dare not ask Anabel, for fear of spoiling things, but I am agog with curiosity!"

He laughed. "What makes you think something has happened?"

She looked at him, and he laughed again. "If Anabel has not told you—"

"I believe I shall scream with vexation," interrupted Lady Goring.

He relented. "We are going to be married."

She clasped her hands before her. "Truly? And Norbury?"

"Anabel is to tell him tomorrow. I imagine that is why she didn't mention it. She wished to speak to him first."

"Oh, I have never been so glad about anything. Does your sister know?"

Hanford looked surprised. "No. I was waiting until all was settled."

"May *I* tell her?"

He stared at her.

"We have conspired together to match you and Anabel," she explained, "and though our efforts came to nothing, I know her interest in the matter."

He smiled. "I suppose you may. But…"

"Oh, I will be discreet. I will call on her tomorrow morning. My dear Mr. Hanford, or Christopher, as I shall call you now, how pleased I am!" She held out her hands and gave his a firm squeeze. "You will both be very happy."

"I believe we will," he answered, returning her glowing look.

Georgina came back, followed closely by Anabel and the children. The latter threw themselves upon Christopher at once, effectively ending conversation, and it was not until they were going into the dining room that he was able to speak privately to Anabel. "How are you?"

"Splendid." They smiled into each other's eyes.

"You haven't told the children?"

"Not yet. I thought we would do that together."

He nodded, pleased. "Tonight?"

"I think tomorrow afternoon would be better. By then everything will be…" She gestured.

"Yes. I will call then. I hope they will be pleased."

"Can you doubt it?" They watched the children climbing into their seats at the table. "They will be delighted. Almost as happy as when I told them we are going home soon."

"It will be good to be back."

"Very!" They smiled at each other again. Anabel started to move away toward her chair.

"Oh, Anabel?"

"Yes."

"I'm afraid I wasn't able to resist telling your mother the news when she asked."

"Mama? Why didn't she ask me? I wonder."

His eyes danced. "I believe she was afraid to."

"Afraid?" Anabel giggled.

"I told Miss Goring also. She, ah…"

"I know. You have been very kind to her. There were moments when I found it quite annoying."

"If I had only known!"

Anabel laughed again. She felt like laughing all the time now.

"I'm hungry!" declared Susan from the other side of the room. Anabel and Christopher exchanged a last amused glance and went to their places.

It was a lively, hilarious meal. The children were in high spirits, anticipating what they would do when they were home again and wondering about all their friends there, human and animal. They pelted Christopher with questions he could not answer, as he, too, had been away for some time, and formed all sorts of plans for the future. They addressed an equal number of remarks to Anabel, their strategy of silence abandoned. Even Georgina and Lady Goring were urged to come down and be introduced to Susan's remarkable pony and William's amazingly intelligent spaniel. "Daisy is very happy too," said Susan. "She can't wait to see the country. I have told her all about it."

"That is one of the blessings of this affair," replied Lady Goring with mock asperity. "That *malevolent* animal will be out of my house. Perhaps I may keep my cook after all."

While Susan puzzled over the meaning of "malevolent" and prepared to defend her pet, Nick said, "We should leave him here. He will kill all the birds within two miles."

"Nick!" Susan glared at him. "Daisy will do no such thing. She loves birds!"

"To eat," her brother mumbled into his plate, but he did not take up the argument.

"Rex will keep the cat away from the coveys," said William.

"Mama! You will not let William's dog hurt Daisy, will you?" appealed Susan.

"It would probably be the other way about," murmured Nick.

"No one will hurt your cat, Susan," replied Anabel. "But you must try to train, er, her better. Daisy is a little wild."

"*I* think she's perfect," declared the youngest Wyndham.

Her brothers glared at her as if to say this was only natural, considering her own temperament. All the adults laughed.

"Do you see what you are taking on?" dared Lady Goring.

Christopher met her eyes, his own twinkling. "With great joy." He and Anabel exchanged a fond look. Georgina's smile trembled a little.

"What do you mean?" asked Nicholas, his eyes moving intelligently from one to the other.

"Nothing, dear." Anabel suppressed her smile. It was not the time to make their announcement. "Here is a Chantilly cream, your favorite."

Nick was diverted but not fooled. During the rest of the meal he often glanced from his mother to Christopher and back again.

When they finished, the party gathered in the drawing room for a very successful, and noisy, game of lottery tickets. Georgina soon forgot her sadness in the excitement of it, and she looked much younger than her eighteen years as she dickered with the children for counters. Even Lady Goring, who had joined in only after much persuasion, enjoyed herself hugely. And Susan, who came out the winner, could hardly be torn from the table to go to bed. Indeed, she resisted mightily, and would have gone on playing all night if allowed.

At last, however, the children followed Nurse upstairs,

leaving the older members of the party in the drawing room. Lady Goring sighed and stretched her arms.
"What a pleasant evening. Who would have thought we
should enjoy a silly game so much?"

Georgina agreed. "I have not played lottery tickets for
five years."

"I feel quite exhausted by it. I believe I shall go
straight up to bed. Are you coming, Georgina?" The girl
rose and joined her aunt. "Good night, Christopher,"
added Lady Goring. "We will see you again tomorrow?"

"Yes."

"Splendid." Amid a chorus of farewells, they went out.

"Are you very tired?" Hanford asked Anabel, going to
sit close to her on the sofa.

"A little."

"You should sleep." He touched her cheek gently
with his fingertips.

"Soon." She looked into his blue eyes. "I am very
happy, Christopher."

"As am I."

"I feel so fortunate, being prevented from making
such a mistake."

"Not half so fortunate as I!"

They laughed.

"We should make plans. When will you go home?"

"Soon. But there is no need to decide anything tonight.
Tomorrow will be better, when you are rested."

Anabel nodded and rested her head comfortably on his
shoulder. "But I am eager to leave now."

He kissed the top of her head. They remained so for
a while, Hanford feeling a great contentment spread
through him. He could not remember being so happy.
"I think Nick suspects us," he said finally. Anabel did not
reply and, looking down, he saw that she was fast asleep.
He smiled, then eased his arm from behind her and went
to ring for the maid to take her upstairs.

Sixteen

ANABEL WOKE THE FOLLOWING MORNING WITH A sense of oppression, and she lay in bed for a while wondering why. Everything was wonderful. She and Christopher and the children were going to be tremendously happy. She glowed at the mere thought of it. Then she remembered Sir Charles. Today she must face him and break off their engagement; that was what weighed on her. He would be very angry, she knew, and she had always shrunk from acrimonious scenes, preferring to agree rather than to argue. She had seen how he resented any interference with his wishes, and although she didn't have any great faith in his love for her, she knew that he was determined on the marriage. Perhaps, she thought, he did love her in a way. But his sort of love was wholly selfish, a matter of his own desires and visions alone. Somehow she conformed to his image of a wife, and he was set on placing her in that position. He would not give up his plan without a battle. How different from Christopher!

For a while she drifted in a pleasant reverie, recounting Christopher's sterling qualities. She was brought abruptly back to earth by the entrance of her maid with tea, the drawing of the curtains, and the other familiar rituals of rising. What would she say to Norbury? she wondered as her hair was brushed. How would it be best to begin?

This question threw her into the dismals again. Anabel was still far from accustomed to upholding her own decisions. The knowledge that she loved Christopher and had made a mistake with Norbury had been almost instinctive. It was quite another matter to plan rationally how best to convey that news and bear down opposition. She did not question her choice—far from it—but she was uneasy about her ability to explain it. Her first marriage had been so much simpler. Her father had presented a fait accompli, and she had merely acquiesced. There had been no necessity for explanations. And Norbury had been much the same. He had impressed his will on her and expected her to yield, as she had. This time all was different. *She* had decided, and it was up to her to take the actions that would bring her own happiness.

Briefly Anabel wished for Christopher. If only he could be with her today, to confront Sir Charles at her side. But that was impossible, she knew. It would make everything ten times worse. In any case, this was her tangle. She had been foolish, and she must right her mistake. Anabel sensed that it was very important for her to see this matter through alone. This season in London had been good for her, she realized. It had shown her a great many things about herself, and she must use this new knowledge rather than retreat into outworn habits. She and Christopher would help each other. She would not rely on him for every decision.

This train of thought was fascinating, if not very comforting, and Anabel remained distracted throughout breakfast, not even hearing the remarks Lady Goring and Georgina addressed to her. After a while they exchanged a glance and abandoned the attempt at conversation, talking quietly to each other. Anabel ate little and soon went up to the drawing room to wait and think. She still had not determined how she would speak to Norbury. Should she simply plunge in as soon as he arrived, or should she wait for an opening? He would bring up their wedding date again; perhaps she could begin there.

Pacing back and forth across the drawing-room carpet,

Anabel twisted her hands nervously. It was all very well to vow to change. In actuality it was very difficult.

The sound of the bell made her jump. She heard a footman going to the door and voices below. It was Sir Charles. Her heart speeded up, and she took a deep breath, going to the sofa and sitting down, trying to appear calm and collected.

"Good morning," said Norbury from the drawing-room doorway. "Are you more rested today? It is so pleasant, I thought we might go for a drive." He came toward her, smiling, and took her hand. "It will do you good to get out."

"Oh…I…" Anabel felt confused. All her faculties had been concentrated on the coming confrontation. She didn't want to go out; she wanted to get it over as soon as possible. But she couldn't seem to think of objections.

"Come," said Norbury. "It is really a lovely morning. You will enjoy being out." He continued to smile pleasantly. He knew that he had not come off well in the events of the last few days. He had allowed his temper to get the best of him again, and Anabel had been annoyed. He was anxious to erase this damaging memory and remind her of his manifold attractions. It would be a simple matter, he felt, to drive the uninteresting Mr. Hanford out of her mind.

"I would prefer to stay here," managed Anabel.

"Nonsense. This is only because you have not been out and seen the day. I insist. Go and fetch your hat."

"But—"

Slightly annoyed but feigning laughter, he took her shoulders and marched her toward the door. "I won't hear it. You will thank me in the end, wait and see."

Defeated, Anabel went upstairs and got out a bonnet and shawl. She could not summon the energy to fight Norbury on this; she was saving it for the larger issue.

It was indeed a lovely day, the air soft and fragrant and

the sky a brilliant blue. Norbury had his phaeton, and as he helped Anabel into it he told the groom holding the horses that he might wait here for their return. This, at least, was a relief, Anabel thought. It would have been impossible to talk with a servant hanging on behind.

They started off briskly through the busy streets. "A turn around the park?" asked Sir Charles, and she nodded, her thoughts still on what lay ahead. They said little during the short journey to the gates. Norbury was occupied with driving, and Anabel was abstracted. But when they turned into the quieter avenues of the park, he said, "I hope the children are completely recovered from their adventures?"

"What? Oh, yes, they are well."

"I realized that I never actually heard where they had got to." He was determined to counteract her previous impressions.

"Uh, the boys went after Susan." Anabel couldn't concentrate on this when she was continually wondering how to bring up their engagement.

"Went after?"

Seeing that he was not going to leave the subject, she quickly explained what had happened. Her references to Christopher were inevitably warm.

Norbury carefully ignored them. "I see. Well, I am very glad it is all straightened out again. I know you were terribly worried."

She nodded.

"It is time I saw the children again," he added. "Perhaps we might take them out tomorrow?" He put all the eagerness he could muster in his voice. Though this was the last thing he wanted to do, he felt it was necessary to restore his position.

"No."

He glanced at her, surprised.

"They are being punished for going out without

leave," she continued cravenly, intimidated by his look. "They are not to have outings."

"Ah." He was relieved. "I suppose that is wise."

Anabel was berating herself for avoiding the true reason behind her refusal. She had to get it over with. "I must speak to you about something," she blurted out.

"Yes?"

"It...it is very difficult. I don't know precisely how to begin, so I shall simply say it. I wish to end our engagement, Charles."

"What?" He spoke blankly, as if he had not understood her words.

"I am very sorry, but I do not think we shall suit after all. It is my fault. I made a mistake. And I sincerely apologize for any pain I may have—"

"Are you joking?" He still seemed chiefly astonished.

"N-no. I—"

"I suppose Hanford is behind this. He put you up to it, and because you are grateful for his rescue of your children, you agreed. You do not really mean it."

"That is not true!" Anabel was flustered. This was not how she had expected things to go. She had not thought Christopher would come into it, and she could not precisely deny that he was behind it, though not as Sir Charles claimed.

"Have you thought that he may have arranged the whole crisis merely to win your sympathy?" asked Norbury.

"What?"

"You say your daughter went to him. How do you know that? Perhaps he took her from the house, knowing that your sons would follow. Or perhaps he simply took the three of them, taught them what to say, and brought them back at the proper moment to earn your gratitude." He warmed to this idea. "Yes. He would wait just long enough so that you would fall into his arms when he returned them."

"That's ridiculous!"

"You didn't fall into his arms?" inquired Sir Charles sarcastically and, seeing Anabel's expression, added, "Naturally you did. I'm sure he counted on that."

"He did no such thing!"

"Indeed? You are not breaking off our engagement to marry Hanford, then?"

She hesitated. Would it be better to tell him or not?

But he saw the answer in her face, and was at once filled with a murderous rage. "I see. His little plot has succeeded. Or so he believes."

"There was no plot. Christopher would never do what you suggest. He is not that sort of person."

"Is he not?" Norbury sneered.

"No! I have known him for years."

"Yet only now have you decided to marry him. Odd."

For a brief moment Anabel was shaken by doubt. Was it possible that he was right? Christopher had said that he was desperate over her engagement. Could he have planned to end it this way? But the thought was no sooner considered than rejected. He would do no such thing; she knew it. "It is of no consequence what you think. You are wrong. And this has nothing to do with my decision. I am breaking it off."

"This is not the time to discuss it. Wait a few days, until your anxiety over your children has faded. You will see then that you are being hasty." It was his last attempt at appeal.

"No, I will not. I am quite certain."

Sir Charles's rage flooded him. How dared she speak to him so? he thought. He had done her the unique honor of offering his hand, and now she was throwing it aside as if it meant nothing—and for a nonentity like Hanford! *His* plans and wishes were to be swept aside so that these two could have their way. He was to be balked of the woman he had chosen and the life he had envisioned. It was intolerable!

Did she not realize that he might have had any woman in London? Yet he had chosen her, despite her widowhood and her pack of whining brats. He *would* have what he wanted. "I refuse," he said.

"What?" Anabel didn't know what he meant.

"I refuse to allow you to dissolve the engagement. I won't agree to it."

"What do you mean? You must."

"Why?"

"Well…that is…"

"If *I* were the one who wished to break my promise, society would protest," he countered. "It would not be 'the act of a gentleman' to draw back. Yet you may do as you please in the matter. Well, I will not go along. We *shall* be married."

"You would marry me even though I do not wish it?" Anabel was astounded and confused. She had never imagined such a response to her announcement.

"You will come round eventually." His tone was smug, and he spoke as if the matter were settled.

"You're mad. I certainly will not. And you cannot force me to marry you. I shall send a notice to the *Morning Post* today saying that our engagement is at an end. And now I want to go home. Turn around!"

She expected another angry outburst, but Norbury merely frowned thoughtfully. Thinking he was reconsidering his ridiculous ultimatum, she added, "We should be very unhappy, Charles. You would regret it as much as I. When you have thought over the matter, you will see that."

He said nothing. He was gazing out over the horses' heads as if weighing some idea.

"We are not at all suited," continued Anabel hopefully. "I find I do not care to live in town, and you are not overfond of children, I think. Your mother was not pleased with the match."

"Nonsense!" he snapped.

Anabel abandoned this line. "You deserve someone who can take a place in society to match your own. I could not." He was ignoring her again. Anabel gazed at his set profile and wished fervently that she had not come out with him. At home she could ask him to leave; here she was trapped. "Truly, Charles, you will be glad in a very few days."

With a sudden jerk on the reins, he turned the phaeton left, then left again into another avenue, heading back the way they had come. Anabel breathed a sigh of relief and relaxed a little in her seat.

They drove in silence for a while. Anabel was happy to have things over and wary of upsetting the balance established, and Norbury was too angry to speak. He had never in his life been put aside by a woman he deigned to distinguish, and to have this occur when he had actually proposed marriage was more than he could bear.

Outside the park, he turned into a busy street and wove in and out among wagons, carts, and pedestrians. Anabel sat slumped beside him, ignoring the spectacle, waiting to be home again. She was thinking how fortunate it was that she and Christopher did not want to live in London. She could not have faced Norbury day after day and maintained a pretense of polite indifference. When would they reach her mother's? she wondered. Looking around, she was startled. "Where are you going?"

Norbury did not reply.

"This is not the way back. We should have turned long since. What are you doing?"

He ignored her, guiding the phaeton past a wide lumber cart.

"Charles!" Anabel gazed about, trying to identify the street.

"This is another way home," said Norbury.

"I don't believe you! Turn around at once."

In answer, he urged the horses forward at a faster pace.

"If you don't turn around, I shall jump off."

He laughed a little. "No, you won't. You would be seriously injured on the cobbles, if not killed."

Anabel looked at the pavement rushing by beneath them and tried to steel herself to leap. She couldn't. He was trying to frighten her as a punishment, she decided. If she refused to be intimidated, he would give it up and take her home. She sat back with folded arms and stared stonily ahead.

But Norbury merely drove on, satisfied with her silence. They left the neighborhood of the park and the fashionable part of London, and continued into an area of small houses, neat but by no means elegant. Anabel had never been here before. Her resolve wavered. "Charles, where are we going?"

He didn't answer.

"Why are you doing this? I shan't change my mind. Can you not be a little charitable and…"

With a quick jerk on the reins, he pulled up. The horses plunged and reared. And before Anabel could gather her wits to jump down, his hand had closed firmly on her upper arm, keeping her in her seat. "Here, you," he said to a grubby boy standing on the pavement below. "Go to their heads." He was holding the startled team with one hand. The boy ran and took the bridles.

"Let go of me!" demanded Anabel.

In response, he pushed her before him out of the phaeton, almost knocking her to the ground from its high perch. She struggled, but his grip on her arm was cruelly tight; she could not break it.

"Hold them for me," he told the boy, then pushed her toward the narrow brick house in front of them.

Anabel struggled harder. He transferred his grip from her arm to her waist, pinning her against him and propelling her up two steps to the front door. She hit at him as he took a ring of keys from his pocket and applied one to the lock, but he paid no heed. "Help!" she cried, twisting her head to try to see the boy. There was no one else visible in the street. "Help me! Get someone."

The child merely gaped at her. Sir Charles flung open the door and pushed her into a narrow hall, slamming the panel behind him.

"Have you gone mad?" asked Anabel. "What do you think you are doing?"

In one quick movement he gathered her wrists in one hand behind her back. Then he forced her forward again, up two sets of twisting stairs. Anabel exerted all her strength to break away. She strained against his grip, threw herself from one side to the other in hope of overbalancing him, and kicked at him with her feet, all to no avail. He was amazingly strong. Nothing she could do seemed to have any effect on him.

He paused on the second landing to open a door there. Then he forced her into a small bedchamber and released her. Anabel backed away from him, chafing her bruised wrists. He remained between her and the door.

"This is a house I sometimes use," he said. "You will stay here."

"What are you doing?" she cried. "You are mad!"

"On the contrary, I am carrying out an extremely rational plan to make you keep your promise. You will remain here until tomorrow, at which time I will escort you home. Having been away all night in my company, as it will appear, you will have to marry me." He looked complacent.

Anabel's blue eyes widened. "What? You…you…"

"No harm will come to you. This house is perfectly safe; it is a very respectable neighborhood." He smiled a little.

"I will never marry you!"

"Oh, I think you will. Your friend Hanford may not

be quite so attentive when he knows you have spent the night with me. And the scandal would be shocking. Your children would suffer if you refused me."

Anabel flushed with rage. How dare he mention her children? "I will take them back to the country. We shall do very well there."

Norbury shrugged. "We will discuss it further in the morning. I think you will change your mind. And now there are some arrangements I must make, if you will excuse me."

"How can you wish to marry in this way?" cried Anabel. "Do you want a wife who hates you? Because that is what I should be, if we ever married."

He met her eyes. "Oh, I think you would put that aside quite soon. You are overwrought now, and you have been worried in the last few days. When you are calmer, you will see things differently. You *did* accept me, after all. You did not hate me then, and you do not now. You have simply allowed your concern for your children to cloud your mind, and Hanford took advantage of that."

"Nonsense! I had grave doubts even before the children ran away, and I am certain I would have broken it off in any case."

He frowned and took a step toward her. "You do not mean that. You are angry with me and trying to wound."

"I do mean it!"

But he shook his head. "When you have had time to think, you will change your mind. I have no wish to hurt you, Anabel. Nothing will happen to you here. And I take such extreme measures only because I love you and cannot bear to lose you."

"Love," she repeated derisively. "You do not know the meaning of the word!"

His fists clenched, then relaxed. "You are mistaken. I do love you. I have never wished to marry a woman in my life before."

"What you call love is just another form of selfishness. If you love me, you would put my happiness before yours and let me go." She saw his eyes flicker and felt a sudden hope.

Then he said, "You will be happy with me." And before she could speak again, he turned and strode out of the room, locking the door behind him.

Seventeen

ANABEL WAS FURIOUS. SHE COULDN'T REMEMBER EVER having been so angry in her life. She had been suppressing her own reactions in the hope that reason would sway Norbury, but now they surged up. She ran to the door and listened to his footsteps retreat down the stairs. "I shall never marry you!" she cried, pounding her fist on the panels.

There was no response. She tried the lock and found it firm, then ran to the single window at the opposite end of the room and looked out. The distance to the street was intimidating, and when she pushed on the sash to open it and get a better view, she found it was immovable. She could break the glass, she thought, sitting back on her heels, but she could not see how that would do her any good. There was a floor above this, so she was not near the roof. And she doubted that she could climb to safety from the shattered window.

Standing, she went to the only article of furniture in the chamber—a bare, narrow bed—and sat down. Charles might do as he liked, she told herself; he would accomplish nothing. She might be forced to remain here until tomorrow, but she would do nothing else. She would *not* marry him. She would go home as she had planned, with Christopher and the children. He would believe her and stand by her, she was certain. And if scandal arose, they would simply ignore it. They could be happy without society if need be.

Resolutely pushing aside doubts about her children's

future under these circumstances, she rose again and paced the narrow confines of the chamber. If only there were some way she could get word home. Or if she had not consented to go out with Charles in the first place. But though she had had a low opinion of him, she had never suspected he would try something so despicable. She still could not quite believe that he would wish to marry a woman who despised him.

Remembering something, she went to the window again and gazed out. The boy who had held Norbury's horses was gone, as was his carriage. If she could attract the attention of some passerby, perhaps he would take a message for her. She bent and slipped off her shoe, grasped the toe firmly, and rapped the glass with the heel. Nothing happened. She hit it again, harder. The pane cracked. Abandoning caution, she struck once more with all her strength, shattering first one square, then two more. When she stopped, she had three small openings surrounded by jagged spears of glass, and she eyed them doubtingly. She couldn't get her head out. It would be very difficult to stop anyone by shouting from this height. Nonetheless, she must try. Putting on her shoe, she suddenly recalled that she had no way of writing a message or any money to offer the carrier. She had come out with little more than a handkerchief. Discouraged, she sat on the bed again and tried to think what to do.

Sir Charles, meantime, was removing his carriage to a livery nearby, where he could leave it out of sight. His plans were not yet fully formed—he had acted on impulse—so he was also thinking furiously. He could not go home; indeed, he could not go to any of his usual haunts in London. He must not be seen until tomorrow. But he could communicate with his servants. As he thought of this, a self-satisfied smile dawned on his dark features. Yes, that was it. At the livery, he asked for pen and paper, and was dubiously led to a small office and supplied with very inferior examples. Still smiling, he composed a note to his valet—the only personal servant he kept—informing him that he and Lady Wyndham had decided to elope, and that he was to tell no one of their plan. As he sealed this missive and offered one of the stable boys a coin to deliver it, his smile widened. Turvey was constitutionally incapable of keeping anything to himself, and this irritating trait would be very convenient today. The news would undoubtedly leak out; Anabel would be trapped.

When he had finished, it was well past midday. Norbury adjourned to a tavern in the neighborhood, where he was most unlikely to meet anyone he knew. To make certain, he took a private parlor and settled contentedly to cold meat and claret. He would pass the day here, he decided, perhaps even take a room. It would be easier to carry out his plan if he did not have to face Anabel. Her final accusations had shaken him more than he would admit. Pushing this thought aside, he called for another bottle.

Christopher Hanford called at Lady Goring's at three, to hear from Anabel how her talk with Norbury had gone, and was very surprised to be told that none of the ladies were at home. Frowning at the footman who had given him this news, he said, "Are you certain of that? My name is Hanford, and I believe Lady Wyndham is expecting me."

"I'm sorry, sir. She isn't here." The servant's normally impassive face showed a tremor of some emotion, but he merely waited, holding the door.

"Uncle Christopher!" hissed a voice from farther along the hall, and Nick's head appeared from the library. "Come here."

The footman looked uncertain. Hanford brushed past

him and strode into the room. "Nick? What are you doing down here? Where is your mother?"

The boy pulled him forward and shut the door. His face looked pinched, and his blue eyes were worried. "*She's* run away," he whispered.

"What?"

"Quiet! I'm not supposed to know, and I don't want William or Susan to hear. They may be looking for me."

"What are you talking about?" asked Hanford in a lower voice.

"I heard Grandmama telling Georgina before luncheon. Mama went out with Sir Charles Norbury, and she didn't come back. They have gone out to look for her." Nicholas was puzzled and dejected. "Do you think she ran away with him? She told us she wasn't going to marry him after all, but perhaps she changed her mind, and she didn't want to tell us because she knew we would be unhappy. We should never have objected to—"

"Nonsense!" snapped Hanford, his fists clenching and unclenching at his sides. "It is nothing like that."

"You think not?" The boy was hopeful.

Hanford became aware of the resolutely suppressed fear in his eyes. "I'm certain it is just a mistake," he replied firmly. "Your mother forgot to tell them of another engagement, I daresay. She will be home for dinner."

"That's what Grandmama said," replied Nick doubtfully, "but she didn't sound sure."

"What else did she say?"

"Well, they said Mama had gone out driving with Sir Charles at eleven, and that she should have been back hours ago." He glanced at the clock on the mantelpiece. "It's three now."

"They went *driving*?" Nick stared, and Hanford controlled himself. "Anything else?"

"No. But Grandmama seemed worried."

"Everything will be all right. But you mustn't speak to anyone else about this."

Nicholas shook his head, frowning.

"I will be back later today."

"Are you going after her?" He sounded hopeful again.

"It is not a question of that. I have some business." Hanford stalked out, and Nick watched him with unallayed worry in his face.

As soon as he was out of the house Christopher gave way to rage. It was obvious to him what had happened. Anabel had tried to break it off, and Norbury had made away with her. *Why* had she gone out with him? She might have known...but he paused, just even in his fury. She could not have predicted that the man would act this way. Even he had not imagined such villainy.

Seeing a hackney cab, he signaled it to stop. He would have to find them and bring her back. But before he did, he would teach Sir Charles Norbury the lesson of his life. The idea made him smile humorlessly.

He overcame the first obstacle—his ignorance of Norbury's address—with ease, obtaining it from an acquaintance at White's. But when he pulled up before Norbury's lodgings in Ryder Street and knocked, he was told by the retired gentleman's gentleman who looked after the chambers that Sir Charles was out. "This is a matter of great urgency," replied Hanford. "Is anyone in his rooms? I must find him."

Something in his eyes seemed to impress the man. "His valet Turvey is here. Would you wish to speak with him?"

"Yes!"

The other drew back. "This way."

Turvey, who was pressing a coat in the kitchen, was startled at the interruption, for Hanford had insisted upon accompanying the man downstairs. When asked for his master's whereabouts, he gaped and bridled. "I'm sure I don't know," he answered. But he exchanged a speaking look with the proprietor.

Christopher was in no mood for evasions. Stepping forward, he grasped the valet's neckcloth and pulled it tight, shaking him slightly. "Tell me where he is!" he said between his teeth.

Turvey choked and gabbled. "Sir!" exclaimed the other man. "Please, sir!"

Hanford merely shook Turvey again, watching the man's face purple with savage satisfaction.

Turvey goggled desperately at his friend, who held out his hands in helpless query, then croaked, "He's eloped."

"What?" Hanford let go, and the man fell in a heap.

"With Lady Wyndham, to whom he is engaged," added the valet haughtily, readjusting his collar. Now that the news was out, he seemed to savor his superior knowledge. "Very romantic, ain't it?" He smirked.

Christopher bent over him. "If you dare to repeat that tale to anyone, I shall make you regret it. Do you understand me?" He took his lapels again and shook him.

Turvey gaped again, turning pale at what he saw in Hanford's eyes.

"Where is the groom who went out with Sir Charles this morning?"

Turvey's mouth dropped open. Hanford looked murderous.

"Round in the stables," said the other man, who had been increasingly worried. He was eager to get Hanford out of his house before he caused some damage.

Christopher released the valet. "And where might that be?"

"In the mews." He pointed toward the rear of the house.

"Does that door go through to them?"

Reluctantly the proprietor nodded, and Hanford pushed past them and out. Turvey, rubbing his neck, met the other's eyes. "A rum go, and no mistake," he said.

His companion agreed. "I wonder if your master's finally met his match, Turvey. That gentleman was in a fine rage, he was."

The valet nodded, and the two of them contemplated the probable outcome with avid eyes.

In the stables, after one look at the groom, Hanford gave up violence for monetary persuasion, and he was soon informed of the circumstances of the morning drive and of the fact that the phaeton had not returned. Picturing a high-perch phaeton on the country roads, Christopher shook his head. "Your master has another place in London, does he not?" he asked. "A house somewhere he uses? You have driven him there."

"Have I, guv?"

Hanford held out a ten-pound note, and the man raised his eyebrows. "Happen I have."

"What is the address?"

The groom looked at him, then at the money. He grinned and told him.

Hanford left Ryder Street almost weak with relief. He had hazarded everything on a theory, and it had paid off. Anabel was in that house; he knew it. It had been the only possible explanation. Norbury could not drive an unwilling woman out of town in a phaeton, and he could not have taken her to a public inn. Now it remained only to get there and free her. In another hackney, Christopher cursed every cart and pedestrian that delayed his progress to her.

Eighteen

NORBURY POURED THE LAST OF THE SECOND BOTTLE OF claret in the late afternoon. He sat at his ease in the inn parlor, his legs stretched out, turning the wineglass by the stem and watching the light dance in the ruby liquid. He was not foxed, but the fumes of the wine surrounded his brain and filled it with self-congratulatory images. He remembered past triumphs and pleasures; he recalled the series of mistresses he had kept in the small house where his future wife now waited. The juxtaposition amused him. It seemed somehow apt. He had dismissed the last occupant soon after he had offered for Anabel, feeling extremely virtuous and domestic, but the lease had several months to run, and he had done nothing about getting rid of it. Now it was serving a final purpose.

He wondered what Anabel was doing and, in thinking about her, frowned. He was a bit disappointed in his promised bride; she had limitations he had not seen until today. How could any woman prefer Hanford to him? The man was a nobody, a country squire without pretensions to fashion or *ton*. He had no wit and, as far as Norbury had seen, little intelligence. He was like a thousand others. Norbury could only conclude, as he had told Anabel, that Hanford had tricked her. He had played upon her maternal feelings in a vulnerable moment. The more Norbury thought about it, the more certain he was that Hanford had staged the children's disappearance, then used it to his own advantage. It was the only possible explanation.

Still, Anabel should not have been so easily taken in. She was absurdly attached to those children. It came of shutting herself up with them in the country for so many years. Her perceptions had become distorted. But that would soon change. Norbury sipped his wine, smiling slightly. He had no doubt whatever of his ability to bring Anabel around to his own way of thinking. He had done as much so many times in the past. Women had resisted him or rebelled against his strictures, but in the end, they had capitulated to his powerful personality and physical charms. In the one or two cases where they had not, he had abandoned the field in disdain.

Anabel would soon change her tone, when he was able to exert the full force of his persuasive powers. He had been hampered with her, as he had not with his mistresses, by convention and propriety. Once they were wed, she would be very pleased that he had not let her break it off.

His smile widening, Norbury imagined the scene. There was always a thrill in overcoming a woman's initial opposition, and in this case it would have a particular spice, for his feelings for Anabel were truly quite strong. In a way he loved her, and drawing out her eager response would be vastly exciting. The picture, heightened by the claret, inflamed him, and he suddenly realized that there was no need to wait. Anabel was his now. Transfixed, he gazed at the wall of the tavern parlor. His determination to marry her remained firm—they *would* marry, and soon—thus they were practically married already. And how much easier it would be to have a willing, fervent bride than to force her through the ceremony. He would make her see her mistake first, now.

His pale green eyes gleaming, Norbury stood and tossed off the last of the wine. Leaving a few coins on the table, he retrieved his hat and strode out into the street. The afternoon was waning; dusk was near. It would be the perfect time for a seduction. His expression eager, he set off to walk the short distance to the house.

❧

Anabel watched the day ending with resignation. She had run the gamut of emotions as it passed, from anger to hope to despair. She had had no luck in attracting the attention of passersby. Those who had heard her calling through the broken window had ignored her, and most had shown no sign of even hearing. Now she was simply waiting for this outrage to end. She knew what she would do tomorrow—depart for home at once—and she had finally admitted that there was nothing to be done before that.

She was lying on the narrow bed, hoping for sleep to make the time pass more quickly, when she heard the footsteps on the stairs. She sat up at once and listened; she had not expected Norbury to return before morning. Could this be someone else? She stood and moved around the bed, putting it between her and the door.

The lock clicked, and he came in, scanning the dim room for her and smiling when he saw her position. "Anabel, my dear. Are you comfortable?" With a twist of his hand, he relocked the door, putting the key in an inner pocket.

"Why have you come back?" She didn't like his tone.

"To see that you are all right, of course. I was worried you might be frightened, all alone in an empty house."

"I should be much better at home. Perhaps you've reconsidered this ridiculous scheme?"

He shook his head, still smiling, and moved closer.

"It is not going to work, you know. I shall weather the scandal. I prefer it to marrying you." He didn't seem to hear. He stepped still nearer, and Anabel caught the scent of wine. For the first time a hint of fear shot through her. In the gathering twilight Norbury seemed very large and strong. What did he mean to do? "I thought you were coming back in the morning," she added.

"A better plan occurred to me."

He was very close now, and Anabel straightened, refusing to cower in the corner. "What better plan?"

Instead of answering, he moved swiftly, catching her shoulders and pulling her against him, his lips fastening irresistibly on hers. He propelled her backward toward the wall and imprisoned her body with his.

Anabel twisted and struggled, but she could not break free. When she brought her hands up to claw at him, he grasped her wrists and encircled them with one of his behind her back. She could not even avoid his kiss; he kept his lips on hers and pressed her head against the wall. His free hand roved about her body, teasing and seeking to inflame, expert in the ways of passion. She could feel his excitement growing, and she stopped struggling, fearing that her resistance increased rather than quenched his desire.

Norbury felt it and laughed a little. "You see? You were wrong. I am the man for you." His voice was thick with desire, and he began to force her around the headboard to the bed.

Anabel, frantic, suddenly remembered the key. It was in his pocket; she had seen him put it there. If she could get it away... Slowly, so as not to arouse his suspicions, she relaxed in his arms. Norbury laughed again and released her wrists, the other hand fondling her breast as he buried his face in her neck. Anabel carefully moved her hands along his sides and across the lapels of his coat. It was the left waistcoat pocket, she was sure.

In another moment she had the key! She threw all her strength into one effort to break his hold, and failed. It didn't even loosen. Indeed, her momentary lapse had allowed him to maneuver her to the bed, and now he forced her down upon it, covering her body with his.

"The key, eh?" he murmured. "Keep it, and see if you want to use it after a while." One of his hands pulled at her skirts and moved up her leg under them; the other remained on her breast.

Anabel saw that her tactics had been to no avail, and she struggled desperately again. It was no use; he was too strong. "I hate you!" she cried. "And I always shall, whatever happens."

He raised his head, surprised. He had thought she would be yielding by now. He kissed her throat, her lips, her forehead; she remained rigid, her face turned away. Reining in his passion, he redoubled his efforts to arouse her, using every trick he had gleaned in a long and varied amorous career. She was unmoved. Puzzled, Norbury drew a little away, while keeping a firm hold on her, and looked into her eyes. She looked back at him with fear and contempt.

They stared at each other for a moment, neither in the least understanding what was in the other's mind. Then the tension was broken by a rhythmic crashing sound downstairs. The volume increased to a crescendo; there was a splintering of wood, then the sound of running footsteps on the stairs.

Norbury sat up with a jerk. He twisted the key from Anabel's hand and rose, listening to the noise with a scowl.

"Anabel!" called a male voice. "Anabel!"

"Christopher!" she cried, sitting up also. "Here I am."

The footsteps pounded to a stop outside the door of the room. "Are you all right? Can you open the door?"

"No, it's locked and—"

"I have the key," roared Norbury, striding toward the entry. His brief puzzlement had exploded into rage at this appearance of his rival and the thwarting of his desire. Whatever qualms he had felt had been swept away. He felt murderous.

The door shook under a heavy blow, then, at a second

blow, the hinges on the ancient, poorly made door ripped from their foundation and Christopher burst through. "To the rescue once again, eh?" sneered Sir Charles.

With an inarticulate cry of rage, Hanford threw himself upon the man, and they fell together and rolled over and over on the dusty floor. Anabel stood and looked for a weapon, but there was none. She strained forward, trying to decipher the tangle of limbs in the fading light. Each man had his hands locked around the other's throat, and Norbury was gouging Christopher with his knees. She stepped forward, hoping to help him, but they rolled again at that moment, and she could get no clear opening.

The battle was all but silent. The only sound in the room was the ragged breathing of the combatants, very loud in that enclosed space. Suddenly Norbury twisted and straddled Christopher, his grip on his throat tightening. Christopher heaved ineffectually.

Anabel, seeing her chance, darted forward and struck Norbury's head with all the strength in her arm. The blow did not really hurt him, but it surprised him so that he slackened his grip on Hanford, who immediately reversed their positions, pinning Norbury to the ground. The latter gazed at Anabel, stunned by her action.

Christopher's blue eyes burned with rage. His hands tightened until Norbury made strangled choking noises and clawed at his fingers desperately. "Christopher!" cried Anabel. "Don't *kill* him!"

Her voice brought him upright, and he drew his hands back and gazed at them as if seeing them for the first time. Norbury did not take advantage of the opening. He lay where he was, rubbing his neck and scowling.

"Let us go home, Christopher," urged Anabel, putting a hand on his arm.

Dazed, he nodded and rose, stepping away from Sir Charles's prone figure.

"You hit me," said the latter, slowly sitting up and gazing at Anabel.

She turned away from him.

"You *really* prefer him to me." It was not a question, but he sounded astonished.

"Yes, I do!" she snapped, pulling again at Christopher's arm. "Please, let's go."

Hanford rubbed his face with his hands. It was difficult to move from a murderous rage to normality; he felt disoriented. And the fact that he had been perfectly ready to kill Sir Charles still stunned him. With a massive effort he recovered himself. "Yes. By all means, let us go." He turned to Norbury, who remained on the floor. "A notice of the dissolution of your engagement will appear in tomorrow's *Morning Post*. If you try to create a scandal, I—"

"I shan't." He shook his head with weary incredulity. "I can see when I am beaten."

Anabel and Christopher left him sitting there and hurried from the room.

Nineteen

AT THE BOTTOM OF THE STAIRS, SEEING THAT NORBURY did not intend to follow them, Christopher and Anabel fell into each other's arms. A great wave of relief and happiness washed over Anabel as she rested there, and she nearly cried at the joy of their reunion. How could she ever have overlooked Christopher's perfections? she wondered again. He was everything she wanted in a man.

"Are you all right?" he said.

"Yes, I am perfectly all right now."

"I came as soon as I could. It took a deucedly long time to find out about this house."

She raised her head from his shoulder. "How did you find it?"

"I knew you must be in London, so I bribed his groom to tell me where." He shrugged, and she smiled. "Come, I must get you home. They are worried." Keeping an arm around her, he started toward the door, then stopped.

"What is it?"

"We have no carriage. I took a hack." He looked so chagrined that Anabel burst out laughing. After a moment's indignation Christopher started to smile, then he laughed with her. The tensions both had experienced during this day were released in great gusts of merriment, and at last they had to hang on to each other to keep from doubling over with laughter.

"Sir Charles will think we have gone mad," gasped Anabel.

"Fortunately we do not care a whit what he thinks," responded Hanford, trying to catch his breath.

Their eyes met, and they both laughed again, more moderately, both thinking that there was no one else in the world with whom they could have shared this amusement.

"Not a proper rescue at all," added Christopher. "The knight in shining armor always has his horse. But I have been rushing about London without a plan, so frantic to find you that my brain was addled." His smile died. "Indeed, I have never felt such terror. If I had not discovered where you were..." He shook his head.

Anabel nodded, also sobering. She did not want to think of what would have happened if he had not come when he did.

"I was truly ready to murder him," continued Hanford thoughtfully. "It is a daunting prospect."

Their eyes met again, serious. Without words, they communicated their love for each other.

"Let us find another hack," said Anabel, taking his arm. "It will be an adventure. I have never ridden in one before."

Arm in arm, they left the house and walked along the darkening street until Christopher saw a hackney cab and signaled it to stop. They sat close together on the drive home, holding hands but saying little, and when they climbed down before Lady Goring's town house, Anabel paused to look at it. "I feel as if I've been away for days," she said.

He nodded. "It seems a long time since I came to call on you here; yet it is only a few hours." He rang the bell, and they were admitted by an eager footman who looked as if he would very much like to ask what had happened.

"Is my mother at home?" asked Anabel.

"Yes, my lady. She is—" He was interrupted by the sudden appearance of Susan on the landing above.

She surveyed the hall, and the newcomers, and started determinedly down.

"Have you seen William down here?" she asked.

"No," said Anabel. "What are you—"

"Or Georgina?"

"We have just come in." The prosaic welcome made Anabel smile a little.

"I know *someone* came down," replied her daughter. "I heard them. Do you think it was Grandmama?" Seeing their uncomprehending looks, she added, "We are playing hide-and-seek."

"Grandmama too?" asked Anabel, amazed.

Susan shrugged. "It was Nick's idea. He insisted that everyone play."

Christopher and Anabel exchanged a glance. He had told her of Nicholas's knowledge of her disappearance.

A sudden scrabbling sound made them all look up. Daisy was galloping down the stairs, his ginger fur disheveled. Ignoring Susan's cry of welcome, he streaked past them and shouldered his way into the library, the door of which was on the latch. Soon they heard protests from within, and Susan ran after him. "That wasn't fair," declared Nick. "He clawed me behind the curtain. *You* wouldn't have found me for a long time." A triumphant Susan reappeared, leading her scowling brother. But when he saw Anabel, his face lit. "Mama, you are home!" He threw himself into her arms.

Susan put her hands on her hips. "Well, of course she's home. It's nearly dinnertime. Now you must help me find the others before we are made to stop."

Anabel smiled into Nick's eyes and caressed his soft brown hair. "There is nothing wrong," she said.

Nick swallowed, then looked at Hanford.

"For dinner," Christopher said. "I promised, remember?"

The boy nodded, blinking rapidly.

"Come *on*," said Susan, starting up the stairs again. "Daisy's here."

The cat had indeed emerged, and Susan was trying to carry him, very much against his inclination. Nick hesitated. "Go ahead," said Anabel. "I must change." They walked up together, and Anabel parted from the others at the drawing-room doorway. She was eager to wash the dust from her face and hands, and exchange her crumpled morning dress for a fresh gown.

She did not linger in her bedroom, however. In a quarter hour she was down again to find the drawing room empty. Puzzled, she walked to the stairs and looked down. No one was about. What had become of them? As she walked back down the corridor Christopher suddenly peered out of the back parlor, then emerged to join her. "I have been recruited into the game," he said, smiling. "I thought to end it, but Susan was very insistent. So I offered to be the seeker. I meant to find your mother and Georgina, and give them the news." He shrugged, smiling wryly. "But I cannot. And now Susan and Nicholas have hidden again, and there has been no sign whatsoever of William."

Anabel laughed. "We will find them together. And then we will announce our plans to everyone. I have an idea where Mama may be."

They found Lady Goring in the small writing closet adjoining her bedchamber, just as Anabel had suspected. She was writing a letter and looked up with slight annoyance when the door opened. But when she saw Anabel, she was on her feet at once and embracing her. "Where have you *been*?"

Anabel explained, her account punctuated by her mother's cries of outrage. "How dare he?" she exclaimed when the story was finished. "I can hardly credit it, even of him."

"It is over now," answered Anabel. "He will not trouble us again. I prefer to think of the future." She smiled at Christopher, and he squeezed her hand. "In fact, Mama, we want to tell the children of our plans. You must help us find them."

"Hide-and-seek in earnest?" responded Lady Goring with a smile. "Very well. And we will have some champagne with dinner, to celebrate."

"Where do you suppose Georgina has gone?"

Lady Goring shook her head. "She was deep into the game when we separated. She might be anywhere from the attics to the cellars. And the children…!" She spread her hands eloquently.

Hanford grinned. "We will start in the attics, then, and move downward, with you guarding the stairs, Lady Goring, to see that no one slips past. We will soon uncover them."

Anabel laughed at him. "You are enjoying this."

"Why not?" He put an arm about her as they started toward the stairs. "I shall enjoy every moment of my life from now on."

Discreetly Lady Goring moved ahead, and she refrained from comment when the others joined her with flushed faces and sheepish smiles.

Georgina was in the attic. She had settled behind two ancient wardrobe trunks, where a dusty window gave just enough light so that she could read a novel. With the increasing darkness, she had to hold it almost at the end of her nose, and she was so absorbed that she did not even hear them approach. Only when Hanford said, "Found!" did she start and look up.

"I didn't think anyone would find me here," she replied, disappointed. Then she saw who it was. "Anabel! Are you… That is, we were worried about you."

"All is well," answered her cousin. "Except everyone is hiding. Come and help us find them."

"Did you discover me first?" she said. "I thought I had been so clever."

"We have Lady Goring," Christopher assured her. "And we started at the top of the house."

The rest of the attics were untenanted. On the nursery floor below, they were just about to give up when Anabel remembered a tiny storage room under the stairs. Holding their candles into its dimness, they discovered William crouched among the discarded furniture and linen. He bounced out at once. "Where is Susan? She's supposed to be looking."

"We have taken her place. Come along and help search for her and Nick."

William looked disgusted at being found before them. "Oh, I know where Nick will be. Behind the curtain in the library; he always hides there."

"I think he has left it for another spot," replied Christopher with a smile. "Daisy routed him."

"Truly?" The boy laughed. "How he hates that cat. If he would but ignore it, it wouldn't torment him so."

The adults exchanged a smile at this bit of wisdom.

"He is probably in the kitchens, then. Once, when we were playing, he hid there eating cake the whole time!" He frowned. "Why didn't I remember that before? I'm hungry."

"It is nearly dinnertime," said Anabel. "We will eat as soon as we find the others."

William started forward. "I'll look in the kitchen."

Christopher caught him. "No, we will stay with our system. First, the drawing-room floor."

There was no one there; nor did they discover Nick or Susan on the ground floor. "They must have gone to the cellars," marveled William. "I should think Susan would be frightened."

Taking a large branch of candles, all but Lady Goring descended the cellar stairs. The foundations of the house were a vast, echoing space supported here and there by a stone pillar and piled with stores.

"Nick! Susan!" called William. "Come out."

There was no response.

"They mean to make us find them," he added, disgusted.

"Do come out," urged Anabel. "It is nearly dinner-time, and we have something to tell you."

In the far corner of the cellar, Nick's head appeared from behind a pile of boxes. He was very dirty. "All right," he responded, moving toward them.

"Where is Susan?" asked his mother.

"*I* don't know. Hiding with her wretched cat, I suppose."

"Didn't you come down here together?"

"No. I went back into the library." Here William made a small triumphant sound. "But the stupid cat came after me and wouldn't let me be, so I shut it in and tried the cellar."

"Where can she be?" Anabel frowned.

"I didn't see the cat in the library," replied Hanford.

"It wasn't there," agreed Lady Goring. "I *always* notice Daisy."

"We must have overlooked their hiding place," said Anabel. "We shall have to search again."

Without obvious enthusiasm, the group returned to the ground floor and began to look for Susan. When they had scoured the house yet again, they congregated in the nursery and wondered what to do. It was past dinnertime. Cook was becoming annoyed, and the rest of them were hungry. The boys favored sitting down to eat and letting Susan take her chances, but Anabel wished to find her first. "I am a little worried," she admitted.

"She is crouching somewhere and laughing at us, Mama," sighed William. "She is so small; she might be anywhere. And if she will not come out when we call her…"

"She had to hear us," put in Nicholas. "We shouted in every room."

"Perhaps she is hurt, or…"

Both boys gazed at their mother skeptically. They had played such games with Susan often. Anabel hesitated. "Well…"

"Let us at least go down to the drawing room," declared Lady Goring, who was looking irritated. "And let us announce dinner. Perhaps that will bring her out." She glanced meaningfully at the boys, who rightly interpreted this as a signal to shout her announcement.

It was thus a very odd descent from the upper floor. William and Nick went first, advertising dinner at the top of their lungs, followed by the older members of the party, looking variously concerned, amused, and annoyed. Their own noise obscured a rising disturbance lower down for quite a while, but finally, in a lull, they heard a confused shouting and thumping from belowstairs. "What is that?" asked Anabel, hushing her sons.

"It sounds as if it is coming from the kitchens," replied Georgina, who was fighting a smile.

"That cat!" exclaimed Lady Goring, picking up her skirts and hurrying down the staircase.

It was not only Daisy. It was Susan, too. The cat was racing round and round the kitchen, claws rasping on the brick floor, ginger fur wild, with one of the kitchen maids in hot pursuit with a cleaver. Susan, her face smeared with a dark substance, was standing before Cook, her head hanging, but when the others burst in and she looked up, a spark of unrepentant mischief gleamed in her green eyes.

"What is happening here?" demanded Lady Goring in a penetrating voice.

The kitchen maid froze, allowing Daisy to escape into the scullery. Susan bit her lower lip, and Cook turned, arms akimbo and scowling, to reply, "Miss Susan was found in the larder, if you please, ma'am, eating the chocolate cake I baked for tea tomorrow. Indeed, she has as good as finished it, and I expect she will be sick now."

Susan shook her head. Her brothers eyed her with half-admiring outrage. "Nick's trick," murmured William.

"Well, she shan't have any dinner, then," said Anabel, moving to take Susan's hand—then shifting to her upper arm when she saw the sticky state of that member. "Come along and get washed."

With a malicious grin at the boys, Susan allowed herself to be led away.

Some twenty minutes later, they were all gathered around the table eating dinner. Anabel had relented and allowed Susan to join them, in view of the momentous news that was to be imparted there, but the girl was not eating. She watched the others devour roast chickens and a ragout of beef with some contempt, and her superior little face caused more than one of the adults to suppress a smile during the course of the meal.

When the servants had brought the last of the dishes and retired to the kitchen, Anabel looked around the table. "We have something to tell you all," she said.

The boys raised their heads, and Susan turned. Under their collective gaze, Anabel quailed a little. The last time she had made such an announcement, the reaction had been far from favorable. And though she knew the children loved Christopher, there was no predicting what they would think. She glanced at him, and he smiled reassuringly. "Uncle Christopher and I have decided to marry," she finished.

There was a moment's silence. Lady Goring smiled benignly, and Georgina more fixedly. Then the table erupted in shouts of wondering glee, and all the children spoke at once.

"Hurray!" exclaimed William.

"I'm very glad," said Nick.

"Will Uncle Christopher live with us?" asked Susan.

Anabel laughed with relief and happiness. "Yes," said Hanford in reply to this last question, "and you had best beware, young miss, for I shall be a very strict disciplinarian. It was obvious today that you require one."

Susan giggled. "Daisy likes you too," she answered.

"Does he? I am deeply honored."

"This is wonderful," put in William. "Everything is coming out splendidly just after it seemed that nothing was right."

Anabel sat back, listening to the happy chatter and watching Christopher talk with the children. William was right. She had never felt happier in her life.

When dinner was over and the children had been taken upstairs to bed, Lady Goring and Georgina left the engaged couple alone in the drawing room. They settled on the sofa and let out identical sighs of contentment.

"I'm glad that is over," she said.

"Did you really doubt their approval?"

"No, I suppose not. But..."

"But you weren't certain they had ever considered me in that light," he finished teasingly.

"Christopher! How can you remind me of my idiocy? I was stupidly blind for so long. It makes me blush with shame."

"Ah, but I mean to extract full payment."

She smiled. "What sort of payment?"

Instead of answering, he bent and kissed her, slowly and gently at first, then more passionately. Anabel felt again that thrill of response through her whole body. She put her arms around his neck and gave herself totally to the embrace.

It was some time before she could speak again, and when she did, she was breathless. "That is the sort of debt I shall never wish to pay off," she murmured.

Christopher's blue eyes shone as he gave the only conceivable answer to this, pulling her close once again.

Bride to Be

One

disreputable friend of her father's would be flicked off and put in the middle of dinner.

She loved her parents dearly, but she didn't share their artistic temperament. And the maternal life was frightening to wear on her. She was almost twenty years old, where would she be when she was twenty-five, or thirty? Still helping her family cope with daily disasters? Lately, she

EMILY CRANE WALKED BRISKLY ALONG THE PATH THAT rambled through the property behind her house. On either side, meadow grass bent under shimmers of morning dew. The line of ancient willows that marked the course of the brook rustled against a crystalline blue sky. The sound of water bubbling over rocks came to her ears. It was an idyllic early spring scene; and she savored it, and her solitude, to the full. Her companions had gone on ahead. She could enjoy a brief respite from the continual upheavals of her home.

This morning, she had finally realized that her parents enjoyed chaos. Indeed, they seemed to thrive on it. When bailiffs pounded on the door, or another landlord threw them out, or the sight of a half-clothed model in the studio caused the cook and maidservant to give notice, they ranted and railed and bemoaned their fate. But they did it with such gusto, Emily thought. Why had she never noticed that before?

Once, when she was fifteen, she had asked her mother how she could bear the endless alarms and disruptions. Her mother had considered the question with bright interest and then decided that it must be a reaction to her upbringing. Emily's parents had been born into noble families—"the stifling atmosphere of upper-class convention," as her mother put it. Emily wondered what it would be like to be surrounded by a large family, never to wonder where one would be living this time next year, or whether the boiler might explode, or whether some disreputable friend of her father's would be hauled off to jail in the middle of dinner.

She loved her parents dearly, but she didn't share their artistic temperament. Paints and canvas didn't console her for every setback. And the itinerant life was beginning to wear on her. She was almost twenty years old; where would she be when she was twenty-five, or thirty? Still helping her family cope with daily disasters? Lately, she had been dreaming of a more settled existence—of tranquility and even, perhaps, a touch of the conventional.

How outraged her father would be by such thoughts! Smiling, Emily parted the curtain of trailing willow branches and stepped through. Wouldn't it be pleasant if she had played in this spot as a child? If she had scores of happy memories of this secret hideaway? In fact, she had forgotten most of the places she had lived as a child. There had been so many.

A movement on the other side of the stream caught her eye. Two rough-looking men were dragging a third along the ground, tugging him toward the spot where the brook widened into a small pond. When one of the men stepped aside for a moment, she saw that the victim's hands were tied.

Emily grimaced. She had wanted only a quiet walk. In a life full of the unusual and unexpected, she had asked for just a few minutes' peace. Was it so much? Evidently it was, replied a dry mental voice. And was she going to allow a helpless man to be drowned? For that was clearly what the two attackers intended.

She sighed. It must be her fate to resolve other people's difficulties. She had been doing it for her parents for so long that she had begun to attract other victims of circumstance. It was a lowering reflection.

Emerging from the willow branches, Emily started across the stream on a line of stepping-stones. "David! Jonathan!" she called.

Her escorts came running.

"What are you doing there?" she cried to the men. She didn't feel a trace of fear. She had been confronting various adversaries since she was thirteen. Indeed, the mob in Essex who had wanted to tar and feather her father had been much fiercer looking than these two disheveled individuals.

Startled, the two men let go of their burden and straightened. Then, seeing David and Jonathan racing toward them, they took to their heels.

They were heading for the road that ran along the back of the property, she saw. Confident that they wouldn't be back, she went to examine the man lying on the bank of the pond. His ankles were tied as well as his wrists, and he had been knocked on the head. A bruise was swelling at his temple. Emily sighed again. Did other young ladies, out for a soothing stroll, encounter such difficulties? She didn't think so. Perhaps her parents somehow *attracted* trouble.

She looked down at the bound man. He had an impressive physique. It was no wonder it had taken two ruffians to subdue him. His skin was bronzed, and his brown hair streaked gold by the sun. His hands were callused, but he didn't wear the clothes or quite have the look of a laborer. Even unconscious, his straight brows and chiseled features held a proud fierceness. Her father would paint him as a Roman legionary, Emily thought. Or, no, a gladiator. It was oddly easy to imagine this man in a brief tunic, his arms and legs gleaming with oil, his… Emily shook her head, startled at the immediacy of the picture and her uncharacteristic flight of imagination.

David and Jonathan came running back. "Have you chased them off?" asked Emily. "Good."

After giving the matter careful consideration, Emily untied the ropes that bound the man. She went to soak her handkerchief in the pond and then applied it to his bruised temple. The chilled cloth elicited a groan, and she moved back out of reach as the man drew in a deeper breath.

He opened his eyes, and blinked at the formidable pair of fangs poised inches from his face. With a speed that was truly startling, he jerked away and reached for Jonathan's throat in one fluid movement.

"Jonathan!" cried Emily.

The dog hadn't needed the admonition. He had already retreated from the look in the man's eyes. "Sit," said Emily.

The man stared at her blankly. Slowly, he sat up, biting back a groan. He put his hands to his head. When they encountered her embroidered linen handkerchief, he removed it and stared as if he'd never seen such a thing before in his life. Then he looked around at the pond, meadows, willow trees as if they too were strange and disorientating.

Had the attack addled his wits? Emily remembered the time her father had brained the local squire with a vase he had been using in a still life. That poor man had been incoherent for quite half an hour. Of course, with the squire it was mostly fury. And then they had had to move again and...

The man turned his head and then swayed dizzily. He squinted up into the sunlight and, looking at her, blinked.

"Are you all right?" Emily said. "You've had a knock on the head."

He put a hand to his temple, and winced.

"I believe you were attacked on the road," she added helpfully. "But we scared them off."

Sinking back, the man blinked again as if to clear blurred vision. He surveyed her more closely. "You?"

Emily snapped her fingers. Immediately, she was flanked by two gigantic Irish wolfhounds, nearly three feet at the shoulder and fiercely alert. Her father didn't let her go walking without them. She watched with some amusement as they regarded the man and each gave a soft growl. "David," she said, gesturing left, then right. "And Jonathan."

"I see." He looked well aware that those jaws would shatter bone.

"Why were those men trying to throw you in the pond?"

He looked at the water behind him. "What?"

"They had tied you up." She indicated the ropes lying in a tangle beside him. "And they were dragging you to the pond. They meant to drown you, I think."

He cradled his head as if it ached. "They must have been footpads. I was riding toward London when they…" He frowned. "One of them jumped from the hedge and started to pull me from my horse. I was fighting him off when the other came out of nowhere and hit me." He fingered the bruise on his head. "He must have had a cudgel."

"Common thieves wouldn't tie you and drag you across a field," she pointed out.

The man shrugged. "Perhaps they were angry that I had nothing to steal." He frowned again. "Except my horse. It's gone, I suppose." He looked around as if the animal might magically appear.

"They might have kicked you for that, or taken your clothes, but they wouldn't have bothered with more."

"You are an expert on footpads?" With an obvious effort, the man made it to his feet.

The top of her head barely reached his shoulder, Emily noticed. He really was quite large. And impressive, somehow, despite his condition.

"I appear to owe you a debt," he added. "You have my thanks. I won't trouble you further." He turned away and then stopped, swaying and putting out a hand to catch his balance as he staggered.

Emily slipped under his arm and steadied him. "You probably shouldn't move."

"I am not going to lie here in the grass. I must find my horse."

"You can't even walk."

"Of course I can." But when he tried to push her away, he almost tumbled to the ground again.

Emily looked up at him, the latest in a seemingly endless line of dilemmas that she had had to solve. "You had better come to the house. We'll send for the doctor."

"I don't need a doctor."

"Yes, you do."

The man managed with some difficulty to gaze down at her, tucked under his arm. "You are a very odd young woman."

It always came to that, Emily thought wistfully. Everyone she met—particularly every young man she met—found her dauntingly eccentric. It was her parents' fault, with the life they had given her.

"You seem to take highway robbery quite in your stride," he added.

And so would he, if he had spent just about all his life moving from one emergency to another. Her father had a weakness for rogues. Over the years, he had befriended a variety of beguiling confidence men, at least one of whom made his living by highway robbery.

"Yet you have the face of a Botticelli angel," he said.

Emily looked up at him, meeting his intelligent hazel eyes from a distance shorter than she had ever experienced before—a rather unsettling distance, if the truth be told. Her eventful life had not included many compliments or the attentions of attractive young men. Her father's freewheeling ways most emphatically did not extend to his only daughter. He never allowed her to be alone with a man, let alone plastered against one's side holding him upright. Papa was going to be apoplectic if he found out. She needed to get her charge home and safely out of her arms. "Come along," she said, giving him a slight push.

He took a step, and stumbled. She wrapped her arm around his ribs to give him more support. With a naturalness that surprised her, his arm draped itself over her shoulders. The warmth of his body against her side was disturbing. "Move," she said, pushing him slightly again.

"I can walk," he declared, stepping away from her. But to his obvious frustration, vertigo returned, and he reeled.

"Why can't you be reasonable?"

"Reasonable? There is nothing reasonable about this situation. Any reasonable young woman would be sunk in a fit of the vapors by this time, wringing her hands and praying for aid."

"Would she?" Emily let her hands fall to her sides and frowned. Could this really be how a gently reared girl would behave? "That wouldn't be particularly helpful," she had to point out.

"No," he agreed, fixing a fascinated gaze upon her. "Who are you?"

It was a very good question, Emily thought. She often asked it of herself. "My name is Emily Crane." She waited, and when he said nothing, added, "And yours?"

"I beg your pardon. I am Richard Sheldon."

"Well, Mr. Sheldon, if you really wish me to have a fit of the vapors…"

"I don't," he put in hastily.

"Good. You will be spared a disappointment." She approached him once again. "We must go to my house."

She put her arm around his waist. His arm settled over her shoulders once again. "Come," said Emily, pressing closer to urge him forward. Richard stiffened a little and nearly toppled both of them to the ground. "Are you going to faint?"

"No," he snapped.

Pressed together, they made their way slowly across the meadow, the massive dogs gamboling at Emily's heels like puppies. Fortunately, the stepping-stones in the stream were large and flat, and they got across without mishap. Now and then, Richard would lurch unexpectedly as dizziness caught him. Each time, she supported him, and each time he stifled a curse.

The journey was beginning to seem endless when he said, "We are going to the house of…?"

"My parents. We are nearly there."

And with any luck, they would evade her father, she thought as she helped their unexpected visitor across the last bit of meadow. The Honorable Alasdair Crane might be outrageous. He might wear Turkish robes and stand before his easel barefoot. He might threaten the local vicar with a cauliflower. He might send his Irish wolfhounds to the post office with a parcel. But his daughter was supposed to be a model of propriety. And this did *not* include dragging large virile strangers home from country walks.

Emily stole a look at his face through her lashes. He seemed to radiate heat. Perhaps the blow had given him a fever? But that didn't explain why fitting her head into the hollow of his shoulder was so disconcertingly pleasant. Nor why she was so intensely conscious of his hand on her arm.

Although Emily's experience of humanity was far broader than that of most young ladies, she had never encountered anyone like Richard Sheldon. His voice and bearing had an aristocratic polish, but his clothes and hands were not even those of a gentleman. He had come within an inch of throttling Jonathan, and in that moment he had been—ferocious. Yet he spoke to her with civility.

Emily shook her head as they stepped up onto the weedy flagstone terrace that ran along the back of their current house. It didn't make sense. She couldn't figure him out.

Perhaps it would be easier when she no longer had her

arm around him. His proximity was distracting. He was so large, looming over her, and the scent of leather and soap and…man were so heady.

The French doors that led inside were propped open, which was fortunate because one of them was loose on its hinges and continually threatening to fall. Now if only she could get Mr. Sheldon seated in their shabby drawing room before her father discovered his arrival…

But here Emily's luck ran out. Her father appeared in the archway opposite before they had taken two steps into the house.

"What the devil is this?" he shouted. "Get your hands off my daughter, you blackguard!"

He surged forward with his hand raised to strike, obviously forgetting that he held a loaded paintbrush. "Father!" Emily cried. "This man was attacked on the road. He's hurt."

Knowing that the words wouldn't penetrate at once, she pivoted somewhat clumsily and dropped Richard Sheldon into an armchair.

"Footpads," she added loudly. "In broad daylight."

"Eh?" Her father came to an abrupt stop before them. "What? Footpads?"

"Yes," said Emily. "They knocked him on the head and stole his horse. I found him in the meadow, ah, er, crawling toward the house for help."

A stifled exclamation escaped Richard, and Emily sent him a silent command to be quiet. Simple explanations worked best with her father.

"Crawling?" he repeated.

Emily nodded, gazing innocently up at him.

The hand holding the paintbrush dropped, leaving a streak of brilliant crimson along his pants leg.

"I was *not*—" began Richard.

"Isn't it a terrible thing?" put in Emily quickly. "Do you think we should inform the magistrate?"

"That jumped-up country squire?" exploded her father. "He wouldn't know a footpad from his own backside. Of all the dim-witted, bad-tempered, rag-mannered blusterers…"

Satisfied with her diversion, Emily let her father's ranting run its course. She threw Richard Sheldon a fierce glance, signaling that he should keep quiet.

"We should send for the doctor," Emily said when her father at last fell silent. "Mr. Sheldon has suffered a severe blow to the head."

Her father stared at their guest suspiciously. His eyes narrowed. His dark brows drew together. "Olivia!" he bellowed.

Wherever they lived, each of her parents always had a workroom. In this house, they were at opposite ends, which Emily found far more restful than some arrangements she had been forced to endure. But in this case it meant that her father had to shout at the top of his lungs before he gained her mother's attention.

"I was painting the petal of a golden poppy," she said reproachfully as she entered the drawing room. "You startled me and made me spoil it, Alasdair."

"Emily's brought this fellow home with her," he explained, in the same aggrieved tones he used when one of the dogs dragged in a half-dead rabbit. "Says he must have the doctor."

The Honorable Olivia Crane raised slim red-gold brows and surveyed her unexpected guest. There was no question about where her daughter got her looks, Richard thought. They were both petite women; red-gold hair, a pointed chin, arched brows and a wide, serene forehead, eyes of heavenly blue. No wonder he had thought of Botticelli.

As Emily repeated the story she had concocted to her mother, Richard looked about himself. It was certainly an odd family. They spoke and moved like members of the nobility, yet their clothes and surroundings were bohemian. The mistress of the house had a smear of yellow paint on her cheek. The master carried a paint-brush as if it were part of his hand. Richard wondered if he was related to the Earl of Radford, who was also a Crane. Now that he thought about it, there was a resemblance. Indeed, his host looked a great deal like the old earl's two sons, whom Richard had often seen in London drawing rooms.

A memory intruded. There were actually three sons, but the third was some sort of black sheep. He had heard the story—what was it?—something about a painter's studio and a nobleman's daughter caught posing nude.

"Good God!" Richard exclaimed, his eyes irresistibly drawn to Emily's mother. "You're Shelbury's lost daughter." The flaming hair of Marquess Shelbury's line was unmistakable. This eccentric pair had caused one of the great society scandals of the 1790s.

Olivia Crane's brows rose again. "My father knows perfectly well where I am," she answered without embarrassment. "I'm not the least bit 'lost.'"

Something like a growl escaped her husband.

Richard flushed. For a man famed for his conversational skills, he had been remarkably clumsy. It was another measure of how much had been left behind in the last eleven months.

"Just the opposite," asserted Alasdair Crane.

"I found myself in my art," his wife agreed. "And, of course, I found Alasdair." They exchanged a smile that seemed more suited to the wild young lovers who had fled for the border than a middle-aged married couple with a grown daughter.

"We should send for the doctor," said Emily.

Richard turned to gaze at her. Once again, she looked unperturbed. She obviously knew her parents' scandalous story and was thoroughly accustomed to their behavior.

It must have been fascinating to grow up in such a household. "I'm feeling much better. I don't need the doctor."

"You can't even walk," protested Emily.

"Yes, I can." To prove it, he stood. The dizziness was still there, but it was receding. He took an experimental step. "You see?" He raised his eyes to find all three Cranes staring at him.

Emily looked slightly dazed. Her mother seemed suddenly thoughtful. The Honorable Alasdair appeared rapt. "Samson," he murmured dreamily. "Chained to the pillars, straining to bring the temple down."

"I beg your pardon?" replied Richard.

"A tunic?" was the incomprehensible response. "No, no. A breechclout."

The two Crane women blinked. Emily's cheeks flushed a delicate pink.

"I could invent the hair," continued her father. "It would take weeks to grow it out." He grasped Richard's forearm. "Just come with me. I must make sketches…"

"Father!" cried Emily.

"Alasdair," admonished her mother at the same moment.

He turned to gaze at them as if he had forgotten their presence. His grip on Richard's arm remained tight.

"You cannot paint him, Father," added Emily. "He is a stranger, a traveler. You cannot just…"

"He would be very glad to pose," answered Alasdair, in a tone that suggested he was used to getting his way.

"No, he wouldn't!"

Emily looked distressed, and her mother irritated. It was all very awkward. And he hadn't the least desire to become an artist's model. "If you would just lend me a horse…" he began.

"I will if you pose," said Alasdair, looking crafty.

"Nonsense," said his wife.

"Lively" didn't begin to describe the discussion that

ensued. It ranged from high dudgeon to broken pathos and back again. After a while, Richard realized that the Cranes were enjoying themselves far too much to come to any conclusion. It was better than many plays he'd seen, Richard thought, suppressing a smile at a particularly clever exchange.

Emily plucked at his sleeve. She didn't seem to find the argument amusing. "Come," she said, urging him out into the hallway.

Her parents' dispute had upset her, Richard concluded. The kindest thing was to ignore the shouting. "If I could borrow a mount," he said.

Emily frowned. "Are you sure you can ride?"

"Quite sure. I'm fully recovered."

Although she looked doubtful, she led him out to the stables and ordered the groom to saddle a horse.

"I'll be sure you get it back. And I must thank you again for—"

"Must you?"

She wanted to get rid of him, Richard decided. She was embarrassed because he'd witnessed the family dispute.

The groom brought out a good-looking bay, and Richard prepared to mount. It was rather a pity that he would never see her again. After his unwanted adventure of the last year, it was clear that nothing about his old life would be right, including the women who had been part of it. Emily Crane might be just the sort of girl he could admire now—free and forthright, with a mind of her own, not bound by senseless convention. The memory of her slender body against his came back with warm vividness.

He put it aside. He had a great many things to accomplish. He had already lost eleven months—or twenty-nine years, some might say—of his life. He had to get on with it. "Good-bye," he said. "Thank you once again."

Emily raised a hand in farewell, then turned back

toward the house. Richard hesitated a final instant before directing the horse out through the gate.

It was no wonder he had been eager to get away, Emily thought as she made her way to her bedchamber. Her parents' voices still echoed from the drawing room. He must have thought they were all demented. People generally did.

She was truly tired of it. It wasn't the moving, the tantrums, the upsets, so much as the loneliness. Her parents had each other, and that would always be enough for them. She had her parents, but it wasn't the same. She wanted what they had—a consuming love, marriage to a man who matched her in every particular, a companion to share the rest of her life. It would be different from her parents' life, of course, a bit more stable, even conventional. Emily smiled slightly. But she longed for the same compelling bond.

Impossible. She would never fall in love. There was no one to fall in love *with*. On her rare encounters with a young man, he was appalled by her bizarre household, just as Richard Sheldon had been today. Everyone just assumed that she was like her parents.

No, she was doomed to a single life. She would have to find some useful profession, make her own way. But as usual, at this point in the reasoning process, she was stopped. Her education had been spotty, so she couldn't be a teacher or a governess. She despised sewing and fancywork. She had no talent for acting, even supposing her father would allow her to go on the stage. Perhaps she would set up as a highwayman. It was one thing her life had suited her for. Her father had taught her to shoot a pistol. She had a fine seat on horseback. And who would suspect a woman of taking to the High Toby? There was nothing else for it. She would sustain her old age by highway robbery.

In the drawing room, the quarrel ended, as they always did, with an embrace. "Come upstairs," murmured Alasdair, stroking his wife's paint-streaked cheek.

"In a moment." Olivia raised her limpid blue eyes to his. "We must talk about Emily."

"What? By Jove!" He scanned the room. "Where has that blackguard taken her?"

"I imagine that *she* has taken *him* to the stables and lent him a horse. Emily is such a practical girl. But that is not the point."

"Not the point! She comes in with her arm around some vagabond, practically glued to his side, and—"

"*That* is the point. Emily must be put in the way of meeting some suitable men. She cannot stay with us forever."

Alasdair scowled, his black brows bristling. "Suitable?" he growled.

"Emily does not share our passion for art," Olivia pointed out. "She has no wish to devote her life to it."

His shoulders drooped a little as he conceded this.

"And I must admit that I don't know if I would do so if I did not have you to share that life."

This earned her another embrace, and it was some time before she was able to continue.

"My sister would introduce Emily to society," she said then. "If I asked her to do so."

"You want to send my daughter to the house of a duchess? What the devil would she do there?"

Olivia looked suddenly haughty. "Do you imagine she wouldn't fit in?"

"I *imagine* she's far too good for 'em." Alasdair shook his head. "And Julia'll fill her head with all sorts of nonsense."

"Emily is a very sensible girl. We have done all we

can to give her a proper perspective on what is important in life."

"*You* have," replied her husband admiringly.

"You are a wonderful example of a man following his true passions."

The look that passed between them then was incendiary. Further talk was unthinkable, but Olivia was well aware as they retired to their bedchamber that the issue was decided. She had learned to manage Alasdair three weeks after she met the fiery young artist all those years ago. And how much else she had learned, she thought, just before all thought was swept away.

Two

RICHARD SAT IN THE TAPROOM OF THE BLUE DRAGON nursing his pint of ale and listening to a pair of shop-keepers at the next table vilify the Duke of Wellington. Londoners were a fickle lot. They had worshiped the man as a hero not long since, but now that the war was over and the duke was involved in politics, he had become fair game.

He shouldn't be here. He ought to be in quite a different part of town, taking up the obligations and responsibilities that had brought him home. The attack on the road was the least of the obstacles he had overcome to reach London again. But now that he was here, he found himself delaying. From the moment he contacted his mother, there would be no turning back.

It was inexcusable to leave his mother thinking that he was dead, asserted a stern inner voice.

He acknowledged it with a nod. But he didn't rise to hurry to her house in the heart of fashionable Mayfair. The problem was, he was no longer the son who had embarked on a voyage to the West Indies. That Richard Sheldon, Baron Warrington, had been a pink of the *ton*, a wit, a habitué of White's and Almack's. And he had expired in the first few days after the ship foundered off South America and a longboat had deposited him on a stretch of unexplored coast. The baron had not been prepared to scrabble for grubs to survive, thought Richard wryly, or to fashion a spear and kill his own food. In a very real sense, he had succumbed to the rigors of the wild. The man who had returned was someone else entirely.

But who?

That was a question he couldn't answer. He felt less like a single person than a bundle of fragments. There was the old Warrington—heedless, improvident, sardonic. Looking back, Richard didn't like him much. He had been overindulged by a widowed mother, he saw now. And then he had lived off his stepfather's bounty without a scrap of gratitude or any appreciation of the older man's virtues. Indeed, he had thought him a prating old stick. When Sir Walter Fielding died unexpectedly, the old Warrington's first thought had been of money, and how he would continue to live in high style. He had actually been surprised, Richard remembered with wonder now, that his stepfather had left him only a token legacy to add to his ruined patrimony. What else had he expected? Sir Walter had made it clear enough that he disapproved of his mode of life.

And so he had gone off in a fit of the sulks, Richard thought, abandoning his mother in her grief, behaving as badly as he possibly could. No one would miss that Richard—least of all himself.

But in England there was little call for the skills of a jungle savage. The Richard born out of sheer need to survive had no place in this city, in this tavern. He could kill with his bare hands, endure plagues of leeches, fade invisibly into a screen of foliage. With a thin smile, Richard sipped his ale. No, that Richard had served his purpose and must now take his leave.

And then there was the silent, determined man who had paid his passage home by working the sails of a merchant ship. He had had just one goal in life—to reach England—and now it was achieved. He didn't appear to have suggestions about the future.

On the docks in Cartagena, there had been ships

departing for Barcelona and Shanghai and Boston. That
Richard had toyed with the idea of hiring himself out
on one of those and disappearing for good. A disorderly
chorus of inner voices had dissuaded him. Duty called.
Warrington deplored the hardships of a common sailor's
life. The man who had fought his way out of the jungle
resisted such confinement.

And so, he had come home.

Richard grimaced as he lifted his tankard once again.
He was damned if he knew *who* had come home. In
Southampton, he had encountered the shipping agent
who originally booked his passage. The man had been
astounded to see him, of course. He was barely recogniz-
able, even to himself, Richard thought. Just now, he felt
more like a committee than a man. Would his mother
be happy to see the son who had returned? She'd reared
him to become a darling of the *haut ton*, and her pride in
his success had been vast. What would she think of the
rough-handed man who came back from the dead?

She would expect him to revive his former self as
quickly as possible. That was the dilemma that kept him
in his chair. Not that he would do so. The cut of a coat
or the latest gossip held absolutely no interest for him
now. But what was he going to do?

Life spread out before him, a blank slate. Once he had
assured his mother of his continued existence, he would
have to find some occupation, some task that would use
his skills and not drive him mad, as his former pursuits
were likely to do.

He might try to discover if anything could be salvaged
from the wreck of the Warrington estates, which his
father had nearly managed to waste before his death.
Richard, succeeding to the title at the tender age of six,
had rarely spared a thought for his tumbledown patrimony. His mother's remarriage had ensured his comfort
and he hadn't cared for anything else.

What an insufferable puppy he had been. He had never willingly moved a muscle to help anyone, and he hadn't cared a snap of his manicured fingers for his heritage or posterity. He would have to make a push to save his estates, though frankly, he wasn't drawn to land management. But it was a step toward finding a Richard Sheldon he could tolerate. He had been stripped down to the bare essentials of humanity. He had survived. He would build, step by step, on that. Perhaps, along the way, he could find a pursuit that consumed him.

It occurred to him that Alasdair Crane had exactly that. The man's passion for painting, and for his wife, had been striking. Crane had known what he wanted, and he had taken it. All the strictures of society had not been enough to stop him. That was what he wanted—that certainty, that savor. And perhaps, someone to share it; a…a kindred spirit.

Richard blinked, surprised at where his thoughts had led him. Even in his lonely fight to escape the jungle he had not indulged in such philosophical ruminations. He sighed. Every person he knew would think he had gone mad. No one would begin to understand such ambitions.

Emily Crane might, stated this new, rather disconcerting inner voice. She had been reared by parents who set their chosen work above society. She would know precisely what he meant. Memories of her red-gold hair, her delicate face and form pressed close against his own, lingered, even haunted his dreams. What if he rode back there now? Would she welcome him?

Shaking off these recollections, he drained the tankard and set it down. First, he had to see his mother and assure her of his safety and good health. After that…he would see.

◆

As he strolled toward his mother's town house in the fading light of a fine spring day, Richard's mood was far from mellow. A visit to his bankers had been annoying. They had treated him like an idiot. And though he acknowledged that he had usually behaved like an arrogant young fool in the past, their condescension had filled him with rage he could barely contain. He had become far too used to strangling any entity that opposed him. London wasn't that sort of jungle.

In truth, it had been unsettling. Had he lost his ability to deal with people? An unfamiliar emotion crept over Richard then—a distrust of himself and his own impulses.

He had reached his mother's door. This wouldn't do. He was a civilized man—overcivilized many had said before his departure. The last eleven months hadn't destroyed that entirely. Perhaps he no longer knew just who he was, but he hadn't spun completely out of control. He could manage the conflicting forces that beset him. After a brief internal struggle, Richard pulled on the mask of his former persona, raised his hand, and rapped on the oak panels.

The door was opened by a footman he didn't know. The man surveyed Richard's clothes with rising insolence and said, "Yes?"

Richard pushed past him and into the front hall. He experienced a flicker of surprise at how easy this was, despite the servant's impressive physique, before saying, "Fetch Henley." It was no good asking a stranger for his mother.

"Mr. Henley is not available," answered the footman, looking ready to wrestle him out the door again.

"Nonsense. He will be sitting in his pantry at this hour, probably reading some tedious volume of military history. If you don't summon him at once, you will be very sorry."

The footman took a step back, clearly impressed

by the way Richard spoke as well as his knowledge of the household.

"I've known Henley since I was a boy," Richard added. "Get him."

The servant retreated another step from the look in his eyes, and then obviously decided that this was a matter for the butler to judge himself. He disappeared through the rear door with a flutter of coattails.

The place looked exactly the same, Richard thought, gazing at the gilt sconces and curving staircase, the furnishings of the parlor on the left. Which was odd. His mother had a penchant for redecorating, particularly in those rooms most seen by guests.

He heard no sound of conversation or music from above. He could just run up the stairs to the drawing room. But he hung back, postponing the moment a little longer. Henley would know everything that was going on in the house and how his mother was likely to receive his return. He envisioned the coming scene with a grimace.

The door at the back of the hall opened, and the tall spare figure of Henley strode through. "How may I assist…?" he began in freezing accents, then stopped. He peered at Richard, came closer. "My lord?"

"Hello, Henley. I'm back."

The old butler seemed stunned.

"I survived the shipwreck," said Richard, to give him time to recover. "But I was flung ashore in the middle of a jungle. It's taken me all this time to make my way home."

"Is it really you?" Uncharacteristically, Henley approached and took hold of Richard's forearm, as if to verify that it was indeed living flesh.

"Alive and well."

The butler released him, then glanced up the stairs apprehensively.

"My mother's all right, isn't she?"

"Her ladyship is at this moment holding a séance to contact your spirit, my lord," was the emotionless reply.

"What?"

"She began them three months after you were declared lost."

Richard started up the stairs.

"My lord, if you appear in the middle of..." But his lordship obviously wasn't listening. It really *was* young Richard, Henley assured himself. He did recognize him, although it had taken a moment to see that pampered exquisite in the powerful man who had taken his place.

❧

The drawing room was so dim that Richard couldn't see anything at first. An odd humming sound emanated from the center of the chamber, where he gradually made out a group of people sitting at a round table illuminated by one wavering candle. They were holding hands, he realized disgustedly. And the rather disturbing sound was coming from someone who faced the other direction. All he could see was a bulky silhouette with an outsized head that must be some sort of turban.

"We call across the great gulf of dissolution to the other realm," chanted a high, nasal voice. "We reach through the mists and darkness that obscure it. We seek this woman's son, Richard, tragically lost at sea in the flower of his youth."

Richard snorted softly.

"Bring him hither my messengers," commanded the voice. "Azrael. Phileto. Bring him!"

Richard was about to interrupt when he was startled by a whoosh like a great rush of wind. How the devil did they manage that?

"He is coming!" claimed the voice. "He is near. Spirit, give us a sign. Show us your presence."

Richard could take no more. He strode forward. "Mother, what the devil are you doing?"

An ear-splitting shriek rent the air, followed by a confusion of other shouts and exclamations. People started up in the dimness, overturning chairs, stumbling into each other, and crying out again. Someone started sobbing. Realizing that he had not chosen the ideal moment to address his mother, Richard moved to secure the candle, which was in danger of being knocked over. Taking it up, he began lighting others in the sconces around the room.

"There he is!" cried a male voice. "Good God!"

Richard continued lighting candles. The drawing room grew brighter, and he was able to see that it held eight people besides his mother. He didn't know any of them, though the orchestrator of the supposed séance was obvious—a burly, square-shouldered man wearing a massive jeweled turban with a feather. Ignoring them, he went to the chair where his mother sat and knelt beside it. "I beg your pardon for bursting in on you at such a moment," he said.

"You did it, Herr Schelling. You brought him back!" was the dazed reply.

To Richard's disgust, the large turbaned man put a hand on his breast and bowed in acknowledgment.

"Mother, I was not dead." He felt ridiculous saying it. "I was cast ashore in South America, and I had to make my way back on foot. I'm sorry I could not get word to you."

His mother simply stared at him as if he were indeed a ghost.

She was a bit thinner, but her gown was still in the height of fashion and her hair and ornaments exquisite. She looked like the mother he had left—a dedicated member of the *haut ton*. He took her hand, both to comfort her and to show her that he was solid flesh. "The ship I took began to go down in a storm," he added, hoping that details would make his return real to her. "The sailors put me in a longboat. Before they could join me it was swept away. I came ashore in a jungle."

His mother put her free hand on his cheek. Her hazel eyes, very like his own, brightened with a haze of tears.

How could he have considered not coming back? Richard wondered. It would have been cruel, unforgivable.

"I thought you were gone," she whispered, too low for anyone else to hear. "My God." She gripped his hand so hard her knuckles whitened.

"I'm back," he assured her, "and perfectly well."

"You won't go away again!"

He wouldn't be able to, Richard saw. Not for a while anyway. He shook his head.

"Brought him back from the dead," someone in the room murmured with a hush of awe. Richard was annoyed to see the turbaned man preen a little in response. He had to get rid of these people. "Mother…"

A tear spilled and ran down her cheek.

Richard stood, meeting the fascinated gazes of an ill-assorted group of strangers. "Perhaps you would all go now. I would like to talk with my mother."

Several left immediately. Others lingered a few minutes to make formal farewells. Finally, only the large turbaned man was left.

"Richard, this is Herr Schelling," said his mother in a shaky voice.

Schelling gave another of his deep bows. "I have been privileged to study with the Adepts of the East," he said, with a slight but noticeable German accent.

"Have you?" said Richard.

"We have much to learn from the Masters of the Hidden World."

"Indeed? But not tonight, perhaps. If you would excuse us?" The man was a pompous charlatan, but Richard had no desire to argue with him.

"I would not dream of intruding on this tender reunion," Schelling answered, without making any move to go. "My dear Lady Fielding, you are serene? Your humors are balanced?"

"No," said Richard's mother. "I am feeling quite agitated."

"Very natural," Schelling practically crooned. "Hardly to be avoided in the circumstances. You must visualize the Great Light, allow your unbalance to flow into it and be floated away."

Richard was appalled to see his mother actually close her eyes and take a deep breath. His disappearance had affected her far more than he had imagined it would.

Schelling, too, had closed his eyes. His hands rose and waved like seaweed in an ocean current. "Yes, I feel the balance being restored, the serenity returning." He opened his eyes. "Perhaps you would like to join us, Richard?"

He couldn't believe the fellow's effrontery. He gave him a look designed to wither him where he stood and said, "No, thank you. The balance of my humors is perfectly satisfactory."

Schelling looked pitying. He shook his head.

He was going to see that this faker never crossed his mother's threshold again. In fact, it would be a pleasure to send him back to Germany, if that was where he really came from. "I'll see you out," he said to Herr Schelling, and took the man's elbow in a grip that made him gasp.

He was not daunted, however. Over his shoulder, he said, "I will see you on Wednesday then, my dear Lady Fielding."

"Oh," replied Richard's mother. "Yes, I suppose… why not?"

For any number of reasons, thought Richard as he hustled the man out and handed him over to Henley. When he returned to the drawing room, his mother was still sitting amid the overturned chairs. "You look so different," she said.

He could only nod. It didn't seem the right time to deal with such a large question.

"It doesn't matter. You're home." She gazed at him as if trying to see the old Richard in the man who stood before her. "Thank God, you're home."

"Yes, Mother." He took her hand once again. She clutched it like a lifeline.

Three

EMILY SAT BESIDE HER AUNT AND WATCHED DANCERS turn like flowers across the parquet floor. The musicians at this, her first ball, had struck up a waltz, and she was not allowed to waltz, because she had not yet been approved by one of the powerful patronesses of Almack's. The rule echoed in her head, along with the many others her aunt had set out for her. There was an intricate code of behavior involved in a London season, she had found. She hadn't known there were so many rules in the world. It was the chief difference between her former life and the new existence that had so unexpectedly opened up before her. Emily felt as if she had traveled to a foreign country, where the culture was totally unfamiliar. Yet there was something alluring about it, too. This new country was full of clear expectations, of calm routines that were extremely soothing after all her years of turmoil.

Her aunt Julia was her native guide, Emily thought with a slight smile. She was also a duchess, of course, and just a little bit frightening. It was odd, because her aunt looked so much like her mother—the same red-gold hair and large blue eyes. Her chin was a bit squarer, and her nose a trifle more arched. But anyone would guess that this woman and her mother were sisters. Which made it all the more disconcerting that they appeared to have nothing at all in common. Aunt Julia lived in a magnificent town house in Grosvenor Square. The vast scale of it all had taken her breath away—the tall footmen and butler who had ushered her through the wide door, the richness of the furnishings, and the formality of every small detail. And her aunt's manner, her bearing, couldn't have been more different from Emily's easygoing mother's. She was serene, cool, affable without sacrificing an iota of dignity. Emily couldn't imagine her ever shouting or throwing a piece of crockery. No guest at her table would stand on a chair or topple out of one in a drunken stupor. It was quite relaxing.

And Aunt Julia had thrown herself into Emily's introduction into society with an endearing enthusiasm, declaring that it had always been a great disappointment to her that she had no daughters. She had been efficient, decisive, always utterly clear—like a general planning a campaign, assembling her stores and ammunition, preparing to launch an offensive. Emily had been impressed, and appreciative, though it was a little uncomfortable being the object of so much concentrated attention after her unregarded youth.

Her aunt's efforts seemed designed to refashion her from head to heels. And wasn't that all to the good? She had wanted a different sort of life. It was logical that she should change to meet it.

Above all else, her aunt was plotting to introduce her to legions of the "right sort of young man." This was the goal of all their activity, all the admonition and advice. Emily wondered what these young men would be like. As far as she knew, she had never encountered such a creature. The right sort of young man, she repeated silently, watching the dancers. She tried to picture one in her mind. Tall, with an athletic figure, an expression that promised intelligence, strength, generosity. He wouldn't have to be incredibly handsome, but there would be something appealing about him that… She was picturing Richard Sheldon, Emily realized with a shock.

Something had seemed very right about him, she

acknowledged. When they had walked together across the field, she had felt so...alive. She had felt his heartbeat under her hand.

Emily shook her head. What was the matter with her? She was never going to see him again. Why had she thought of him at all?

"Sit like a queen," said her aunt Julia. "How you carry yourself is very important."

Guiltily, Emily straightened. She was so used to leaning back in her chair and daydreaming. It was the one thing she was worried about—her errant imagination and the remarks that came out of her mouth as a result of it. There were things one was supposed to talk about, and many more things one was never to mention. Most particularly, the thousands of questions that buzzed in Emily's head were not acceptable conversation. Indeed, she had already shocked her seemingly imperturbable aunt more than once with the things she knew—and those she didn't.

Holding her head high, she gave her aunt a sidelong glance. Her mother had assured her that Aunt Julia knew everything there was to know about society and that she could have no better advisor in negotiating its intricacies. Emily felt deeply grateful to have such a guide.

In her aunt's house everything ran so smoothly that her needs were fulfilled almost before she recognized them. It was completely unlike home, as if she had been transported into one of those fairy tales where magical servitors anticipate every wish. And then the poor heroine makes a mistake and is plunged into disaster, Emily couldn't help thinking.

Realizing that she was leaning back again, she sat straighter. A London season couldn't be any more difficult than the vicissitudes of her life so far. In fact, she was thoroughly trained in dealing with the unexpected. Why, her father had once invited a pickpocket to dinner to meet the dean of the local cathedral. Could she encounter a more awkward situation among the *haut ton*? Not likely.

"That is Elsmere," murmured her aunt, discreetly indicating a young man dancing by. "Very eligible."

Emily turned back to the dance floor. The waltz was graceful. To be held so close to a man one hardly knew must be rather interesting. The dancers shifted and Emily gave an involuntary gasp.

"What is it?" said her aunt.

"That gentleman there—dancing with the woman in yellow."

The duchess searched the crowd.

"Isn't that...Mr. Sheldon?"

Her aunt examined him for a moment. "He looks a bit...different. But yes, his name is Sheldon. Not mister, however. He is Baron Warrington." She frowned. "Someone told me he had been lost at sea."

"Baron," echoed Emily. He had said nothing about that.

"You know him?"

"He...he had an accident on the road and stopped at our house."

"Really?"

Her aunt's tone made Emily uneasy. "Just for a few minutes."

"Don't tell me you developed a *tendre* for him?"

Intimidated by the ferocity of Aunt Julia's expression, Emily shook her head. "We scarcely exchanged five words." Which was true. No need to mention the walk across the field.

"Quite unsuitable, you know. He hasn't a sou. That family's been all to pieces since my father's day."

Mr. Sheldon—Baron Warrington—waltzed quite expertly Emily noticed. "So he is not the 'right sort'?" she wondered a little wistfully.

"Emily! You must *not* say such things!" Aunt Julia looked around, making certain no one had overheard.

A young lady showed no interest in the question of matrimony, Emily remembered. All that sort of thing was handled by her elders. Which was a splendid thought, really, particularly after years of having to deal with everything herself. "I beg your pardon," she murmured.

Satisfied, her aunt turned back to the crowd. "No, he isn't," she conceded very quietly. "Not only is he penniless, his manners aren't exactly…engaging."

This surprised Emily. "He was perfectly polite to Papa, even when he wished to paint him as Samson."

"Emily!"

She flushed. "I'm sorry. I forgot."

Aunt Julia had informed her that her parents' ramshackle establishment and their scandalous past was a social liability. The gossips would like nothing better than to revive the story about their elopement, which would be very embarrassing.

"He met Alasdair?" The duchess looked distressed.

When Emily nodded, her aunt looked despairing.

"He will wreck everything."

"How?"

"He is a famous wit," replied the duchess bitterly. "He will make a fine story of Alasdair. Oh lud, Olivia, too. If I had known…"

"He didn't seem like the sort of person who would…"

"He ruined the Stanley chit. Caused her to retire to some godforsaken place in Scotland and breed terriers. Only because her nose was a trifle…large. What he will say about Alasdair…" She struggled for control. "It was long ago, of course. Perhaps he never heard the story."

"He called Mama 'the Marquess of Shelbury's lost daughter,'" Emily felt obliged to tell her.

The duchess moaned.

"Mama wasn't the least bit embarrassed."

"She never comes to London," was the acerbic reply.

"It is easy to care nothing for society's opinion when you don't get within a hundred miles of it."

Emily acknowledged the truth of that. But she still couldn't reconcile the Richard Sheldon she had met with the man her aunt was describing. "B-baron Warrington was quite civil to all of us."

The duchess turned and focused her gaze on Emily. "Why?"

"What?"

"Did he need help from you?"

"He…he wanted to borrow a horse."

"Hah." Aunt Julia looked triumphant. "You see."

"But aunt…"

The duchess's attention had shifted. "He has been away for an age," she murmured. "Where, I wonder? If there was anything disreputable about it…"

"Aunt!"

"Warrington has no scruples. So we can't afford any."

The waltz ended. The baron escorted his partner off the floor. He was dressed in the height of fashion now, Emily noted, and he looked irritated.

"The best defense is a frontal assault," muttered Aunt Julia. She appeared to be running calculations in her head. "Come. You will have to renew your acquaintance. I have met his mother," she announced in more normal tones.

"Perhaps later," Emily ventured, her feelings wildly mixed. "He is probably already…"

"Nonsense. Come."

She had no choice but to follow her aunt across the floor. Richard Sheldon had gone to stand beside an older woman who somewhat resembled him. He looked very handsome, but there were a number of very handsome men in the crowded ballroom. He stood out like a hawk among roosters. What was it that made him so different? It was something in his stance, Emily decided, in the way his hands hung at his sides and his body moved inside his clothes.

"Lady Fielding," said her aunt, very much the duchess. "How do you do?"

The woman standing next to Richard looked surprised, and then very pleased, to be addressed. "Very well, thank you, duchess. You know my son, Richard?"

"Warrington, isn't it?" replied Emily's aunt. "I believe you are acquainted with my boy Philip." There was no trace of concern in her aunt's expression or tone, Emily noted.

Richard nodded. He hadn't taken his eyes off her, Emily thought. He was staring as if he were a hawk indeed. Her aunt had assured her she looked lovely. Her ball gown was finer than any garment she had ever owned, of pale blue satin overlaid with white gauze and trimmed with blue ribbons. A matching ribbon threaded through her hair, which had been sculpted into an intricate mass of curls. It had taken almost an hour to achieve the style, and the wisps and ringlets that the fashionable haircutter had teased out around her forehead and cheeks tickled and made her want to brush them back, which she had been strictly forbidden to do.

"May I introduce my niece, Emily Crane," said Aunt Julia grandly. "I am presenting her this season."

"Indeed?" Lady Fielding gave Emily a polite smile. "I hope you are enjoying yourself."

Before Emily could speak, her aunt said, "This is her first ball. She knows very few people in London as yet."

Lady Fielding looked at her son. So did the duchess.

Richard gave a small bow. "Would you care to dance?" he said.

Emily's eyes flew to her aunt, expecting some excuse for a refusal. After what she had said about Mr. Sheldon, she couldn't send Emily off alone with him.

But the duchess merely smiled benignly.

What was she up to? What did she expect her to do? They were all looking at her. She stammered out an acceptance. Richard took possession of her hand as if he owned it and swept her out to join the country-dance just forming.

The transformation was amazing, Richard thought as they began the first figure. The pretty young woman he had met in the country had been polished into a fashionable beauty in an amazingly short space of time.

They moved down the line of dancers and turned at the end, holding up their arms for the next couple to pass under.

Emily outshone most of the other women in the room—which wasn't really surprising if the duchess of Welford had taken her in hand.

"I didn't realize you were coming up to London," he said as they turned.

"It was decided later."

Perhaps it wouldn't be so bad being stuck here in town after all. Up to now, beset by his mother's anxiety whenever he was out of her sight, he had despaired. The simple act of replenishing his wardrobe—a task that had once occupied all his faculties—had rubbed him raw. The fact that all his old things were too tight in the chest and arms, which he once would have seen as a marvelous opportunity to rig himself out in the very latest mode, now was merely an annoyance. Emily Crane promised a refreshing break from the irritations of society.

He looked down at her, remembering the feel of her slender body against his, her calm acceptance of the oddest events. That memory was more vivid than anything that had ever happened to him in rooms like this. Her eyes were downcast. He ought to speak Richard realized. "Your mother remained in contact with her sister?"

She threw him a quick glance, looking almost frightened, then nodded.

"I wouldn't have thought they would get on. It's hard to imagine people more different."

This earned him another glance, but no reply.

"One of the leading hostesses of the *ton* and a woman who doesn't care a whit for society," he elaborated, thinking that he might not have been clear. "It's amazing to think that they grew up in the same household."

He expected that Emily would expand on this interesting conundrum, but she only nodded, her expression stiff.

"I wouldn't have thought your father would send you to stay with a duchess," he added, smiling to show he meant it as a small joke.

Emily made a choking sound.

What was wrong with her? She hadn't seemed at all shy when he met her before, certainly not tongue-tied or missish. "What do you think of London?" he asked, confident that she would have an original perspective.

"It is very interesting. My aunt took me to see the pictures at the Royal Academy."

"Indeed? An odd choice of amusements."

She gazed up at him, her blue eyes wary.

"Paintings are hardly a novelty in your life, growing up, as you did, with artists. Your aunt might have chosen something less familiar." She was acting as if he spoke a language that she scarcely comprehended; and as if she weren't very happy to be dancing with him.

"What did you think of them?" he inquired, a bit curtly.

"Of…?"

"The paintings at the Royal Academy. I assume your father's work is more…animated than what the Academy hangs?"

Emily bit her lower lip.

What had happened to her? Or perhaps he had been mistaken in his first impression. He had been rather groggy. Tonight, she was as boring as any deb—more so.

"Which pictures, precisely, did you like?" He heard the sarcasm in his voice.

"The portrait of the Duke of Wellington was very fine."

"So *everyone* says."

"Yes, well, they say the likeness is—"

"Striking. So I have been told. *Repeatedly*."

The snub made her flush.

Richard felt a twinge of regret, immediately submerged by impatience. He had a strong desire to walk away. It took a considerable effort of self-control to keep dancing.

"You…you haven't been to see the show?"

"No. I've been rather busy." Richard's mind wandered back to his own concerns. Busy trying to reassure his mother and separate her from Herr Schelling, busy fending off his friends' assumptions that he would be resuming his old life as if he had never been away. They were all fools, he thought, looking around the ballroom. What would they do if their luxurious life were suddenly snatched away?

He realized that Emily had said something. "What?"

She flinched slightly. "I wondered if you are in town for the whole season?"

"I hope not."

She looked surprised at his vehemence.

"You are, I suppose?"

Emily nodded.

"My felicitations."

Her chin came up at this, but it was a pale shadow of the spirit he thought he had seen in the country.

"My aunt has been very generous," she declared.

"Has she?"

Emily blinked at him.

"What else has she to do? Gossip?"

This elicited a look so timorous that he lost all desire to converse with her. Clearly, he had mistaken her character.

They completed a figure of the dance in silence.

"I trust you are fully recovered?" said Emily then.

"Recovered?" he echoed.

"From the…the incident on the road."

"Ah." Couldn't she dare the word *attack*? "Of course."

"And you have not had any further…?"

Richard waited, but she didn't finish the sentence. "What?" he asked finally.

"Nothing."

Nothing was the word for it, Richard concluded. She had nothing more in her head than any of the other wide-eyed young debs. He had never had much interest in such creatures, and he had absolutely none now. The music ended; and with relief, Richard returned Emily to the duchess and left her there.

❧

Emily watched him walk away, feeling rather low. Baron Warrington was quite a different creature from the man she had met at home. He was cold and sarcastic. He spoke as if he were setting traps. She had tried to behave as her aunt had instructed, to show him that she could be at ease in society, where he seemed so perfectly at home. But she had been thrown off by the fear that he meant to gossip about her parents to all his London acquaintances. Would she turn the details of her home into anecdotes for the sniggers of the *ton*? She had experienced that kind of snide mockery often enough in her life, and she didn't like it in the least.

"Did you enjoy the dance?" asked the duchess sharply.

"Not particularly."

"Emily."

A young lady does not have strong opinions, Emily remembered, especially negative ones. "I…I mean, yes, aunt, it was very pleasant."

Her aunt nodded like a governess acknowledging a correct answer. "Was he rude to you?"

"No. Not exactly."

"What do you mean?"

"He was just…rather sarcastic."

"He is well known for that."

She had totally mistaken his character in their brief earlier meeting. Her aunt did seem to know best about these unfamiliar creatures—the denizens of society.

"We will call on Lady Fielding tomorrow," declared the duchess.

Emily gaped at her.

"We must lose no time in cultivating the acquaintance."

"But aunt, I don't really want…" She could do without further setdowns from Richard Sheldon.

Aunt Julia waved this aside. "If Warrington is seen to spend time with you, escort you here and there, it will be far more difficult for him to spread scandalous stories about your family."

"I don't think he will wish to escort me anywhere."

"His wishes are irrelevant."

"But…"

Her aunt silenced her with a gesture. "You needn't be concerned about this. That is why a girl has a sponsor in society—to manage such things."

Her cousin George, Aunt Julia's second son, joined them. He had been drafted as Emily's official escort this evening. Large, blond, and good-natured, he closely resembled his father the duke, who had greeted Emily's arrival in his house with absent courtesy. She had a strong suspicion that the duke, and all three sons of the household, viewed her chiefly as an amusement for Aunt Julia, as if she had suddenly taken up horticulture or knitting.

"That Anne is queer as Dick's hatband," said George. He had been dancing with the daughter of the house, whose presentation ball this was.

"Slang, George," admonished her aunt.

"I beg your pardon, ma'am. But she is a bit much."

The countess of Holburn's daughter Anne was tall and sturdy with dark hair and somewhat prominent green eyes. She had an almost insolent air, and when they were introduced, she had concentrated all her attention on George, scarcely glancing at Emily or her aunt.

"You will clearly outshine her," said the duchess, scanning the room critically. "I haven't seen Maundseley's girl since she was ten. Have you, George? You know her brother."

"Bad skin," replied her son.

"Ah," said the duchess with obvious satisfaction. "And the Wetherby chit seems frightened of her own shadow. No threat there."

"You make the Season sound like some sort of contest, Aunt," Emily ventured.

"Not at all," was the airy response. The duchess didn't shift her gaze from the crowd.

George caught the eye of a servant and provided them all with champagne. Remembering her instructions, Emily merely sipped.

A few minutes later, when her aunt was diverted by an acquaintance, Emily looked up at George. He seemed very much at home in this setting. "Do you know Lord Warrington?" she asked him.

"Eh?" He started as if one of the gilt chairs had spoken to him. "Warrington? Of course." He seemed miffed at the suggestion that he might not know someone.

"What sort of man is he?"

George goggled at her.

It probably was the sort of question she wasn't supposed to ask, but she didn't care. Fixing her cousin with a steady gaze, she waited.

"Er…he's…" George frowned in unaccustomed concentration. "Got a deuced sharp tongue. Modish; up to every rig and row in town." His gaze sharpened suddenly. "You ain't setting your cap in that direction, are you, because…"

"No." She gave him a look that made his mouth snap shut. "Is Lord Warrington a great gossip?"

"Fellows don't gossip," George protested. At her raised eyebrows, he added, "Know all the *on dits*, of course. Warrington tells a dashed good story. A wit, you know. I remember one time he was…" He flushed and stopped abruptly.

"At others' expense?"

George didn't seem to understand what she meant, but his account agreed with his mother's. Emily felt a lowering of her spirits.

"Ah, here is Beatrice with a partner for you," declared the duchess. "Young Hanford, I believe. Very good."

The countess stopped in front of them, facing her aunt. Emily had a sudden image of two duelists extending their pistols, preparing to fire. The air seemed to quiver as the two women smiled at each other.

Emily took the hand of the smiling young man, and moved into the dance. And into the small hours of the morning, this process went on. Either the countess or Aunt Julia would approach with a gentleman in tow, present him, and then send them out onto the floor. Their appearance varied, but all of them were the honorable this or lord that, and they all seemed to say the same things to her. And to expect the same responses. The one time she ventured to stray from the accepted subject, her partner looked down with such a startled expression that Emily subsided, afraid she had made a terrible gaff.

How had Cinderella really felt at the ball? she wondered on the way home. How would she have liked hours of fittings for her new finery, instead of having it conjured up in a moment by her fairy godmother? And what had she found to talk about with Prince Charming?

Four

"YOU HAVE A FITTING FOR YOUR NEW RIDING HABIT AT eleven," said the duchess the following morning at the breakfast table. "Henry's chosen you a horse." She ticked off two items on a long list that lay beside her plate. "Tonight is the Wetherbys' rout party. We'll call on Lady Fielding in the afternoon."

"Perhaps another day would be better," ventured Emily.

Her aunt shook her head. "On the contrary. It is vital that we move quickly, before he has time to…" She waved her hand, indicating disaster.

"I don't think… That is, couldn't we wait…?"

Her aunt looked at Emily with raised eyebrows. "I thought you had decided to be presented?"

Puzzled, Emily nodded.

"You yourself decided?"

What did she mean by that?

"Making one's entrance into society is a delicate process. Particularly when you have certain…disadvantages."

Emily frowned at her.

"That is not a criticism, merely a statement of fact. I know the system intimately and am expert in working it. I thought you had accepted my guidance."

"Yes, but…"

"Good. I do have your best interests at heart, you know."

She did, Emily thought. She had opened her home; she had spent a great deal of money on Emily with apparent pleasure. She was totally engrossed in advancing her niece's interests. And this was familiar territory for her, alien as it seemed to Emily. She reminded herself that she *did* want a more settled life. Aunt Julia was trying to get it for her.

❧

This reasoning did nothing to calm Emily's nerves as they drove the short distance to Lady Fielding's house. Richard probably wouldn't even be there. Of course he wouldn't be there. Undoubtedly he had his own chambers elsewhere. Reassured, she relaxed in the seat.

When they pulled up, however, they found another carriage waiting. They had barely stepped down when Richard emerged from the front door with his mother on his arm.

"We appear to have called at an inopportune time," commented the duchess.

"No, no. We were just going to the park," said Lady Fielding. "Take the carriage back to the stables, Ben. Please come in, duchess."

Richard looked annoyed, Emily thought.

"Why don't we all go to the park?" said her aunt. "We can take my barouche."

With a small flurry of conversation, it was settled. Richard handed the three ladies into the carriage and climbed in after them. The driver slapped the reins, and they were off.

"A delightful day for a drive," suggested the duchess blandly. Lady Fielding agreed, and the two older women initiated a flow of commonplaces to fill the silence. Emily risked a glance at Richard, sitting beside her on the forward seat. He looked intensely bored. Her aunt was staring at her, Emily realized. Guiltily, she straightened in her seat and smiled. Her aunt nodded very slightly and looked away.

The park was busy, as it was, in fact, a very fine spring day. The duchess and Lady Fielding acknowledged acquaintances as they passed. Emily had just concluded that this outing would not be so difficult after all when the duchess said, "Perhaps you would like to walk a little, Emily?"

She had to repress a start at being called back from her own thoughts. "Oh…yes."

The carriage was stopped and the footman jumped down to open the door. Emily stepped to the gravel drive and hesitated. Was her aunt coming? But both the older women were looking at Richard, who responded by joining her and offering his arm. Not joyously, Emily noted.

"Would you care to see the Grecian temple?" asked Richard in a colorless voice.

Emily glanced up at him. He looked like a man going through the motions. There was no trace of the person she had helped across the fields, the one who had spoken to her forthrightly and without affectation. That was because she had imagined him, Emily told herself sharply. "Yes, thank you."

He led her along a landscaped path toward a small building ornamented with columns and carvings. Flowers had been planted all around it, and in urns along the pediment. "It's pretty," Emily ventured.

"If you like fakery."

This silenced her. They strolled toward the temple, properly in full view of the duchess and Lady Fielding, who sat chatting in the carriage.

His arm was hard and unyielding under her hand. His face was equally stiff. No one was going to believe that he was enjoying her company. Her aunt's scheme was doomed. She looked around the park, desperate for some suitable, interesting topic. A spot of color caught her eye. "Look."

Richard turned and the boredom vanished from his expression. "It's a balloon."

"What?" Emily watched the gaily striped sphere drift upward. It was high above the rooftops already.

"A balloon. A silk bag filled with gas that is lighter than air. That's why it rises."

"Lighter than air? How could anything be lighter?"

"The various gases it contains have different properties. If one separates out the less dense element, it will lift even quite heavy objects." His gaze was fixed on the still rising balloon. "It gives us flight."

"Us?" echoed Emily.

"Mankind. There are aeronauts in the basket hanging below the bag. You can just see it."

She squinted. There was indeed something dangling from the bright sphere.

"An ancient dream finally coming true," Richard murmured.

"Wishing for wings, you mean?"

He stared down at her with such intensity that Emily was abashed. "How will they get down?" she asked to divert him.

He continued to gaze at her for another moment. "They let out gas to descend, drop weights to rise higher."

"You know a great deal about it," said Emily, impressed.

Abruptly, he looked self-conscious. Turning away from the balloon, he led her along the front of the Grecian temple. "I have read about such things," he answered, his voice once more emotionless. "Shall we return to the carriage?"

Emily started to ask another question. But something moved in the corner of her eye, and she turned, startled. An urn on the roof of the temple was toppling slowly over the edge of the pediment. In the next instant, Emily was snatched off her feet and tumbled to the ground in

Richard Sheldon's arms. The urn crashed into the pavement where they had been standing and shattered in a rain of soil and stems.

Emily felt the flying shards of pottery strike Richard's back. His body had wrapped around hers, shielding her almost completely from the projectiles and taking most of the impact of their fall. She rested in his embrace, breathless and a little dazed. He had moved so fast, and so decisively. There had been no time to think. He had somehow just known. It had been the same when he lunged at Jonathan in the field behind her house, Emily remembered; this very large man suddenly became a blur of lethal motion.

A man shouted behind them. Shrieks sounded from the direction of their carriage.

Richard's body was all muscle, like sprung steel. It felt as if he could hold her forever, effortlessly. Emily began to feel odd, tingling with energy and languorous all at once.

"Are you all right?" he asked.

His lips were inches from her ear, which made the question seem intimate and intensely personal. A flush of heat washed over Emily. She made a soft affirmative sound that surprised her.

Richard untangled himself and rose, pulling her up after him. Emily swayed a little on her feet.

In the next instant, Lady Fielding hurled herself at Richard, keening at the top of her lungs. He caught her and held her against his chest. "It's all right, Mother. No harm done."

"You were nearly killed!"

"Not at all. We had stepped out of the way. Mother, calm yourself."

Stepped out of the way? That hardly described it. But watching Lady Fielding wail and wring her hands, Emily could see why he would make light of the incident. She

took a deep breath. There had been something just before
the urn fell, some small movement barely glimpsed. She
took another breath, regaining her equilibrium. Emily
started around the temple to look for some sign of what
it might be.

"Are you all right?" asked her aunt.

"Yes, I am just going to…"

"What a very distressing accident."

"I'm not sure…"

"I believe we had better get Lady Fielding home. She
is quite…distraught." The duchess's expression showed
her low opinion of such displays of emotion. It also
seemed to contain a glint of satisfaction.

"I want to look behind the temple."

"Behind it? Whatever for?"

Emily didn't feel her aunt would respond well to
her suspicions. "We should tell someone about this…
accident," she ventured instead.

"You may be sure I shall. Disgraceful carelessness."

Lady Fielding had descended into hysterics, Emily
saw. She could not keep her from home. With great
reluctance, looking back over her shoulder more than
once, she returned to the carriage. On the drive back,
she bent all her faculties to recalling that moment when
she had seen—what? A movement? The urn itself, or
someone pushing it?

The duchess was soothing Lady Fielding with her
vinaigrette. The latter had subsided into weeping now.

At the house, the duchess took over, sending a
messenger for Lady Fielding's physician and sum-
moning her dresser and a covey of maids. All of them
supported Richard's mother up the stairs, leaving
Richard and Emily standing in the front hall gazing
after them.

"She is easily upset since my…absence," said Richard,
as if to himself.

Emily had, of course, heard the story of his shipwreck. It was a choice bit of gossip among the *ton*. "I'm sure she'll be all right."

He nodded, eyes still on the stairs, then turned to her. "You should sit down. Would you care for anything? No doubt you are quite shaken by the—"

"I think someone pushed that urn. I may have seen… well, I'm not sure."

Richard looked skeptical.

"There was something," she insisted. "A movement. Why should the urn fall otherwise?"

"A crack in the base," he suggested. "A flaw in the wall under it."

"But after the way those men attacked you on the road…"

"Footpads."

"They did not act like footpads. Don't you think it suspicious that they—?"

"My dear Miss Crane, you read too many sensational novels."

"I don't read any."

"You will *not* mention this foolishness to my mother."

Emily drew herself up. "I would never do such a thing."

"Or to anyone else either." He shook his head. "What an *on dit* that would make. Warrington thinks himself persecuted. I suppose I was deliberately marooned in the wilderness as well?"

Emily hadn't thought of this. "Could it have been arranged?"

Richard gave a harsh laugh. "Indeed. By someone in direct communication with the Almighty. Or perhaps a sorcerer who summons storms? I beg you to curb these idiotic flights of fancy, Miss Crane."

"You have to admit—"

"Stop it!" His voice was like a whip. "I have no patience with this lunacy. You will drop it at once."

Before Emily could reply, her aunt appeared at the head of the stairs and began to descend.

"How is she?" asked Richard.

"Better. She is asking for you."

Richard started up, then hesitated. "Do you need...?"

The duchess waved him on. "No need to see us out."

With a nod of thanks, he strode up the stairs. Emily turned to walk out with her aunt. She didn't see Richard pause on the upper landing and stare intently after her.

"A volatile woman," commented the duchess as they returned to their carriage. "She has endured a difficult time, of course. But a bit more fortitude..." She shook her head as they started off.

What was behind the attacks? Emily wondered. If she was right, a determined killer was after Lord Warrington. She bit her lower lip. Was she right? Was she imagining things? She frowned. The men at the pond had been solid and very real. But today...she couldn't be sure. Perhaps the movement had been the balloon? There was no way to know. And it was no business of hers, in any case. Lord Warrington clearly did not want her opinion. She should put the matter from her mind. But she couldn't.

❧

Stepping down from the carriage in Grosvenor Square, Emily noticed that a caller was departing from one of the neighbors, escorted by all four daughters of the house. That was odd. Only the eldest was out. The younger sisters would not be receiving callers. As her aunt entered the house with a sweep of draperies, she hesitated. The caller made his final farewells and sauntered down the pavement toward her. "Daniel Fitzgibbon," she blurted out.

The man stopped, stared at her, and then came forward slowly. He didn't look gratified by her notice. And no wonder—the last time Emily had seen him, he had been head of a company of motley traveling players just one step ahead of a magistrate.

Coming up to her, he bowed most elegantly. "Miss Crane."

"How…how are you?"

"Very well, thank you. And you?" He glanced up at the imposing mansion behind them.

"I'm staying with my aunt."

"Ah."

"What are you…?" Emily hesitated once again. Her father had befriended this man, and she rather liked him herself. But he did have some dubious habits; things had been known to go missing from the towns where his company of actors performed. If he was playing these tricks on her aunt's neighbors… Emily glanced uneasily at the house. Aunt Julia would *not* approve of the connection.

Fitzgibbon smiled as if he could follow her thought processes. "I am an exceedingly fashionable dancing master to the young ladies of the *haut ton*," he told her.

Emily couldn't help but stare.

The man raised his eyebrows, waiting.

"Dancing master?"

He gave her a slight bow. "I am a very fine dancer."

Emily remembered the complicated dances in some of his performances. "Yes, but…how did you come to be teaching?"

The footman holding the front door coughed discreetly. Emily heard her aunt's questioning voice from inside.

"A complicated story," said Fitzgibbon. He made a gesture indicating that he did not wish to tell it in a public street. "Will you bubble me?" he added with some urgency.

"No. That is… I don't…"

"Emily?" said her aunt, appearing in the doorway.

Bowing once again, Fitzgibbon handed her a card, tipped his hat, and walked quickly away.

"Who is that you were talking to?"

Emily slipped the card into her reticule. "The Talbots have engaged him as dancing master for the girls," She hurried up the steps and into the house.

"Dancing? Is that the fellow everyone's talking of? Maria Talbot was telling me he's even got Margaret moving with a bit of grace." She frowned. "But I do not understand why you were speaking with him."

"I…I was thinking I could use some lessons," Emily said in a rush. "I have had so little practice dancing."

"Hmm. Perhaps." Her aunt turned and started up the stairs. "I am glad to see you taking an interest in your social skills," she added with more warmth.

Emily kept her head down as she followed Aunt Julia upstairs. She hadn't exactly lied to her. No, she had simply neglected to tell the truth, jeered another inner voice.

In her own room, she took out Fitzgibbon's card, only to discover that the name engraved on it was Edwin Gerrity. What if she had mentioned his name? She sat down abruptly in the armchair under the window. How many of her father's collection of eccentrics were now in London? she wondered suddenly. They included a great many disreputable figures, and a few out-and-out scoundrels. If Daniel Fitzgibbon, thieving actor, could so easily become Edwin Gerrity and enter the houses of the *haut ton*, what else might happen? The possibilities daunted her. Aunt Julia would be furious.

Emily went to the small writing desk in the corner and put the card safely inside. She had to keep her two lives firmly separated. There was no room in this household for characters like Fitzgibbon/Gerrity. Imagining him here was as difficult as picturing her Aunt Julia among Papa's

paints. She swallowed. Completely separate, she thought.
It was the only answer. Everything would be fine as long
as she held to that resolve.

☙

Richard folded his arms across his chest as his mother's
carriage started off along the cobblestones. He glowered at the tufted blue velvet lining the interior. He
had tried to forbid this expedition. But his mother
had resorted to tears and laments about the incident
in the park, and he had had to yield. He had also had
to accompany her, wasting his time and spoiling his
temper. But he wasn't about to send her alone into the
clutches of Herr Schelling.

She sat happily beside him, gazing out the window.
When would she recover her spirits? When would she
be able to contemplate his leaving London without falling into a despond? This fearful, clinging woman was so
unlike the mother he remembered.

A wave of compassion overtook him. He had changed.
No doubt she felt the same bewilderment over the son
who had returned to her. And she had mourned his death
for a long time. She could be allowed more than a week
or two to recover. "Are you warm enough, Mother?"

She turned and smiled at him. "Yes, thank you, dear."

Her expression touched him. He had given her a good
deal of pain over the last year. And in the years before
that. The old persona was all too easy to resume, but he
wasn't going to do that.

"It is so good to have you home again," she added.
"Nothing was the same with you…gone."

A year ago, he would have dismissed this as maudlin
sentiment, Richard thought. But he could see the emotion in her eyes.

"Even the Season seemed a lot of silly posturing."
She looked self-conscious and gave a brief laugh. "How

people would stare to hear me say that. Of course, it is all right now that you are back."

Richard watched her visibly gather the elements of her social self around her. Family connections went deeper than the roles individuals played in the world, he saw. But one didn't always understand that until a crisis struck.

"I'm afraid Herr Schelling lives quite out of the world. In Kensington," said his mother in another tone entirely. "But he says the vibrations there are good for his work."

"Indeed?"

She nodded. "There is a rift in the etheric envelope that allows him to reach through to the other realm."

"A what?"

Lady Fielding gestured airily. "A rift. I don't understand it precisely, of course."

"Of course." Because it was gibberish, Richard added silently.

"But it does help Herr Schelling do the most amazing things."

"Such as?"

His exceedingly dry tone earned him a doubtful glance.

"Besides communicating with my supposedly deceased spirit," he added.

"That was a mistake," she acknowledged. "But Herr Schelling was wondering… You do not think, Richard, that you received any sort of etheric communications when you were trapped in that awful jungle?"

"No, Mother, I do not."

"You might not have noticed them, you see, because they are very subtle…"

"Vanishingly so."

"Richard."

He subsided. He had promised to keep his sentiments to himself on this expedition. It was going to be even more difficult than he had imagined.

Herr Schelling lived in a respectable looking house

on a quiet street in this unfashionable suburb. The maid who admitted them looked quite ordinary, as did the furnishings Richard glimpsed, though they were rather luxurious for a man in his position. Apparently, Herr Schelling paid some heed to the physical plane as well as the etheric.

The upstairs room to which they were taken was different. Its only furniture was a large round table in the center, set on a circular carpet decorated with stars and surrounded by straight chairs. All the walls were muffled with heavy dark draperies. The only light came from a branch of candles set on the table.

A few people stood about the room, talking softly. Herr Schelling surged forward from among them and held out both his hands. "My dear Lady Fielding. How splendid to see you in my humble abode once more."

Richard almost snorted. What sort of man could actually utter the words "humble abode"?

"Lord Warrington," said their host. "You also are most welcome."

Restraining himself, Richard merely nodded.

"I believe we are ready." Schelling turned and gestured. Richard followed his mother to a pair of chairs and sat beside her. When they were settled, a large weeping woman was led in and seated. Herr Schelling materialized next to her, wearing his bulging turban now. When had he put it on? Where had he gotten it? Richard looked around the room, noting how hard it was to see anything in the shrouded corners. The man was slippery as a barrel of eels.

Schelling snuffed all but one of the candles, then sat in the last empty chair. Those seated next to him took his extended hands and the entire group began to link hands as well. Richard allowed his mother to grasp his hand, but he nearly balked when the other was taken in a limp clammy grasp. Turning to protest, he found a thin, timorous woman who evaded his gaze as if it were a blow. The limp fingers trembled in his. Grimacing, Richard turned away again. He should have forced his mother to stay home. He should have argued much more vehemently.

Their host moaned, and the circle stirred with anticipation. The candle flame fluttered in an errant breeze.

"We call across the great gulf of dissolution to the other realm," Schelling chanted in a high, nasal voice. "We reach through the mists and darkness that obscure it. We seek Wendel, newly passed over in the prime of his life."

Some relative of the weeping woman, Richard concluded. His distaste for this farce nearly overwhelmed him.

"Bring him hither, my messengers," continued Schelling. "Azrael. Phileto. Bring him!"

The draperies stirred. The candle dipped and smoked. There was a creaking sound.

"He is coming!" intoned their host. "He is near."

A dog began barking somewhere. Richard almost laughed aloud at the intrusion of this prosaic noise. Did Herr Schelling keep a pug?

"Wendel?" cried a tremulous voice. "Is that you, Wendel?"

The barking grew more rapid.

"Wendel!"

A strangled choke escaped Richard, the product of outrage and laughter colliding and being stifled by consideration for his mother's feelings. All this rigmarole for a dead dog? This put him in his place—the group apparently ranked deceased sons and pets about equal.

"He cannot speak," said Herr Schelling, to Richard's disappointment. "But I sense he is well."

"Does…does he have enough to eat?" quavered the large woman.

This was unconscionable, Richard thought—playing

on the grief of this woman, as on his mother's. He was going to see that Schelling was thrown out of England.

There was not much more. Schelling made a few more moaning sounds and then "came back to himself." The candles were relit. Clasped hands were released. The maid appeared to invite the group downstairs for refreshment, Schelling pretending to be too drained to act the host. Richard hung back a bit to let the others go ahead, then took his mother's arm firmly. "We're going," he said.

"But the evening isn't…"

"Now," he insisted. He led her down to the entry and out into the street. "How can you tolerate that man?" he asked his mother.

"He has abilities."

"To contact a dead dog?"

Lady Fielding looked doubtful. "It was a little odd, wasn't it? We never had a dog before."

"I think you should give up seeing him."

"He was such a help to me."

"He is a charlatan. Do you imagine that nonsense tonight was real?"

His mother looked thoughtful. "It does seem strange that there are dogs in the spirit realm."

Richard rubbed his eyes with one hand.

"It might have been a hoax," she added.

He blinked in surprise and pleasure. "Of course it was a…"

"Myra has given him a number of gifts, you know. Perhaps he wished to make some return for her generosity."

"Gifts?"

Lady Fielding nodded. "He doesn't ask for anything, naturally."

"Doesn't he?"

"Oh, no. Too proud. But his assistant lets one know how difficult it is for him to sustain his work."

"Indeed. What is her name?" That would be a place to start, he thought.

"Umm. Sarah, I believe." She nodded to herself. "I have been thinking of asking him to contact Walter."

Richard sat bolt upright on the cushions.

"I do miss him, you know."

He nodded. He could acknowledge now that his step-father had been a kind and generous man. How much more his mother must feel.

She frowned. "Perhaps you think I should look for your father instead."

Richard scarcely remembered his father. Even had he believed in Schelling's powers, he wouldn't have thought to seek him.

"But it has been so long…"

"You cannot reach either of them, Mother. Schelling's claims are utterly false."

"It would be wonderful to hear Walter's voice once more," she replied, as if she hadn't heard a word. "He always knew just the thing to say. He was so…comforting."

"He was a good man. But—I'm sorry, Mother—he is gone."

"Well, I know that."

Her change of tone gave Richard hopes for a moment.

"I would just like to talk to him, you know," she went on, deflating them. "I'll send a note round to Herr Schelling tomorrow. He'll know just what to do."

Staring grimly out into the night, Richard made no reply.

Five

THE DUCHESS CAME INTO EMILY'S BEDCHAMBER AND ran an expert eye over her. Emily shifted a little under that critical gaze, telling herself that her gown of sea green muslin was impeccable and her hair was styled in a most becoming cloud of curls. "Very nice," her aunt said.

This was high praise from Aunt Julia. Emily gathered her dark green wrap and followed her out to the stairs.

"I think you will like Vauxhall Gardens," the duchess declared as they walked. "The fireworks are very pretty." Emily murmured her agreement.

"We have received a prodigious number of invitations. I do believe you are making a hit. And we certainly needn't worry about Warrington any longer after his disgraceful behavior in the park."

"Disgraceful?"

"Throwing you down in that odious way and positively rolling about on the ground. Everyone is talking of it." She raised a hand. "No one blames you, of course. It was all Warrington. He was...ferocious." Her expression showed how shocking she had found the incident.

"He saved me from being crushed by that urn," objected Emily.

"A gentleman would have done so in quite another manner."

"How?"

The duchess gave her an admonitory glance. "I don't know, my dear, but he certainly would not have grabbed you so...aggressively and thrown you into the dirt." She shook her head. "Warrington's unfortunate experience at sea must have upset the balance of his mind."

"He acted boldly to save us both from being hurt. I don't know what you expected him to—"

"You sound almost admiring. Emily, you must not—*must not*—get some romantic notion in your head that—"

"It is nothing of the kind."

The duchess frowned at her, looking every inch the outraged duenna.

It took Emily a moment to realize the extent of her transgression. "I'm sorry I interrupted you, Aunt."

"You must watch your tongue, Emily. We have spoken about this. A young girl does not have opinions, let alone such very…insistent ones."

Emily nodded. It was rather hard, to have been encouraged for her first twenty years to have strong opinions and now to be told that this was not what was wanted at all.

In the front hall, two of her cousins, George and Philip, were waiting to escort them. Tall and blond, they looked elegant and imperturbable in their evening dress. Did they mind being commandeered to take her about London? She never could tell how the men of this household felt about anything. Her father, the only male she knew well, was such a different creature. *His* feelings were never in doubt.

All such concerns fled when they reached the river and embarked for Vauxhall. The gardens glittered on the other side of the water, and music drifted in the soft spring air when they stepped to shore again. There were colored lanterns hanging in the trees, Emily saw with delight. Paths wandered through the vegetation. She could see a glowing fountain at the far end of one and a small pillared structure down another. "It's beautiful," she said.

Philip looked down at her. "Mater thought you'd like it."

Fashionably dressed groups strolled here and there, chattering like exotic denizens of a fairy story. Her aunt was truly making an effort to see that she enjoyed her London season, and she was very grateful.

They walked down the broadest avenue, George and the duchess in front. Emily tried to see everything at once. All the paths looked intriguing. The colored lights through the new green leaves were lovely. The music was growing louder. It was an enchanted landscape. "Can we go there?" she asked her cousin, indicating a particularly enticing walk.

Philip shook his head. "Mater likes to sit in the Pavilion. Nothing down there but trees. George'll order the ham and some rack punch," her cousin promised her kindly.

"Can't we walk a little first?"

Philip started to refuse. Emily looked for her aunt, who had drawn a good way ahead. A large raucous group surged out of a path on the left and engulfed them in a tipsy, jostling mass. "Here now," said Philip indignantly, but no one paid any attention. The group went careening around them laughing and gesturing, heading for the gates. They looked like law clerks or shop assistants, Emily thought, and they looked like they were having a very good time.

One of the young men stumbled hard into Philip and clutched his lapels to stay upright. Philip roared with outrage and cursed him. Some of the others began to jeer, laughing more than ever when Philip raised his walking stick and threatened to thrash his assailant.

Emily backed up a step, then another. Philip was red in the face and shouting, but it didn't seem to her that he was in any real danger. She had seen mobs bent on violence, and this wasn't one of them.

She took another step back. The temptation was irresistible. She would just go a little way down the path that had so drawn her and then find Philip when his dispute was settled.

The walk was as enchanting as she'd expected, winding through the lantern-hung trees like a secret path through a magic forest. Emily was lured farther, first by a gazebo that was a fantasy of wrought iron and glass, and then by a series of sculptures that seemed to be Greek gods and goddesses. By the time she remembered that she must get back to her aunt, she had lost track of the turns she had taken and the direction she had come.

Aunt Julia would be livid. She had never meant to stay away so long. Her cousins were probably searching for her, and none too happy about the task.

Quickly, she started to walk. Coming to a place where two paths crossed, she tried to remember which one had brought her here. But she had been engrossed in the sights of the place, letting her feet take care of themselves. She had no memory of this turn.

Taking a breath, she chose a path, telling herself it looked quite familiar.

Ten minutes later, Emily had to concede that most of the paths looked alike. She had not come upon the gazebo or the statues again. She was lost and there was no one to be seen. She had obviously wandered into a deserted area of the gardens, and she didn't need to be told that this was not a wise idea. If she could just find a busy avenue, someone would direct her to the Pavilion. She stood on tiptoe, trying to see over the bushes for the direction that offered the most light. It was impossible to say. She would just have to walk.

She moved down the paths rapidly, her expression set.

But she couldn't seem to find a populated place. Emily was beginning to feel the first tremors of panic when she passed under an arch of branches and into an open space where two men sat at the edge of a dry fountain looking down into it. "Lord Warrington?" she said, astonished.

He stood, as did the other man. "What the deuce are you doing here?"

Emily hurried forward, too relieved to notice his scowl. "I'm lost. Could you tell me how to find the Pavilion, please? My aunt will be so worried."

A wordless exclamation from the unknown man drew her attention. He looked like a superior sort of workman. His hands were covered with something green and slimy looking.

"Why the devil are you wandering around Vauxhall alone?" asked Richard.

"I...I was just looking at a path, and then I made a turn..."

"Easy to lose your way here," said the other man.

Richard threw him a look that Emily couldn't interpret. "I will escort you to the Pavilion," he said stiffly.

"If you just tell me the way..."

"Naturally I will not send you off alone," he put in, as if she had arranged this whole incident just to inconvenience him. He stepped forward and offered his arm. Since she really didn't want to go alone, Emily swallowed her protest and took it.

They started off along a path that seemed quite the wrong direction to her. Which was no doubt the problem, she thought wryly. It was enormously comforting to hold Richard's arm and watch him choose the way with complete confidence. "What were you doing with that man?" she asked, her curiosity returning.

"Nothing that concerns you."

There was a fleck of the green stuff on his coat, she noticed. It looked like the scum one found growing in ponds. "Was he working on the fountain?"

Richard nodded.

"But why were you—"

"It is none of your affair," he interrupted almost savagely.

Emily's chin came up. "I *beg* your pardon."

A stiff silence descended. He really was an insufferable man.

"I am interested in the waterworks they have here," said Richard suddenly. "They are very complicated and intricate."

"Oh."

"Not a fit pursuit for a man of fashion," he added with a sneer. "Your new friends among the *ton* will find it vastly amusing."

She looked up at him. His mouth was tight, his face half turned away. He seemed both angry and humiliated. "Why would they find it amusing?"

He didn't appear to understand the question.

"Why shouldn't you be interested in how things work?"

Richard stopped walking. He stood there looking down at her. "It isn't…done. A nobleman doesn't care about machinery, or new inventions." His lips turned down. "Or the future."

"You are a nobleman, and you do."

"*I* am…" He stopped and looked perplexed. "I have never let it be seen. Not even by…"

Emily waited for him to go on. When he didn't, she said, "It was very interesting about the balloon. Far more interesting than hunting and horse races and silly wagers in the clubs."

He gave a short laugh. "You have been talking to the bright young sprigs."

"It is all they talk about. What is so intricate about the waterworks here?"

Richard hesitated.

"My aunt said they have a great many fountains."

Enthusiasm struggled with doubt in Richard's expression. "A huge number. They pump water from the river and run it through pipes under the entire garden. There is a marvelous system of valves to move the water from place to place. Finch oversees it all."

"The man you were with just now?"

He nodded. "He knows a vast amount about machinery."

"How did you meet him?" It seemed reasonable to her that Richard should be interested in the subject, but she couldn't imagine how he had become acquainted with someone like Mr. Finch.

"I sought him out," was the defiant reply. "Since I have been back in London…" He stopped, his jaw set. Deeply interested, Emily waited for him to say more. But he didn't.

"That was clever of you," she offered finally.

"Clever?" He looked baffled. Richard's gaze bore into hers. He seemed to be searching for something in her face. Emily couldn't look away. She realized that she wanted him to find whatever it was he sought.

The lanterns and leaves and strains of music seemed to recede. She was conscious of nothing but Richard and the wary amazement that had crossed his face. Emily was suddenly very aware of his height, of the strength of his arm under her fingers. She could hear her heart beating.

He continued to gaze at her as if she were some fantastic creature that he couldn't quite believe in. Emily found herself longing for that belief. Lost in the timeless moment, she leaned closer.

Richard's head bent. His lips touched hers, and something glorious flamed into life, astounding her. The touch sent a tremor through every nerve in her body. It ignited her, made her want to melt into his strength.

The kiss deepened. Richard's arms slid around her and drew her tight against him. His hands moved, exciting and dangerous, along her back. The hard angles of his body enticed her toward total surrender.

Emily had never imagined anything like this. She hadn't known that she could catch fire, go up in a conflagration of sensation that promised worlds. She gave herself up to it, letting his touch guide her in this fabulous, unfamiliar universe.

Richard pulled away, and Emily nearly cried out with disappointment. He let his hands drop to his sides. He was breathing hard, and his eyes looked wild. "I beg your pardon," he said thickly. "I…" One of his fists clenched on the word. He fell silent.

Emily suddenly remembered all her aunt's strictures. What was Richard thinking of her? Did he imagine she habitually kissed men she scarcely knew? She drew away from him, trying to show that was the furthest thing from the truth.

He responded by taking a step backward.

She wanted to say something to ease the tension that vibrated between them, but she couldn't find the right words.

Richard turned away. Her hand reached out without conscious volition, then dropped again.

"This way," he said, starting off. He didn't offer his arm again. Emily followed, and in a few minutes, they emerged from the trees onto a broad, brightly lit avenue full of fashionable strollers. Richard's expression became more even distant. "The Pavilion is down here."

They walked side by side along the crowded pathway. Emily wondered if she looked as self-conscious as he did. She fumbled for something to say. Her aunt was wrong about Richard. He was not the supercilious, malicious man she described. He was…she couldn't say precisely, but she knew she wanted an opportunity to find out.

The Pavilion loomed ahead. When would she see him again? Her aunt was unlikely to arrange another outing with Lord Warrington. Something she had heard at a party popped into her mind. "Have you seen the steam locomotive on Hampstead Heath?" she blurted out.

Richard looked startled. "Not yet."

"I should so like to. It is quite amazing, I believe."

He gazed down at her. She couldn't decide if he was apprehensive or bemused.

"Perhaps you would escort me?" added Emily breathlessly.

"I…if you like."

"Thank you. Thursday?"

He nodded just as Emily heard a sharp exclamation up ahead. In the next instant, she was swept up by her aunt and being questioned and scolded for her heedlessness. Somehow, Richard was dismissed in the midst of the explanations. And from the remarks made in the carriage going home, Emily was very glad she had made her own arrangements.

⁂

Emily walked along the busy London street, conscious of her fashionable clothes, the smart maid who walked beside her, the tall footman who escorted them both. It was so very different from anything in her life before the last few weeks, and yet she was on her way to visit one of her father's disreputable old friends.

Her Aunt Julia had made inquiries about Gerrity, the dancing master, and had agreed that Emily could benefit from some expert instruction. The only thing was, there was no dancing class this afternoon. She was going to see Daniel Fitzgibbon—Gerrity, she reminded herself—for quite a different purpose.

Emily was received with careful ceremony. The servants were safely disposed belowstairs, and she was ushered up to the drawing room by a solemn butler. Only when the door was closed and latched did her host grin at her and say, "Mary's here too, y'see."

Emily smiled at Mrs. Fitzgibbon, a small plump woman of unshakable placidity. She smiled and picked up a teapot. "Lemon or cream, dear?"

A tightness that she hadn't even recognized relaxed as Emily sat down opposite her and accepted a cup. She needn't worry about saying or doing the wrong thing here, or about letting slip some forbidden bit of information about her family.

"Your parents are well?" asked Fitzgibbon.

"Yes. I had a letter just yesterday. Papa has acquired a ferret."

Mary Fitzgibbon laughed quietly. "For ratting?" inquired her husband.

Emily shook her head. "He thought it would pose for a painting he's working on. It stole one of the apples from the still life and ran up a curtain to eat it. He shouted at it until Mama came and suggested another subject."

"What became of the poor animal?" wondered Mary.

"It's living on top of the hall clock, stealing food from the kitchen."

The three of them shared a smiling moment, appreciating the Honorable Alasdair Crane's well-known eccentricities.

"How do you come to be in London?" asked Emily then.

"Mary wanted a more settled life. She was tired of traveling. And Sarah wanted to see the city."

"She's here?" The Fitzgibbons' daughter, Sarah, was Emily's own age, and they had played together as children. She got only a nod in return. Sensing some awkwardness, she added, "It is so good to see old friends. My aunt's house is…very formal."

"She's known as a high stickler," said Daniel.

"But she is kind to you?" asked Mary.

"Oh, yes. Are there others from home in London?"

"Jack Townsend's here," Daniel replied. "Fleecing young sprigs at the gaming hells." He cocked his head. "Not that he cheats, mind. Well, he don't need to. He's deuced clever with the cards."

Emily nodded, remembering this dapper adventurer from her parents' dinner table. "Gentleman Jack" had saved her father from being horsewhipped by an irate neighbor whose foxhounds had had an altercation with David and Jonathan.

"Flora got herself on stage in Covent Garden," her host continued. "Seems to have hooked a great swell, too. He's set her up in style in…"

"Daniel," admonished his wife.

"Eh? Oh." He eyed Emily uneasily. "Mrs. Taylor has a boardinghouse in Kensington. Rooms for displaced gentlewomen."

"And work for them?"

He shrugged.

Emily took it as agreement. Mrs. Taylor was an unusual breed of crusader. She deplored the way society treated certain classes of women, exploiting them as governesses, companions, or poor relations and then often abandoning them with a pittance when they were older. She gave them refuge and taught them a variety of dubious skills, from genteel thievery to confidence tricks.

"There's others about as well. Here and there."

"It's odd to know they are nearby, and I probably shan't see them."

"There's more than one London," responded Daniel. "You could live all your life and never venture from one to the other." He nodded sagely. "Hardly anyone does."

"Do you think Papa's…friends would help me with something?" Emily asked.

"Of course they would, dear," said Mary Fitzgibbon. When it appeared her husband would object, she gave him a look. "Her father has put himself out for most of them."

"I know, but I can't speak for Jack, or Eddie. Besides, what could they do for her?" He turned to Emily.

"Begging your pardon, but you're staying with a duchess and moving in circles quite above their touch."

"I just want them to watch out for someone. An… acquaintance of mine. Papa knows him too."

"What did he do?"

"Nothing. That is…I don't think he did. But someone is trying to kill him."

Both of the Fitzgibbons looked startled.

Emily knew it sounded outlandish. But she had been doing a great deal of thinking in the last few days, and she had come to some clear conclusions. Lord Warrington was in danger, which he refused to see. Someone had to do something.

And it was so much more interesting than simply going to balls and evening parties. The Season was amusing and interesting, but a trifle limiting, Emily admitted. Watching out for Lord Warrington would add a fascination to events that didn't seem to require all her abilities. She was used to watching out for her parents. Could it be she actually missed this? Of course not. She was happy to be free of the endless alarms and debates, living in ease and luxury.

But she couldn't allow a fellow human being to be harmed, she added righteously. Her conscience would rebel. She was obliged to help. She could do a good deed, and occupy her mental faculties at the same time. Splendid. Praiseworthy, even. There was nothing more to it than that.

"They tried to drown him back home, and then to crush him with an urn here in London. He was in a shipwreck too, but I'm not sure… He thinks it is all accidents. I could not convince him otherwise. So he is not being careful, you see. And I cannot watch over him all the time, because I am not free to come and go as I like."

"Why should you watch over him?" asked Mary, her eyes glinting with curiosity.

"I don't wish to see him murdered," Emily answered a bit quickly. "And they tried first right outside our house. I feel…responsible."

"That's nonsense." Daniel looked perplexed. "Why should you?"

"Well, I…I was there, you see. I untied him. And when the urn fell in the park. And he isn't paying the least heed to it. It is…it is like watching a runaway team about to trample someone. You must try to pull them away."

Her host seemed about to dispute this, but Mary spoke first. "Who is he?"

"His name is Sheldon. Lord Warrington, that is."

"A lord?" snorted Daniel. "We've nothing to do with lords."

"You're visiting among the *ton*," said Emily. "Jack is in the gaming houses, and Flora at the theater. And I'm sure all of you hear things." She spoke the last words firmly, knowing quite well that they gathered information along with other valuable commodities.

"We can pass the word," agreed Mary. She ignored her husband's surprised look. "What does this lord look like?"

"Oh." Emily blinked, unaware of Mary's close scrutiny. "He's tall," she began, "and, and very…well muscled. His skin is bronzed; he has been in the Indies. Brown hair and hazel eyes that are extremely…penetrating."

"Engaging manners, I suppose?"

Daniel gaped at his wife. Emily bit her lower lip as she struggled to form a reply. Richard was abrupt and sarcastic. But his rare smile was certainly engaging. He acted decisively in a crisis. She had felt so safe in his arms. Hurriedly, she banished this thought. "His manners are…indescribable."

Mary nodded as if she had gained important information. "We'll see what can be done." Her husband shrugged, then nodded.

"Thank you."

"Your dad shielded us from the magistrates," was the placid reply.

Emily smiled at them, then rose to go. "You will let me know if you hear anything?"

The Fitzgibbons said they would and stood to see her out.

"May I call again to see Sarah? I so love talking to her."

The earlier awkwardness returned. Daniel shifted from one foot to another.

"She is all right?"

There was another pause, then Mary replied. "She's not ill or anything. But we're a bit on the outs."

"Why?"

"She's gone to work for some German feller who reads fortunes," Daniel blurted out.

"Not fortunes," corrected Mary. "He contacts their dead relatives."

Daniel made a derisive noise.

"Dead?" said Emily.

"He holds—what d'you call them—séances. Pierces the veil and gets messages from those who've passed on."

Daniel snorted again. "He's supposed to have brought some swell back from the dead."

"People, mostly women, give him gifts," explained Mary. "He pays Sarah well, treats her well, too."

Her husband growled. "So she says."

"So I know," was the confident reply.

"You don't wish her to work there?" ventured Emily.

"It's not that I object to taking money from marks," stated Daniel, as if he had made this argument many times before. "But I draw the line at making light of death and the hereafter. It ain't a game, you know? There's some things not to be meddled with."

"I'll tell Sarah you were asking after her," said Mary.

Smiling her thanks, Emily turned to the door.

"No good'll come of it," Daniel muttered. "She ought to stick to honest thievery."

A bit bemused by his unexpected philosophy, Emily went on her way.

Six

"THERE IS NO MORE INCOME TO BE SQUEEZED FROM your Somerset properties," declared Elijah Taft.

Richard looked at the craggy old man who sat opposite him in his mother's library. He had known Taft all his life, a dour West Country man with a daunting knowledge of estate management. Taft's belligerence was completely justified by their history. In the past, Richard had condescended to see Taft only when he wanted money and had berated him soundly when there wasn't any. Yet Richard still found that the man's attitude galled. "They're in poor shape, aren't they?"

Taft bristled. "When you put nothing into your land, my lord, when you pull our every spare penny and let buildings fall to ruin and fields…"

Richard held up a hand. It was true; he had never made the least effort to manage his patrimony, or indeed to learn much about it. The decaying house depressed him. But even if he had tried, there was no money to mend anything or salvage acres that had been neglected for more than a generation. "Cottages and barns need to be repaired, I suppose. And other things."

"A thousand other things, my lord. And there's no more income to be gotten out of…"

"I know," Richard said sharply. The man might be right, but it made the situation no easier to face. "The problem is, there is no money. That's always been the problem, hasn't it?"

"There was a reasonable income—once."

"But my father was not a reasonable man."

Taft said nothing. He didn't need to. His face showed his agreement.

"And my grandfather not much more so, I understand."

"He did his best," was the gruff reply.

Taft and his grandfather had grown up together, Richard knew. They had been fast friends from early boyhood, and Taft had taken on the management of that Lord Warrington's affairs as a mission as well as a job. He had made the property his lifework. No one knew it better or cared more for every inch of the land. "I don't have the thousands of pounds that are no doubt needed to set things right," he pointed out.

"If every cent was put back in," Taft began.

"You wish me to live on nothing at all?" He would be more dependent on his mother than ever.

Taft's glower was familiar from days gone by.

Richard was assailed by an unfamiliar bitterness. It was all well and good to decide to change. But circumstances didn't always allow one to do so. "The house is falling to pieces, full of mice and damp. Perhaps we should just pull it down and have done with it."

The flare of rage in Taft's eyes was almost daunting.

He didn't really mean to tear the place down, Richard thought. He was only dispirited by the damage that generations of neglect had left behind. The task of saving the estate seemed overwhelming, and rather lonely as well. He started to withdraw the words.

"You worthless excuse for a man," Taft blurted out, obviously laboring under intense emotion. "You don't deserve the place—"

"You forget yourself!" snapped Richard.

As Taft struggled for control, Richard grappled with a fury that he acknowledged as unfair. But that didn't make it any less fiery. It was one thing to criticize oneself; it was quite another to have accusations thrown in one's face by an employee. "If you find my character so distasteful, perhaps you would like to end our association."

He couldn't help feeling a twinge of satisfaction at Taft's stricken look. "I...I beg your pardon, my lord. I have devoted my life to keeping..."

Guilt made Richard brusque. "Yes, yes. Very well." The clock on the mantel chimed. "I have an engagement."

Taft rose. He had recovered somewhat, the lines of his face once more hard and craggy. He bowed his head in curt acknowledgment and went out.

He would have to find a way to begin repairs, Richard thought. Perhaps he would allow Taft to make use of all the income for a time. If nothing else, he would leave the land in a better state than he found it. But this sounded long and difficult even to the new Lord Warrington. He couldn't imagine being like Taft, spending his whole life in a hopeless cause.

Putting these thoughts from his mind, Richard called for his curricle to be brought round. The steam locomotive he was to see this afternoon intrigued him far more than estate management. He would always be more interested in new mechanisms and inventions than in land and crops. It was another of the things that made him so different from his peers.

Different. And open to ridicule and blank incomprehension if he showed it—except to one person in London. Taking his hat and gloves from a footman, Richard allowed his thoughts to linger on Emily Crane. He could still feel that kiss on his lips, feel the effect in every fiber of his flesh. She was damnably alluring.

London was turning out to be more enjoyable than he had expected, Richard mused. Perhaps he would stay in town for the whole of the Season.

Richard dropped his hands and let the team increase its pace on this straight stretch of road. It had been an odd afternoon. The locomotive had been fascinating, but Emily Crane had been…he didn't know what to call it. Impertinent? Her conversation had veered from his relatives to his position in society to the dangers of holding a grudge. She had gone on for quite some time about the possibility of making enemies among the *haut ton*. She seemed to see it as some kind of battleground, rife with verbal rapier work and relentless vendettas. What had she been up to in her short time in town? She was a decidedly unusual girl.

To top it off, the groom perched behind them in the curricle appeared to have overindulged during their luncheon at the inn. He was continually nodding off and then jerking awake again to gaze around blearily. Richard was beginning to fear that he would lose his grip and fall.

Emily cleared her throat nervously. Richard braced himself for another odd remark. "Lord Warrington?"

"Yes?"

"I…there was something I wished to speak to you about." Emily took a deep breath and then spoke in a rush. "My aunt tells me that gossip about my parents could be quite harmful to me. So I wanted to ask you please not to mention that you…that is, that they…your visit to them."

The request surprised Richard, and annoyed him. "Do you imagine that I spend my time gossiping?"

"I…I didn't mean…"

"Do you imagine I tell malicious tales for the pleasure of it?"

She bit her lower lip.

Richard was assailed by a rush of wholly unprecedented embarrassment. Had Emily Crane heard all about the old Lord Warrington? Embarrassment became humiliation. No doubt she had, and had probably despised the man described.

The emotion he felt then stunned him. In all of his twenty-nine years, he had never worried about what a woman might think of his character. He hadn't cared. The old Warrington had had only one purpose for a woman.

"I don't spread rumors or indulge in tittle-tattle," he added stiffly, wondering if she would believe him. "I have more important things to do with my time."

"You talked to me of nothing but my parents at the ball," Emily snapped. "How was I to know that you would not…"

"I didn't know you were trying to conceal their identity. That scheme is unlikely to fly, you know."

"I am not trying…"

"What *are* you trying to do?"

Emily hesitated. "My aunt is very knowledgeable about society."

"Undoubtedly."

"I am not."

Richard felt a spark of interest.

"I must be guided by her advice."

"Must you?"

Emily looked up at him. She was an enigma, he thought. He couldn't predict her as he could so many people he met. "You wish to succeed in society?"

"Why shouldn't I?" She looked him straight in the eye as if daring him to answer.

Richard was startled by a strong pulse of desire. His hands had found her body delightfully rounded in all the right places, he remembered. Her red-gold hair, brushing his chin, had been like threads of flame. Sternly, he called himself to order. This was out of the question—he certainly didn't need any more complications in his life.

The sound of hooves pounded up behind them. Richard pulled a little to the side to let the other vehicle pass. It came abreast of them—a light carriage and four going flat out. The driver had a hood pulled up over his head, obscuring his features. How the devil did he see the road with that thing on? If this were some young blood racing for a wager, he would most likely be foxed as well. And deadly dangerous.

Richard started to slow the curricle, but at that moment, the other carriage veered slightly and slammed into it, rocking the lighter vehicle. Both teams shied, one of the leaders squealing. Richard fought the reins, every muscle in his body taut.

The other carriage hit them again. The driver must be sodden drunk, Richard concluded. He pulled hard on the ribbons, trying to halt his thoroughly spooked horses. The leader threw back his head in a challenge and tried to bite his opposite number.

Richard hauled harder as the other carriage careened into them again. In the midst of the chaos, he noticed a small gloved hand clutching the seat beside him. Emily wasn't making a sound, he noted with approval. Then all his attention was claimed by the plunging team. There was something wrong. They were moving away from the curricle to the left. Risking a glance downward, Richard saw that the traces had parted. The only links between the curricle and the horses were the reins in his hands.

The team turned farther, eager to get away from the melee now that it was free. Richard gripped the leathers, but it was no good. They weren't pulling the curricle any longer, and if he held on he was likely to be dragged from the seat. With a supreme act of will, he let go. The horses raced off, dragging the broken traces behind them. He heard a muted cry from Emily just as the rogue carriage hit them again and sent the curricle plunging down a hill toward a grove of trees. He had a bumping, reeling vision of sky, branches, a huge spray of water, then blackness.

Richard woke to darkness and rain pounding on his face and chest. When he tried to sit up his whole body protested in one great ache. Where was his spear? His sling? Groping for them, he searched the area for predators.

He found mud. He was half-submerged in it. Then his hand brushed his coat tail, came up to his shirtfront. He sniffed the air. He wasn't in the jungle. He had come home, he remembered. He was home. No great spotted cats or bone crushing snakes were likely to drop on him.

Bringing his hand to his face, he rubbed his pounding head. There had been a carriage…a fall. Struggling up, pulling his boots from the sucking mud, he squinted into the darkness. There was a full moon behind the rain clouds. He could make out the hulk of the curricle, sagging in the middle of a small pond. There seemed to be trees beyond—probably the trees they had crashed through, he decided, as memory sharpened. He had been thrown clear.

He scanned his surroundings. The rain was letting up a bit. He could hear something else, a rhythmic sound. Squelching his way toward it, he discovered his groom, flat on his back on the sodden soil, snoring. Richard shook him. When he got no response, he hauled the man up by his lapels and shook hard. The groom snorted and gurgled, but he didn't wake. How could the idiot sleep in these conditions? He must have emptied a barrel of ale. Richard dropped him, resisting the strong urge to give him a kick. He had to find Emily, yet he was almost afraid to. With her more fragile frame, was she lying broken somewhere nearby?

A movement caught his eye. A pale figure staggered upright, wavered. Striding over to it, he was just in time to catch Emily in his arms.

She clung to him. A hint of warmth penetrated his

soaked shirt from her body. She was shuddering with cold and probably shock. "Are you hurt?" he said.

"B-bruised and battered," she responded, her teeth chattering.

She said it remarkably calmly, all in all.

The rain intensified again, pouring over them, the drops beating on his head. The spring night wasn't frigid, but with the wet and the wind, it was enough to do them harm. He had to find some shelter. Holding Emily close to his side, he led her over to the somnolent groom. "Wait here. I'll find someplace out of the rain."

She nodded, then sank down next to the groom. "Is he sl-sleeping?"

"Apparently. I'll be as quick as I can."

Richard left them there and took his bearings. The road was beyond the trees and up a bank if he remembered correctly. He could scramble up there and hope to flag down a passing carriage, but travelers would be few or none on a night such as this. He needed a house. Peering through the rain, he looked for a light. There was nothing. He walked up the low bank of the pond. Rain pounded on his face and shoulders and dripped from his fingertips. He would have preferred the jungle, he thought ironically. There, at least, he could have built a shelter. But this landscape offered no convenient plants with great broad leaves.

He walked a little farther, straining to penetrate the curtains of rain. There seemed to be something…a dark mass against the slightly lighter clouds up ahead. Moving faster, he came to it. Not a house, not even a barn; it was a small three-sided shed for storing fodder. But the overhanging roof kept out most of the rain. There were mounds of dry straw inside. It would do.

Returning to the others, he told Emily about the shelter as he helped her up. "I can walk," she said when he would have supported her. "Help your poor groom."

"Poor!"

"There must be something wrong with him to sleep like that."

"He's drunk," retorted Richard. But he grasped the man's shoulders and began to drag him across the muddy field.

Slowly, they made their way to the shed. "Oh," said Emily when she stepped inside. "It is so good to be out of that rain."

Richard grunted his agreement as he deposited the groom on a pile of hay. Emily had wrapped her arms around herself, still visibly shivering. "I have no means to make a fire. There may be a house nearby, but to find it in this…"

"You mustn't go out there again," she objected.

"I don't intend to. We will have to cover ourselves with the hay."

She turned to it immediately, surprising Richard at the lack of argument. Burrowing into one of the piles, she started to create a nest for herself. After a moment, he bent to help her pile the hay on top. He could not see her face, but his hand encountered hers and paused. "You're freezing," he said. Her fingers were like ice.

"I am cold. The hay will help." She nestled down into it.

Richard turned to throw some of it over the groom, then made his own place in the cramped shed. When he was done, there were scarcely six inches between him and Emily, and little more separating him from the servant.

He lay there in the darkness waiting for the chill to fade. The rain beat on the slanted roof. The groom snored. He could hear Emily's teeth chattering, the rustling in the hay caused by her shivers. She made no complaint. She didn't cry or moan or accuse. She was simply lying there, quietly freezing, not asking for anyone's help.

An unfamiliar pressure arose in Richard's chest. He had never experienced anything like it. Did it have something to do with the new Richard Sheldon? Was it something he'd acquired during his ordeal?

It was almost painful. It pushed him, without words, to act.

Reaching out, he pulled Emily into the crook of his arm. She fit neatly under his open driving coat against his side.

She made a small sound of protest.

"You must get warm," he said.

She didn't reply, but neither did she draw away. She was shivering violently now. But as heat began to spread between them, the shudders lessened, and finally faded. She relaxed slightly in his embrace, though he could tell that she still wasn't completely at ease.

How could she be? It was not a situation that encouraged nonchalance. He could feel the soft curve of her breast against his ribs, the pressure of her thigh on his own. Her breath ruffled against his cheek, and the beat of her heart made a counterpoint to his accelerating pulse.

He remembered the kiss in Vauxhall Gardens, and the way she had responded to his touch, with an innocent eagerness that had driven him wild. The feel of her lingered in his fingertips, on his lips. He could recall every nuance of those moments—the delicate, yielding texture of her mouth, the slender suppleness that nestled against him now. Making love to Emily would be glorious. She was such a beguiling mixture of inexperience and wisdom.

Her contours softened into his, and Richard almost groaned aloud. His body was demanding the pleasures his mind had visualized so clearly. It was all he could do to keep his hands still, to discipline the drive of desire.

Emily's breathing grew more regular. She had fallen asleep.

Richard clenched his jaw. She trusted him. She had

little reason to do so, but she did. She snuggled closer, and this time Richard caught his breath. He was unbearably aroused. He wanted her as he couldn't remember ever wanting any woman. And he wasn't going to do anything about it.

The thought made him smile slightly. How the old Richard Sheldon would jeer at this restraint. Nothing had been allowed to interfere with his desires. He would have found Emily's trusting openness laughable.

Of course, no one had trusted him, Richard acknowledged. It was different, seemingly, when one had to deal with such complications. Because there was more going on than simple physical arousal, compelling as that was. He felt odd. When he considered Emily, he felt—pity, or no—that wasn't it.

Her reaction to their plight had impressed him, he reasoned. She had been brave, astonishingly uncomplaining. He admired that.

She turned slightly in his arms, and Richard let out a quick breath. Her hands were curled on her breast. They would only have to move a little to caress…

He stopped himself. This was not acceptable. He was losing his grip on himself. And that was a thing he no longer allowed. If he had learned one thing in his fight for survival, it was control.

He'd taken a sharp pummeling in the accident, he told himself. That was it. Perhaps he was slightly delirious. He would take more care.

He looked around their crude shelter, then down at Emily, curled so confidingly against him. He had a sense of consequences rippling out from this night, already far beyond his control. He ought to have gone on searching for a house or…something.

The sound of the rain contradicted him. He had done what he could. And now he would simply have to endure. He would hold her, keep her safe and warm, until he could get her home again. And he would resist the urge to touch her, to see if he could rouse the desperate need he was feeling in the exquisite body pressed against his. It couldn't be any harder than slogging through a steaming swamp for days on end. It had to be easier than facing a jungle cat with little more than his teeth and nails to defend him.

But it wasn't. The heat they'd generated burned through him, and the soft caress of her breath drove him mad. It was hours before the rhythm of the rain and the rush of wind finally lulled him into a restless sleep.

Around dawn, the groom stirred. He sat up, holding his head as if it might split in two, then staggered out into the long grass. He squinted at the daylight, spat, and reeled off in the direction of the pond like a desert wanderer spotting succor.

⁓

Emily woke to the sound of voices. Her aunt was calling her, she thought groggily. Perhaps she had overslept. Aunt Julia equated early rising with virtue and steadiness of character. Why hadn't the maid brought her tea? She moved, and was rewarded by a whole medley of aches and strains, a prickle of hay in her face, and a sudden stunning awareness of another body pressed close to hers. She blinked to clear her vision and found herself gazing at Richard Sheldon's face from a distance of inches. She was folded in his coat. His arm was draped over her. So was one of his legs. Even as her face flamed, Emily realized that the position was not precisely unpleasant. It was unprecedented in her life, of course, and very unsettling. But the pounding of her heart and the shortness of her breath were…stimulating.

An earsplitting shriek cut through these ruminations. It also caused Richard to jerk awake just as Emily was struggling up out of their cocoon. When she managed to sit, she found herself facing her Aunt Julia, her cousin George, and two of the duchess's footmen. All of them looked profoundly shocked.

"Emily," cried the duchess. "What…?" Her mouth opened and closed, but she appeared unable to find words.

Emily struggled to escape the hay. It was clinging to her clothes and no doubt her hair as well. She must look like…well, she didn't want to think about it.

A strong hand helped her rise. Richard came to his feet beside her. Emily tried to gather her wits.

"What are you doing?" her aunt managed finally.

"The curricle overturned," said Richard.

The duchess gazed at him with horror.

"I…we were all thrown. It was some time before we recovered, and then…with the rain and…we were forced to shelter here. My groom was…ah…injured."

"What groom?" asked George belligerently. He was tapping his stick against his thigh.

Richard looked around the empty shed.

"This is dreadful," moaned the duchess. "This is disastrous. Olivia will…" She turned even paler. "Alasdair! He will have an apoplexy. He'll kill someone." She looked at Richard as if in no doubt of the victim.

"But Aunt, we only…"

"Don't tell me what you did!" She started to wring her hands. "Lady Jersey will make such a story of this."

"Not if Lord Warrington is a man of honor," said George. He looked thunderous.

Richard looked worse, thought Emily. He looked murderous. Muscles shifted in his jaw as he stood rigid. His hazel eyes burned. She worried suddenly that he would go for George's throat.

"I will call on the duke as soon as I am able," he said, spitting out the words.

George gave a curt nod. His mother wrung her hands a final time, then clasped them tight together.

"Miss Crane should be taken home," Richard added.

The duchess surged forward to gather Emily. George ushered them both out of the shed. "I will tell my father to expect you," he said over his shoulder.

"Count on it," was the clipped reply.

Emily stumbled a bit as she was helped over the rough ground. She still felt disoriented. She couldn't seem to think. It seemed an endless way to her aunt's carriage.

"But will it do?" said the duchess to her son.

"I've left Ned to find that groom. We should be able to hush it up."

"Nothing…improper occurred," stammered Emily.

Her aunt looked scandalized. "Nothing? Do you call lying in a man's…? I can't even speak of it. What would your parents say to me if they heard?"

Her father wouldn't say anything, Emily thought. Aunt Julia had been right before. He would kill someone. She wasn't sure about her mother. "No one will know."

The duchess shook her head. "We will do our best. But such things get out. The servants will gossip. If Warrington doesn't…"

"He would never tell anyone," interrupted Emily.

Her aunt and cousin stared at her as if she had lost her wits.

She remembered their opinion of Richard's sharp tongue and tendency toward malice. But it wasn't true. He wasn't like that at all. Was he?

"He won't if I have anything to do with it," answered George grimly.

She didn't believe it, Emily decided. He had never maligned her parents, after all. Despite what nearly everyone said, she found she trusted him.

Exhausted by her ordeal, Emily climbed into the carriage and sank back on the cushions. Things would be clearer when she was rested.

Emily was sitting in the morning room the next day when her aunt entered with Richard in tow.

"Lord Warrington has something to say to you." The duchess looked strained but resolute. "Your uncle and I have given him our consent."

"Consent?"

Her aunt merely slipped back out of the room.

Richard came closer. His gaze was cold and his expression grim. "I've come, of course, to ask you to be my wife," he said without preliminaries.

Emily had been half expecting this, half rejecting the idea as ridiculous. "Of course?"

Richard waited in icy silence. His expression was forbidding. He might have been carved from stone.

She wasn't going to go along with this. Her aunt had arranged the scene, but no one could make her follow the prescribed steps. "That carriage attacked us."

He blinked, startled.

"It was absolutely blatant."

Surprise made Richard look a little less intimidating.

"And I have been wondering if your groom was given some drug. The way he was sleeping," she pointed out. "It was unnatural."

One corner of his mouth twitched.

"And the traces were cut, weren't they? I could see that."

"Could you?"

She nodded, pleased to have elicited a reaction. "They had to befuddle the groom to do that."

"They?"

"Whoever did it," she added impatiently.

"Ah."

At least he was looking a little more human, Emily thought, not so frightening. "You must admit now that someone is trying to harm you."

"I am not required to admit anything." He grimaced. "Except stupidity that goes beyond all bounds."

She chose to ignore this. "Whoever was driving that carriage deliberately ran you off the road."

"If they did, it is no business of yours."

"You do admit it!"

He brushed off the statement with a gesture.

"The urn, the footpads, it is all…"

"An odd series of…occurrences."

"Occurrences? They were plain murderous attacks!"

"Whatever they are, they are my affair. I will deal with them."

"But you must—"

"I will judge what I *must* do," he interrupted angrily. "Indeed, I already have."

Like come here today and offer for her when it appeared to be the last thing in the world he wanted to do. A tremor of unhappiness shook her, and she closed her fists against it. He wasn't going to listen to sensible advice. He wasn't going to take steps to protect himself. Would he even try to discover what was behind the attacks?

"You have not answered my first question."

He was going to let himself be killed through sheer stubbornness.

"I don't imagine you've forgotten it."

He needed help. But he would never admit it. On the contrary, he would act like a fool to prove he didn't.

Richard raised his eyebrows. His gaze was stony.

It would be much easier to watch over him if they were engaged, Emily realized. Later, of course, she would break it off. She would never entrap a man into marriage.

"Well?"

She took a shaky breath. It was all for his own good. She cared…she cared only that a fellow human being was in jeopardy. She swallowed. Her heart was beating very fast. "Yes," she said.

Richard winced. "Yes?"

"I…I accept your proposal."

He looked like a man who has received dire news and is just apprehending the full extent of the disaster.

Stricken, Emily swallowed again. It would only be for a little while, and then she could explain to him that she had never meant to go through with it. He would be safe by then, and she would be…she would have figured out the puzzle. She struggled to pull in some air.

"I see." He stood straighter. "That is clear then."

The coldness of his tone and the anger in his face were too much. Emily opened her mouth to retract everything.

The door opened and the duchess peeked around the panels. "Have you settled things between you?"

"It appears we are engaged," replied Richard.

The duchess came into the room and gazed at Emily with a kind of despair. Then she visibly pulled herself together. "I'll send the notice off to the *Morning Post* at once."

"I'm sure you will," replied Richard contemptuously.

At that, Aunt Julia was every inch the duchess. She raked him with a look so haughty that Emily quailed.

This was supposed to be one of the happiest moments of her life, she thought. An accepted proposal should mean excitement about the future, tender emotions, and a flurry of felicitations. Instead she felt a sinking sensation and, when she looked at Richard, a tremor of tears. Should she take back her acceptance?

"You have subjected my niece to mortal danger," said the duchess through her teeth. "You have very nearly destroyed her position in society. I don't believe you have anything to complain of."

Richard looked as if he might explode. Emily braced

herself for she didn't know what. But when he finally spoke, he said only, "As things appear to be settled, I will take my leave."

Her aunt began a protest, but he didn't wait for it. He was striding out the door before she managed two words. "Well," she said. "Well."

Emily reminded herself that the engagement would only be temporary. She would find the assailant and end the attacks, and then she could show Richard that she was above all this sort of thing.

"It is not the match I hoped for," said her aunt. She paused to grapple with this prodigious understatement. "But under the circumstances…" She swallowed as if something was caught in her throat. "Oh lud," she murmured.

She was going to have to move fast, Emily thought. She had to find the solution before all this flew right out of control.

Seven

RICHARD SAT IN THE LIBRARY OF HIS MOTHER'S HOUSE, his legs extended, a glass of brandy held loosely in one hand. It was past midnight. The household was asleep, and the streets outside had grown quiet. How he had dreamed, six months ago in the jungle, of sitting just so, of being home again. Now, he was, and he almost wished himself back in the wilderness.

Trapped into marriage. It was the last thing he would ever have expected. In fact, he couldn't quite believe it even now. Since he had first entered society, he had had the address—some had called it ruthlessness—to discourage any scheming females. A woman who approached him when he didn't wish it was soon sorry. Not that many pursued a man without fortune. It wasn't a record to be proud of, he acknowledged, but it had kept the question of marriage at bay.

Yet here he was. The notices would appear in the papers tomorrow. It was out of his control. He was as helpless as he had been when the storm swept over the ship and he'd been marooned two thousand miles from home.

He hated it.

Richard sipped his brandy and wondered if Emily Crane had somehow engineered the whole, from the moment of their meeting at her house. But after a moment, he shook his head. It was impossible. All that Emily had done was acquiesce. His mouth hardened; not that he forgave her for that. He would never forgive her.

He tossed off the rest of the brandy and refilled the glass. A toast to his coming nuptials, he thought bitterly. He had meant to marry, of course, someday. He owed it to his name. An heiress was clearly called for to repair his fortunes. But this had always figured as a distant event in his mind. He had never imagined such a humiliating position. Grimacing, Richard addressed himself to the brandy once more. It didn't matter what he wanted. He'd gotten Emily Crane.

He'd gotten the thing he had always hoped to avoid— one of those society marriages where husband and wife shared little more than a residence. They were common enough; and in the past, he had even found their vicissitudes amusing. But he had vainly imagined he could evade that fate, even with the illusory heiress.

Richard snorted in self-mockery. It seemed the old Warrington had had some mawkish romantic notions, despite his careless treatment of women. Perhaps this forced marriage was no more than he deserved.

He turned from this depressing subject to the other matter. He saw again the hooded driver, heard his carriage slam against the side of the curricle. Whatever he might say to Emily Crane, to himself he had to admit that the crash had been no accident. The man had meant to overturn them.

And someone had definitely tampered with the traces. When he examined them, they'd been cleanly cut through. The groom denied imbibing more than a mug of ale. He might be lying, of course; but his record was spotless, and the butler vouched for him. It seemed that someone had actually slipped him a drug and cut the reins.

Richard shifted in the chair, conscious of the aches and bruises throughout his body. He might easily have broken his neck in that spill. Had that really been the idea?

If so, then the other incidents that seemed to obsess

Miss Crane might deserve his attention after all. He had dismissed her suspicions, seeing them as fanciful embroideries, female hysteria. Even though Emily had never shown a single sign of excessive sensibility, an inner voice pointed out.

Richard rubbed his forehead, as if that could ease the tension in his brain. He had not seen those other incidents. She might have been mistaken about the footpads, the urn. And they had seemed so trivial after all he'd been through. But taken together...

He sipped brandy. Why should anyone want him dead? He had no enemies on that scale. He had no money to tempt his heir. The idea that his cousin Donald, a wealthy man in his own right, would kill to assume a mere barony—it was ludicrous. There was absolutely no reason for him to be the victim of a murderous plot, and yet he was very near to conceding that he was.

The door latch clicked. Richard's muscles tightened reflexively. But when the panels swung open they revealed only his mother in a long white nightgown and mobcap, a paisley shawl swathing her shoulders. "Richard?"

He rose and went to her. "Yes, Mother. Why aren't you asleep?"

"I was just wondering if you were all right."

A complex question. "Of course I am."

"That awful accident." She gestured vaguely. "So worrisome."

"But I came out of it perfectly well. You should go back to bed. You look tired." She did indeed, he thought. Tired, and older than her fifty years.

His mother sighed, looking around the room. "I hardly ever come here since Walter died. He always sat here."

His stepfather had loved books, Richard remembered. He had indeed spent countless evenings in this room with a favorite volume and a glass of brandy. How strange that he had chosen the same retreat, when he had scarcely entered it during his stepfather's life. A pang of regret startled Richard, as unfamiliar as most of the feelings that plagued him lately.

His mother had wandered over to the bookshelves, scanning the spines as if they held some message for her.

"Would you like a little brandy?" Richard asked. "Perhaps it would help you sleep."

"And this engagement," she said, still gazing at the books, not appearing to have heard him. "It is so sudden."

"Come and sit down, Mother." He guided her to an armchair and poured out another glass of brandy before sitting opposite. They had been through all this earlier, but clearly it had not sufficed. He could hardly blame her.

"I didn't even know you liked the young lady. You've known her such a short time."

"These things happen quickly sometimes," he offered.

"And you say she has no fortune at all?"

He shook his head.

"I don't wish to interfere, but do you think that is really wise, Richard?"

It was the antithesis of wise. It was a disaster from start to finish.

His mother sampled her brandy. Gazing at the amber liquid with approval, she repeated the dose. "One can't live on love, you know. I thought your father was the most glorious young man on earth. But once we were married, it was…difficult." She drank again.

"Mother, I—"

"My family opposed the match, but I wouldn't listen." She looked straight at Richard, not the least bit befuddled.

He was amazed, and wholly at a loss. It seemed grossly unfair that he had to defend an engagement he had never wanted in the first place. "Miss Crane is…" He grimaced slightly, not knowing how to finish.

She waited. The silence stretched out uncomfortably. Finally, his mother sighed and sipped from her glass again. "It is a good family. The duchess has been very kind."

Richard refrained from comment. He was picturing his mother's introduction to Alasdair Crane.

"If you need some help with setting up your own household—"

"I won't take your money," interrupted Richard harshly.

She looked surprised. As well she might. He had never refused her money before.

"But how will you…?"

"I don't know! But I will manage it on my own." Perhaps he would take Emily to live on his Somerset estates, he thought savagely. A few weeks of leaking roofs and rotting floorboards—not to mention the odd rat— would show her what sort of bargain she'd made. She'd demonstrated a remarkable fortitude, a treacherous inner voice commented. He stifled it by draining his glass and reaching for the decanter.

His mother looked a bit daunted. She seemed to cast about for a new subject. "Did I tell you Lydia is coming for a visit? I haven't seen her for an age. She's Walter's niece, you know."

Lydia Farrell was one of the members of his step-father's family who had received a legacy from him, Richard remembered. He had resented them fiercely at the time.

"Such a lovely girl."

Lydia must be well into her thirties, Richard calculated. He thought she was married and had a couple of children. He hadn't seen her since he was a stripling. In his hazy recollection she was a skinny, silent creature with little to recommend her. "She lives in Wales?"

"I'm sure she must be heartily sick of the country. We'll show her a bit of town life."

The idea appeared to please her, which was enough for Richard. His mother badly needed a diversion.

"I wonder if I can get her vouchers for Almack's." She looked down into her glass, found it was empty, and held it out to him.

"You are going to be thoroughly foxed, Mother."

She gave a trill of laughter. "Don't be silly. Just a sip more."

She didn't laugh nearly as much as she used to, Richard thought as he poured it. He sent a silent thanks to his almost cousin Lydia. Though she didn't know it, her timing was impeccable.

❧

Emily sat very straight as one of the footmen placed a filet of sole on her plate, then moved along to her uncle, who sat at the head of the long table. She never quite got used to the formality of dinner in a ducal household. A liveried servant was posted behind every chair. And there were always two full courses and a remove. Her aunt and uncle, and tonight her cousin George as well, seemed to take it for granted. They only remarked on the ceremony if something went amiss, or if a dish was particularly good.

"What did you do today, Emily?" inquired the duke.

She smiled at him. He tried to be kind, she knew, but he spoke to her as if she were twelve years old instead of almost twenty. "I rode in the park."

He nodded as he sampled the sole. "Your horse is satisfactory?"

"Yes, thank you. You couldn't have found a better one for me."

He acknowledged this benignly.

"She's a spanking rider," said George.

"Slang, George," said the duchess automatically.

Under other circumstance, Emily would have told

them that her father had taught her to ride, and that he was ridiculously proud of her fine seat. But she wasn't to mention her parents. Under other circumstances, they might have been chatting about bride clothes and wedding arrangements, but that topic was equally awkward. In fact, she couldn't think of a single thing to say, even though she found the scrape of cutlery in the silence oppressive.

Thankfully, the gentlemen fell into a discussion of the duke's racing stables, which obviously interested them far more than anything Emily might have said. She finished her fish and sipped her wine. She had wished for more stability and convention, she remembered. She hadn't realized her wish would be granted with a vengeance.

The sound of raised voices drifted back from the front of the house, followed by a thud. A door slammed. Emily's aunt frowned and cocked her head at the noise.

An argument had broken out in the entry hall. There was another thud. "What on earth?" said the duchess. "John, go and see."

One of the footmen bowed and went out. The apparent altercation continued.

"What is that?" asked Uncle Henry, apparently just noticing the disturbance.

His wife shrugged. "I have no idea. I've sent…"

"I damned well will interrupt them," declared a masculine voice. "Get out of my way, idiot."

"What in blazes?" George started to rise, but Emily was well ahead of him. "Papa!" she cried to the rakish figure who came striding into the room just then, and threw herself onto his chest.

Alasdair Crane embraced her with one arm while gazing around the room with a mixture of contempt and amusement. "Hullo, Julia," he said. "Duke."

"Alasdair," responded the former in a faint voice. "Where is…?"

"Right here," said Olivia Crane, walking gracefully into the dining room. "I beg your pardon for descending on you unannounced."

Emily transferred her hug to her mother, who returned it full measure.

"Alasdair was in a hurry," she added, looking amused.

"Hurry?" bellowed Alasdair. "Damned right I was in a hurry. What the devil have you been up to, Julia?"

The duchess raised her eyebrows and gave him a look that would have withered any member of society on the spot.

It had no effect whatsoever on her brother-in-law. "We send Emily to you, against my better judgment, mind." He glowered at Olivia, who smiled serenely back. "And before she's been in London a month, we hear she's engaged."

As she watched her aunt struggle with her temper, Emily was overwhelmed with relief and affection. She was incredibly glad to see her parents. Though it had been only a few weeks, she had missed them far more than she realized.

"Engaged!" roared Alasdair. "Without so much as a by-your-leave. To some fellow I've never heard of. It's insupportable." He had stepped close to Aunt Julia and was looming over her in a way that she clearly disliked. "Nothing to say for yourself?"

"I see that your manners haven't improved, Alasdair," was the cold reply.

"Not likely to, since I haven't any."

"Indeed," murmured the duchess.

"Are you Philip or George?" Emily's mother said.

Her cousin made a strangled noise in his throat. "Er, George."

"I am your aunt. Your other aunt."

"I know."

His stunned expression seemed to amuse Olivia a good deal. "Hello, Henry," she said to the duke.

The latter nodded. Of all his family, only he seemed unperturbed by the interruption.

"I *am* sorry for the sudden arrival, Julia," she added. "But once we got the news, we had to come up, of course."

"How did you get the news?" wondered her sister faintly.

A good question, Emily thought. She hadn't had time to write herself, and she was certain her aunt had not done so.

"Not from you," exploded Alasdair. "Is there something havey cavey about this business? Because I'll have you know I won't stand for any…"

The duchess went pale. George choked again. Emily's mother seemed to be enjoying herself. "I still have a few friends in London," she said. "Cynthia sent me the notice."

Her sister's lips turned down. "She always was a little sneak." Her expression showed that she regretted the remark as soon as it was made.

"What's there to be sneaking about?" demanded Alasdair. "I'll have the whole story, by God. And if there's anything smoky about it, someone will pay." He glared around the room pugnaciously. George gulped.

"It was rather…soon for an engagement," said Olivia. Alasdair growled.

"Emily is lovely," countered the duchess. "Can you be surprised that she captivated a young man…"

Another rumble from Alasdair made her falter briefly.

"And there was a prior acquaintance," she added. "So it is not really…"

"What?" Alasdair glowered. "Emily wasn't acquainted with any young sprigs of fashion."

"It was the gentleman who had trouble on the road," Olivia told him, clearly not for the first time.

"Eh?"

"The one you wanted to paint as Samson," explained

Emily, then wished she'd held her tongue as her father's irate gaze swung in her direction.

"That vagabond?" He looked incredulous, then enraged. He turned on the duchess again. "You've engaged *my* daughter to some wandering scoundrel who can't even keep a horse under him?"

This seemed unfair even to Emily. "He is Lord Warrington, Papa."

As usual, he ignored any point that might weaken his argument. "This will all have to be gone into in detail. I have not given my consent, and I think it highly unlikely that I will do so."

"We will certainly talk with the young man," said Olivia soothingly. She smiled. "And as long as we are in town, we can renew some old acquaintances. You can put us up for a few days, Julia?"

Her sister looked horrified.

"I...that is...are you sure you would not be more comfortable...Papa..."

"Well, Papa did say that I was never to darken his door again," Olivia pointed out. "And he and Alasdair have never really gotten on."

From the way her aunt's eyes widened, Emily took this to be a considerable understatement.

"And with Emily here..." Olivia let her voice trail off and fixed her sister with a steady gaze.

The duchess looked wildly around the room. Her son evaded her gaze. Her husband shrugged, disavowing responsibility. Emily kept her eyes on the floor. While she felt some sympathy for her aunt, her longing for her parents' company was far greater. "Of course you are... welcome," she murmured at last.

Her sister gave her a genuine smile. "Thank you, Julia. Really, we won't trouble you in the least."

If the duchess believed that, Emily thought... But clearly, she didn't.

Later that evening, a more expected arrival was taking place as Lady Fielding greeted her late husband's niece. Richard returned from dinner at his club in the midst of these effusions and in time to admire Lydia Farrell's dashing traveling costume and the favorable changes time had wrought in his relative by marriage.

She was no longer skinny and diffident. Quite the contrary. The years had generously rounded her figure. Her face was slightly fuller as well, which became her, her complexion was ruddy rather than pale, and her dark brown hair gleamed with vitality. All the country air, he decided. "How do you do, Lord Warrington?"

"Oh, you must call him Richard," exclaimed his mother. "We are all family here."

"I don't think I could do that," was the cool reply.

The look that went with it told Richard that he had been even ruder than he remembered when they had met years ago. "Please do," he said.

She seemed surprised, and examined his expression before saying, "Then you must call me Lydia."

"Good," said Lady Fielding as she led the way to the drawing room. "I'm so glad you've come. It has been so long."

"More than ten years." Lydia threw him another sidelong glance. "I believe Richard was still at school the last time we met."

"A scrubby schoolboy, in fact. And you were barely out of the schoolroom."

She smiled ruefully. "It has been a long time. But I don't think I ever called you scrubby."

"Even though I richly deserved it."

He had startled her again.

"You were extremely polite," he added.

"I expect I was a mass of nerves. My upbringing was very retired, you know. I had no idea how to go on in society."

"You grew up in Wales?"

She nodded, turning away. "What a lovely room." She sank gracefully down on a sofa. "And how wonderful not to be bouncing in a carriage any longer."

Lady Fielding prepared to pour tea; and Richard leaned back in a chair, taking a cup when he was offered it. Lydia raised one brow. Clearly, she had expected him to excuse himself.

"How is your family?" asked his mother.

"Very well, thank you. Jeremy and Thomas—my sons—are at school now. William is deep in the spring planting, as he is every year. I tried to convince him to come with me, but he hates society. He said he would rather be shut in a cellar for a month than trapped in a ballroom for one night."

Richard smiled at his mother's incredulous expression.

"But you must… Surely even in Wales there is some society?" she said.

"Oh yes. We dine with friends, and there is even an assembly hall not too far away." She gestured as if dismissing this topic. "Tell me about London. I have only been here once before, when I was presented years ago."

As his mother began to relay all the latest gossip, Lydia appeared amused and interested. His mother was more animated than he had seen her for a long time. This visit was really a fortunate accident. Perhaps it would solve one of the host of problems that beset him.

❧

Emily signaled a hack near the duchess's town house, and quickly climbed in. The household was in disarray this morning as her parents settled in and her aunt brooded about the consequences of their visit. No one had seen her slip out alone, and no one was likely to miss her for an hour or two.

The cab let her out at the Fitzgibbons' house.

"Have you heard anything?" she asked when they were seated in the drawing room.

Daniel looked solemn. "There's a whisper—no more than that, mind—that some bullyboys have been after your Lord Warrington."

"He is not my…"

"We saw the announcement in the paper," put in Mrs. Fitzgibbon. She smiled at Emily over her knitting.

"Oh." It was public knowledge now. Emily's heart quailed when she remembered the evening party they were to attend tonight and all the attention the news would draw. Her parents would probably want to go along. A small shudder shook her.

"We wish you very happy," added Mary Fitzgibbon.

"Oh. Er, thank you." Mary was eyeing her dubiously. She would have to learn to do better than that. She would be pelted with congratulations—sincere or not— tonight. "Bullyboys?" she managed.

Daniel shrugged. "The sort you can hire to cosh a bloke or slip him into the river."

"Killers, you mean?" Her voice squeaked a little on the words.

Her host nodded. "Nobody we would know, you understand. Or our friends, either. I don't hold with violence, so I don't hear, you might say, directly. Can't vouch for the truth of it."

"He has been attacked, though."

"Well, there you are then."

Emily sat still for a moment, trying to take it in. It was one thing to have suspicions, and quite another to have them confirmed. Confronted with actual flesh and blood killers, she felt daunted.

"So that's that," added Daniel. "Happy to have been…"

"Can you find out anything more about these men? Particularly who hired them?"

Daniel shook his head. "I don't care to get mixed up with…"

"We could ask the Bruiser," suggested Mary.

He glared at her and made a gesture as if cutting off further talk.

Mary absorbed it placidly. "It's her promised husband. We can't just let it go."

"The Bruiser'd be no help," was the response. "And dealing with the likes of him ain't what I like at all."

"I don't want to get you in trouble," began Emily.

"You're exaggerating, Daniel," declared Mrs. Fitzgibbon. "And the boy was a great help when Jack had his…little problem."

"Boy!"

"You know quite well he is little more."

Daniel looked extremely unhappy. "There'll be a price."

"I would be happy to pay whatever…"

"If money's all he asks," growled Daniel.

"You worry far too much," said his wife. She smiled at Emily. "It's what's kept us one step ahead of…difficulties. But this is quite all right."

"If you're sure." Emily frowned at Daniel's woebegone expression.

His wife gave him a look.

"I reckon it'll be all right," he conceded.

She let out her breath. "Thank you. I don't know what I would do without your help."

"Happy to do it, my dear," answered Mrs. Fitzgibbon. Her husband merely grimaced.

In the hack on the way home, Emily thought over what she had heard. The worst sort of ruffians were apparently after Richard. She must tell him this right away. She would have to get him alone, make him listen.

Then she remembered; they were engaged. They would be expected, and allowed, to talk privately together. She relaxed a little in the seat. She had been right to go along with the betrothal. The matter was even more urgent than she'd known. But now she would be able to really help Richard resolve it. And then, of course, she would break off the engagement. It wasn't going to do anyone any harm. It was all going to work. There would be difficulties, but she would overcome them.

She was feeling quite sanguine as she slipped back into the duchess's house and made her way upstairs. It wasn't until she heard her father's bellow from an upper room that she remembered the difficulties might be greater than she knew.

Eight

"OH DEAR," SAID EMILY WHEN SHE WALKED INTO THE party and discovered the hostess's scheme of entertainment. She was calling the event "Homage to the Arts," and she had various examples stationed around the edges of the reception rooms. Emily could see a burly man in the far corner applying a chisel to a block of stone and a group of actors playing a scene on the other side. There was music in the air. Undoubtedly a painter sat in some other part of the house plying his craft. Nothing could be more calculated to enrage her father, who was already out of sorts at the mere thought of attending a *ton* party. She moved quickly into the crowd, putting some distance between herself and the inevitable explosion and callously abandoning her aunt, whose worst fears were about to be realized. Several acquaintances offered their felicitations as she moved through the rooms. Emily accepted them without pausing, searching for a refuge from complications.

Richard was standing in the far salon, watching a pair of dancers stationed in the corner, in an area set off by velvet ropes twined with flowers. In this constricted space, they were taking poses from a ballet, unable to really execute the steps. Richard looked torn between amusement and disgust at the sight.

Emily went to stand beside him just as a young sprig of fashion offered the dancers a bottle of champagne, which they eagerly accepted. "That should make it a bit easier for them," she said.

Richard turned and discovered her.

"Perhaps we should do the same for all the 'arts,'" she added.

"You don't approve of our hostess's scheme?"

"It's insulting."

He raised his eyebrows.

"She's exhibiting artists as if they were animals in a zoo. And all these people"—she indicated the crowd around them—"are treating them just that way."

"You are an unaccountable creature."

Emily was taken aback.

"Your conversation is a muddle of inanities and impertinence. But then you come out with an interesting observation—like that one. I cannot make you out."

"Inanities?" she glared at him.

He was nodding when the festivities were interrupted by a roar and clatter from another room.

"What was that?" Richard moved in the direction of the sounds.

Emily sighed. "I expect it was my father."

"He is here?"

"He and Mama came up to town yesterday."

"Ah." His expression hardened. "Come to see the new son-in-law, have they?" His tone was cutting.

"To thrash him more likely," Emily couldn't help answering. At his startled look, she added, "My father is… He is not like other people, you know."

"I did observe that. His arrival must be very awkward for you."

"Oh, I'm used to him." She had to smile. "My aunt is in quite a taking. When he said he was coming here tonight, I thought she would faint."

"I thought you wished to conceal your parentage."

"What?" She drew herself up straighter.

"You asked me not to speak of them—not to gossip, if I recollect correctly." His voice implied that he certainly did.

All of her aunt's fears would be realized now, Emily realized. If Aunt Julia were right, her own debut in society might be wrecked by the gossip. She looked around the room at the glittering crowd. It would be too bad; but the truth was, she had much more important matters on her mind. "My aunt was worried. And she convinced me that I must be too."

"But you have changed your mind?"

Emily nodded impatiently. "I must speak to you about something important."

"Now that you have snared a husband," he added.

"What?"

"You needn't care about society's opinion, since you have gotten what you came for?"

Emily struggled briefly to contain her outrage. He didn't understand anything, she told herself. Taking a calming breath, she bent a little toward him and lowered her voice. "I have some information that you must hear."

"Information?"

"Yes. There are—"

"You are a mass of contradictions."

"You must listen to me."

"Either you are the most devious, heartless little schemer I have ever encountered…"

Emily glared at him.

"Or you are demented. I suppose, given your upbringing, I should be charitable and choose the latter. But it is difficult for a man who has been entrapped into marriage to be charitable."

She stood very still, telling herself again that he had a right to be angry. But his words and contemptuous expression still cut her to the quick. "I did not mean…" she began, and found she couldn't continue.

"You do understand that I have no fortune?"

Emily fought to hide her agitation from the people around them. Eventually, Richard would understand.

She took another calming breath and rushed on before he could stop her again. "Some…friends of mine have heard rumors about the attacks on you. Ruffians may have been hired to harm you."

Richard stared down at her.

"They are trying to find out who this may be," Emily added hurriedly. "If we could find them, then we could discover who is behind…"

"We?"

His gaze made Emily falter. "Well, that is…"

"I have told you it is none of your affair," he continued, but he said it as if he were mystified, rather than offended, by her persistence.

"You admit that someone is after you, then?"

His frown didn't seem directed wholly at her. "I have been forced to acknowledge that something odd is going on."

"Thank God," replied Emily, feeling immense relief.

"Why should you care?"

He really had the most piercing gaze, she thought. It took her a moment to gather her faculties. "I care about anyone who is in trouble."

He obviously found this unsatisfactory.

"And I was there at the beginning, you know. When those two men were trying to drown you. I have some… some responsibility, since I chased them off."

"You?"

"The dogs and I."

He looked bemused.

"And it's interesting," she finished.

"What?"

Instantly, she regretted that final phrase. "It's an… an obligation."

He examined her as if he had never seen such a creature before. "Having, as you see it, saved my life, you now feel obligated to safeguard it?"

"That's it." Relieved, Emily smiled at him.

"Ridiculous," he pronounced. "The obligation—if one did exist—would be on my side."

"But if you save something, you cannot just abandon it afterward."

He looked offended. "We're not talking of a half-dead kitten, or an injured fox." There seemed to be amusement in his voice as well, though she couldn't be sure.

"So I should just let you be killed?"

"I assure you I am exceedingly difficult to kill."

"But a systematic attack…"

"Where did you hear of such a thing?"

"I told you. Friends of mine…"

"What sort of friends would be privy to that kind of information?" He looked around the crowded room, his lip curling a little. "Certainly not those you have made in London?"

"Old friends."

"Miss Crane, you are being deliberately unhelpful."

"I cannot tell you who they are. They would not wish to be known to you." The Fitzgibbons would be exceedingly unhappy if she betrayed their true identity, or their connection with some of the town's more unsavory elements.

"Indeed. But I am to take the word of these mysterious individuals…"

"Well, what other clues do you have?"

He raised an eyebrow.

"How else will you find out who is after you?"

"I have certain resources of my own."

"Are you going to refuse help just because it comes from me?" Emily was horrified to hear her voice break slightly as she spoke.

He seemed to be trying to formulate an answer when a low musical voice interrupted with, "I beg your pardon."

Emily turned, and almost collided with a tall attractive woman bearing down on them. Emily stepped out of her way.

"Richard, you must rescue me," said the newcomer. "I believe your mother has introduced me to everyone here, and I have forgotten all their names."

Emily watched Richard smile down at her. The woman was dark haired and quite beautiful, and she had an enviable ease and confidence.

"And some mad earl smashed the painter's easel," she continued. "He threatened to slather the hostess in red paint for 'mocking creative life blood.' I had no idea that *ton* parties were so…active."

A small sound escaped Emily. That had to be her father, though he was only the son of an earl.

The woman was looking inquiringly at her, as if wondering why she didn't take herself off.

"This is Emily Crane, Lydia," said Richard. "Miss Crane my, er, cousin Lydia Farrell."

"Ah. Miss Crane, I'm sorry I didn't recognize you. I've just come up to London. May I offer my felicitations." Her gaze was speculative and appraising.

"Thank you," answered Emily faintly.

Lydia looked from her to Richard. "Am I interrupting? I don't mean to intrude on your tête-à-tête."

Emily had a strong desire to say yes, but she held her tongue as Richard assured his cousin that she was quite welcome. He certainly seemed to find her so. The conversation had been a fiasco from start to finish. It was hard to see how it could have been worse.

"Sheldon," bellowed a deep voice behind her.

Emily closed her eyes in despair. Things can always get worse, she reminded herself.

"Or Warrington, whatever you call yourself," continued her father, descending on their little group like the wrath of God. "I want a word with you."

Richard merely waited. He didn't look the least intimidated.

"I have not given my consent to this engagement!"

Was that a spark of hope in Richard's eyes? It certainly looked like one. People were starting to turn and listen. A few were drawing closer as if part of the entertainment was beginning.

"And I don't like it above half," her father went on. "Puffing it off in the papers without consulting me." Alasdair Crane huffed like a goaded bull. "Not quite the thing, eh?" He waited for an answer, but no one gave him one.

Emily watched a series of expressions pass across Richard's face. To her, they looked like temptation, compunction, and regret. She wondered what the crowd made of them. "Have you, er, spoken with the duchess?" asked Richard finally.

"Julia has nothing to do with the matter. We're talking about *my* daughter." He glared at the other guests, who now surrounded them in a clump. "All of you hear me?" he demanded. "Did I speak loud enough for you jackals?"

Emily was shaken by a crazed desire to laugh. Since she also felt utterly humiliated and unaccountably afraid, what came out was more like a bleat.

"And you, my girl. You ought to have known better than to accept him without consulting your parents."

The laugh was in her throat, side by side with a moan. She gulped and nodded.

Her mother came gliding up and put a hand on Alasdair's arm. She whispered something to him.

"I've said what I meant to," he answered aloud. "You come round and see me," he commanded Richard. "I have some questions for you."

Richard was actually smiling, Emily saw with incredulity. He bowed his head in acknowledgment.

"Come along," added her father peremptorily to Emily. As she followed her parents through the murmuring crowd, Emily saw Richard's cousin thread her arm through his and smile warmly up at him.

❧

When Richard presented himself at the duchess of Welford's splendid town house the next day, he found he was looking forward to the visit with a surprising amount of anticipation. He had been summoned by Alasdair Crane, after all, and he could only foresee the unexpected.

The butler ushered him into a small parlor near the back of the house. It was well away from the main rooms, he realized with a smile. The duchess must have given orders to keep her unpredictable brother-in-law as far from her as possible.

The door opened, and Alasdair Crane came in. But the bluster and outrage of their last encounter was gone. The man looked almost forlorn, Richard thought.

"I have no studio here," he said, as if this would naturally be Richard's first concern. "I cannot paint. And Olivia is making me buy new clothes." He fingered the lapels of his coat—which did indeed look new—as if the mere sight of it pained him.

"That…that is too bad." Richard had to hide a smile.

"It's intolerable. She knows that."

Was he supposed to offer some sort of solution? "Perhaps you could use a room on the upper floors for a studio?" The place must have thirty rooms.

Crane shook his head. "Julia claims the smell of paint makes her ill." He grimaced. "I've always doubted that she and Olivia were really sisters. Old Shelbury's such a dry stick. I shouldn't wonder if their mother played him false." This idea seemed to cheer him. "Olivia's father must have been a different sort altogether—an artist even."

Richard couldn't contain a short laugh.

It attracted Crane's full attention. "What are you doing here, anyway?"

"You summoned me, sir."

"I did? Oh yes." He shook his head again. "Can't think clearly when I'm not painting. It's this engagement, isn't it?"

"I believe so," answered Richard, making an effort to keep his voice steady.

"Yes, that's it." Emily's father walked over to a sofa near the fireplace, his steps heavy. "May as well sit down."

He did so, and Richard followed suit. Silence fell.

"Look at that light," said Crane suddenly.

Turning to follow his gaze, Richard saw a shaft of sunshine streaming through one of the windows and pooling on the yellow carpet.

"Like butter. Butter spangled as an opera dancer's tights."

A bit surprised, Richard nodded. The motes of dust floating in the light did make it look rather like that.

"It'll be gone in half an hour and I won't have touched a brush to canvas."

"I'm sorry." He actually was, Richard realized. The man's deprivation was so real, his face so forlorn. Moved by a sudden impulse, Richard said, "When did you know you wanted to paint?"

Alasdair didn't look the least bit surprised by the question. "I was four years old. I was playing with some building blocks in the nursery when my sister's governess began a lesson in watercolors." His dark eyes bored into Richard's. "Her brush swept across the paper like a bluebird's wing, and suddenly I couldn't see anything else. She let me try, and…" He made a gesture signifying that everything had flowed from there.

"So it was a gift, a talent. You didn't have to struggle and wonder what your purpose might be."

Alasdair Crane shook his head, his attention fully on

Richard for perhaps the first time in their short acquaintance. "You don't want to paint?"

Richard smiled slightly. The man's obsession was almost endearing. "No, I've never wanted that. But I do want…something like that," Richard blurted out. Part of him couldn't believe he was confiding in a stranger, but another pushed him to get any guidance he could. "A task or a pursuit that compels me."

Alasdair nodded as if this were the most reasonable statement in the world.

Richard felt a curious relief, along with satisfaction. He had known Alasdair Crane would understand this desire.

"What do you love?"

Richard frowned, at a loss.

"Think about it. Find what you love, and follow it, and that will be enough for you."

"But…" This seemed both too simple, and immensely complicated. "How will that tell me what to *do*?"

"The doing's not the problem." Crane waved a hand. "Or, it is. But not the main one. When you have the passion, wrestling with the details of the work is a splendid fight."

Richard puzzled over his words. They sounded good, but he was no further along in finding a next step.

Giving the shaft of sunlight a longing look, Crane said. "So you want to marry Emily?"

Richard gathered his wits. There was no suitable reply to the question. It would not be honest to agree, and to disagree would create considerable havoc. He could understand the duchess's decision not to tell the Cranes the circumstances behind the engagement. Emily's father would probably try to call him out. Or just shoot him.

"Olivia reminded me what it was like to have one's wishes opposed." Crane sat a bit straighter on the sofa. "I would have killed anyone who tried to keep her from me. I still would." He gave a sharp nod.

"You are to be envied, sir."

"I know it." He grimaced. "It was damned unsettling, finding myself in Shelbury's shoes, acting just like him."

"I'm sure you could never be like the marquess."

"You would have thought so, but now that it's a daughter of my own…" He scowled. "Hostages to fortune, that's what the bard called them. And with only the one child…" He sighed. "The important thing is to see her happy. That's what Olivia says, and I agree. So if it's you she wants…" He examined Richard and seemed to find him wanting. "You're mighty cool about this."

Richard groped for words.

"In your place, I'd've made it clear by this time that I didn't give a rap what her parents thought—or anyone else." He peered at Richard. "I'd've consigned them all to perdition."

"Perhaps we are of different temperaments." Oddly, Crane's accusations stung.

"You're not afraid of me. I can see that."

"No."

"You don't much care what I think." He frowned.

"I hope for your good opinion, of course."

Alasdair snorted. "Fustian."

"Not at all. You have shaped your life to your own design. I admire that."

"Trying to turn me up sweet?"

Richard shrugged, letting him take or leave his remarks. He had meant them, though.

"I don't understand you." Crane leaned forward as if decreasing the distance between them would help. "You've said nothing about Emily in all this."

They were back to the sticky part. To tell the truth would be to go back on his word. It occurred to Richard that this was the first time in his life that he had seriously inconvenienced himself for another person. He had a sudden sense of vertigo.

Crane sat back, resting his hands on his knees. "Well?"

"Not everyone can…express himself as fully as you do."

This brought no break in the hard scrutiny.

"I'm not an artist. It is not so easy to say how I feel."
That was certainly true.

The older man continued to watch him, though his
gaze seemed slightly less hostile.

"You will be wondering about my prospects," said
Richard, attempting a diversion. "I have to admit
they are not good. My estates in Somerset are heavily
encumbered, and one in Wales left me by my stepfather
is mainly rock. My income is…limited."

Crane shook his head as if bewildered.

"The cottage at Morne is Elizabethan. There are
some beautiful vistas. Very paintable." Paintable? he
thought incredulously. This eccentric man was reducing
him to idiocy.

"I don't know how to do this," replied Crane. He
sounded pathetically bewildered. "I'm not some sort
of old Roman paterfamilias." He blinked at Richard,
then rose. "I need Olivia. Where is Olivia?" He made
his way to the door, leaving Richard alone in the
small parlor.

It was a relief. He felt as if he'd been interrogated,
though he hadn't really. It would have been enormously
satisfying to declare a great love, to fling his passion in the
face of all opposition, to dare anyone to thwart him. He
longed to have such feelings, such certainty…

There was very little sound here at the back of the
house. The silence enveloped Richard. He wondered if
Crane meant to return, or if he should go? Sitting back
on the sofa, he waited.

❦

In her bedchamber upstairs, Emily had been enduring a
similar trial. Her mother had come to her about the time

Richard arrived and settled in for a cozy chat. "It seems so long since we had a chance to talk," she began.

They didn't talk very often at home, Emily thought, and braced herself for difficulties.

"I didn't expect that you would become engaged so soon. I thought you would have a season at least." She made a deprecating gesture. "Of course one cannot control these things. When you fall desperately in love…"

She paused, giving Emily the opportunity to profess her passion. Emily swallowed. Should she tell her the truth?

Looking a little concerned, her mother went on. "I remember the first time I spoke to your father. It was a rout party. His mother had made him go, and he was so magnificently angry." She smiled. "He tried to be quite savage with me, reviling my dress and the petty emptiness of society." Her blue eyes twinkled. "And I told him it was all a kind of art. I had heard about him, you see, and made it my business to meet him. It wasn't two weeks before we…" She broke off with a self-conscious laugh. "Well, never mind that ancient history. We were talking of you."

Emily had to tell her something. When I met Richard Sheldon, two men were trying to kill him, she thought wildly.

"I suppose you found Mr. Sheldon—Lord Warrington, that is—ah, interesting when he was at our house?" Olivia prompted finally.

"Yes."

"And then you met again in London."

"At a ball. We danced." That had been quite unpleasant, she remembered. "And walked in the park, and…" In a sudden panic, she wondered whether her aunt had confided the whole story to her mother. She hadn't told Papa, of course. No one would do such a silly thing as that.

"And you fell in love," said her mother. "He is a handsome man."

The concerned look that accompanied this spurred Emily to action. She nodded vigorously. "He…he was shipwrecked in the jungle and had to fight his way out. It took months and months. There were huge snakes and, er, panthers."

"Really?" Her mother was looking a bit puzzled.

"I think that is admirable," Emily blundered on. "It shows true courage and, er, initiative, don't you think?"

"Umm."

"He is quite at home in society, too. He knows everyone."

"Does he?"

And someone is plotting to kill him, and I want to find out who, so I agreed to an engagement when my aunt found me sleeping in his arms. No, it didn't sound good. Emily stole a look at her mother. She wasn't afraid she would be scandalized. Quite the opposite, actually. She would undoubtedly feel that nothing warranted a forced marriage, and the whole thing should be called off as soon as possible. Despite everything, Emily didn't want that.

"But, my dear…"

"So he is just everything I want in a man."

"You make it sound like a recipe," objected her mother.

"I'm not like you. I don't get swept away by great gusts of feeling." It was true, Emily thought, with a brush of melancholy.

Her mother frowned. "You have always been such a practical, self-possessed girl," was the worried response.

Emily almost smiled. "Some parents would find that reassuring."

"We love you very much, Emily. And we want to see you happy—as happy as we have been."

"Perhaps that isn't possible," she muttered.

"What?"

"I'm sure I'll be very happy," she declared.

"But the way you speak of…" They were interrupted by her father's voice, bellowing Olivia's name. "Oh dear."

Her expression alarmed Emily. "What has Papa been doing?"

"Talking to Lord Warrington. At least, I hope that is all he has been doing."

Emily rose in consternation. But before she could make another move, her father burst into the room looking plaintive. "I can't make him out," he complained. "He don't seem to give a farthing for…"

"What did you do to him?"

The intensity in her voice seemed to gratify both of Emily's parents. They exchanged a glance.

"I didn't do anything. You should see him, Olivia. You're much better at ferreting out…"

"I will see him." Emily started for the door. "You stay here."

In a flurry of skirts, she was gone.

"Well, *that's* more like it," said Alasdair.

❧

Emily peered into four empty rooms before she found Richard in the small back parlor. He was standing by a window looking undecided when she burst in and came to a sudden halt just inside the door. "Oh, there you are." Having achieved her object, Emily could think of nothing else to say.

"Here I am," he agreed.

He always looked so at ease. It was admirable, and rather irritating. "I hope my father did not…" Did not what? Of course he had ranted and accused and done all the other things that had made any young man she encountered think they were all mad.

"He is a very interesting man," replied Richard. "I envy him his passion for his work."

"You do?"

He nodded. "It is a gift—to know so clearly what you wish to do, and to concentrate every faculty upon it."

This sort of reaction was unprecedented in Emily's experience. She couldn't quite believe it. "He didn't shout at you?"

Richard shrugged. "Oh, yes, a bit. More last night, you know."

She certainly did. "And you… Didn't you mind?"

"It seems to be just part of what he is," was the astonishing response.

Her mouth was a little open, Emily realized. She closed it.

"Perhaps it comes of being an artist."

Maybe being in London, in her aunt's house, had muted her father's usual outrageous behavior. Then she remembered the smashed easel. That wasn't it.

"I'm glad you came down. I wanted to speak to you," Richard added.

For some reason, Emily's pulse accelerated.

"About what you said last night—these rumors you mentioned. I suppose I shall have to look into them." He grimaced. "Ridiculous as the idea still seems."

"You were attacked—"

"I've conceded the point. If you will just tell me where to find these friends of yours." She started to speak, and he waved her to silence. "And don't tell me again that you cannot say."

"I can't." Daniel would be furious. "I'll find out if they've learned anything else and tell you at once."

"Unacceptable."

"I won't betray them to you."

"Betray? What am I, the Inquisition?" He frowned at her. "Just who are these people? They are beginning to sound rather unsavory."

Emily gave a small shrug.

"What would your father say if he knew you were associating with dubious characters?"

She couldn't restrain a laugh.

Richard raised one dark brow. "Ah. I suppose they are friends of his." He surveyed her. "Perhaps I should ask him about them, then?"

Her hand went out in an involuntary gesture. "No!"

"Ah?"

"You mustn't tell him about…any of this."

"Because he would prevent you from seeing these 'friends'?" He watched her. "No, I can see that isn't it."

"If he knows about the attacks, he might find out about other things as well."

"What other…?" Richard appeared to understand suddenly. "About the true nature of our engagement, perhaps?"

She avoided his eyes. Silence lengthened. Finally, when she could stand it no longer, she looked up. He was gazing at her as if she fascinated him.

"I am beginning to have serious doubts about you."

"What?"

"You do understand that I have no fortune whatsoever. In fact, I can scarcely support a household of my own. It will be a very poor one."

"I don't care…" began Emily, then was stopped by the expression on his face.

"I am not known as a pleasant or a generous man." His scrutiny intensified.

She tried to keep her expression blank.

"Yes, I can see that you've heard that."

He was watching her as the hawk does a rabbit. She needed to say something sensible, Emily thought, to divert him. But nothing occurred to her.

"So, we have a man of uncertain temper and no

resources. And we have a beautiful young woman who is likely to attract many admirers."

She glanced at him, and quickly away. The look in his eyes was making her breathless.

"Miss Crane, precisely why did you become engaged to me?"

She looked down. "The...the scandal. My aunt said..."

"Yes. She alarmed us both with her hysteria over the scandal, didn't she?"

Emily risked another look. He seemed exhilarated, like a man on the trail of a promising quarry.

"Or did she?" He was staring as if he wanted to see right through her. "When you first came to London, you took instruction from the duchess."

"She knows all about society," Emily protested, understanding just how the fox feels.

Richard was nodding. "She does indeed. And so you followed her advice." He looked triumphant. "And it was a dead bore, wasn't it?"

"I don't know what you mean."

"No?" He shook his head. "I couldn't fathom the difference in you—from the decisive young woman I met in the country to a simpering ninnyhammer."

"I was not!"

"Oh, you were." He smiled mockingly at her. "I assure you, you were."

"Young ladies of fashion..."

"Are simpering ninnyhammers. I will certainly grant you that. And the duchess would be just the person to mold one." Richard looked as if he were having a wonderful time. "So you found it a dead bore. And you fixed on these...incidents."

"Attacks," corrected Emily.

He made a dismissive gesture. "And you began to think about them, because they were vastly more interesting than a London season."

"I enjoy going into society. Having new gowns and meeting new people."

"You did for a while." He smiled at her. "A short while."

Emily tossed her head. "You know nothing about it."

"Don't I?" His smile was more like a grin now. "So you asked these mysterious friends for help, and busied yourself in other ways. And then there was the carriage accident."

"Attack," she corrected again. She was beginning to be angry at his teasing.

He nodded. "And the night in the fields."

He looked a little self-conscious then. Emily felt her cheeks warm at the memory.

Richard cleared his throat. "The duchess reacted predictably. And you accepted my suit." His gaze sharpened. "Why?"

"She told me I would be ruined if…"

"Yes, yes." He brushed this aside. "I cannot believe that Alasdair Crane's daughter would give a snap of her fingers for that."

"Let him find out about it, and see how wrong you are!"

He digested this. "Well, yes. But it was extremely unlikely that he would find out. Your aunt would never tell him, and he sees no one in society."

"Someone would have told my mother," she protested. But she knew it sounded weak.

"Possibly. But from what I have seen of your mother, she would be inclined to listen to your side of the story. And she appears eminently capable of handling your father."

There was no denying this.

"You wanted to stay on the trail of the attacks," he mused. "And it would have been almost impossible to do so unless…" He watched her with deepening fascination. "Do you have the slightest wish to marry me?"

"No!" declared Emily, goaded beyond endurance. "And I have no intention of doing so."

For the first time in the conversation, he appeared at a loss. "Yet, you did accept me."

"I intended to break it off as soon as…"

"You had solved the mystery. I knew it!"

"You don't know anything!"

"Indeed? Are you claiming that I'm wrong?"

She would have liked nothing better. The fact that she couldn't made Emily even angrier. He was so despicably smug.

"So you weren't trying to get your hooks into me. It all begins to make sense."

"My…?" Rage choked her for a moment. "I hope they do kill you!"

"Now, now, when you have made such efforts on my behalf?"

"You don't deserve them." She smoldered at his amused expression. "I should have let those men throw you in the pond."

"And miss everything that has happened since? You can't mean it."

He was laughing at her. Emily folded her arms and gritted her teeth. "I am declaring the engagement at an end as of this instant."

This penetrated his mockery. "Just like that?"

"Precisely like that."

He considered.

In a moment, he would show his relief at being rid of her. Despite her anger the idea stung.

"There's no need to be hasty," he said.

"What?"

"You had a certain plan in mind," he went on slowly. He seemed to be working something out in his head. When he met her gaze she felt an odd sort of tremor. "You won't introduce me to these useful friends of yours?"

"I can't."

He ruminated further. "Why shouldn't we work together?"

"Together?"

"You appear to have some valuable…acquaintances. I am more able to act on their information."

She felt a thrill of excitement. She did want to see the thing through to the end—even if he was the most infuriating man on the face of the earth.

"The engagement is in name only," he added.

Emily nodded. "Absolutely."

"We will find a way to end it when the game is up."

"I will certainly do so."

He gave a nod, and after a moment, held out his hand. "We are agreed then?"

She hesitated. "We will pursue the attackers together?"

"In our individual spheres."

She wasn't sure she liked this.

"You appear to have the only information on how to begin," he added.

Slowly, she took his hand. It was very large, and warm.

He eyed her with something like admiration. "You are very like your father after all."

"Don't be ridiculous. I am nothing like my father."

Richard's answering smile was as irritating as ever.

Nine

THE FOLLOWING MORNING, EMILY SET OFF RIGHT after breakfast to visit the Fitzgibbons. She found only Mary at home. Daniel was holding a dancing class at the mansion of one of his noble patrons.

"Did Daniel speak to the...Bruiser?" Emily asked her.

Her hostess nodded placidly. As usual, her hands were busy with knitting needles. "The poor boy's wits are a bit addled by this time, but he said he would see what he could discover among his friends."

"Addled?" This didn't sound promising.

"It happens to the best of them, which I'm afraid the Bruiser never was. No one can take that sort of punishment forever."

"Punishment?"

Mary nodded, then noticed Emily's confusion. "He is a fighter, my dear. Fisticuffs."

"Oh." Emily had heard of the bare-knuckle matches that were so popular with the sporting set.

"Not a very successful one. That's why he may be useful."

"I don't understand."

"It's men like the Bruiser who would be engaged to do someone harm. They have no other profession, you see, and if they do not win their matches...they are discarded by the Fancy and must turn to other shifts."

"It sounds dreadful. Perhaps I shouldn't have asked you to speak to him."

"Oh, we've known the Bruiser since he was a lad.

He'll be all right. Some of his friends now"—she made a disapproving sound—"we steer clear of them."

Emily nodded. "But if his wits are addled…"

"He has enough left to ask a few simple questions. He was a right sharp little boy." She sighed. "We tried to keep him out of the ring, but he was mad for boxing as soon as he saw it."

Suppressing her doubts, Emily thanked her for their efforts. "You will tell me as soon as he finds out anything?"

"Of course, dear."

Emily sat with her a few minutes longer, chatting about Daniel's success in London and some old friends. She was just rising to go when there were sounds of an arrival below. They heard voices outside the room, and then a slight brown-haired girl walked in, grinning when she saw the two of them.

"Sarah," exclaimed Emily and Mary at the same moment.

"I didn't expect you this morning," added the latter.

"Herr doktor isn't feeling the thing. He's laid up in bed."

"Is it serious?" asked her mother.

Sarah shook her head. "A feverish cold, though you'd think it was the cholera from the way he carries on. Hullo, Emily."

"How are you? I've been hoping to see you."

Sarah grinned again. "Could have come to one of our 'evenings.' My gentleman could call up a spirit for you. Maybe Rex, eh?"

"He was a dog." With a nasty temper and yellow fangs. She had no desire to see him again.

Sarah made an offhand gesture. "Schelling does dogs, cats, people, whatever you like. We had a pony once, come to think of it. This weepy cove loved it when he was a little lad."

"Language, Sarah," admonished her mother.

"This 'melancholy gentleman' had loved it," she amended.

"You are working for this…?"

"Student of the Adepts of the East," Sarah supplied. "That I am. I nursemaid the visitors. Talk up his powers and tell them stories of what he's done for other poor souls. The usual line of patter. And I keep them out of the way of…things they don't need to see."

"Do you like it?" wondered Emily. She remembered Sarah as an enthusiastic child actress and an endlessly inventive playmate.

"I've learned some new dodges. Dad doesn't like it, I know. Says we're taking advantage of the bereaved. But some of them find it real comforting."

"What sort of people come?"

"All sorts." Sarah gave her a sidelong look. "That fiancé of yours has been to see Herr Schelling."

"What?" Emily was dumbfounded.

"Warrington, isn't it? That's what the paper said."

"Yes, but…"

"He was escorting his mother. And he seemed right put out about it."

"Lady Fielding came to Schelling's?"

"Oh, she's one of our regulars. Herr doktor uses her case as a draw."

"Her…?"

"Her son was lost at sea. Well, you must know all about that. Lady Fielding was broken up about it. Schelling gave her a good show, and then his lordship up and walks in on one of the sessions! Scared the living daylights out of everyone there and made Schelling's reputation, I can tell you."

Richard must have hated that, Emily thought.

"So you're actually getting married?"

For a moment, Emily thought she had some-how divined the reality behind her engagement.

Then she realized that it was just the amazement of a childhood friend.

"I don't intend to get leg-shackled for a good long while."

"Sarah," exclaimed her mother, who had been calmly knitting through this conversation.

"Contract a suitable alliance," corrected Sarah with fond mockery. "The other says it a lot better, Ma."

"I don't want you to use…"

"Vulgar cant phrases. You didn't send me to school so I could talk like a navvy." Sarah grinned at Emily, who couldn't help grinning back.

"Well, we didn't."

"Your lord's a big handsome fella," said Sarah teasingly.

Emily nodded uncomfortably. She didn't like deceiving her friends.

"When's the wedding?"

"Oh…not for a while." Struck by inspiration, she added, "Mama and Papa have come up to town to meet him."

"They're here in London?" cried Mrs. Fitzgibbon.

She nodded. "Papa's already created a small scandal at a *ton* party."

Mary laughed. "Mr. Crane has his own ways. But he's always been very kind to us."

"I'll tell him you're here. I'm sure he will want to see you." It would be a relief for her father to spend time with old friends like these. Then a reservation surfaced. "I'd rather you didn't tell him about the inquiries we are making. He might not… That is…"

They gave her identical shrewd stares, which showed Emily that Sarah had been brought fully up to date on her previous visit.

"Men are much happier if they don't know *every-thing*," replied Mrs. Fitzgibbon.

"Their brains are limited," agreed Sarah. "It doesn't do to tax them."

Relieved, Emily nodded.

"He and Daniel will be too busy reminiscing to worry their heads about anything else."

"Do you recall that time Dad and your father were lifting a pint at the pub?" Sarah paused. "Don't recall what town it was. We were always on the move."

"And so were we," said Emily. The Fitzgibbons' acting troop had always found them in whatever house they had shifted to from year to year.

"It was Kent, I think. Anyway, the local vicar came in, and it seemed he was very low church."

Emily nodded in recognition. "He started haranguing them about the evils of playacting and wanton actresses parading their 'nakedness' on the stage."

"We certainly never had anything like *that*," huffed Mrs. Fitzgibbon.

"And so Dad told him," supplied Sarah.

"But he didn't listen. That sort of person never does." Emily was smiling broadly by this time.

"They can't hear for talking," put in Sarah's mother.

"And so your father stood up and gave him one of his 'earl' looks," continued Sarah. "Told him he wasn't wanted and to take himself off."

"Which didn't set well with the vicar at all."

"He called your father a maker of graven images."

"And Papa upended a pint of bitter over him. Someone else's pint."

"It's fortunate the townspeople didn't like that vicar above half," commented Mrs. Fitzgibbon. "Otherwise both of them would have ended up in gaol." She was smiling, though, at the girls' laughter. "Aye, we did have some good times."

"I'll send Papa over soon," said Emily, rising to go. They would be starting to wonder where she was.

Saying her good-byes, she left the house with a smile. She was still in a mellow mood when she reached the duchess's house and heard that a "family party" had been arranged for that evening. Richard would be bringing his mother to see them. The possibilities in such a gathering were enough to sober her most thoroughly.

❧

Richard barely listened to his mother chatting with Lydia Farrell. As their carriage made its way through the streets to the duchess of Welford's house, he was thinking about Emily and the odd succession of events that had brought them to this moment. He had never known a woman like her. Most probably, considering her eccentric upbringing, there was no other woman like her. He could imagine her, he realized, at his side in South America, hacking her way through the jungle vegetation, eating whatever they managed to capture with their own hands.

The mental picture surprised him considerably. Why should he be thinking such a thing? That was the past, and Emily Crane had nothing to do with it. She had nothing to do with anything. She might be of some small use in this matter of the supposed attacks on him. He ought to be thinking about those.

"You're very pensive," commented Lydia.

Richard looked up to find her watching him.

"I suppose this first family party is enough excuse," she added.

"First…? Oh, yes."

"You have met Miss Crane's parents before?"

He nodded.

"I have heard they are exceedingly odd," complained his mother. "And of course there was that scandal, years ago. This really wasn't a very wise choice, Richard."

He repressed a grimace.

"They are staying with the duchess, and she is the best

of good *ton*. But after his behavior at Geraldine's artistic evening, I declare I am afraid of Mr. Crane."

"It was only an easel he broke," Richard reminded her.

"Yes," agreed Lydia in an ironic drawl. "He only threatened to cover the hostess with paint and box her ears."

Richard's mother groaned.

"Don't worry, Aunt. Richard will protect us."

She seemed to enjoy mocking him, Richard thought. Apparently he hadn't convinced her that the old reprehensible Warrington was a thing of the past. "I'm sure that won't be necessary."

"You must stay by me, Richard," demanded his mother. "Don't leave me alone with him."

"I confess I am looking forward to this evening with the liveliest anticipation," commented Lydia.

"It will be a perfectly conventional visit," Richard assured her. "I daresay you will be rather bored."

"Surely not. I've never met anyone who eloped to Gretna Green, let alone the daughter of a marquess."

Richard's mother groaned again.

❧

They were conducted upstairs to a large reception room in the duchess's house—not the main drawing room, Richard noticed. Nor was there any sign of the Welford family. Emily came forward to greet them and made the introductions with a certain constraint. Everyone sat down. There was a short silence.

"So, you are an artist, Mr. Crane?" said Lydia.

He scowled. "When I am allowed to be."

"Allowed?"

Richard could hear the amusement in his cousin's voice. He hoped she could restrain herself from doing mischief.

"I cannot paint here," Crane declared belligerently. "The landscape of London does not inspire...?"

"Inspire?" He made the word a curse. "I am always inspired. Olivia's damn sister won't have the smell of paint in her house."

Richard heard his mother gasp.

"She can't be any kin of yours," Alasdair complained to his wife. "I mean to say—the smell?"

"But Mrs. Crane and the duchess resemble each other so closely," said Lydia.

Richard tried to signal her to silence.

"Are *you* enjoying London, Mrs. Farrell?" said Emily.

"Prodigiously." Her lazy smile implied that the current scene was a rich source of this enjoyment.

"It is my first time in London." Emily's tone and expression showed a determination to avoid explosions.

"Yes, I know."

"Lady Fielding," said Emily's mother, "I understand you have attended a number of spirit calling sessions."

Richard gave her a sharp look. Where had she heard that in her short time in town? He noticed that Emily was gazing at her mother with exasperation. His mother was nodding with more enthusiasm than she had shown so far.

"Have you found them convincing?" Olivia added.

"I beg your pardon?"

"I believe these people employ all sorts of tricks."

His mother drew herself up. "Herr Schelling is a gifted man. He has no need of tricks."

"Nonsense," answered Mr. Crane. "It is impossible to communicate with the dead. They…dead."

"Just so," murmured Lydia with a laugh in her voice.

"Herr Schelling can reach beyond the veil," insisted Richard's mother. "He brought Richard back."

Everyone turned to look at Richard. Even Emily, he noticed with annoyance. "I wasn't dead," he said curtly, feeling ridiculous.

"You were the next thing to it," argued his mother. "In that dreadful jungle."

"Jungle?" said Alasdair. "I have always wanted to see a jungle. Astonishing variety of color, I hear." He gazed at Richard.

"Very colorful," he muttered.

The door opened. At precisely the same instant, Richard and Emily both said, "Ah, here is the tea tray," and rose, bumping into each other as they moved toward the footman carrying the tray.

Lydia stifled a laugh. Olivia Crane looked at her with raised brows.

Refreshments were offered and poured, occupying a few minutes. But all too soon, everyone was settled again. Richard was searching his mind for a safe topic when his mother addressed Emily's. "How do you occupy yourself in the country while your husband is painting, Mrs. Crane?"

"I paint as well."

"You paint...?"

"Pictures," was the dry response. "A woman is fully as capable, artistically, as a man."

From Emily's expression, Richard judged that this was a common topic, and not one she was pleased to have broached here and now. He felt a rush of sympathy for her.

"Though, of course, it is made much more difficult for a woman."

"Is it?" Lady Fielding murmured.

"Hampered by ridiculous conventions, refused admission to the studios." Olivia Crane shook her head in righteous indignation. "As if the sight of a naked body could corrupt anyone."

Lydia and Lady Fielding choked on their tea.

"But a girl must be protected..." ventured Richard's mother after a moment.

"Protected from learning? From expressing herself in any way? What rot!"

Richard covered a bark of laughter with a cough. He had never heard a lady of Olivia Crane's standing use such an expression, and he was sure his mother never had either. She looked as if she had been turned to stone. His cousin, however, appeared fascinated.

"But you must admit, there are those who would take advantage of a young girl's…enthusiasms," Lydia said.

"Oh, yes. Girls should be given pistols, and taught to shoot them, as soon as they reach twelve years of age. If I had not found Alasdair…"

The Cranes exchanged a searing look. Richard was at the same time shocked and envious. Emily appeared to have dropped into despair, he noticed. His cousin was avid. His mother was eyeing Emily with suspicion, as if wondering whether she had firearms concealed in the folds of her skirts. Should he overturn his teacup? Simulate a fit?

"Can't we just have a normal conversation?" cried Emily.

Everyone turned to look at her. She quailed slightly, but didn't retreat.

"What is a normal conversation?" asked her mother.

"Seems quite normal to me," grumbled her father at the same time.

"You must have had them when you were young?" Emily answered desperately. "When you went about in society."

"You mean the sort of thing Julia talks about?" Her mother seemed genuinely perplexed, and interested in what she meant.

"Gossip and sport?" barked Alasdair.

"How would I know? I have never seen it. You never talk about anything…"

"Normal?" wondered Lydia.

Richard gave her a look, asking that she be quiet. She pressed her lips together obediently, though her eyes continued to dance.

"Never mind," said Emily. She looked at Richard's mother. "Please forgive my outburst."

Her father looked outraged at this apology. He would have spoken, but his wife put a hand on his arm. "Have you been to the opera this season, Lady Fielding?" she asked.

The following half hour was filled with irreproachable, and deadly dull, exchanges about the events of the season, the theater, and possible family connections that—after some truly tortuous examination—turned out not to exist. It was, Richard supposed, a normal conversation for members of the *ton* on such an occasion. And he was finding it deuced difficult to stay awake.

"We should be going," said his mother. "So pleasant," she added, fooling nobody.

Their farewells weren't prolonged. Emily looked relieved, Richard noticed, but also miserable. The occasion hadn't gone well, true. But did it really matter? He lingered a moment in the hall, letting his mother and cousin walk on. "Was that the sort of normal conversation you wanted?" he heard Olivia Crane ask.

"How should I know?" Emily replied. "I've only Aunt Julia to go by, and…"

"I haven't been so bored in twenty-five years," complained her father. "And don't tell me you weren't, my girl, because I could see your eyelids drooping."

"No, Papa," conceded Emily in a tired voice.

❧

"You cannot marry that girl," said Richard's mother when he joined them in the carriage. "It's impossible, out of the question."

"Why do you say that, Aunt?"

It was easy for Lydia to enjoy all this, Richard thought. None of it involved her.

"She is utterly unsuitable. That unladylike comment

about 'normal' conversation! What if she were to repeat it in a more public place? And her parents…"

"They are unusual," began Richard.

"They are outrageous. Was she joking? About the pistols? I suppose it must have been a joke—though she didn't *look* as if it was—but it was in the poorest possible taste."

"I think she meant it," offered Lydia.

"Pistols!" repeated Richard's mother. "Can you imagine? Young girls running around brandishing pistols?" She looked from one to the other of her companions. "How can you smile?"

"Well, it is quite a picture," answered Lydia.

Lady Fielding blew out an exasperated breath. "I forbid you to marry her, Richard."

This was an odd twist. He had no intention of marrying her, yet he couldn't tell his mother that without revealing things she wasn't to know. He found he didn't much want to, in any case.

"Do you hear me?"

"I am twenty-nine years old, Mother."

"And acting like a moonstruck stripling. How could you have engaged yourself to such a…a hoyden?"

"You are not being fair."

"Fair?"

"Her behavior is perfectly…" What? Richard wondered. Understandable? Acceptable? Agreeable?

"Dreadful," declared his mother. "You must break it off, at once."

"Even if I wished to, it would not be the act of a gentleman." And he didn't wish to, he realized. He was having far too much fun. How long had it been since he had had fun?

"We must contrive something. Some excuse. It shouldn't be difficult, with *that* girl."

"You aren't to interfere, Mother." He would enjoy

the situation to the full, and then, of course, they would end it. That was clearly agreed.

"You expect me to simply let you ruin your life—"

"I am not doing any such thing. And I am perfectly capable of managing my own life, thank you."

"Oh really?" His mother leaned toward him. "You have engaged yourself to a chit who hasn't a penny to her name. How do you expect to live? I will not help you, not with such a girl as that."

"I have already said I don't want your help," replied Richard through his teeth.

Lydia threw him an unreadable look.

"And *her* parents obviously haven't two shillings to…"

"I will be speaking to Taft about what may be done to…"

"I do not understand you at all any more. This is just a disaster. Tell him, Lydia."

"I don't think, Aunt…"

"Enough." Richard faced their startled looks directly. "This is my affair. You will leave it to me."

He had been a bit too forceful, he saw. His mother, in particular, looked frightened. He had to be more careful. But it was damned difficult when he seemed to be besieged from all sides.

Ten

EMILY WAS ALONE THE NEXT MORNING WHEN Richard was announced. Her father had finally snapped at breakfast and insisted that they find their own lodgings if they were to stay in town. Her mother had seen the wisdom of this without much urging, and so they had gone off to look for a suitable place. It was just as well. Richard could tell her, in that roundabout way people used, that his mother had been horrified by the freewheeling Cranes and that he really could have nothing further to do with her. She had heard the same thing, spoken with more or less finesse, a score of times. Her parents' absence would make it quick and easy. No one said such things to Alasdair Crane's face, of course.

But when Richard was ushered into the small parlor they had been using, Emily felt a pang. She didn't want to hear him trying to spare her feelings as he explained that the visit yesterday had been…really…rather… unusual and—and all the rest of it. "Just say it straight out," she said when he greeted her.

"I beg your pardon?"

"What you have come to say. There's no need to spare my feelings."

He looked puzzled.

"I've heard it all before. Repeatedly."

Richard frowned. "I came to say I thought we should make a clear plan."

She couldn't take it in at once.

"Decide what we are going to do," he added, "how we will proceed."

"Proceed?"

"What did you think I was going to say?"

Emily was too surprised to evade. "That your mother was scandalized by us, and you could not keep up the connection."

Richard looked startled, then self-conscious.

She was right. His mother had reacted just like all the neighbors and acquaintances who had found the Cranes "unsteady" and "unsound."

"You believe I would say something so rude?"

"Plenty of others have done so." At his expression, she added, "Oh, not in so many words. But I soon learned what they really meant when they told me the children I had been playing with could not come out or the girl who had joined in my walks was taken ill or the young man who had called was busy with estate matters."

"They objected to…?"

"Everything. The way we lived, my father's temper, my mother's ideas."

"I see."

Emily berated herself silently. If he really had not come to say those things, she had herself given him the notion.

"That must have been very difficult."

"I love my parents. And I admire the way they have done what they liked." Pity was even worse than avoidance; she knew from bitter experience.

"Yes. But having chosen for themselves, they might have paid some heed to the consequences for you."

"They gave me what they prized most." She could never bear to hear them criticized.

"What?"

"Freedom to find my own way."

"That is a gift indeed."

Emily gazed at him. People of their own station in life never saw it that way. Others—Sarah Fitzgibbon, for example—understood, but never the so-called gentry.

"And a bit of a burden perhaps?"

She blinked.

"Obeying the rules is easy, after all. There is no need to think or choose among alternatives. Still less to chart a new course."

He seemed to be talking to himself rather than to her, but Emily understood exactly what he meant. "Where to begin?" she murmured.

He turned to her with an arrested expression, and started to speak. But then he appeared to change his mind, or not to know it fully. There was a silence that eventually grew awkward.

Emily was about to break it when he said, "Have you found it?"

"What?"

"Your own way."

He wasn't like anyone she'd ever known. And he wasn't at all like the person her aunt and others had made him out to be. It was very confusing, and it made it difficult to answer. Something in his eyes, though, pushed her toward honesty. "Not yet."

Richard nodded once as if he too were searching for a place, a way to function in the world. Emily dismissed the idea as ridiculous. He was firmly established in society.

"Perhaps we should sit down?"

She started. "I beg your pardon. Of course."

They sat opposite each other in front of the hearth.

"Have you any more news from your mysterious friends?"

"They have found someone who may be able to discover the identity of the attackers."

"Someone?"

Emily nodded.

"You do not intend to tell me anything about this person?"

"I can't."

"Because your friends have forbidden you to do so?"

"They would be angry if I…"

"Have you asked them?" he wondered.

"I don't need to ask. I know how they feel."

Richard considered this. He looked annoyed. "You know, it will be impossible to pursue this matter if we do not trust one another."

"It is not that I—"

"And can we? We are barely acquainted. You cannot be sure I will not betray your friends somehow. And I do not know how far I may confide in you."

Protest rose to her lips, and no further.

"Perhaps our collaboration is doomed before it starts."

"I don't…"

He held up a hand for silence. She pressed her lips together. "Unless we are both willing to take a chance."

For some reason, this simple sentence took Emily's breath away. He meant only that they would tell each other everything they discovered. There was no reason in the world for her pulse to pound—no reason for her to feel that he was suggesting a revolution in her life. He was gazing steadily at her, expectant. The risk of speaking seemed overwhelming, as if the wrong words might wreak havoc beyond her comprehension. "I will ask the…my friends if I may tell you," she managed.

He nodded, satisfied. "Good."

Emily's relief was equally out of proportion. What was the matter with her?

"So then. A plan."

Gathering her wits with difficulty, she asked, "You spoke to the groom—the one who was with us when… in the carriage?" Fiercely, she commanded her cheeks not to flush.

"Yes. He seems a trustworthy fellow. He's been with my mother for some years. When we rested the horses at the White Hart, an ostler brought him a mug of beer. It must have been laced with something, and they tampered with the harness while he was drinking it. By the time we set off, he was too befuddled to notice the cut."

Emily leaned forward. "If we find that ostler…"

"I've inquired. No one seemed to know who I meant."

She sank back, disappointed.

"A dead end, though it does tell us that a watch is being kept."

"Someone followed us to Hampstead. And to the park that day." Emily shivered. It was unpleasant to think of spies observing one's movements.

"You really believe you saw someone push that urn?"

"I can't be sure. It was so quick—a movement in the corner of my eye." An idea struck her. "We might hire watchers of our own, to see who is following you."

Richard smiled slightly. "To watch the watchers?"

"Yes."

"I don't wish to become the head of a circus parade."

"But…"

"I can keep an eye out as well as anyone. If someone is following me, I will discover them." He seemed to read Emily's doubts in her face. "I have been stalked for three days running by a jungle cat. I can spot a human hunter. But why am I being hunted?" he murmured. "That is the real puzzle."

"An enemy?" ventured Emily.

He frowned. The old Lord Warrington had certainly made enemies. He had probably offended most of the *haut ton* at one time or another. Some of them may have wished him dead for the insult or slight, but they were hardly the sort of men to plan actual attacks. Besides, he had been out of that world too long. "None that I can think of."

"A quarrel?" wondered Emily. "Someone you bested at…something?"

"I have certainly had disagreements and rivalries. But none that warrants murder."

"Your cousin Donald inherits your title," she pointed out.

"Donald lives happily and distantly in Yorkshire."

"He might have hired these ruffians we have heard of."

"I admit I don't know him well. But all reports make Donald a kindly country-loving man." He shook his head. "No, I do not believe in him as the adversary."

Emily reserved judgment on this point. "Who would wish to kill you?"

He shook his head. "I do not imagine myself a paragon of virtue, but I have never offended anyone so deeply, I would vow. My past holds no ruined gamesters or spurned lovers or jealous husbands."

Emily looked down at her hands.

"A paltry record, really." The old Warrington had been a paltry fellow. "A life without high drama."

"Yet you do have an enemy."

"Yes. Peculiar. And a bit heartening? Perhaps I wasn't such a negligible fribble after all."

She gave him an odd look. "It is not a joke."

Richard let out a breath. "No. But it is far more diverting than I thought London would be."

The look he gave her then made Emily's pulse flutter.

"You are as fascinated as I," he added almost teasingly.

"I am concerned…"

"Nonsense. Why should you care anything about me? We had barely met—indeed, we hadn't even met—when this began. The mystery of it draws you."

He was right, she thought. Curiosity, the challenge, had driven her into this search. But then, oddly, it seemed there was something else. She couldn't quite grasp it.

"Admit it," he insisted.

Emily nodded, unwilling to delve further into this slippery subject.

He smiled. "We are alike in that."

He gave one satisfied nod, and his eyes smiled into hers for a moment. Their hazel depths were mesmerizing. Emily felt a strange little lurch, the sort of tremor she'd felt when looking down from a great and precipitous height.

"So. You will speak to your friends, and I will keep a sharp lookout for these watchers."

"Perhaps you should find out if anything went on while you were away," Emily suggested.

"Went on?"

"You were out of the way," she reasoned slowly. "And someone clearly wants you out of the way. Why?"

"You are suggesting it might not be personal?"

"You said you have no enemies. If not, then it must be something else."

"What?"

She shrugged.

Richard rose. "A question for another day. I must go. I promised my cousin I would take her driving in the park to observe the smart set."

Emily stood also. "Mrs. Farrell?"

He nodded.

"Is she making a long visit?"

"I hope so," was the fervent reply.

He took his leave, and Emily returned to the armchair. She had been so despondent earlier when she'd feared he had come to end their connection. Why didn't she feel better now?

To Emily's astonishment, Daniel Fitzgibbon readily agreed to see Richard. Indeed, he offered to take him to meet the Bruiser at his earliest convenience. He really didn't wish to remain in contact with the fighter and his circle, she realized, which made her a bit wary about the whole matter.

The difficulty arose not over Richard, but when Emily herself insisted on coming along. "You shouldn't be acquainted with no one like the Bruiser," Daniel insisted.

"But I am acquainted with pickpockets and confidence men and ladies of…of dubious reputation…"

"Never mind them. They don't hurt nobody. Not really hurt them."

"And the Bruiser does?"

Daniel looked torn. "It's not him so much. I mean, he beats coves bloody in the ring, but that's the game there. It's the people he knows. They ain't so particular about where they put their fists."

"But we aren't meeting them."

"No." He drew the word out dubiously.

"I promise you I have no intention of doing so."

He shook his head.

"You have no objection to taking Lord Warrington to meet the Bruiser, however? Because he is a man, I suppose."

"Seems he can take care of himself," Daniel declared.

"How can you know that?"

"Fought his way through a jungle full of tigers, they say."

"You've heard of that?" asked Emily, too curious to correct the zoology.

"It's talked of in the pubs."

"Oh." She took this in before returning to the real topic. "I am going," she told Daniel. "I am working with Lord Warrington on this matter, and he never would have found the Bruiser without me. I won't be shunted aside."

"He'll forbid you to go," asserted her father's old friend.

"Forbid me?"

"What sort of man would let his promised bride risk herself that way?"

"The sort who is confident of her abilities," she responded automatically. But as soon as she spoke, she suffered a qualm of doubt. If the question were put to Richard, would he want her to come? Would he side with Daniel against her?

In the end, it was Sarah who convinced her father that it would be grossly unfair to exclude Emily from a scheme she herself had made. Sarah threatened him with various forms of retribution until he gave in, with poor grace, and agreed to escort both of them to a rendezvous with the fighter.

She wouldn't tell Richard of his reluctance, Emily decided on her way home. In fact, she would tell him that Daniel would only do this favor if she were along. There was no sense having the argument all over again. The second time, she might lose.

❧

Two days later, Richard sat in a hack facing Daniel Fitzgibbon as it wove its way through some of the seedier streets of London. Emily, beside him, was silent. She didn't seem the least bit intimidated, however, as the neighborhood grew less savory and the noise outside the vehicle more raucous.

Richard occupied himself by examining Fitzgibbon. He would have wagered a good deal that the man hadn't always been a dancing master, and even more that his career included some shadier endeavors. Why else was he using a false name? How did Emily know him so well? No doubt her father had something to do with it.

"Here we are." Fitzgibbon struck the roof to signal the driver to pull up before a tall narrow house in a bit better shape than others on the street.

Richard opened the cab door and stepped down,

turning to offer Emily a hand. She held up the skirts of her gown as she climbed down.

"The Bruiser doesn't like to leave his own part of town," repeated Daniel.

"So you have said." Richard surveyed the area. In broad daylight, it didn't appear actually dangerous. He wouldn't have cared to come here at night. A mocking laugh drew his attention. There were two burly ruffians leaning against the wall across the way. One of them pointed at Emily and sniggered. Richard caught his gaze and held it. After a moment, the man jerked his head and urged his companion away.

"Come on," said Daniel. "No sense hanging about outside here."

He was nervous, Richard noted. Fleetingly, he wondered if the man was leading them into some sort of trap. Were they to be robbed in this shabby place? But no, it was much more as if Fitzgibbon didn't want to be anywhere near here himself.

"It's a decent boardinghouse," he said, his tone confirming Richard's instincts. He sounded as if he were reassuring himself.

They went upstairs, and Fitzgibbon knocked on a door near the back. It was opened at once by one of the largest men Richard had ever seen. He stood well over six feet, and his heavy frame was overlaid by slabs of muscle, particularly in the arms and shoulders. His head, which looked rather small in contrast, showed scars from his bouts in the ring, and he had the horny hardened knuckles of a fighter. His hair was carrot red, and when he smiled—with surprising sweetness—large gaps showed in his teeth. "Mornin' Daniel," he said, gesturing them in.

Richard glanced at Emily, who looked a bit wide-eyed. Apparently, her father's eccentric circle of friends had not extended quite so far as this.

"This is Lord Warrington," Fitzgibbon was saying. "And…and Miss Crane."

The extreme reluctance with which he spoke the last words roused a sudden suspicion in Richard's mind. *Who* had insisted that Emily come on this expedition? Perhaps it hadn't been Fitzgibbon after all.

"Yer lordship. Miss." The giant moved uneasily. "I only got the one chair."

It was a poor room, Richard acknowledged. There was an iron bed that scarcely looked as if it would support the man's weight, a rickety table with one straight chair, and a broken down wardrobe which presumably held all his possessions. He gestured Emily to the chair. "You know why we are here?"

"Daniel said someone's after you. Asked me to put my ear to the ground, see what I could find out."

Richard nodded. "And were you able to find out anything?"

"Oh. Like I tol' Daniel, a couple of coves ha' been talkin' about a job they got, and the money comin' to 'em when it's done."

"A job?"

The Bruiser grinned, but the effect was far from humorous. "That's what they call it. When they're out to do harm."

"And what made you believe this had any connection to me?" Richard wondered.

The fighter looked confused.

"Was my name mentioned?"

"Oh. No names, yer lordship. They're not as stupid as that."

"Then why do you think they meant me?"

"They bragged as how it was a swell they were to do."

That was probably unusual, but it was a slender connection. "I don't suppose they let on who hired them."

The Bruiser shook his head.

"No, they wouldn't be that careless," said Richard.

"Afeard some other cove would take the job from 'em," the fighter elucidated.

"Like you, perhaps?" Richard was a bit impatient.

The fighter shook his head slowly. "I don't do none of that," he stated firmly.

Emily leaned forward. She didn't look the least bit intimidated, Richard saw. "What is your name?" she asked.

All three men stared at her.

"Your mother didn't call you Bruiser," she added, with a smile that softened the question.

The huge man ducked his head. He was flushing, Richard noticed incredulously. "No, miss. She called me Jerry. Jerry Jenkins is my name."

Emily nodded, still smiling.

Her smile encouraged the man to further confidences. "But it don't sound well, for a fighter, you see. Jerry Jenkins. It's too…lighthearted, like, for the ring. So I started callin' meself the Bruiser." He cocked his great fists and scowled.

"Very effective," pronounced Emily, earning another grin.

The fighter turned back to Richard. "You a member of the Fancy, my lord? Look like you'd strip right well."

"No." He had had no interest in boxing before leaving London; and after the rigors of his journey, he had even less. Fighting for no purpose but money and attention seemed a ridiculous waste after fighting so many months for his life. "Is there anything else you can tell us?"

The Bruiser frowned.

He had either never had quick wits, or they had been pounded out of him, Richard concluded. "Who are these men you spoke of, the ones doing the 'job'?"

"Oh. Bob Jones and Ralph the Thumb, me lord."

"Ralph the Thumb?" echoed Emily.

Richard tried to imagine any other granddaughter of an earl brightly asking such a question, and failed.

"He bit off Ikey Reynolds's thumb in a fight six years ago. So they started callin' him Ralph the Thumb. Ikey put it in a flask of brandy. He shows it for a penny."

"What?" Emily asked.

"His thumb."

At this she finally looked a bit green, thought Richard with satisfaction. "Perhaps we should talk to, er, Bob and Ralph," he suggested.

Daniel Fitzgibbon looked horrified. The Bruiser shook his head in his deliberate way. "They'd cut you as soon as look at you." Thoughts seemed to move ponderously through his brain. "And if they're after you, me lord, then it wouldn't do to meet them."

"And present yourself to be killed," added Emily tartly.

"I suppose it won't do," acknowledged Richard. "But you could talk to them," he said to the Bruiser. "Buy them some blue ruin, get their tongues wagging, see if you can learn more."

"They're partial to the bottle," the fighter allowed.

"I would pay you to do this," said Richard, trying to be very clear.

"I could use a bit of rhino. Ain't gettin' the matches I used to, these days."

"You'll do it then?"

"I'll try me best, me lord. Bob's a mean, close-mouthed cove. Ralph might let somethin' slip, if he was far enough under the hatches."

"Perhaps you should concentrate on him, then."

The Bruiser frowned uncomprehendingly.

"Perhaps you should get Ralph off alone and fill him with gin," Richard explained.

"That's right clever." He nodded in appreciation.

Richard's hopes, never high, sank a notch. "The

important thing to find out is who hired these men and who is their target."

"And you must be very careful," said Emily. "It sounds as if they are dangerous."

Fitzgibbon looked startled, but the Bruiser seemed positively astonished. "You worrin' about me, miss?"

"You are taking a risk to help us. Of course I am concerned."

She really was, Richard thought. He looked at the Bruiser in a new light. The man seemed totally at a loss for words. He was staring at Emily as if she were a creature wholly outside his experience. Undoubtedly, she was. She was rather outside his as well.

"I'll do my best for you, miss," said the Bruiser, with the fervency of a convert.

"Thank you, Jerry." Emily rose and offered the giant her hand. "I'm sure you will do very well."

The Bruiser held her fingers as if terrified of breaking them. It took Richard a moment to recover from the sight. Then he took out a sum he judged sufficient and passed it over to the fighter, along with his card. "You will send word when you have news?"

"Yes, me lord."

"A note will fetch me any time."

"I don't write so good. I'll get the landlady's boy to go."

"Very well."

They moved toward the door, but Emily stopped before going through. "Do you like being a fighter, Jerry?"

The man grimaced. "I used to, miss. But I ain't so quick on my feet now, and my fams ache in the wet so it's hard to mill like I did."

She looked blank. "Fams?"

"Hands, miss." He flexed them. The horny calluses on his knuckles cracked.

"You need some other employment."

"Ain't none for such as me." He frowned. The effect was daunting. "Or none I'd take."

"Nonsense, I'm sure something can be found."

Richard's heart sank at her thoughtful expression. He was not surprised when she turned a speculative eye on him. "We must go," he said quickly.

"Yes, but…"

"We will talk later."

She hesitated a moment longer, then went out. Richard followed with the sure knowledge that he had only postponed the inevitable.

Eleven

SINCE THE CRANES DID NOT INSIST ON A HOUSE IN the most fashionable part of London, they found lodgings without much delay. The house included space for a studio for Emily's father, which sweetened his temper considerably.

Her mother bustled into her chamber. "Do you need anything?"

"I don't think I can fit all my things into my trunk," she admitted. Her aunt had expanded her wardrobe even more than she'd realized until she tried to pack it.

"I'll borrow another from Julia." Her mother started out again, then hesitated. "I've arranged with her to continue chaperoning you. You were promised a whole season, and you shall have one."

Her mother suspected something, Emily knew. She had sensed an oddity about the engagement, though she hadn't quite put her finger on what it was. "I'm surprised Aunt Julia agreed," she said as a diversion.

Her mother smiled. "I made it the price for our leaving her house."

"But…"

"Your father was insisting on going, but Julia didn't know that."

Emily laughed. "We've been a great trial to her."

"It's good for her to be shaken up a bit. I'd forgotten how complacent she is." She gave Emily a searching look. "Was I mistaken to send you to her? We might have found some other way to…"

"She is very kind to me. I have learned a great deal from her."

"Um." Her mother didn't look entirely satisfied. "I'll go and see about the trunk."

When she was gone, Emily sat on the bed, a half-folded chemise in her hands. She and her parents had never communicated well, she realized. They talked, and her parents were solicitous when they noticed there was some difficulty; but remarks on both sides seemed to veer off in incompatible directions, never quite hitting the mark. How had she turned out so different from them?

❧

In the new house Emily had far more freedom than before, and one of her first acts was to invite Sarah Fitzgibbon to tea. The great pleasure she found in this simple act showed her more than anything else had done the constriction she had felt at the duchess's.

"We haven't had a proper talk in ages," said Sarah when they were sitting together over the tea tray. "Now we can say what we like."

"Yes."

"So why don't you tell me what's really going on between you and this Lord Warrington."

Emily's cup wobbled in her hand, though she managed not to spill any tea. "What do you…?"

"I remember when you were wild about the second assistant curate at the cathedral in Winchester. You aren't acting anything like that."

"That was five years ago! And a case of calf love. This is entirely different."

"Why?"

Sarah had always been blunt, Emily recalled. "I am older now," she hedged, uncertain whether to tell her the truth.

"And wiser," mocked her old friend. "And so? You've decided to settle for money and position after all."

"He hasn't any money," Emily replied before she thought.

Sarah stared. "None at all?"

"I don't care about money."

Sarah's answering look was penetrating. "We used to imagine the sort of men we'd marry. Remember our lists?"

"Yours was very long," said Emily with a smile.

"I'm particular. You always said that all you wanted was the sort of love your parents have."

Her smile fading, she nodded.

"Well, I beg your pardon, but your…connection with Lord Warrington doesn't look like that to me."

"You can't tell that," she protested halfheartedly.

Sarah merely continued to look at her.

Her regard was irresistible. And it would be a relief to have a friend who knew her true situation. "You must swear not to tell a soul."

"Haven't I always kept your secrets?"

Taking a moment to gather her thoughts, Emily told the whole story, beginning with Richard's appearance at her house in the country and omitting nothing, not even the night they spent in the hay. "So we will break it off when we have discovered the truth," she finished. "I will, I mean."

Sarah gave a soft whistle. "If it weren't you telling me, I'd have trouble believing such a rigmarole." Her eyes gleamed. "You really got to meet the Bruiser? I've begged to do so, but my father always refused."

"He didn't seem at all dangerous. His real name is Jerry." Sarah's answering grin made Emily feel that they were children again, conspiring over some forbidden treat.

"So it's not love, but an adventure."

Even as she nodded, Emily felt an irrational tug of sadness. But that was exactly what it was.

"He's a handsome man, though," added Sarah. "And he must be brave, getting out of the jungle like he did."

"Yes." Some part of her enjoyed hearing these compliments, though of course they had nothing to do with her.

"He's worried about his mother. He doesn't like her going to Herr Schelling. Can't say as I blame him," Sarah went on. "Most of the women—and nearly all who come are women—just stay a few sessions, get what they want, and go on. But a few keep coming, and those tend to be, I don't know, shaky."

"What do you mean?"

"Like they've lost their confidence or something. They can't break free."

"You mean Herr Schelling plays on their weakness?"

"No." Sarah wrinkled her nose. "Well, he does. But it's not that. It's like…something happens to them, and they never move on and get back to the way they were." She shook her head. "And the strange thing is, he didn't even die."

"Lord Warrington?"

"Right. She was all to pieces when she thought he was gone. You'd think with him back, she'd be set right. But she comes to Schelling's little shows same as ever, and she still seems shaky, like I said. Her son sees it too. I could tell."

Emily felt as if she had gotten a glimpse into Richard's heart. It felt clandestine, and all the more thrilling because of that. She was filled with a sudden desire to do something for him, to help. She wanted to repay him, she realized, for accepting her family as no one else had ever done. Ideas racing, she examined Sarah. "Why do you work for Herr Schelling?"

"It annoys my dad," was the quick response. But at

Emily's look, she shrugged. "Well, it does. He always assumes I'll do whatever he thinks I should."

"Do you like Schelling?"

"He's all right. A businessman, you know?"

"He does seem to take advantage of people's sorrow."

"I've seen churchmen do as much. Get the money for a new window in the church or a fine monument from the grieving relatives."

"I suppose."

"I probably won't stay with him much longer," she confided. "But the thing that really drew me in—it's like the plays we did in Dad's troupe, but it's real. The people come in, and they tell their stories, and they're full of emotion, you know. The things that have happened to them are as amazing as in the plays, but they really happened."

Her expression was intense, and Emily didn't interrupt.

"I used to feel—well, I still do sometimes—like my life was all made up. We wandered around, doing the plays. We had no house or anything…real. So when I watch these people at Herr Schelling's, it's as if that's all reversed. I'm on the other side."

"But you're still…"

"I'm still performing," acknowledged Sarah. "I'm not part of it. But I understand it better, almost so I could go off and do it myself."

"It?"

"Real life," explained Sarah. "A regular life, like most people have."

Emily stared at her, feeling a strong echo of what she meant in herself Where did one find that confidence in life, that contentment? How did you know that you were doing it right?

"I'll be moving on soon," repeated Sarah.

"To what?" Emily leaned forward a little, waiting for her answer.

"That's what I'm figuring out." Smiling, Sarah added, "Perhaps Herr Schelling will give me the answer from the Great Beyond."

Emily smiled back, but her mind was still busy. "If you are really going to leave his employ," she began.

Sarah raised her eyebrows.

"Would you help get Lady Fielding away from him?"

Inquiry turned to surprise on Sarah's face.

"If we could think of some way to discourage her from seeing Herr Schelling…"

"Nothing easier. I know how all his dodges work."

"Then you'll do it?"

"You're dead keen on this, aren't you?"

Emily drew back. "I'm simply trying to help a… an acquaintance."

"Ah, that's what it is, is it?"

"What else?" Emily took care to meet her gaze squarely.

After a moment, Sarah grinned. "What indeed? Sure. I'll do it. Easy." She snapped her fingers.

Emily was overcome by gratitude too intense to be examined.

❦

Richard made a small elegant bow and put out his hand to lead Emily into the dance. He'd been a bit surprised to see her arrive at the ball, chaperoned by the duchess as before. But at the first sight of her, his spirits had risen. "I didn't expect to see you," he said as they began the waltz.

"My mother insisted, and she blackmailed Aunt Julia into bringing me."

Emily appeared to be watching her feet, so he couldn't see her expression. "Blackmailed?"

She nodded, though all he could see was the top of her head. "She promised to remove Papa from my aunt's house as long as she continued to take me about."

"Ah." He tightened his arm slightly, and they turned at the end of the room. He thought he felt her slender frame tremble very slightly. "Is anything wrong?"

At last, she looked up. "No." Her gaze dropped again.

Richard said nothing, and the silence lengthened. "Nothing further has happened?"

"No."

Another couple moved clumsily into their path. Holding Emily closer, he swung out of the way. She gave a little gasp at the quick movement, and he suddenly became aware of the suppleness of her waist under his hand and the grace with which she danced. Her ball gown left her pale shoulders half-bare, and ringlets of hair brushed her white skin as one's lips might. The image was electrifying. It filled his senses until he was conscious of nothing else in the room but her. The rhythm of their dance faltered briefly.

"I'm sorry," said Emily. "I haven't actually waltzed before. I mean, I've practiced, but I've never…"

"So I am the first?"

"Yes."

She met his eyes, and it seemed to Richard that she was as conscious of him as he was of her. Their clasped hands seemed to pulse with heat. Muscles clenched involuntarily in his other arm, seeming eager to draw her tight against him. He remembered the feel of her nestled close in the hay. Shadows shifted in her gaze, and her lips parted slightly. His body was urging him to take them for his own.

This wouldn't do at all, he thought. This hadn't been part of the plan, and desire had no place in their arrangement. He clenched his jaw. Would the music never stop?

"Did I make a mistake?" asked Emily.

"Possibly," he muttered.

"Did I step on you? I didn't think I had…"

"You dance beautifully, Miss Crane." He could

move to the side of the room and suggest they stop. But somehow he didn't. He kept holding her, turning in the dance, her flowery scent clouding his senses.

When the music finally ended, they were both breathing rather quickly, as if the waltz called for great physical exertion. They stood together as the couples moved off the dance floor, still linked by the fever they'd roused.

Richard realized that they were attracting amused glances. He offered his arm and led her out of the ballroom into an adjoining chamber. "A glass of champagne?" he said.

Emily put a hand to her flushed cheek. "Thank you."

When he returned with their glasses, she was composed once more. Indeed, she appeared determined to ignore the past quarter hour. "I don't suppose you've heard anything from our friend Jerry?"

"No." She looked more than ever like a Botticelli, Richard thought. She was drawn on such delicate lines, and her face had that blend of the sensuous and ethereal that made a man want to… "There's scarcely been time."

Emily nodded and drank from her glass. Groups of guests chattered around them, but it was somehow as if they were quite a distance away. She took a deep breath. "We must find some job for him."

"I sensed you would expect me to do so." His voice sounded caressing, Richard realized. This must stop at once. "I don't see why," he added in harsher tones.

"He is helping us."

"And being paid for it."

"But it is so sad, the way he has been treated."

"The world is full of sad cases."

Emily looked at him as if he had disappointed her. Richard felt a pang, but the important thing was to break this unforeseen current of attraction. It complicated matters most damnably, and threatened to take him in directions he had no intention of going.

"Perhaps on your estates somewhere. Surely there are many tasks Jerry could do."

"You think he'd like to herd sheep? Or farm?" answered Richard mockingly. "Or are you imagining him as a footman? I suppose he would be handy for ejecting unwanted callers."

"You're teasing me, but—"

"I have no intention of employing the Bruiser." His reward was a startled, hurt glance, quickly averted. He tried to take satisfaction in it.

"There you are."

Lydia Farrell came up to them, and Richard greeted her with relief. The dance had been a bizarre aberration. Something in the air, or the music. It wouldn't happen again. "Hello, Cousin."

Lydia's tone was rueful. "I'm afraid your mother sent me to fetch you."

"To detach me, you mean?"

They exchanged an understanding smile. "Well, yes."

"I'll go and speak to her. If you'll excuse me, Miss Crane?"

Emily looked mortified. That was probably all to the good, Richard thought as he walked away. In fact, it certainly was. Things must be kept on a clear footing.

"I beg your pardon for sending Richard away," said Lydia.

She used his first name with practiced ease, Emily thought, as if she had done so for uncounted years. "It is of no consequence." She started to excuse herself.

"We've had so little time to talk," objected Lydia. "And we will be members of the same family. More or less."

The last phrase made Emily raise her eyebrows. But Lydia didn't explain.

"It was quite a whirlwind romance, I understand. You'd been in town only a few weeks before the engagement was announced?"

"Yes."

"Charming. Like a fairy tale."

Something in her voice made Emily examine her. Would Richard have confided the truth to this intimidatingly beautiful cousin? Emily found that she hoped not.

"When is the wedding to be?"

"We haven't decided."

"Oh, you must set a date. You have no idea of the planning involved. Your mother...but she might not realize either, I suppose."

Emily choked back a gasp. This reference to her parents' elopement was in the worst possible taste.

"My dear," said Lydia, laying a hand on Emily's arm. "Families have no secrets."

Of course Lady Fielding knew all about it. What else had she expected?

"I would be happy to help with the wedding plans. I do love a wedding. It would be such fun."

If there were going to be a wedding. Richard must not have told her. Emily's spirits rose. "It's kind of you to offer."

"You may call on me at any time."

The look in Lydia's dark eyes was intent. Emily didn't know what to make of it.

If she were truly engaged, she would ask her to convince Lady Fielding that the Cranes were not demented. As it was, she simply smiled and thanked the woman. "My aunt will be looking for me," she added.

Lydia looked as if she were going to speak, but then she just smiled back warmly and nodded. When Emily saw her a bit later in the evening, bent close to Richard laughing over some unknown joke, she wondered whether Lydia had told him of their conversation. But it looked as if they had quite enough to say to each other without that.

Twelve

As Emily was walking home from the Fitzgibbons' house a few days later, still smiling from her visit with Sarah, she was suddenly overtaken by a sense of foreboding. It was so abrupt and unexpected that it stopped her in the middle of the pavement. It wasn't late. Though she had once again slipped out without the maid she was supposed to bring, she wasn't foolish. She looked around.

Everything looked perfectly normal. Emily started walking again, but she couldn't dismiss the uneasiness, and she decided to find a cab for the rest of the way home. It was all very well to get a bit of exercise, but one thing her parents had taught her was to heed the promptings of intuition. She gazed up and down the street. No hacks were visible. Walking faster, she kept an eye out.

She saw nothing more unusual than a cat leaping from a tree branch to a windowsill. But the sense of oppression didn't lift. When no cabs materialized, Emily walked faster still. She wouldn't come out alone again, she vowed. Not ever. Just let her get home today, and she...

There was a loud report from somewhere behind her. Before Emily could react, she heard a whine like a wasp and something pinged on the stone wall of the house beside her. Chips exploded from the stone, hitting her skirts and cutting her arm. She heard a shriek and a man shouting.

"Are you all right?" someone asked.

"Of course she is not all right, Harold," replied a woman. "You can see she's bleeding. Where is your handkerchief?"

A cloth was applied to Emily's arm.

"Find a hack," said the authoritative second voice.

There was an indistinct mumble.

"I'm all right," said Emily, raising her hand to her forehead.

It was pushed aside with surprising gentleness. "Your arm is covered in blood. The wound is superficial. I can see that. But I am surprised you don't feel dizzy."

She did feel a bit dizzy, Emily thought, but she wasn't going to admit it.

"Where do you live?"

She gave the address, and wished fervently that she was there now, or that she could at least sit down.

After what seemed like a very long time, hoofbeats approached. Emily was bundled into a cab over the driver's protests about her condition. Assured by her formidable rescuer that she wasn't anywhere near dying, he finally slapped the reins and started off. In a few minutes, which passed for Emily in a daze, Harold was helping her down and knocking sharply at the house her parents had taken.

The housemaid who opened it screamed. Harold abandoned her at once, slipping back to the cab and away. Emily tried to reassure the girl, and keep her quiet, but it was already too late. Her mother came running from upstairs, and her father started to bellow from the back. Perhaps she could faint, Emily thought. She closed her eyes and tipped her head back. But her consciousness remained stubbornly alert.

"Be quiet, Nan," said her mother to the maid. She took Emily's uninjured arm and led her into the front parlor, pushing her down on a sofa. "Get some water and soft cloths," she told the servant, who ran to do so. "What happened?" she demanded then.

"Something hit a wall I was passing. Bits of stone flew out and some struck me. It's really not..."

"Hit?" The maid returned, and Olivia began bathing her arm.

"I didn't see what it was." Which was true, Emily thought woozily, though she had a pretty good idea.

Though Olivia was concentrating on her task, it didn't prevent her from giving her daughter a searching look. "Were you out alone again?"

"Yes, but—"

"I have *told* you…"

"I will never do it again, Mama."

Her tone appeared to convince Olivia. She finished bathing the wound and began to bandage it. "I still don't understand how this can have happened." Completing her work, Olivia sat back. "We should have a doctor look at you."

"I don't need…"

"You will do as I say."

Emily blinked at her tone of command, which she had heard only a few times in her life. "Yes, Mama."

Olivia continued to gaze at her. "I cannot imagine how such an accident might have occurred. And I have a very good imagination."

"I should have asked the people who helped me." She should have questioned them, Emily thought. "I was too shaken."

Her mother responded to the genuine chagrin in her voice. "Only natural."

"I didn't even get their names." She couldn't believe she had been so heedless. "Well, the man was called Harold, but that is not very useful. I'll never find them again."

Her obvious bitterness had puzzled her mother, she could see.

"I…I didn't get a chance to thank them properly," she added.

"Nor did I." Olivia shook her head. "It is too bad."

Emily sat up straight, only to be urged back onto the

sofa. "You will lie still for the rest of the day," commanded her mother. "In fact, I think you should have your dinner on a tray." She left unspoken the true reason for this—preventing an outburst by her father. Emily understood it immediately, however, and agreed to be helped up to her room and put to bed.

Someone had shot at her, she had absolutely no doubt of that. They had followed her—she'd felt their presence—and then tried a shot. She shuddered when she thought of the whine passing her ear. A tiny deviation, and she would be dead. The certainty made her feel cold, and she pulled the covers up under her chin.

It didn't make any sense. Richard was the one in danger. Had he been targeted as well? Was he all right? Sitting bolt upright, Emily reached for the bellpull, then she drew back. Jumping out of bed, she got writing materials. With shaking hands, she wrote a note and sealed it before finally ringing.

Nan appeared at once, looking worried. "Would you have this delivered to Lord Warrington's house? And have the footman wait for an answer."

Emily tossed and turned for two hours before receiving a reply. Lord Warrington was well and thanked her for her inquiry. Emily smiled in relief as she read this, and in amusement as well. Obviously, her vague note had puzzled him considerably. She savored the thought as she settled down to sleep. He imagined he knew everything, but he didn't.

In the morning, she evaded her father over breakfast, then endured the attentions of an imposing doctor recommended by her aunt. She wasn't entirely surprised to hear a knock on the door in midmorning and be brought Warrington's card. She was very glad he had come, she realized. There was no one else she could talk to so freely.

❧

Richard cast a generally approving eye over the neat entrance hall of the house the Cranes had hired. It was well proportioned, and it appeared there was more room than showed from the street. The hallway stretched back a good distance. There was a faint smell of gum spirits in the air. No doubt the older Cranes were already at their easels.

He smiled slightly. It seemed such a simple way to find contentment—a piece of canvas and some brushes. But it hadn't been simple at all, of course. It had meant giving up the prerogatives of birth, the support of family, everything, in fact. He should keep that in mind.

The maid returned and ushered him into a small parlor. Emily rose to greet him, but the words froze on his lips when he saw the bandages on her arm. "What happened to you?"

Emily made an airy gesture. "The most foolish thing. It was quite diverting, really."

Richard stared at her. What could be diverting that required bandages? Then he heard the parlor door close behind the servant.

Emily took a breath. "Mama will be down in a few minutes. I haven't told her…anything."

"You will tell *me*."

"There is no one else I can tell."

Richard sat down, feeling oddly unsettled by her apparent reliance on him. She could tell him what she told no other? He was puzzling over that fact when her next words drove all thought from his brain.

"Someone shot at me."

It was like a whip cracking overhead. He couldn't believe he'd heard correctly.

"I was out…walking. I began to feel uneasy, and then I heard the shot." She put her fingers on her bandaged arm. "It knocked splinters of stone from a building. That is what cut me."

Richard's throat was choked with surprise and apprehension.

"I was stupidly shaken, and I didn't even get the names of the people who helped me." She shook her head as if she had made some silly social error. "I don't know why I couldn't have…"

"You are absolutely certain of this?"

She blinked, touching her bandage again as if to ask if he questioned its reality.

"You're sure it was a shot?"

"Oh. Yes. The ball buzzed just past my ear."

"Just past… You speak of it as if it were a shuttlecock. Are you entirely out of your mind?"

Emily looked offended. "No. It was an unpleasant experience, but…"

"Unpleasant? Coming within an inch of death was unpleasant?"

"Well, you talk of it in much the same way," she accused.

He scarcely heard her. "Why in God's name would anyone shoot at you?"

She leaned a little forward. "That is what we must discover. I have been puzzling over it ever since. We thought it was only you being attacked. But do you think the carriage incident might really have been aimed at both…?"

Richard couldn't concentrate on anything but the bits of cotton wool affixed to her arm. If she had heard the bullet, it had barely missed. It might very easily have snuffed out her life.

"I was thinking we should have asked the Bruiser…"

"You were a target because of me. Because you are associated with me," he reasoned. "The engagement, perhaps. It was publicly announced."

"Why should someone who wishes to kill you care about that?"

"To frighten me?" he wondered, hardly heeding her. "But what could that accomplish?"

"I think we should…"

Richard rose, unable to sit still a moment longer. "'We' shall do nothing further. This supposed engagement must be broken off at once. We will not be seen together again." He began to pace. The prospect was surprisingly distasteful. But it was necessary, of course. A shudder went through him. He could almost hear the bullet whizzing by her.

"You are abandoning me now that I have been attacked?" said Emily.

"I am not abandoning…"

"Not seen together again?"

She said the words as if they were an insult. "Your association with me has put you in danger. I cannot in conscience…"

"So you think. But you don't know."

Richard didn't understand how he had made her so angry.

"It might be because I have been extremely helpful in the search for the attacker. Where would you be without me?"

"I…"

"Well, dead," she went on. "Drowned in the pond behind our house." She brushed this aside with a gesture, as if he had brought it up. "But that isn't what I meant."

"I cannot see you put in danger," he declared.

"I already am," she pointed out, as if speaking to a simpleton. "I was shot at."

"But if you were no longer connected with me…"

Emily sat up very straight, her chin in the air. "I see. You don't wish to be burdened with any other problems when you are trying to save yourself. It doesn't matter. I can manage perfectly well on my own."

"That is *not* what I meant." He had a fleeting desire to shake her. "You are willfully misunderstanding me. I don't want to see you hurt!"

This silenced her. She met his eyes almost timidly, it seemed. She looked—not frightened, but wary—of what he didn't know. "Do you really think I would be safer on my own?" she said quietly.

"If you had not gotten involved with me, you would not…"

"You may be right. But now that I am…involved, do you think whoever is behind the attacks will simply forget about me?"

He stared at her lovely face, a sinking sensation spreading through him.

"I helped discover certain things," she continued. "If the plot succeeded and you were killed, do you think this person would want anyone knowing anything about it?"

Her voice was so calm, so reasonable as she set out this terrifying case. Slowly, reluctantly, he shook his head.

Emily stood. "If you wish me to break off the engagement, I will do so."

For such a small, delicate creature, she had a great deal of dignity. He was deeply struck by it.

"I can take care of myself. I have been doing so all my life." A melancholy smile curved her lips. "If I can manage my parents, I can manage anything!"

Richard was struck by a memory of their first meeting. She had scared off his assailants with her dogs, half carried him home, and then dealt with her volatile father with marvelous finesse. She did have surprising resources. "All your life," he murmured, trying to picture it.

"Well, since I was quite small." She wrinkled her nose. "I remember offering the local vicar's wife a pansy when I was about three. It just prevented her from beating my father about the head with her umbrella." Emily nodded to herself. "He would have hit her back, you know, which she didn't expect, and then…" Her gesture left the ensuing chaos to his imagination.

Richard smiled. But his amusement was nearly submerged in some other emotion. "A big responsibility for a child."

She glanced at him almost as if he had frightened her, then quickly away. When she spoke again, her tone was brisk. "So, what are we to do?"

"It appears we must leave things as they are, for now."

"I am sorry."

"For what?"

"That you are in such an…uncomfortable position."

Richard shrugged. "That is the fault of this villain of ours."

She started to answer, then stopped.

"You are not to go out walking again," he added, making it a command. "You are not to go anywhere unless I am with you."

Clearly, she had a reply to that, but before she could make it, her mother came into the room and greeted him. "I hope you have convinced her, Lord Warrington. I do not understand just how this…accident happened." She looked at him as if to judge whether he knew more.

Richard attempted a facade of amiable innocence.

She rejected it with a look. "The important thing is to prevent any similar episode."

"Exactly." This time he met her gaze with no qualms. "I shall do everything in my power to prevent it."

Olivia seemed to approve of his tone. "That will be sufficient, I would think."

"I'm still here in the room," said Emily.

"Of course you are, dear. You should sit down. I expect you are still a bit weak." Olivia took a seat and waved Richard into another. "Nan is bringing a tray. You ought to offer guests some refreshment, Emily."

Richard nearly laughed at the look this roused. Emily

was not used to being lectured on manners by her mother, he saw. "You have set up your household very quickly," he commented.

Olivia's smile was impish. "Julia was a great help. She even lent me servants and some bits of furniture."

"She would have given you all her best plate to get us out of her house," said Emily.

"My dear, you mustn't give Lord Warrington the wrong impression about our family."

He had to stifle a laugh at Emily's incredulous expression. When he caught Olivia's eye the next time, he began to suspect she was teasing her daughter. It was a family like no other.

Thirteen

SITTING OPPOSITE HIS MOTHER AND LYDIA FARRELL IN the former's fashionable barouche, Richard watched other members of society parade through the park in the daily display of the season. The stream of carriages, showy hacks, and carefully dressed walkers reminded him of a circus. There were the trainers of dangerous animals—duennas escorting rapacious young debs; the jesters—dandies padded and pomaded into ludicrous shapes; the jugglers—those who had staked every cent on some precarious social scheme. And himself? Some days he felt like a tightrope walker, teetering on a thin line between various sorts of disaster.

"There is Jane Townshend," said his mother. "Look, Richard. In the carriage with the wheels picked out in red."

Automatically, Richard looked. A thin dark girl sat beside an older, stouter version of herself in the carriage.

"A lovely girl. And they say she has four thousand a year, at least."

"Which makes her even lovelier," murmured Lydia Farrell with a sardonic look.

"Drive over that way, Ben," Lady Fielding urged the coachman. "I will introduce you, Richard."

"No thank you, Mother. Ben, stay as we were."

The team swung back into line, and the barouche moved on, passing the Townshend carriage at a distance.

"You are being thoroughly exasperating, Richard,"

commented his mother. "If you have made up your mind to marry, you should take some thought for…"

"That matter is settled." He was already weary of this argument. It would be a great relief when his engagement to Emily was ended. His mother would be delighted. But somehow, the thought didn't comfort him.

"Speaking of which," said Lydia. At her companions' questioning looks, she pointed.

Richard's spirits rose at once. "Pull up, Ben. There is someone I wish to speak to."

"Richard!" objected his mother. But he stepped down from the barouche without responding.

Emily, he was pleased to see, was walking with her mother. When she saw him approaching, she smiled, and Richard's mood lightened further.

"You see I am following everyone's advice," she said when he reached them. "I have not taken a step out of the house alone in three days."

"Commendable." Richard made his bow to Olivia Crane, who carried a sketch pad under her arm. "You are going to draw the parade of fashion."

She made a face. "No. I thought I would do some studies of the flowers, until Emily goes mad with boredom, that is."

"Mama! Of course I am happy to sit while you sketch."

"You know you find it horridly tedious." She turned to Richard. "I have never understood how Alasdair and I could have had a child so utterly uninterested in painting. We got her a watercolor box when she was three, you know, and she—"

"There is no need to tell that story again, Mama."

"But I would like to hear it," Richard said. And it was true, he realized. He was curious about the youthful Emily.

"She ate them."

"I did not!" Emily gazed at her mother in laughing

exasperation. Olivia raised her eyebrows. "One," conceded Emily. Now, she turned to Richard. "The colors looked just like some candies I had seen in a shop window. Papa did *not* explain what they were for when he gave me the box."

"He thought you would know instinctively," put in her mother.

"It tasted quite nasty." Emily looked wistful. "I would have liked some of those candies."

Richard couldn't contain a laugh.

"You, of course, have never been a disappointment to your parents," Emily accused.

"I…"

"Well, until now," she added, with a look that told him she was referring to his connection with her.

"You are not a disappointment," declared Olivia, whose gaze had begun to roam over the flower beds nearby. "You know your father thinks the world of you, as do I."

"I know, Mama." The look Emily gave her was fond and forgiving.

"Those roses are rather fine. The color!" She wandered off the path toward the spill of blooms.

"Perhaps Miss Crane could walk a little with me while you draw?" said Richard.

Olivia agreed with a wave of her hand. She spread her shawl on the grass and sat down on it, pulling a pencil from her reticule, already lost to her surroundings.

"It is providential that they found each other," said Emily. "Can you imagine how unhappy a conventional man of fashion would be with my mother?"

Richard gazed at Olivia, settled on the ground, her pencil busy, oblivious to the stares and snickers of passersby. "I would find it rather…challenging myself."

The look Emily gave him was incandescent with emotion. He couldn't read it all; gratitude seemed to be part of it, and relief. But there was more than he could grasp in a fleeting instant. Nonetheless, the intensity of it shook him. "And your father," he said as a diversion.

Emily laughed. "Aunt Julia wanted to murder him after only two days in the same house."

"Perhaps two such spirits were bound to come together."

She looked surprised; which was no wonder. He was surprised himself. Where had those words come from? He offered his arm. "Would you care to walk?"

"*Not* to the Grecian temple."

"Indeed not." He smiled back at her, feeling an unexpected twinge of something very like joy.

They strolled along the gravel path in silence for a few minutes. The sun set her hair afire, Richard thought. It made her skin glow like pearls. He needed to say something before he lost himself in…

"I have arranged something I hope you will like," said Emily. "I think you will."

Richard dragged his thoughts from the grace of her form with great difficulty.

"It's about Herr Schelling."

"What?"

"I know you don't approve of him and…and you wish your mother would not go there."

She had his full attention now.

"I believe I have a way to stop her."

"You? How?"

"Sarah Fitzgibbon, Daniel's daughter, works for Herr Schelling. And she has agreed to help."

Richard was having trouble taking this in.

"She needs to speak to you about some of the… details." Emily faltered a little under his fixed gaze. "If… if you wish her to do this," she stammered.

"This was your idea?"

She nodded uncertainly.

"You persuaded Miss Fitzgibbon to go along?"

"She didn't need much persuading."

A tightness in Richard's chest kept him silent.

"I...I saw that you disliked your mother's association with Schelling," Emily hurried on. "Well, Sarah noticed it too. And so, since she is there and knows all his shifts and she is going to be leaving anyway, I just thought..."

"You concocted this whole scheme for me."

Emily gazed up at him, looking a bit apprehensive.

"You saw my distaste for the man, and you put yourself out to do something about it," he marveled.

"I didn't really..."

"You had no obligation to do anything."

Emily had flushed a little. "It seemed a simple service for a...a friend."

He couldn't take his eyes from her face. He felt an unsettling mixture of gratitude and excitement and disappointment. "A friend? Of course."

"So you will see Sarah? So she can set it up?"

"Of course," he repeated.

"Good. I'll speak to her and tell you the day." She moved slightly, tugging on his arm.

They had stopped walking, Richard realized. They were standing stock-still in the middle of the path, forcing others to go around them and drawing amused or irritated glances. He moved on at once. "Wherever did you meet the Fitzgibbons?" he said with an attempt at lightness.

Emily's smile was wry. "My father is always bringing home some...unusual acquaintance."

"Ah." Where would Alasdair Crane draw the line? he wondered. Capital crimes? Convicted felons?

They turned a corner in the path and walked back the way they had come. "Oh dear," said Emily.

"What?" He followed her gaze and found that Olivia Crane had attracted a small group of onlookers. As he watched, one of them pointed to her drawing and made a comment.

Emily walked faster. "She hates that."

"No doubt."

When they reached her mother, she was gathering her things. "I can't work here. These people are incredibly rude and will not move on."

Richard wondered if she would expect him to disperse the crowd. Her husband would set on them with his walking stick, he supposed.

But Olivia said only, "Let us go."

"You selling that picture of the roses?" asked a man nearby. "It's dashed good." Olivia was looking slightly less annoyed, when he added, "My little girl could color in the lines."

Olivia drew herself up. Her lack of height didn't detract from the impression of freezing dignity, Richard thought. "You may wish your daughter to be a mindless copyist," she declared, "but I will not be a party to it."

The man goggled at her. Gathering Emily with a glance, Olivia walked away, every inch an aristocrat. If she had chosen the stage rather than the brush, she would have been a sensation, Richard thought, moving to catch up.

There was little conversation up to the gates of the park, where he saw them into a hack and on their way. When they were gone, Richard looked about for his mother's carriage, but as he expected, she had departed as well. He would walk home, he decided. He got little enough exercise here in London.

Strolling down the busy streets, watching the clerks and shopgirls and servants on errands hurry past, Richard's eye was caught by the display in a confectioner's window. There was a box of multicolored candies lying open to tempt passersby. The reds and blues and greens were as brilliant as paints. He looked at them for a long moment, then went into the shop, bought the box, and directed that it be sent to Emily at home. When he came out again, he was smiling.

A different, but perhaps related impulse stopped him at an elegant shop a bit farther along. He examined the display rather longer this time before moving on.

❧

The meeting of Richard and Sarah was soon arranged, but as the hour approached Emily found herself unexpectedly nervous. Richard had reacted so strangely when she told him the plan. And she wasn't at all certain how the two would get along. What if they disliked each other?

As agreed, Sarah arrived first.

"Is it all set?" Emily wondered.

"Lady Fielding's due tomorrow night," was the cheerful response. "We'll be ready."

"Thank you," said Emily, meeting her friend's eyes.

"Can't have your betrothed unhappy," Sarah teased. "Who'd send you sweets then?"

Emily felt herself flushing. The box of candies had been an unexpected, and unexpectedly affecting, gesture.

"Good ones, too," added Sarah.

The parlor door opened, and the maid appeared. "Lord Warrington," she announced.

Emily and Sarah rose as he walked into the room. "Good day," he said, surveying Sarah with obvious curiosity.

"This is Sarah Fitzgibbon, Daniel's daughter," Emily said quickly. "Sarah, Lord Warrington."

"I've seen you at Herr Schelling's," Sarah declared.

"Yes." Richard examined Sarah more closely. She returned the favor. Emily sank down on the sofa again.

"I understand I owe you my thanks," Richard said. "I hope you are not jeopardizing your…position." His tone made it clear what he thought of her line of work.

"I'm not staying with Schelling much longer anyway," replied Sarah. "I've learned all his tricks."

"Going to set up on your own, are you?"

Emily bristled at his tone. "What do you know about it? Sarah is—"

"Not likely," interrupted Sarah. "I expect I'll go back on the stage."

"I thought you disliked it," said Emily, startled.

"Not traveling players. Something here in London." Sarah grinned again. "Perhaps I'll join Flora at Covent Garden and become the next Mrs. Patrick Campbell."

"Laudable."

Emily frowned at Richard's drawling response.

"But before you make your debut…"

"Right." Abruptly, Sarah was all business. "There's a few things I need to know before tomorrow night."

Richard looked surprised at the change in her.

"This Sir Walter Fielding we're supposed to be contacting—what was he like?"

Richard looked at the carpet, frowning. "He was a good man," he said finally.

"He spoke like you, I suppose? His accent, I mean?"

"Yes."

Richard didn't look as if he was enjoying this, Emily thought.

"Were there any expressions he used often?" asked Sarah. "Pet names about the house?"

"Why must you know such things?" demanded Richard, looking revolted.

"We want to make it as convincing as possible, before we blow the gaff," answered Sarah.

His mouth hard with distaste, Richard said, "He called my mother 'dear heart.' And he often said 'by thunder.'"

Sarah nodded. "Good."

"This is intolerable," he burst out. "This kind of deception and trickery…"

"It's for the last time," Sarah pointed out. "If you'd rather Herr Schelling pulled the strings…"

"No." Richard looked grim. "What else?"

"That will do for me." Sarah rose. "I've got to get back before they miss me. And to see to some things." Her smile was wicked.

Richard stood also. "Thank you," he said stiffly.

Sarah gave him a mock salute.

"I'll see you out," said Emily. She wanted a word with her friend.

"No, no. I wouldn't want to separate an engaged couple." Sarah went out, leaving the engaged couple looking self-conscious.

Silence fell over the room. Emily's pulse speeded up, and her mouth felt a little dry.

"An unusual young woman," Richard said finally.

"I think she's splendid."

He held up a hand in defense. "No doubt you're right. It was certainly kind of her to offer to detach my mother from…her employer."

"She is only working there because…" Emily broke off, not wanting to betray any of Sarah's confidences.

"I'm sure she has her reasons."

Silence descended again. Stealing a look at Richard, Emily couldn't interpret his expression. He looked very handsome this morning. His simple blue coat and buff pantaloons set off his athletic figure to perfection. And the bronze of his skin was striking against his snowy neckcloth. She had first imagined him as a gladiator, she remembered suddenly, and flushed. "Thank you for the candies," she said to erase this image.

He smiled. "I thought they looked like the watercolors your mother spoke of."

Her answering smile came without conscious bidding. "They did. But they tasted much better."

"I'm glad."

Their gaze held as the smiles slowly faded. Emily looked away first. "I'm sure Sarah will do the thing just right."

"She seemed very capable."

They were repeating themselves, Emily thought. Why didn't he take his leave? He had gotten what he came for, hadn't he?

"You've known her a long time?" he asked, in the tone of someone making polite conversation in difficult conditions.

"Most of my life. We used to see each other every year when the Fitzgibbons' acting troupe came to our town." She smiled reminiscently. "They always came—wherever we lived."

"You moved about a great deal?"

"Papa is always looking for new places to paint. And escape from irate neighbors. We were rarely more than a year in any one spot."

He frowned.

"It was great fun," lied Emily. "I got to see all sorts of country."

He made no reply. Another silence fell. She would just say she had an appointment, Emily decided. But she didn't move.

"I have something else for you."

She started slightly.

Richard drew a small box from his waistcoat pocket and handed it to her. It was covered in dark blue velvet. Emily held it, gazing at him.

"Open it," he commanded as abruptly as before.

Her hands trembling, she did so. "Oh." Inside was an exquisite ring set with a sapphire flanked by two smaller diamonds. "Oh," she said again. "I can't… You shouldn't…"

"It is the expected thing," he replied stiffly. "Several friends have been asking me what sort of ring I meant to get you."

"But you… We aren't…"

"Try it on."

Emily knew she shouldn't, but the ring was so lovely. She drew it out, fumbling a little, and fit it on her finger.

"Too loose?" he asked, as if there were nothing strange about any of this.

"No. It's just right."

"Ah." He nodded as if satisfied. "I thought the blue stone would suit you."

She slipped it off. "I can't take it."

"Why not?"

"You must see that it is impossible."

"It fits with our…plan."

"Pretending to be engaged. That does not mean you must spend large sums of money on the—"

"I didn't spend anything," he interrupted, sounding bitter. "It is the ring my father gave my mother when they were engaged. She put it aside for my future wife."

"Then I certainly can't accept it." She tried to hand it back.

"You don't care for the ring?"

"It's lovely, one of the most beautiful I've ever seen. But your mother will…"

"She will do as I say." His voice was steely.

"There is no need to carry our charade to such a length." Emily retrieved the box and held out the ring to him.

"I don't wish people to start to doubt it," he answered in quite a different voice. "The only way I can offer you my protection is if we are known to be engaged. If anyone suspects the truth…"

He broke off, but Emily had no trouble finishing the thought. If her true role were known, the mysterious attacker would make every effort to eliminate her.

"Put it on," he said.

She slipped the ring on again. It really was exquisite. When she raised her eyes, Richard was watching her with an odd expression. His hazel eyes seemed almost soft.

"It becomes you."

She swallowed.

His short laugh was derisive. "I was once a veritable pink of the *ton*. My advice was sought after on all matters of dress and decoration."

Richard stood. "Wear it," he commanded. And without another word, he strode out of the room.

Emily remained sitting on the sofa. Her eyes kept straying to the ring. She held out her hand finally, spreading her fingers to admire its rich glitter in the sunlight. She had never had anything so beautiful. Her throat ached with a threat of tears. She cleared it, and dropped her hand to her lap.

The ring had been lent to her. She would return it to Richard when their quest was complete. She mustn't think of it as hers.

She cleared her throat again. It was something precious she was guarding for a friend. She would take very good care of it for the short time it remained with her. Unconsciously, Emily's right hand crept over to cup the other. It was no more than that, she reiterated. It meant nothing, really. Nothing at all.

Fourteen

"THERE IS A BOY ASKING TO SEE YOU," HENLEY TOLD Richard very early the next morning. The butler's tone made it abundantly clear that he did not approve of the individual in question. "He insisted you would wish to know he was here." He waited for Richard to confirm his doubt of this.

"Where have you put him?" asked Richard, laying aside a letter to his estate agent and rising from the library armchair.

"He is waiting in the kitchen." Henley's face had gone impassive at this distressing reaction.

Richard nodded and started for the back premises.

"I will have him brought to you, my lord!"

"No need."

Leaving Henley to recover from the shock, Richard went down the back stairs to the brick-floored kitchen. Suspecting the identity of his caller, he thought the boy would be more comfortable there than in an upper room.

His entrance roused a flurry of exclamations and fluttering aprons. With a smile for the cook, whom he had known since he was in short pants, Richard went over to the raggedly dressed boy who was twisting his cap near the outer door. "I am Lord Warrington," he said.

The boy looked relieved. "T'Bruiser sent me."

"He has news for me?"

"Aye, m'lord. He asked, could you come and see him."

Richard started to ask for more information, but

realized the boy was unlikely to have any. "Tell him I'll be there at two."

The boy's relief increased. He nodded and put on his cloth cap. When Richard handed him a coin, he goggled at it, then looked deeply gratified as he slipped out the door and up the area stairs.

He would have to send word to Emily, Richard thought as he returned to his correspondence. But he set the letter aside again when it occurred to him that perhaps he should not. She really oughtn't visit the Bruiser's neighborhood.

She would be furious if he went without telling her, he mused. Oddly, the idea made him smile. There was something inexplicably enjoyable about quarreling with Emily.

He would go without her, he decided, and tell her the outcome later on.

He took up his pen and tried to frame a few more sentences to his estate agent. It was damnably difficult to know what to say to him. Even if Richard managed to convince the man that he was serious about restoring the land, what could he offer? Nothing could be done without money, and there was no money. It was damnably depressing.

Richard frowned, wrote a bit more, then stopped again. Something was nagging at him. Had he forgotten to tell Taft anything important?

No, that wasn't it.

He reread the letter. It seemed as clear and sensible as he could make it. Taft would very likely doubt him, but…it wasn't the letter. He put it aside once again, scowling at the library wall.

He didn't want to go and see the Bruiser without Emily, Richard realized. The expedition would lack a vital…spark. It would become a duty instead of a foray into mystery. Emily added something indefinable to any outing.

Ridiculous, he told himself. He valued Emily's insights; that was all. She had encountered unusual people and circumstances in her unconventional life, and her unique point of view was very helpful. He simply wanted to take advantage of it.

Richard took out a fresh sheet of notepaper and scrawled a few quick sentences on it. When he had dispatched it to the Crane house, he felt much better.

❦

Emily gripped the side of the seat as the carriage clattered over a rough stretch of pavement. Her ring glinted in the sunlight, and she was startled yet again by the sight of it on her hand. Stealing a glance at Richard beside her, she found him intent on guiding the vehicle through the narrowing streets. He had been quiet since taking her up, and didn't seem to share her anticipation of the Bruiser's news. She wanted to ask him if anything was wrong, but she couldn't, quite. The presence of the groom and husky footman perched behind was inhibiting.

"It's odd that the Bruiser won't venture out of his own neighborhood," she said finally. "It seems he wouldn't be afraid of anything."

"Difficulties in Mayfair are seldom solved with one's fists."

She blinked. The sentiment, and the abrupt tone, were unexpected. "You mean he feels out of his element elsewhere?"

"Undoubtedly."

"We should have invited him to our house. Papa would put him at ease."

A short laugh escaped Richard. "I daresay he would."

"I'm sure he would like to paint him," continued Emily meditatively. "You know, that might be a step in finding Jerry employment. I don't suppose you have thought…?"

"No."

"I'll speak to Papa," she decided.

"How will you account for your acquaintance with a prizefighter?" Richard asked.

Emily couldn't resist. "I'll tell him you introduced me."

"Indeed?" He threw her a look. "Is your father a good shot?"

"Rather good. Why?"

"Because it will be pistols at dawn if you say that. I just wondered about my chances."

She laughed. "He might call you out. But when you met, he would be distracted by the mist on the grass or the color of the clouds and forget to shoot you."

"It almost sounds as if this has happened." The amusement in Richard's voice dissipated the constraint she had noticed earlier.

"It did. One of our neighbors challenged him once. But then Papa wandered off as the seconds were pacing the ground to watch some willow leaves floating in a brook. When he shot them—"

"The leaves?" interrupted Richard incredulously.

"Yes. He was framing the composition, you see, and he forgot he had a loaded dueling pistol in one hand. I understand they go off at the least touch."

Richard made a choking sound.

"The duel was called off. Our neighbor decided he was mad."

"You seem to know a great deal about the occasion."

"I was hiding in the bushes."

"What?"

"I was only nine, and I wanted to see a duel." She paused, remembering. "I was worried about Papa, too."

"That he let you find out…"

"Well, he shouts. One can't help but overhear."

"I would have thought your mother…"

"Oh, she was…"

"What?"

"Never mind."

"She was there with you, wasn't she?"

Emily hesitated, but he looked very certain. "She wanted to make sure he was all right. I think she meant to throw a rock and spoil both their aims."

Richard burst out laughing. "That is outrageous."

"She said the squire had no business offering a challenge. Papa hadn't meant to insult him."

"I doubt that."

"He hadn't. Papa's insults are very…straightforward."

Richard gave another snort of laughter.

"And he only said he didn't wish to paint a portrait of the squire's wife."

"That's all?"

Emily wrinkled her nose. "Well, he did tell him that he couldn't because his life was devoted to the pursuit of beauty. But he didn't mean it as an insult."

"No, indeed."

"He didn't. More of an abstract judgment."

Richard pulled up the horses in front of the Bruiser's boardinghouse. "One can see why the squire might take it personally, however."

"He was not a connoisseur of art."

As he helped her down, Richard smiled in a way that made Emily feel quite euphoric.

❧

They found the Bruiser sitting in his room, as before. "What happened to your face?" Emily exclaimed, distressed by the discoloration and swelling all along his cheek and over one eye.

"Sparring with some of the hopefuls," was the obscure response. "One lad looks promisin'."

He seemed oblivious to his injuries, indeed almost to approve of them, she thought in bewilderment.

"You have some news for us?" asked Richard.

"Aye. Bob and Ralph the Thumb have gone."

"Gone where?"

The fighter shrugged his massive shoulders. "No one knows. They packed up and left."

"Left London?" Richard demanded.

"Well, they ain't anywhere people knows of. And Ralph owes Sam Pierce ten quid." His expression suggested that this should tell them something important.

"Sam collects his debts?" ventured Richard.

"Regular," replied the Bruiser, looking solemn.

"I wonder where they can have gone?" Emily frowned. "If they were indeed behind the attacks…"

"They was after somebody in foreign parts," put in the Bruiser.

"Foreign…?"

"You mean, in another part of London?" asked Richard.

The fighter nodded, waving his huge hand. "Off away west."

"And you have heard nothing of where they went when they disappeared?"

"Disappeared's the right of it. Nobody knows where they are." He shook his head. "Sam has friends in foreign parts."

Richard looked at Emily. "It sounds as if they have left London."

"But why?"

"To keep them from being questioned, perhaps."

"Someone found out we were asking about them?"

"It seems likely." Richard gave the Bruiser a sidelong glance, as if to say that he was not the most subtle questioner.

"So the attacks will end?"

"These men will no longer be involved," he corrected. He frowned. "They must know something useful, or there would be no need to get rid of them."

He turned to the Bruiser. "See if you can find out where they went."

"Right."

"And keep your ears open. If anyone else is offered their job in 'foreign parts' send word to me at once." He rose to go.

"Do be more careful," Emily said, making no move to follow suit. "Do you have something to put on those bruises?"

The fighter stared at her. "Had a beefsteak on my eye yesterday all right and tight."

"A...?"

"A customary remedy," Richard put in. "I believe it's quite helpful."

"I'm going to tell Papa," she said. "Would you like to pose for a painting, Jerry?"

The Bruiser looked uncertain, and apprehensive. "Painting?"

"A picture. Of you. In your...fighting clothes, I imagine."

"Like the ones of Cribb and Molyneaux?" answered the fighter.

Emily looked to Richard for guidance.

"Two famous champions," he explained. "Their bout in 1810 was epic in the world of the Fancy. I believe it has been painted several times."

"A little like that," Emily said. "But you would have to come to Papa's studio in, er, 'foreign parts.'"

The fighter scowled, struggle evident in his face.

"He would treat you well," Emily assured him. Her father was kinder to his sitters than to his aristocratic kin.

"Your dad?" said the Bruiser, and Emily couldn't tell if he found the connection reassuring or intimidating. She simply nodded. "I dunno."

"He's a right one," said Richard. Both Emily and the Bruiser looked at him. "Nothing toplofty about him."

The Bruiser looked half-convinced. Emily felt a rush of emotion at his endorsement of her father.

"Mebbe," allowed the fighter.

She left it at that, wanting to speak to her father before making definite arrangements.

"We should go," said Richard.

Emily rose and offered Jerry her hand.

As she and Richard walked back down the stairs to the carriage, she couldn't help but say, "Thank you."

"For what?"

There seemed too much to say. For not thinking my family bizarre, for not deploring my father's eccentricity or my mother's lack of ceremony. For taking them as they are and, seemingly, liking them.

"Is it so important to you that the Bruiser be immortalized?" he asked, amusement in his voice.

"I would like to help him," she managed.

"And you think this is the way?"

"Papa will pay him a little, and then perhaps we can find something else for him to do."

"Is that how your father gained so many unusual friends? Does he paint them, and then find them employment?" His amusement seemed to have faded to curiosity.

"Sometimes. Not always."

They climbed into the carriage and started off. Richard was silent for a few minutes, and Emily wondered what he was thinking.

"I'll see what I can find for the...for Jerry," he said then.

"I thought you didn't want to..."

"I changed my mind."

His tone didn't encourage questions. He must have been affected by the fighter's battered face, Emily decided, as she had certainly been. Men disliked admitting such sympathies. Which was silly, but that was how they were. She felt a moment's warm cordiality toward the entire male sex. They needed their little ruses and evasions. "It has gotten quite hot, hasn't it?" she asked, and was gratified to see the expected relief in his expression.

❧

Richard maneuvered the carriage through a narrow gap left by a curricle and a wagon full of vegetables. He didn't even notice the approving looks from the other drivers for his steady handling of the reins. He was contending with a tangled mass of feeling that the expedition with Emily had evoked.

He'd given her the ring because he wanted to, he admitted to himself. It wasn't really a necessary part of the charade. He'd become aware of this the moment she settled beside him in the carriage this morning, ring on her finger, and looked up at him with a confiding smile. He had a sudden image of her face when she had first taken the ring from its box and held it out. There had been a glow in her eyes, a softness to her mouth.

His jaw hardened. This wouldn't do. He had to stop it at once. Richard's fist closed and his face reddened. She had engaged herself to him because of the thrill of the chase. There was nothing more between them, and he had been profoundly relieved to find that this was so. Profoundly relieved, he repeated silently. He had important things to think about, a whole life to reshape for himself. He couldn't afford errant impulses of…sympathy.

That was it, he decided. He had felt sorry for her, with her gypsy existence, her unsettled youth, not to mention parents who might be amusing, but clearly did not devote themselves to her comfort.

He had wanted to give her a treat, he thought, as one would a child. The candies were clear evidence of that; the ring had been merely an extension of the same whim.

Excessive, he acknowledged, even foolish perhaps, but no more.

Reassured, Richard guided the carriage into his mother's stable yard and handed the ribbons over to a groom. He seemed to have developed a somewhat maudlin tendency during his sojourn in the jungle, which was odd. Perhaps enduring hardship had made him more sensitive to others' trials? He shook his head. He would have to curb the inclination, which had already committed him to finding work for a broken-down prizefighter. He hadn't time for such things.

Striding into the library, he took up the letter he had been drafting to his estate agent Taft. He needed to get it off. It was time to act, to take control of events. He couldn't waste time chasing an illusory enemy or feeling sorry for individuals he encountered. He had enough to do just hunting down himself. But even as he took up the pen to work on the letter, his eyes grew distant, and he forgot matters of business as he lost himself in the memory of Emily's exquisite face.

Sarah put her finger to her lips, signaling silence. Emily nodded, and her friend led her through a door and into a narrow space defined by a wall on one side and a thick velvet drapery on the other. She could hear people talking quietly beyond the curtain. This was the room where Herr Schelling did his spirit calling, she realized. Sarah had explained to her that it held a number of secret spaces, from which various effects could be created.

The man was a total fake, she thought. Of course, she hadn't believed he was really contacting the dead, but having the tricks explained made it more distasteful. She was very glad they were going to get Richard's mother away from him.

Chairs scraped on the other side of the drapery. Sarah

touched her arm and pulled her a few steps to show her a tiny hole in the fabric. Setting her eye to it, Emily could see a round table with a single candle burning on it. Herr Schelling was facing her, and he seemed to be looking right at her. She drew back quickly. He couldn't possibly see anything, she told herself, and peered out again.

Richard was there. His strong profile was stiff in the dim light. His mother sat next to him. Strangers occupied the other chairs. Her gaze drifted back to Richard. He looked so stern, and so handsome. Emily felt a thrill of excitement and nerves run through her.

Herr Schelling raised his hands and the circle stirred with anticipation. Schelling moaned and chanted. "We seek Walter, beloved husband of one of our circle," he concluded.

Emily saw Richard's mouth jerk. His mother looked anxious and hopeful and distressed.

"Bring him hither my messengers," continued Schelling. "Azrael. Phileto. Bring him!"

Beside Emily, Sarah pushed at the heavy curtain so that it billowed and swished. There was a low sound from high up in the corner of the room. This came from a henchman stationed on a set of wooden steps, Emily knew. Sarah had explained that this fellow—an actor who had fallen on hard times due to a propensity for drink—would provide the voice of Sir Walter Fielding, which would seem to come from above.

"He is coming!" intoned their host. "He is near."

The man on the steps let out a long "Ahh."

"Walter?" said Lady Fielding shakily.

The man gave something between a sigh and a groan.

"Is it you, Walter?"

Emily watched Richard's face. He was obviously having difficulty controlling himself.

"Dear heart?" said the actor in a muffled voice, as if from far away.

A small shriek escaped Lady Fielding. Richard scowled.

"By thunder, is that you?" added the actor.

"Walter. Oh, Walter, I have missed you so."

This was cruel, Emily thought, letting people imagine that they could reach loved ones who were gone. She turned to Sarah with some reproach, but her friend was gone. She had slipped away to carry out the plan.

Swallowing her outrage, Emily did her part, keeping the curtains moving so that Schelling would not notice Sarah's absence.

"And I you, dear heart," continued the actor. "You are always…" The man broke off with a startled exclamation.

"What is it, Walter?" cried Lady Fielding. "Are you all right? Are you…happy where you are?"

"I am serene. Here on the other side…" He stopped again, with an audible curse. Sarah was doing her part, Emily thought with a smile. She made the drapery billow more wildly.

"What is the matter?" cried Lady Fielding. She started to rise from the table.

"There is some disturbance," began the actor. Then, with a whoop, he tumbled from the steps that Sarah had pushed over and fell through the velvet curtains out into the room. "Devil take it," he grumbled as he flailed at the folds. It was clearly the same voice as "Sir Walter's," and just as clearly the man was half-drunk. Sarah had counted on that.

"It's a fraud," declared Richard, standing. "It was all a trick, Mother."

Lady Fielding was staring at the actor. Bewilderment slowly gave way to understanding, then to outrage, in her face. She drew herself up very straight. "How dare you pretend to be my husband?"

The man looked at her indifferently, then shrugged, gesturing toward Herr Schelling as if to say, "It was all his idea."

Richard's mother turned and faced the turbaned German.

Schelling spread his hands. "My dear lady, this is some dreadful mistake. I promise you, I never…"

Lady Fielding's glare cut him off. "All of it a fake. What else is behind these curtains?" She gestured as if she would pull them down. Richard stepped forward to restrain her just as Emily felt a touch on her arm. Sarah was there, indicating that they should go. Emily had to agree, though she very much wanted to see the rest of the scene.

Sarah led her to a room at the back of the house where they put on their wraps and slipped out. Sarah had a portmanteau as well. "That's that," she said as they walked along a back street in search of a hack.

"You aren't going back?"

"No, I'm done with Herr Schelling." She laughed shortly. "I expect he's about done with London as well."

"Good riddance. It was despicable, the way he deceived people."

Signaling to a cab, Sarah agreed. "Though most of them were eager to be deceived."

"Even worse."

They climbed into the hack and directed the driver to the Fitzgibbon house. "Dad will be pleased that Schelling's out of business," continued Sarah.

"Aren't you?"

"Oh, yes. But there are worse folk about, Emily. He gave some of his 'clients' a deal of comfort."

"False comfort."

Sarah shrugged.

Fifteen

"I DON'T THINK SO," SAID EMILY IN RESPONSE TO ONE of Lydia Farrell's questions. The woman always had a lot of questions. And she was nearly always in evidence when Emily and Richard encountered each other at a *ton* party. Had Richard's mother asked her to interfere with the match? Emily examined the handsome older woman more closely. She looked guileless.

"Of course, Richard knows more than I about fashion," Lydia said.

Emily couldn't decide whether she meant to be cutting, but it didn't really matter, because Richard wasn't listening, he seemed fascinated by another conversation entirely.

"A madman," one of the exquisitely dressed gentlemen behind him was saying. "He's built some sort of mechanism that runs along a rail. Belches smoke and steam and makes an ungodly racket. He thinks people will want to ride in the thing!"

"Madness," agreed his companion.

"Worse than that, he expected me to put up three thousand pounds to lay rails across my land. As if I would soil my hands with such an investment."

"The gall!"

"Fools," muttered Richard.

Lydia gave him a sharp glance. "Do you think so?"

The two exquisites moved down the room still shaking their heads.

"They were talking about the steam locomotive,"

Emily said. "We saw…" Seeing Richard's expression, she broke off.

"Locomotive?" drawled Lydia. "What a very curious word." She looked Emily up and down. "Don't tell me you are interested in such things, Miss Crane."

Out of the corner of her eye, Emily saw Richard wince. It seemed he was right about the *ton*'s contempt for new inventions and change. Raising her chin, she said, "Very. I find them extremely interesting."

"How prodigious unfashionable of you," murmured Lydia mockingly.

Richard shifted from one foot to another.

"Locomotives will revolutionize the transport of goods," Emily replied, recalling some of the things Richard had said when they viewed the new mechanism.

He turned to look at her.

"Laying the rails is a large expense, of course," she added.

"Why, Miss Crane, it sounds as if you have made a study of the subject," jeered Lydia.

"No. Merely listened with interest to people who really know. Steam power is changing all sorts of manufacturing, I understand."

"And fomenting riots among the weavers," retorted Lydia Farrell. "Do you care nothing for poor men's livelihood?"

"That is exactly why men of wealth and influence should be interested in such matters. Particularly those who care about their tenants and dependents. They can make certain the new inventions are used wisely." Richard was staring at her, she noticed uneasily. Probably she had made some mistake in what she said. She really knew next to nothing about steam power or anything to do with it.

"What a very novel idea," said Lydia coldly. She seemed displeased with the entire conversation.

"Every day I hear of some new device that will ease men's labor and aid their work," put in Richard quietly.

"Or put them out of work altogether," commented Lydia.

Replying, he spoke very slowly. "Not if it is done properly."

He looked astonished, Emily thought, as if he had been struck by a notion so vast that he could hardly contain it.

"I wouldn't expect Utopia just yet," was Lydia's sour reply.

Unexpectedly, Richard laughed. His cousin appeared to take this as an insult. "Would you excuse me?" she said. "I think your mother wants me."

Emily scarcely noticed her departure. She was transfixed by the joy and excitement in Richard's face. "What is it?"

"You. You are the most amazing creature."

The light in his hazel eyes shook her. She had to swallow before she could say, "What?"

"A few words, a phrase, and you cut through weeks of pondering and confusion."

"I…I don't understand." She couldn't think; she could hardly breathe with him gazing at her in that way.

Richard laughed again. "I know. That's the true beauty of it."

"Of what?" She had to smile, but she was also impatient to understand him.

"I will show you that," he replied with the same maddening obliquity. "In time, I will show everyone."

"Couldn't you just tell me now?"

"I haven't got it all worked out." His smile was tender. "Perhaps *you* should tell me."

"Lord Warrington!" But her protest was cut short by the arrival of the duchess, who was ready to depart.

Emily joined her aunt in the carriage feeling exhilarated and bewildered. What had Richard meant? What had she done to make him so happy? She very much wanted to know that, she realized. She very much wanted to repeat the thing, whatever it was.

She opened her hands and looked down at the exquisite ring. She had no business wanting any such thing. Their engagement was a sham. This ring was a deception and would soon go back to him. She shouldn't be thinking this way.

"It is a lovely piece," said her aunt.

Emily started out of her reverie. Aunt Julia was also gazing at the ring.

"Perfect for your coloring," she added. "And very suitable." She looked regretful. "You know, I am sorry, Emily."

"Sorry?"

"I intended to find you a great match—brilliant even. I did everything I could." She looked bewildered. "Things just somehow…slipped out of control."

"It was not your…"

"Alasdair wasn't even here," murmured her aunt. "I just don't understand how it went so wrong."

You aren't taking into account the interference of a killer, Emily thought.

The duchess was gazing worriedly at Emily. "Lord Warrington is quite different since he returned to town. Not nearly so arrogant. Handsome, too." She grimaced. "But Emily, how will you live?" The last words came out almost as a wail.

Emily saw real concern in her aunt's eyes. For a moment, Emily was tempted to tell her the truth. But she couldn't. "I am accustomed to a…gypsy existence," she said, trying to offer some comfort. "I've never had all the luxuries you take for granted. What you might see as hardship will not be so to me."

"But to have no assured income…" There was fear in the duchess's face.

"Well, I never have," answered Emily, suddenly feeling she understood her aunt better. "Never any significant amount, anyway. I'm used to dealing with the bailiffs."

"I always knew Olivia was mad," whispered her aunt.

Only the horror in her tone kept Emily from taking offense. "She's quite happy, you know."

"That's what I mean. I would be worrying every moment, terrified that…that everything would be at an end."

Emily felt an instant's true sympathy with her aunt. She had had such moments. But she had dealt with the fears, and they had passed, leaving her the stronger for it. She patted her aunt's hand. "You are in a far different position." She searched her mind for a distraction. "You never told me whether Lady Sefton granted vouchers to that girl you mentioned?"

The duchess appeared to gather herself. Her customary blend of dignity and reserve returned to her features. "I doubt it. The chit wore a silk ball gown cut down to her…ahem."

For just a moment, her aunt looked much more like her mother than usual. Emily smiled at her, and received a slightly sheepish smile in return. "If only she had had you to advise her, she would have been quite all right."

Aunt Julia looked surprised, then touched. "Do you think so, my dear?"

"Oh, yes."

The duchess cleared her throat. "Thank you."

Richard paced from one end of the library to the other, his whole body vibrating with energy. It was as if every part of him had come awake. He would be one of those men Emily had described, part of the legion who helped a new age to be born. He wasn't wealthy, true. But he was intelligent, knowledgeable. He could persuade those who had money to use it wisely and well. He could bring the inventions he found so fascinating into the world in ways that made sense for the people already living there. It was the thing he had been searching for—a mission that could consume him.

Richard was flooded with gratitude to Emily. Somehow she had brought it together for him. In a few words, with her honesty and lack of pretension, she had made it all clear. She would understand, as no one else could, exactly how he felt now and the plans that were unfolding so quickly in his mind. He would go and see her, he decided. He longed to tell her everything, to exchange ideas and see the future opening out in this exciting new shape.

He was halfway to the door when he realized that he was picturing their meeting all wrong. He wanted to sweep her into his arms. He wanted to thank her in ways that were out of the question. He had been seeing the future as something they shared, something that involved far more intimate matters than inventions.

Some of Richard's excitement drained away. He stood in the middle of the room for a moment longer, then went to the desk and sat down. This wouldn't do. Emily Crane had never intended to be part of his future; and even if she had, he could give her nothing but gen- teel poverty and an empty name.

There was the thrill of a changing world, he argued silently. But that was his vision, not hers. Asking her to give up so much for an idea… Richard shook his head. That would be offering her the same sort of life her parents had given her. She deserved far more than that.

She deserved everything, Richard thought. She should never have to worry again.

His fists clenched, and the muscles in his jaw hardened. He had let things get out of hand. *Things?* inquired a sardonic inner voice. Richard clenched his teeth. He had let *himself* get out of hand. He had drifted somehow into…into feeling things he should not feel and thinking things that could not happen.

With a great effort of will, he relaxed, placing his hands flat on the surface of the desk. He must put Emily from his mind, and certainly from his plans for the future. His gaze encountered his never-finished letter to Elijah Taft. He needed to make some decision about his estates. Taft had sent a note saying as much, and suggesting he come down to Somerset and observe for himself.

He would do that, Richard decided. Though his true interests lay elsewhere, he couldn't neglect his inherited obligations. And it would be a very good idea to get out of town for a while, to put some distance between himself and a woman he could not have. A woman who had never said she wanted him. Yes, it was time to go away.

❧

"Somerset?" said his mother when he informed her that evening. "I can't bear that house. Besides, it must have tumbled to pieces by now."

Richard pressed his lips together, suppressing a bitter comment.

"But you cannot go now, when Lydia is so stupidly insisting on leaving."

"My husband wants me home," said Lydia.

"I won't be left all alone," Richard's mother wailed. "After that dreadful scene at Herr Schelling's and…everything."

"You could come and visit us in Wales," Lydia suggested.

"Wales?" She said it as if the word were foreign to her.

"The countryside is beautiful at this time of year," offered Lydia.

"But the Season isn't half over," objected Lady Fielding.

"You can certainly stay for it," Richard assured her.

"But you will not," she accused.

He shook his head.

"I don't know what is wrong with you. You haven't shown a particle of interest in society since you returned." His mother looked from his face to Lydia's. The corners of her mouth turned down. "I think you are both extremely disobliging."

Lydia gave her a compassionate smile.

"Well, I *will* go to Wales then." She said it as if someone had dared her not to. "But Richard, you must escort us. I will not travel across the country all alone."

He might have mentioned the servants who would be with her, or the post boys and outriders. But he would concede this much. He could have a look at his property in Wales before going on to Somerset. It was out of the way, but if he meant to set things in order, that property must be included. "Very well. When do you want to go, Mother?"

Lady Fielding's mouth fell open.

Lydia looked surprised. She couldn't seem to accept the idea that he was a changed man.

"You will go?" his mother asked.

"I will escort you down to Wales. I shan't stay long."

"But you…"

"We have plenty of room," said Lydia.

Richard didn't bother to mention that he would be staying on his own acres. It would only provoke another protest from his mother.

"When will we leave?" wondered his mother. Now that her request had been granted, she seemed at a loss.

"You will have to pack," replied Lydia. "What about Wednesday?"

"Two days! I would never be able to…"

"I'll help you get your things together," Lydia soothed. "I know just what you'll need."

His mother looked stunned. Was she regretting her decision to abandon the delights of the Season? "Very well," she said. "Wednesday."

Back in his study, Richard drafted a new letter to Taft, detailing his travel plans and assuring the man that all would be settled when he came to Somerset. After that, there was nothing more to do but resolutely suppress his regret.

*

"He didn't mean anything by it," Emily told the cook.

"He called my ragout of beef a 'glutinous mishmash,'" countered the stout older woman, hands on her hips.

Emily wished, for perhaps the hundredth time in her life, that servants did not so relish repeating her father's intemperate remarks. If they had not told the cook…

"What is 'glutinous'?"

She wasn't about to answer that.

"And he overturned a perfectly good dish of oyster fritters."

And rather enjoyed seeing them rolling around on the tablecloth, Emily suspected. "He is an artist, you see. His feelings, er, run away with him. But he does not mean…"

"It's not what I'm used to."

Emily was sure it wasn't. She was a good cook, highly recommended by Aunt Julia. No doubt she had worked only in calm, regulated households. "I know my father thinks your cooking splendid. He has said so." She hurried over this small white lie. "When his painting goes badly, he is out of sorts, you see. He needs to…to grumble. But he does not really mean it."

The cook considered this.

Emily watched her, hoping she wasn't going to give notice. "You know how gentlemen are," she ventured.

The cook sighed.

She was going to stay, Emily saw. She made a mental note to get her mother to compliment the dishes at dinner.

"I suppose they all have their little ways."

Emily nodded, though it was difficult to imagine other gentlemen with "ways" like her father's.

"We just have to get used to them."

"Thank you."

"I'd best be getting back to the kitchen." The cook turned, and gave a wordless exclamation at the sight of a figure looming in the doorway.

"They did not tell me you were occupied," said Richard, stepping farther into the parlor.

That was another thing, Emily thought as she rose and the cook sidled out. Their housemaid had picked up her father's free and easy manners, and let anybody in whenever they knocked.

"A domestic crisis?"

How long had he been standing there? "A misunderstanding merely."

"Ah."

He had been there a while, she concluded. She offered him a chair and sat down again herself.

Richard seemed about to speak, but he didn't.

Emily tried to think of something to say. She could ask a question about railroads or steam engines. But somehow, with him sitting across from her, handsome in his blue coat, she couldn't think of any.

"I came to tell you that I am going out of town," he said.

"Oh." She hadn't expected this.

"My mother has formed a desire to visit Wales. I am taking her to stay with my cousin there."

"Mrs. Farrell."

He nodded. "I have some business in the area as well. An estate my stepfather left me."

A fine excuse to spend more time with a relative he obviously found fascinating, Emily thought.

"I believe you will be quite safe in my absence," Richard added. "The attacks have stopped, and the culprits have apparently fled. You will continue to take care, of course."

"You seem eager to get away." The remark had escaped her lips before she knew it.

"It will be pleasant to see the countryside," was the bland reply.

Emily wanted to protest, but she had no grounds. Richard was not really her promised husband, despite the ring on her finger. She had no claims on him. "Wales is very beautiful, I understand."

"So they say." Before she could answer, he was rising. "I must go. My mother has all sorts of commissions for me."

Emily stood. "How long will you be gone?" she couldn't help asking.

"I'm not sure."

In other words, it was none of her affair, she thought. Stung, she did not offer her hand. "I hope you have a pleasant journey."

"Thank you." He hesitated a moment, then bowed and went out.

He would have all the time he wanted to talk with Lydia Farrell. Staying in the same house, they would naturally form an even closer connection. She had a husband, Emily thought. But from what she had gathered during her brief time in London, that often made no difference whatsoever.

⁓

Over the next few days, Emily found that she had completely lost interest in London. When her aunt offered to escort her to a ball, she could scarcely muster the energy to refuse. The streets seemed dirty and the amusements pallid. Despite the hordes of people, there was nothing to do in town. One sat about waiting for something to happen, but it never did. She would almost have welcomed a sign from Lord Warrington's attackers, but of course there was none.

Was the threat really over? Had Richard's obscure enemy given up and called off the vendetta? It seemed so. Nothing even slightly suspicious had occurred in days. When he returned to town, she would give him the ring back, and announce to the world that their engagement was at an end, Emily decided. There was no reason to delay. And then…then she would get on with her life. This resolution provoked a small nod. It was very important that she get on with her life at once.

"Are you quite all right, Emily?" asked her mother at breakfast the following morning.

"Yes."

"Feeling well?"

"Perfectly."

"I thought you seemed rather silent."

"I don't really have anything to say just now, Mama."

Olivia Crane seemed pleased rather than disapproving of this bad temper. Indeed, the look she gave her daughter held equal parts of relief, gratification, and compassion. "When does Lord Warrington return to London?"

"I have no idea."

Another mother would certainly have reprimanded her offspring for impertinence. Olivia hid a smile instead.

Emily rose from the table and went into the front parlor, where she took up her station for another day of boredom. Her parents would be laying out their palettes, she thought. They would soon be deeply engrossed in their painting. What was she going to do? She must make a plan. She never had a proper plan. That was her problem.

But her mind remained blank when the question of the future arose.

She turned instead to the book she had gotten from the circulating library on new inventions and industries. The subject matter was more interesting than she had expected. She might have enjoyed reading it, except for the fact that every paragraph reminded her of Richard. She put the volume aside without regret when she heard the bell ring, followed by footsteps in the hall.

Sarah Fitzgibbon hurried in, waving aside the maid who would have announced her. "I must speak to you."

"Of course. I'm so glad to see…"

"There's something wrong."

Emily blinked. "Your parents? What…?"

"No. They're fine. It's the Bruiser. He sent a messenger to Lord Warrington. When he found he was gone, he came to Dad."

"Sit down and tell me," commanded Emily.

Her friend sat. "The Bruiser heard that those two men, the ones you suspected of being the attackers, have gone into Wales. And they went in the company of someone very frightening."

Emily sat back, shaken. "Frightening to London toughs?"

"It's very odd," agreed Sarah. "But he heard it from one of their, er, lady friends. He seemed quite sure." She hesitated, biting her lower lip. "Lord Warrington went to Wales, didn't he?"

All Emily's faculties were painfully alert. She nodded. "When did they go?"

"That's what I don't know."

"It was today you heard this news?"

"Just now," replied Sarah. "I came right over, though Dad didn't want me to."

Emily sprang to her feet. "What if the killers are lying in wait for him?" Emily moved toward the door. "I must get word to Lord Warrington at once." She hesitated, turned, then turned back again. "I must go after him."

"What could you…?"

"We are working on this matter together!"

Sarah looked startled at her vehemence. She drew back slightly when Emily grabbed both her hands and added, "Thank you for telling me this. If only it is not too late."

"I don't think you should be—"

"Forgive me, I must go," Emily interrupted. "There is so much to do."

Sarah was beginning another protest as Emily swept out of the room. She stood still for several moments, frowning. Then she seemed to come to a decision. She contemplated it, nodded once, and also left the room.

❧

Emily found her father in his studio. By great good luck he was not immersed in a painting, but rather was setting up a still life on a tabletop. He was humming too, which was a good sign. "Papa," she said, rather loudly.

"Eh? Oh, yes, my dear? What do you think of these figs?" He held one up with the tips of his fingers. "That purple sheen along with the…"

"Very nice, Papa. But aren't you tired of painting fruit and flowers? And you have so little room here."

He acknowledged it with a look around the cramped studio, then put a hand on his heart. "I would make any sacrifice for my daughter's happiness."

"But I am not happy, Papa."

He looked astonished. "You aren't?"

Emily felt a twinge of guilt. Papa was so very easy to manipulate. But it was for a good cause. "I don't like London."

"You don't?"

She shook her head.

"I don't like it either."

"I want to go back to the country."

"But I thought… Olivia told me you should attend all these balls and other idiocy so that you could…"

"They're so dull, Papa."

Her father looked at her with pride. "Exactly so. I knew you were too much my daughter to like that sort of thing. We'll pack up and go home at once."

Emily gave him a brilliant smile. "Oh, thank you, Papa. But, I've been thinking, I should like to see some really dramatic country—to get the cramped streets of London out of my head."

"Dramatic?" he echoed, his attention truly caught now.

"I have heard that Wales is very beautiful. Mountain crags and torrents. Ancient trees and rock."

Her father's eyes grew distant. One could almost see pictures composing themselves in his head.

"Waterfalls," said Emily.

"We must go to Wales," declared her father. "At once. Today. I shall tell Olivia…"

"I'll tell her." She didn't want to risk a diversion. "I'll go right now."

"Good girl." He started putting tubes of paint in a wooden case. "Mountain crags," he muttered.

If Emily had expected opposition from her mother, she soon discovered her mistake. Olivia Crane seemed positively gleeful at the idea of packing up all their possessions and moving them on an instant's notice to the wilds of Wales. In any other mood, Emily would have noticed the sidelong looks and knowing smiles her mother gave her. But all of her faculties were concentrated on one goal—reaching Richard and saving him from whatever plot the killers had hatched.

Sixteen

RICHARD WATCHED THE FLAMES RISE AND FALL IN THE wide kitchen fireplace of Morne. The kitchen was one of the few habitable rooms. He had a passable bedchamber as well, but the rest of the old house was barely furnished. Lydia had sent some of her servants over to scrub out the dust and cobwebs, all the while urging him to join his mother at her far more comfortable house.

He listened. There was the crackle of the fire, the rustling of a breeze outside, an occasional creak of ancient boards. But no human voices, no chattering or demands for attention. That silence let something inside Richard relax, let a tension he had scarcely been aware of ease. He had grown accustomed to solitude in the jungle. He had regretted it most bitterly then, but it had set down roots. He would need occasional doses of it from now on. He took a deep breath, feeling as if his spirit had expanded to its full extent. Here in this house he had neglected and ignored, he felt a measure of content.

Here was something about the man he had become. Here was one trait to mark down as his own. He savored it.

Then he smiled and rose to add wood to the fire. These philosophical ruminations weren't much like the old Richard either. Of course, the old Richard wouldn't have spent half an hour in this primitive place. It was hard to imagine what circumstances would even have lured him to Wales.

Richard walked through the other rooms. The walls

and roof were tight; the windows, small and mullioned, still kept out the weather. He suspected that the old man who lived down the hill had kept an eye on the place and made repairs. The way he had spoken of Morne showed that he loved it.

Opening the front door, Richard looked out over a narrow valley and the crags of mountains beyond. Morne sat on the knee of another such range with a view that went on for miles. It was beautiful, but not the sort of land for anything other than sheep.

A rider approached along the rough lane that meandered up from the valley floor. Squinting against the afternoon sun, he recognized Lydia. She waved, and he lifted an arm in response, trying not to resent her appearance. She was just trying to play the good host.

"Hello," she said as she dismounted and looped her horse's reins around a post. "I just wanted to make sure that you were settled in all right."

"Very well. Will you come in? I can offer a mug of cider, if nothing else."

Looping up the skirts of her riding habit, she followed him into the kitchen. "Betty brought you supplies? If you need anything…"

"She did, along with offers to come round every day and cook them. I am perfectly satisfied with the arrangements."

Lydia looked around the nearly bare room. "You're certain?"

"Completely."

She gave him a rueful smile. "Well, you've said I mustn't bully you any more about staying with us, so I won't. But you know that any time you wish to…"

"I know."

"Yes." She put her riding crop on the long wooden table in the center of the kitchen, then picked it up again. She walked a few steps toward the fireplace, then turned back restlessly. "Actually, I came to talk with you about something."

He gestured toward one of the three wooden chairs, but she didn't notice.

"William and I have been thinking about it for a while."

Richard waited, curious. Lydia's husband had seemed to him a bluff, hearty man who thought very little.

"We wondered if you would sell this place to us."

The unexpectedness of the offer kept Richard silent.

"Now that you have had a chance to see it again," Lydia continued, "you must have realized that it is not particularly productive. But it borders our land, and we could use the extra grazing. We do not need another house, of course." She looked around the shabby room. "Another buyer would want a place to live." Her tone implied that Morne would never be livable.

"I hadn't thought of selling."

"You don't visit or pay the least heed to the place."

"I haven't," he acknowledged.

"Cash is always useful," she added diffidently.

There was no denying that. He could use the money—though he didn't expect it would be any great sum—to improve his Somerset acres. But his stepfather had left him this place. It was the only legacy he would ever have of the man he should have revered as a father. The only sign of respect he could show now was to value the gift. And on this visit he had found himself drawn to the wild landscape and the silences. "I don't think I want to let the place go."

Lydia looked surprised, and predictably displeased. "Why not?"

"I didn't properly appreciate it before. I want to get out into this country, explore."

"You could do that on any visit to Wales. There is no need to burden yourself with an estate."

"True. But as I said, I am beginning to like the place."

"I see."

"If I ever should decide to sell…"

"You will think of us, I hope." Her tone was brusque, and she moved toward the door as if impatient to end this conversation. Lydia strode out to her horse. She waved aside Richard's help and mounted at the block. She looked down at him for a moment before departing. "You're quite sure?"

He nodded.

Lydia flicked her horse with the riding crop and set off down the hill at a brisk pace. Watching her figure grow smaller with distance, Richard wondered at the visit. She had made rather a long ride to ask a question she could have put to him at any time during their journey. But she had wanted him to see Morne. She had thought he would be repelled at the dilapidation.

And so he would have been, not long ago. Lydia still thought of him as Lord Warrington, pink of the *ton* and perpetual annoyance. He wondered how long it would take for her to see that man was gone.

Richard stretched and breathed in the clear cool air. He decided to go out riding himself. The slant of light across the crags was golden and alluring.

Emily rode up the rough lane toward the low, steep-roofed house that she was almost certain must be Morne. This place matched the description she had been given in all particulars. She had meant to arrive in early afternoon, but the innkeeper's directions had failed her more than once today, and she had been thoroughly lost for more than an hour. She looked more closely, and didn't see any lights in the windows. What if Richard wasn't home?

Weariness weighed her down. There had been the hurried packing and the long jolting journey by coach.

Settling on an inn had been the usual chaotic process, with her father ranging up and down stairs criticizing the accommodations. Then she had gone to Lydia Farrell's house, only to be told by a servant that Richard was not there. At least she had avoided encountering Lydia and Richard's mother, she thought as she reached the small yard before the house and found the mounting block.

There were no lights. Evening was blurring the edges of things, and she couldn't see a place to stable her horse. It was growing cool here in the mountains.

Emily rubbed her forehead. No doubt her father had discovered her absence by this time and was wreaking havoc in the village. She had no idea how to find her way back in the dark.

With a sigh, she pulled the long skirts of her riding habit over her arm and went to the front door. As she expected, there was no answer to her knock. She waited a moment, then knocked again. The only response was the call of an owl. Emily tried the latch. The door opened on a small entryway. "Lord Warrington?" she called.

There was no reply. But she did see a glimmer of light through a doorway at the back. Following it, she came into the kitchen, where the embers of a fire glowed and there were signs of habitation. Pulling off her gloves, Emily put logs on the fire and lit an oil lamp, filling the room with warm golden light.

She unpinned her hat and laid it on the table beside her gloves. She was extremely hungry, having had nothing since the bread and cheese she took from the inn this morning. Searching the pantry, she found half a ham, some dried apples, a loaf of bread, and a crock of pickles. A jug of cider sat on the table. Emily put the apples in a pan of water on the hearth to soften and proceeded to make a meal with the rest. She was just thinking that it was too bad there was no sugar or cinnamon to put in with the apples when she heard sounds outside.

A male voice cursed as something fell with a clatter. A horse snorted. She had to find somewhere to put her horse, Emily thought, starting up guiltily. She would be hungry, too.

Old hinges creaked, and then there was the sound of footsteps behind the house. Somehow, they sounded angry. The back door burst open. Richard stood silhouetted in it, lamplight gilding his face and figure. He stared at her as if he couldn't believe his eyes. "What the devil are you doing here?"

Emily took a step forward. "There is something I must tell you."

Richard scowled. "I took the wrong trail coming back and was nearly lost in the mountains overnight. I'm tired. I'm hungry. My horse needs attention. You'll have to wait."

Years of dealing with her father had taught Emily that this wasn't the time for argument. Instead, when Richard lit a lantern and went back outside, she fetched her horse and led it around to the shed where he was tending his own mount. She was struggling to pull off the saddle when two strong arms suddenly enveloped her and lifted it from her hands, "Go in," he said roughly. "I'll be there directly."

Once again, she obeyed. In the kitchen, she cut ham and bread and poured a mug of cider. Checking the apples, she found them palatable and set them out in a bowl. Life with her father had also taught her that gentlemen listened much better when their stomachs were full.

Dinner was a silent affair. Emily had a bit of apple and bided her time. She could almost feel Richard's irritation fading with the food and the firelight. He even began to show that expression she had seen so often on her father's face—a mixture of sheepishness and stubbornness that meant he was sorry but wasn't going to apologize.

"What are you doing here?" he said finally.

"I came to warn you."

Richard frowned.

"Sarah came to me after you had left London and said those ruffians had gone to Wales."

His frown deepened.

"You aren't safe here," she insisted.

"You came all the way from London to tell me this?"

"I didn't want them to catch you unaware."

"You didn't come alone?"

"With my parents. Have you understood what I...?"

"Where are they?" He looked around the kitchen as if someone might be hidden in the room.

"The killers?"

"Your parents."

"Oh. In the village, at an inn."

"Even they would not allow you to go out alone after dark."

"It wasn't dark when I left. I got lost. What do you mean, 'even they'?"

Richard stood. "I'll take you back there."

"Why aren't you listening to me?"

"You've told me nothing of consequence. Come along."

"Sarah is not a fool, and she thought it important."

"And did she tell you to come haring down here rather than sending a message?" Richard came to stand over her. "If there is danger here, all you have managed to do is put yourself in the middle of it. And then you ride out alone, lose yourself, generally behave like an idiot."

He was really angry, Emily saw. His hazel eyes glittered with it. Mustering all her dignity, she stood. He loomed over her, very large, and very close.

"You had promised not to go wandering about alone," he accused.

"That was in London."

"It applied to everywhere!"

"I was only thinking of warning you. I…I forgot."

Richard grasped her upper arms, his fingers digging into her flesh. He shook her slightly. "Forgot?"

"The attacks in London had stopped."

"So you came down here where you think they will begin again."

"You were here!" The words came out with such emotion that Emily herself was surprised. They seemed to stun Richard. He stared at her. She could hear him breathing. His grip on her arms tightened. And then he pulled her closer and kissed her, hard.

Emily was too shocked to react for a moment. He had been shouting at her, and now suddenly his lips were crushing hers. She pulled back. But even as she thought to struggle, the kiss changed. It grew softer. His mouth moved on hers, coaxing, instructing. The demand was still there, but it beguiled and taunted her, sought to lure her into matching it.

Richard's hands slid down to her waist. He pulled her against him, every hard line of his body joining in the kiss somehow, which went on and on overwhelming her senses. Emily found her hands slipping under his coat and along the fine fabric of his shirt over his ribs. She gave herself up to the strength of his embrace, melting into the contours of his body so naturally it amazed her. She hadn't understood that a kiss could be so wildly intoxicating.

She felt his heart pounding to match her own. Her fingertips explored the muscles of his back, her lips parted under his coaxing and her senses swam.

Richard raised his head and looked down at her. He blinked as if dazed, then grimaced. "Oh God."

She wanted him to kiss her again, Emily realized. She pressed closer, and he groaned. "We are engaged," she murmured.

He gave a little laugh. Then, as if he couldn't help

himself, bent to capture her lips again. Emily gave herself up wholeheartedly to the kiss, following where he led. His mouth was warm and sure. His hands evoked promises of delight she had never dreamed of. She felt weak with yearning and charged with energy at the same time. He had stirred a sense of sweet urgency that felt likely to carry her completely away.

Richard ripped them apart. "No," he said.

Emily's hands were reaching for him. She pulled them back.

"This won't...do." He was breathing hard.

So was she, Emily noticed. Her knees were trembling, too.

"I have to get you out of here."

Without conscious thought, Emily took a step toward him. Her feet tangled in the long skirts of her riding habit, and she stumbled. Richard caught her, off balance, and they both went down in a flurry of broadcloth.

She landed on top of him, clinging. And then he was kissing her again, crushing her to him as if afraid she would escape. She surrendered to his lips gladly, shifting so that her knees rested on the floor to either side so that she could press closer. When she felt his hands through the cloth running up her thighs, she shivered with pleasure.

But they closed on her waist to lift her away from him. He thrust her upright, then stood himself, moving around the kitchen table so that it separated them. "I'm going to saddle the horses."

"We'll never find the way back to the inn in the dark," she pointed out breathlessly.

"Yes, we will." He moved abruptly.

In the same instant the window behind him shattered and a bullet whined between them to explode in the plaster wall. Richard dove, catching her in his arms as he hit the floor just as the other window erupted, showering them with bits of leaded glass.

Richard started to crawl along the floor, pulling her with him. They wormed their way into the windowless hall, where he stood, yanking her upright.

There were voices outside. Emily couldn't tell how many, though it seemed like more than two. And they seemed to come from all sides of the house.

Richard ran to the front door and dropped a wooden bar into place across it. "Not that it will keep them out," he muttered. His face showed intense concentration, and perhaps anger, but not a trace of fear.

The hinges of the kitchen door creaked, then immediately fell silent. Richard put an arm around Emily's waist and swept her silently down the hall and into a room at the opposite corner of the house. At a window he listened intently before pushing the casement open. Emily heard branches scrape softly as it moved.

Richard listened again, then leaned out the window. In the next instant he was pushing himself through it, his shoulders sticking briefly in the small opening. Once out, he turned and practically lifted Emily through. He pushed the casement shut and crouched beside her.

They had come out into a thicket of some kind. In the moonlight she could see that the bushes had grown into a mound, and dying branches in the center had broken off to leave a sort of vegetative cave.

Richard grasped her shoulder and pointed. Emily nodded and started to crawl in the direction indicated. She stopped briefly to hike her long skirts out of the way. Richard's fingers encircled her ankle as she did, sending a thrill through her despite the danger. And then they were both moving on hands and knees through a dark tunnel of underbrush away from the beleaguered house.

There were occasional shouts behind them. Once, a flurry of shots made Emily falter. But the sounds gradually faded as they drew farther away. And though her knees were being lacerated and her hands torn, she didn't consider stopping. It was obvious the killers had struck again, and there was no doubt about the outcome if they found them.

Seventeen

CROUCHING IN A TANGLE OF UNDERBRUSH IN THE darkness, Richard listened for sounds of pursuit with all the intensity he had learned in the jungle. He heard a hunting owl, a whisper of breeze, the trickle of water in the gully below. He heard the rapid breathing of the woman kneeling next to him. They had been working their way steadily uphill, as fast as they could manage under the circumstances, and it had been taxing.

He listened. He didn't hear voices, or hoofbeats. It seemed that they had eluded the attackers for now. But they had to get farther from the house before daylight, and confuse the trail.

They began to move cautiously along the slope. Emily made no protests, thought Richard; no sign of tears or the fear she must be feeling. He hadn't been wrong about her—pluck up to the backbone, someone to count on.

He was shaken by a tide of feeling that kept him motionless. He had tried to run. He had put the width of a country between them. When he had felt the bond with her deepening in London, he had fled. It was the only honorable thing to do. Their sham engagement must be ended, his internal judge pronounced. He had to let her go before things became even more complicated.

But she had come after him, he protested silently. She had worried about him. Of course he hadn't been able to resist. No man could have resisted that tone in her voice, the delicate glory of her hair and eyes and that delectable body.

He heard echoes of her soft murmur—they were engaged. Engaged in chasing assassins the judge replied, and nothing more, as he well knew. Taking advantage of their agreement was not the act of a gentleman, even if her response had been so warm and eager that it nearly drove him mad to remember it.

Emily stopped and waited. No doubt she was looking back at him, wondering at his stillness. Richard started after her.

He steered downward now, with a ridge between them and the house. Near the bottom, the gully grew steeper, and he signaled for Emily to stop. Worming his way forward, he came to an overhang that dropped sheer to the small stream running through the bottom. The moon was fully up now, and its gleam on the water showed him only empty countryside. There was nothing to do but risk it.

He swung over the lip of the overhang and hung by his hands briefly. When he let go, he fell only a few feet to packed sand. Emily was already looking down at him. He made a motion and held out his arms. With only a moment's hesitation, she jumped into them.

It was like catching an armful of steel and velvet. He held her against his chest for a moment, relishing the feel of her slender strength. Then he set her down on the sand and bent to whisper in her ear. "We need to obscure our trail. We'll walk in the stream."

She nodded. The moonlight frosted her hair and gave her skin a pale sheen. She looked directly back at him with a clear confidence. She was relying on him to get her out of this. She seemed to have no doubt at all that he would. That was far more daunting than simply saving himself had ever been.

She went over to the stream and Richard used a branch to sweep away their footprints as he moved after her. The water was shallow, fortunately, but lined with rocks and pebbles. They would have to wear their boots, and soak them. There was no other way to navigate such treacherous footing.

Richard prepared to step in, then noticed that Emily was holding up the trailing skirts of her riding habit with one hand. The extra cloth would hamper her damnably if they had to run. He knelt beside her and began to cut away the hem with his penknife, trimming the skirt well above her ankles. After one small sound, she turned to allow him to reach the other side.

When he finished, he rolled the cloth into a tight cylinder and shoved it into his pocket with the knife. It wouldn't do to leave it for their pursuers to find. Then he retrieved the branch broom, which would also alert hunters, and stepped into the stream.

The water was cold seeping through his boots, but not icy. They could probably manage it for quite a while. Waiting for Emily to go ahead where he could keep an eye on her, Richard scanned the walls of the gully once more. They were visible here, and vulnerable. But he still heard nothing other than natural sounds. By daylight, he intended to be far away, leaving no track to follow.

They moved through the night, splashing as little as possible, following the meanderings of the streambed. Richard estimated that two hours had passed when the gully began to narrow and the sound of falling water came to his ears. A little way ahead, the stream fell about ten feet to a pool before continuing.

He surveyed the dim scene. The gully widened and flattened, offering less cover. The moon was descending; soon their light would be gone. It was time to go to ground.

He held out his hand. Emily took it without hesitation, her fingers small and cold. Yes, he thought, she would have fought at his side through the jungle. She would keep going without complaint until she dropped of fatigue. He squeezed her hand in reassurance. She smiled up at him, and his heart faltered momentarily before beating faster. He let go.

Taking advantage of the slanting rays of the moon, he picked a way across the stony incline that caused the waterfall. It steepened ahead, suggesting the possibility of caves, which riddled this countryside. The moon had nearly set before he found one, and it was a shallow cup above head height in the rocky wall. Not ideal, Richard thought, but it was going to have to do. Deep darkness was just ahead and Emily must be exhausted.

Reaching up, he hooked his hands over the rim of the cave. He groped for a foothold in the cliff and heaved himself up. The depression was scarcely ten feet deep, he saw then. But it was dry, and there were no signs of animal inhabitants. Also, it faced west. Sunrise would not reveal its recesses to the world. He knelt at the edge and held out his hands for Emily's, half pulling, half balancing her as she made her way up. "We'll stay here till dawn," he murmured.

She nodded and sank down inside the cave, her shoulders drooping and her head down. After a few moments, she tugged at one of her wet boots.

"Let me." He knelt and pulled off first one, then the other. "We should try to get your stockings dry, at least," he said very softly.

Emily half turned away from him, embarrassed he thought, and reached under her skirts to unfasten the stockings. She slipped them off quickly, shivering a little at the night air on her bare feet.

Richard took the cloth torn from her skirt out of his pocket and began to dry her feet. With a small sound of protest, she pulled the cloth away and did it herself. He picked up the wet stockings and hung them over a projecting bit of stone, knowing that they wouldn't actually dry by daylight.

"Shall I help you with your boots?" she murmured.

Wild laughter bubbled up in Richard's chest, almost impossible to choke back. She had sounded so matter-of-fact—as if they often removed each other's boots in the dead of night, in the back of beyond while men stalked them with murder on their minds.

"Are you all right?"

"Yes," he managed. He pulled off his boots and stockings, hanging them next to hers. He took the piece of cloth and dried his feet. She had tucked hers under her skirts, he saw, rather envying the source of warmth.

"What will we do in the morning?" she asked quietly.

"Figure out where we are, and head for the nearest house or village, someplace with enough people to make an attack impossible. My cousin's house, by choice."

"We're lost now, aren't we?"

"In the dark, yes. But by daylight, I can get my bearings." The problem was, it was several miles to any safe place, and their pursuers would certainly be mounted. "See if you can sleep a little."

"Are you going to sleep?"

"I'll keep watch. I'm used to it."

She was silent. After a little while, she leaned back against the wall of the cave and appeared to relax.

Richard watched the slope below and listened. The moon was gone now, and there was little to see. But he could hear night sounds. He could test the breeze for scents. There was no danger on the wind just now. He thought Emily had dropped off, and was fighting his own drowsiness, when she suddenly spoke very softly.

"When you were first lost in South America, were you frightened?"

He turned toward her voice, but he couldn't see her in the dark. Briefly, he debated his answer. He didn't want to make her feel any worse. But he couldn't offer Emily anything but the truth. "Terrified," he replied. "The closest I'd ever been to wilderness was a foxhunt."

She gave a little spurt of laughter, quickly stifled.

"I'd never even been in at the kill," he added, remembering the old Richard with something near disbelief. That man had receded so far that he seemed even less than a memory.

"Were you wet?"

The question made him smile. "Soaked in salt water and cursing my fate. I spent most of a year wet. In the jungle, it rained every few hours." He heard her small shiver. "It was hot, though, so one didn't mind as much. Are you cold?"

"A little."

They seemed doomed to huddle together outside the confines of civilization, Richard thought wryly. First a shed full of hay, and now this. They were coming down in the world. He didn't know how he would bear being so close to her, but he couldn't let her shiver alone. Shifting, he slid an arm around her and pulled her to his side.

Emily nestled in as if she had done so a thousand times. Despite the rough surroundings, and their peril, Richard's body began to demand things he had no intention of giving it. He could control himself, he insisted.

Emily's head burrowed into his shoulder. He could feel the curve of her breast like soft flame on his ribs. She trusted him, he thought, with her honor, with her life.

The mixture of fear for her, self-doubt, and determination that Richard felt then was more intense than any emotion he had ever suffered. He wanted more than anything to deserve that confidence. The thought of failure was intolerable. Failure meant that Emily Crane would disappear from the face of the earth.

She stirred a bit, like a cat getting comfortable. Her breathing grew more regular. She had fallen asleep in his arms. She had given herself up completely to his vigilance.

The determination strengthened, filling his consciousness, steeling him against the voice of doubt. He would see her safe. He would do whatever that required. And any man who stood in his way…would regret it to the end of his days, which might be brief indeed.

Emily sighed in her sleep. She turned, and her arm fell across his chest. He wanted her, Richard thought. He had never wanted anything half so much. But that was irrelevant. He could keep his desires in check. His right hand, resting on the cave's stone floor, clenched.

At least sleep was out of the question, he thought sometime later. The unceasing demands of his body were keeping him wide awake on his watch. He dared a feather touch on Emily's hair. But the result was enflaming rather than soothing, and he stopped at once. He must think about tomorrow, plan their moves. He wouldn't rescue her by sheer desperate longing.

With a massive effort of will, Richard shifted his attention to the future, and ways they might evade their attackers and find their way out of the wilderness.

❧

Dawn arrived by imperceptible stages, a slow diffusion of pearly light. Mist pooled in low places and drifted in veils among the crags. It would hamper their attackers, Richard thought, but it was a disadvantage for them as well. It would be much harder to get their bearings or travel in a consistent direction. Sound would be deceptive too, difficult to pinpoint.

Emily woke. After a moment's disorientation, she smiled at him in a way that made his pulse jump. Part of him wished fiercely that she had never come here from London, but another part exulted in her presence by his side. "Are you all right?" he asked quietly.

The smile turned rueful. "I'm hungry."

"I'm afraid the servants have neglected to set out breakfast."

"How careless of them." She reached up and took

her stockings from the stone, wrinkling her nose as she felt them. "Still damp. But I suppose it is only what one should expect when one is being chased by murderers."

Richard smiled. "It doesn't lend itself to luxuries." He watched her check her boots. "Are you ever afraid?"

Her azure eyes met his directly. "I'm terrified right now. But I've found it doesn't help in the least to give way to emotion on these occasions."

"Having been so often chased by murderers?"

"They were usually after Papa," she admitted. "But it's hard to tell the difference when you're small. Perhaps there isn't any."

Some weeks ago, he might have laughed at this. This morning, he couldn't. Indeed, he felt an unaccustomed tightness in his throat.

"Not that most of them would have actually murdered him," Emily added softly. "Well, maybe one or two."

"You haven't deserved the life you've had. You should be given every luxury. You should be cared for and cosseted, and never have to worry."

Emily didn't seem to know what to say. Her cheeks flushed, and she gave him a doubtful look. "I'd settle for a cup of hot coffee," she replied finally.

Richard called himself to order. Turning away, he put on his stockings and boots and let himself down from the cave into the mist below. It swirled about his shoulders, completely obscuring the ground. "We'll have to get above this," he muttered.

"What?" Emily's head appeared in the opening.

He gestured for silence, then helped her down. Keeping a hand on the cliff face, Richard moved away from the sound of the waterfall.

It was rough going at first. They couldn't see their feet, or obstacles that tripped them up. But finally the ground began to rise and the mist to recede. Richard judged that they had been walking about an hour when they reached the top of a ridge and looked out over a sea of fog broken by similar heights. Very conscious of their exposure, he led her down a little, until they were mostly hidden, and then went over his sketchy mental map of the area.

"Do you know where we are?" whispered Emily.

"We left the house going east," he told her softly. "The stream flowed northeast. We are still on my land, I believe. My cousin's estate borders it on the north, so that is the direction we want. The difficulty will be keeping to it in this weather."

"How far?"

"Six or seven miles." In a straight line, he added to himself; not taking into account the mountainous nature of the country.

"That isn't far." She attempted a cheerful smile. "And it will be hard for them to find us in the mist."

"As long as we're quiet."

They set off at the best pace they could manage and were soon struggling down slopes into narrow ravines and up the opposite sides. Now and then, one of them would send a stone rattling into the depths, making him wince. His only consolation was that their pursuers would have the same problem. At intervals, he stopped and listened intently, but the morning passed without any sign.

Around noon, the fog began to dissipate. Richard left Emily resting beside a trickle of water and climbed up to reconnoiter. He didn't stand on the peak this time, but crouched among some boulders to take bearings.

He could see the country spread out now, mist covering only the lowest places. Some of the hills would be landmarks to a native, but they told him next to nothing. All they could do was continue going north. When he judged that they had gone far enough, he would cast about for the Farrells' house. He made his way carefully back down. But when he reached the place where he had left Emily, it was empty.

Richard had to bite back a cry. His first instinct was race down the ravine shouting her name. It took him a long moment to control it, and to quell the panic surging up inside. Clenching his fists, he mastered his fear.

He knelt, searching the ground. It was stony and showed no footprints. However, the vegetation wasn't disturbed. There was no sign of a struggle. Nor was there evidence that anyone had forced his way through the bushes upstream. Setting his jaw, he walked down, all his senses straining.

He found her barely ten yards away. A curve of rock had hidden her, and she was standing still, making no sound. She turned as he approached and started to speak. "Look at this…"

Richard grabbed her upper arms and shook her. "Don't ever move from the place where I've left you," he hissed.

She blinked, startled. "I only…"

"And keep your voice down!"

Emily took a breath, her eyes wide on his. "I only went a few steps," she whispered.

He couldn't help shaking her again. "You are to stay exactly where I put you."

"But it was…"

He started urging her upstream. "I chose a spot sheltered by an overhang and concealed by bushes. If I had been taken above, you might have stayed hidden."

Emily looked uneasy. She struggled in his grasp. "I'm sorry. But I noticed this odd…"

"It doesn't matter what you noticed."

She jerked away from him and took a step back. "My observations are worthless?"

Richard's anger was ebbing now that he knew she was safe. "No. But you shouldn't go off alone. If we were separated, I couldn't protect you…"

The stubborn look didn't entirely fade from her face, but it moderated. "All right. The next time I will wait until you come back."

He nodded. His pulse had returned to normal. "We should move on."

"Look at this first." She led him back a bit and pointed to the wall of the ravine.

Richard looked, frowned, and moved closer. Reaching up, he broke off a loose piece and rubbed it in his hand.

"Isn't that coal?" Emily asked. Her reading had not been entirely in vain.

"It certainly looks like it."

"It gets wider as it goes down the hill." She pointed to the broadening seam of dark rock.

He walked a little way, seeing that she was right. Farther along, most of the cliff face was black—here, on his own land. He reached up again to verify the evidence of his eyes. Coal was the lifeblood of the inventions that so fascinated him.

"Do you…?"

A clatter of stones sounded in the distance, followed by the whinny of a frightened horse. All of Richard's faculties focused in an instant, calculating the direction of the noise, the terrain, the nearness of the threat. Demanding silence with a savage gesture, he scanned the stony ground. They had left no sign.

He moved quickly downstream, drawing Emily along with him. A man called out, too far away for Richard to catch the words. Using every ounce of skill he had gained as a castaway, Richard guided Emily north.

Eighteen

EMILY TRIPPED OVER A SCATTER OF ROCKS AND staggered. Richard caught her arm and urged her on. They had been moving fast and quietly down a series of gullies for what seemed like hours. There had been no further sounds behind them. They didn't even know if the one they'd heard was their attackers, Emily thought. But they couldn't afford to assume it wasn't. She was coming to the end of her strength, but didn't dare ask that they rest.

She watched Richard moving ahead of her like a wild creature. In the last few hours something about him had changed.

He turned to check on her. His hazel eyes seemed exultant as well as intent, lit with a kind of triumphant determination. He frightened her a little. Since they had fled his house together, his presence had seemed to guarantee safety. Until now.

"We must keep going," he said.

When Emily nodded, he took off again with the loping stride that looked so effortless and was so hard to match. Emily followed as best she could. The sun was past noon, and the air had grown unseasonably warm as the last of the mist burned away. She had taken off the snug jacket of her riding habit, but even carrying it over her arm, she was hot. Her blouse clung to her back, and her still-damp boots were a penance.

Up ahead, Richard had stopped. He was listening again, she saw. She heard nothing but natural sounds—birds, the rustle of leaves. By the time she reached him, he was moving again. It had been that way all day. He drew ahead, waited for her to catch up, and then set off again, having had a rest, Emily thought resentfully, while she never got a moment's respite. A trickle of sweat ran down her neck. It was as if some other personality had taken over in him.

She stumbled again, this time knocking two rocks together with a sharp crack. Richard whirled, crouched for battle. His eyes took in every shadow. His lips were drawn back in something very like a snarl. Emily went dead still. For a moment, she was convinced that some terror menaced her from behind.

He straightened slowly, then he came back to where she stood. "I...I kicked a stone," she admitted as he loomed over her.

He bent toward her. Emily swallowed. But it was the old familiar Richard who said, "You're tired, I know. I'm searching for a place where we can rest." He gestured at the open valley around them. "This is too exposed."

"I'll be more careful." She got a glimpse of compassion in his face before he moved off again.

Emily trudged on, watching where she put her feet and taking particular care around stones. The sun started down the western sky. The emptiness in her midsection made her a bit dizzy. She had never been so hungry in her life.

At last, she had to stop. She would sit for just a few minutes. She looked ahead for Richard, to signal her intention, and saw nothing but empty landscape.

She rubbed her eyes. The valley was narrowing. There were walls of stone on either side, a few trees and brush ahead. But it wasn't so thick that she couldn't see clearly to the end of the declivity. Richard was gone!

Emily's heart began to pound. Her mouth went dry, and her legs trembled. She hadn't known what fear really was until now, she realized. Richard's presence had been sustaining her in ways she hadn't begun to understand.

How could she have lost him? She turned in a circle. There were no side trails. He couldn't have turned off without her noticing. Had he fallen? Was he hurt? Frantically, she ran forward, glancing left and right, watching for a hidden obstacle, something he might have fallen into or behind. There was nothing. Had he been captured? Were their pursuers waiting to pick her off as well?

Emily stopped and listened as she had seen Richard doing. She heard nothing helpful. Clasping her shaking hands together, she tried to think what to do. Keep searching, she thought. She had to find him.

Some sound made her look up. Richard was standing not five yards from her, gesturing for her to come along.

Emily gaped at him. One minute, she had been alone; the next he had reappeared like an apparition. She must be going mad. Relief and bewilderment overwhelmed her. Her legs gave way and she sank to the rocky ground, shaking.

Richard rushed over. "Have you hurt yourself?"

She managed to shake her head.

"I've found a place to rest." He took her arm and pulled her up.

Leaning against him, Emily walked. This was how they had met, she thought fuzzily; only then she had supported him.

"It isn't far," he assured her.

His arm was steady around her. Emily let herself relax.

They were heading straight for the wall of the valley. It towered over their heads at this point and was nearly sheer. Had he climbed that cliff, and then somehow jumped down when she wasn't looking?

"This way." Richard guided her right up to the wall of rock, around a projecting bit, and *into* the cliff. "Turn sideways. It's narrow."

There was a crack about two feet wide through the whole mass of stone, Emily realized. You couldn't see it unless you stood in exactly the right spot behind a thicket. The fissure seemed to go very far back. She couldn't see the end.

"How did you find this?" she murmured, astonished.

"An unlikely coincidence. A wren flew in just at the moment I was looking that way," Richard told her. "No one will find us here."

The opening was just wide enough to allow passage. Stone scraped Emily's back.

"This is the narrowest part. You have to squeeze through."

She wriggled a bit, and was through. Richard had more difficulty, but he was soon behind her again. Emily saw light ahead and walked faster. When she emerged from the dimness of the fissure, she gasped at the scene that opened before her.

The crack widened to form an oval the size of a ballroom. Trees grew thickly around the edges, shading a small pool in the center fed by a spring trickling over a slab of stone. Shafts of sunlight gilded the leaves and glowed in the water. The earth was cool and carpeted with ferns.

"Help me move this," said Richard.

Turning, Emily saw that he was pushing a boulder toward the opening. She lent a hand, and it rolled into place, blocking the way. Richard picked up a smaller rock and set it on top. She helped him make a small pile, and soon they had the passageway effectively closed.

"The trees hide us from above," he said. "But we must be very quiet. If we are heard, they can find their way here."

She nodded, already walking under the trees toward the water. Cupping her hands, she drank from the spring. Then she splashed the clear liquid over her face and neck, sighing at the wonderful feel of it. She pulled off her boots and stockings and sat on a rock at the edge of the pool to dangle her feet in it. It was heavenly. But it wasn't enough. Emily turned to see what Richard was doing.

He was watching her with a smile. "Go ahead," he said. "I'll sit here." And he sat on a rock with his back turned, facing the blocked entry.

Emily hesitated, but the lure of the water was irresistible. With another look at Richard's back, Emily began to unbutton her blouse.

She shed her clothes quickly and slid into the pool. The water slid over her skin like silk, washing away the dirt of the journey and even, it seemed, some of the aches and bruises. It made her feel charged with energy, as if she could swim for miles, leap like a salmon, or flip like an otter.

She ducked under and shook out her hair under the surface. Coolness enveloped her head. She spread her arms and swooped back up, breaking the surface in a scatter of golden droplets. An even brighter glint drew her eye to Richard's ring on her finger. It was the only thing on her body at this moment.

She glanced quickly at him. He sat as before, turned away. Emily experienced an odd qualm of disappointment, immediately dismissed. She swam a few strokes to the edge of the pool, turned and swam back. It was as if they had entered another world through that narrow passage in the cliff.

Something touched her foot. Emily gave a startled cry and jumped onto a rock slanting into the pool. Gazing into the water, she saw a glint of tiny fish, and felt foolish.

"What is it?"

Emily looked up to find Richard on his feet, facing her, poised for rescue.

The universe seemed to stand still. Emily didn't feel the slight breeze on her body or the water dripping from her hair. She couldn't move. She was conscious only of Richard a few yards away.

The tension in his face and stance slowly drained away. His hands dropped to his sides. His eyes stayed on her as if he was helpless to shift them. She couldn't read the expression in them. She had never seen it before.

A bird called. Emily started and grabbed her skirt, holding it up before her like a curtain. "It was nothing," she stammered. "A fish. It startled me."

Richard turned his back. He stood there, rigid, giving no sign of what he felt.

She had spoken too loudly, Emily realized, not to mention standing there like a stick without anything on.

Richard folded his arms. Every ounce of his attention appeared to be focused on the pile of stones blocking the entrance. He was keeping watch, the pose seemed to say, not squeaking at shadows and possibly bringing their enemies down on them.

Emily yanked on her creased, stained riding habit. It had been a silly mistake, she acknowledged. But she wasn't accustomed to bathing outdoors. There was no call for him to be so superior about it.

She marched over to Richard. "Your turn," she whispered. "I'll keep watch." She would show him that she could be as responsible as he.

He stared down at her, his hazel eyes hot.

Emily took a step closer. He moved quickly back. "Go," she murmured. Commandeering the rock, she sat down in his place, facing the cliff.

There was a period of silence. Emily was acutely aware of his gaze on her back. At last, she heard him walk away. There was another silence, which seemed very long, before she caught a quiet splash and knew that he had gone into the pool.

Emily felt a brief glow of satisfaction. He had succumbed to this small indulgence. He wasn't immune. She heard water ripple against rock, the sound of swimming. Unbidden, her imagination began to build a picture. It grew more and more detailed, filling her senses until she was conscious of nothing but the liquid sounds behind her and the images in her mind. Her cheeks reddened. Had he done this when she was in the water?

Without realizing it, she had inched around on the rock. She was perpendicular to the cliff now. Shocked, she started to turn back. But splashing stopped her. Emily bent her head, letting her damp hair hang down along her face. Twisting her head slightly, she sneaked a look at the pool.

Richard had just climbed out. He stood at the edge, shedding water like dripping gold. His body was dappled with shadow from the overhanging trees, and it was gloriously formed—broad shoulders, lean muscled arms and legs, a deep chest that narrowed to…

He raised his head and caught her looking.

Heat flooded Emily's face, washing down her neck to prickle over her whole body. She was transfixed by his unwavering stare. Even if she turned now, pretended she had been looking in quite another direction, it wouldn't matter. He knew. And she didn't want to turn away. She wanted to keep looking. She wanted to memorize the contours of his body. Remembering his kisses at the beginning of this journey—so long ago it seemed now—she realized she wanted even more.

Richard simply stood there. He didn't reach for his clothes. He didn't seem to breathe, though Emily's breath was rapid. It was as if he was waiting for a sign. She had the sudden sense that he would follow whatever lead she gave. This moment, full of portent, was in her hands.

She found herself on her feet, facing him, unclear how she had gotten there. Her body seemed to have made the decision on its own. She walked to the opposite side of the pool from where Richard was standing, following her with his eyes. Quickly, she slipped off her riding habit once again and stepped into the water. Her pulse was pounding. Part of her was silently shrieking at her temerity. With the water softly lapping about her shoulders, she looked at Richard again. A tremor of nervousness shook her. What if he…?

In one swift movement, he returned to the pool. In another instant, he had her in his arms, his lips warm and urgent on hers, nothing between them but a film of water.

The flood of sensation was dazzling. Emily felt him along every inch of her skin. His kiss made her dizzy as they floated together. His hands on her back made her shiver. Her arms crept around his neck as his mouth coaxed and enflamed hers. They sank slowly beneath the surface, hardly noticing the water close over their heads.

The kiss was endless. It took her breath away even more than the liquid atmosphere. It seemed that she had never experienced physical sensation before. Nothing that had happened to her body up to now had had this intensity, this irresistible demand.

With one kick of his powerful legs, Richard brought them up again. When they broke the surface, he pulled Emily toward the rocks at the edge of the pool. But she slipped out of his arms and dove, twisting around behind him, touching the back of his knee fleetingly before darting away.

He came after her at once. In the small pool, they circled and danced. He caught her once from the back, letting his hands slide up and cup her breasts, pulling her back against him so that she felt his arousal unmistakably. His fingers teased her into gasping before he let her go again and arced away through the water. She pursued him then, slipping up from below to brush along the length of him, evading his hands by an inch as hers moved featherlight over his skin.

At last, though, he caught her and crushed her to him in another shattering kiss. Emily gave herself up to it completely, and it carried her to a level where she ached for more. As if he knew, Richard lifted her out of the pool and carried her to a shaded bank of ferns. Sinking down beside her, he began to drop soft kisses over her whole body until she vibrated with longing.

She pushed her fingers through his brown hair and down over his wide shoulders. Tugging at his arm, she brought the kisses back to her lips, holding him close, reveling in the things he was making her feel.

His knee slid between hers, and his hand moved upward along the tender skin of her inner thigh. It stopped a bit above her knee, and his kiss deepened. She was drowning in it when his hand moved a little farther, then stopped again. Emily trembled with anticipation so intense it astonished her. Richard's lips strayed to her neck, her breast. He made her gasp again. Then his hand moved up a little, and stopped.

She shifted to encourage him. He gave a low laugh and captured her lips again. She pleaded with her body, curling one leg around his, pressing closer. And at long last, his fingertips caressed the aching center of her desire.

Emily went rigid with pleasure. His kiss, his strong body against hers, the overwhelming sensations he was drawing from her, all of it combined into an urgency like nothing she had felt before. She would have cried out if he had freed her mouth. But he kept it for his own as he drove her wild with longing.

It built and built until she knew nothing but him. They were rising; he was carrying her into unimaginable places. It built to the unendurable. And then shattered into glorious pieces blinding as lightning flashes.

Richard shifted, and she felt him inside her. She clung and moved with him, still caught in the waves of passion he'd evoked. He took her lips again, moving faster. She

felt the urgency driving him and exulted. She had the
same power as he; she could wipe out the universe for
him as well. He reached a crescendo, crushed her in his
arms for heartbeats, and relaxed against her.

Emily listened to his breath rasp. She felt the pounding of his heart and the sheen of sweat that coated them.
She felt her pulse gradually slow and the world seemed
to slow with it. The sun had dipped behind the cliff to
the west, throwing their refuge into shadow. Above, the
sky was still blue, but the ferns wore a cloak of evening.
Birds called in the trees. A pungent green scent rose
from the ferns crushed under them.

Tired from days of unaccustomed exertion, Emily
nestled into Richard's arms and dozed.

Richard raised himself on one elbow and looked down at
Emily, sleeping innocently as a wood nymph in a bower
of ferns. Her skin glowed in the fading light. He allowed
himself a lingering gaze along her legs, the curve of her
hip, the lovely arc of her breasts and creamy shoulders.
Her face was peaceful, a fringe of copper lashes hiding
her eyes. Her lips were slightly parted, and it was all he
could do not to bend to them and coax her to wakeful-
ness and passion once again.

But he slid carefully from her side and rose. He gathered her clothes and put them beside her, then slipped
briefly into the pool again before donning his own.
These mundane tasks gradually pulled him back into the
reality of their situation.

He had strayed from it somehow. When he had felt her
eyes on him at the edge of the water, the very atmosphere
had seemed to thicken and change. Thought had given
way to something more primitive. Caution had—not
disappeared—but retreated, perhaps, to the further reaches
of his consciousness, leaving only Emily in the foreground.

What fire she had. He looked at her pale form under the trees. He had been wanting her for weeks, he admitted now. Resisting had taken all his strength. And now he'd lost the battle. Richard smiled slightly in the gathering gloom. He ought to feel remorseful about that, he supposed. On the contrary, all he wanted was to do it again.

He turned away. They had to reach safety, but after that, with the altered circumstances… His smile broadened in anticipation.

A breath of cooler air touched his skin. Emily should dress before she took a chill. Richard wondered if he dared make a fire, and decided that would be tempting fate. He walked over and bent to touch Emily's bare shoulder. When she started, he said, "It's getting cold."

She sat up, looked around as if dazed, then reached for her clothes. Richard strained to make out her expression, but though there was still light in the sky, darkness had come to this hidden place. He could see only her pale skin being obscured by the darkness of clothes. She might not feel as he did, he realized. He had not been too entranced to notice her inexperience. "Are you all right?"

"Perfectly." She stood.

Saying the wrong thing loomed suddenly as a fearful risk, one Richard had never faced before. He considered a whole spectrum of remarks. This was ridiculous, one inner voice declared—inexplicable.

Emily took a step closer. "Is something wrong?"

Yes, Richard wanted to say. I've become a tongue-tied idiot. "No."

"You sound…odd."

"The circumstances are…unusual," he managed, then cursed himself for a fool. He had never in his life sounded so stiff. But the emotion that seethed below the surface seemed to translate into paralysis.

Emily gave a breathless little laugh. "If my aunt knew of *this*," she murmured.

It wasn't a moment when he wanted to recall the duchess.

"You'll have to marry me now, or I am quite ruined."

Richard felt a surge of resentment. Was this all she could think of? "As I told your cousin, I'm a man of honor."

Emily pulled back. "I know that. I…"

"So you needn't worry." He turned away. Her first thought had been for the proprieties—not for the way he knew he had made her feel, not for any bond their caresses forged. She had not engaged herself because she cared for him, Richard reminded himself. She had never said that she did. They had agreed that their association was purely practical. And then he had broken the agreement.

Emily had enjoyed their lovemaking. He was certain of that. But who knew better than he, Lord Warrington, that such physical pleasure could mean little else?

She wanted a haven after her—what?—her brief lapse under the strain of their flight? He set his jaw. "We should get some rest," he added in a hard voice. "We'll move at dawn." Taking out his penknife, he began cutting ferns to cushion the rocky ground.

Emily said nothing. He could feel her gaze on him as he worked, but she made no sound. When he had accumulated a good pile of vegetation, he said, "You can sleep here." Moving off a little way, he started cutting again. He heard the rustle of the ferns as she lay down on them. And why not, he thought bitterly. She had gotten her assurances. No doubt she would drop off at once, while he was certain that he would be awake for hours yet—if not all night.

His bed of fern complete, Richard sat down beside it. In the morning, he would climb the nearest peak and take bearings. It couldn't be much farther to his cousin's house.

Emily stirred, and all his senses came alert. But her even breathing didn't change. It was the worst fate he could imagine, Richard thought—to be so attuned to a woman who wanted nothing more than the protection of his name.

He made himself lie down, but turned restlessly. Memories of the silk of Emily's skin, the scent of her hair, plagued him. Try as he would to push them aside, he kept hearing the gasps of pleasure he had drawn from her. His body betrayed him, hungering for things his mind denied.

She belonged to him now, a sharp inner voice insisted. She had made the bargain clear. He had no reason to deny himself. Or she to refuse him.

Richard rose in one swift movement and went to where Emily lay. Her face was a blurred white oval in the darkness. Kneeling beside her, he slipped his hand under her skirts and ran his fingers along the skin of her leg.

"Richard?" she murmured, waking.

He caught her lips in a hard kiss, not wanting talk, and pulled roughly at buttons and fasteners. He stripped the cloth away, and ran his hands over her lucent contours possessively.

She murmured his name again.

"Don't speak," he commanded.

He cupped her breasts, let his hands wander down over her skin. He could see every inch of her clearly in memory, dappled with the shadows of leaves, the sparkle of water. The feel of her under him was driving him to a fever pitch of desire.

He pushed her knees apart with his own and freed himself from the encumbrance of breeches. He was rock hard and aching for release, and he would have it. She was his to take, a glow of warmth and surrender in the dark.

She lay still. She said nothing. The last time, her body had begged for his touch.

Something like anger flashed through him. Something like pain. Richard was assailed by a savage need for her to beg for his touch.

Fighting his own pounding demand, he set out to make her beg.

He ran his fingertips lightly up her inner thighs, pausing just long enough to tantalize before moving over her hipbones and along the curve of her waist. He teased her breasts until he elicited a breathy gasp, then let one hand slip down again to rouse her. He touched and caressed until she was straining against his hand.

When she cried out softly, he felt a flare of satisfaction. He took his own pleasure with a hard, driving rhythm that surged through his body like storm surf. The tempo rose and rose, and exploded in a wave that slammed through every nerve and fiber with an intensity that left him panting. She was his, declared his scattered thoughts. His.

Emily's hands moved gently on his back. He pulled away from her and stood. There was no way to see her expression in the dimness, and he didn't care about it anyway, he told himself. He strode over to the pool and stripped off his clothes, finding a grim satisfaction in the fact that he hadn't taken off his boots during the encounter. The cool water damped the remains of his fever, soothing him toward sleep. He staggered over a stone once going back to his bed of leaves, and once there, he felt exhaustion dragging at him. He gave himself up to it gratefully, falling into a bottomless pit of black.

Insensible, he dreamed. He was running, not away, but toward some unimaginable reward that continually eluded him. The harder he searched, the more it receded. He despaired, dreaming, of ever finding the thing that he sensed would make his life complete.

Birdsong woke him at first light. The sun was still below the clifftop, and the air was cool and damp with dew. Richard sat up, his gaze drawn to Emily, who slept in a tangle of clothes and bright hair. He felt a pang, and rejected it. He had to concentrate on getting them out of here.

Leaving his coat on the pile of ferns where he'd slept, he moved silently off toward the wall of stone he meant to climb.

Nineteen

EMILY OPENED HER EYES ON A DAZZLE OF LEAVES AND the cry of a jay. The morning was golden and green. She was lying in a nest of her clothes, mostly covered by them, and she was alone.

How did she know that? Raising her head, she looked at the spot where Richard had slept. Only his coat was there. She surveyed the ground around the pool. There was no sign of him.

She didn't know if she was glad or sorry. Yesterday had ended in such a muddle. She hadn't known how to speak to him, and her feeble effort to joke had obviously gone wrong. Her mind was dizzy with memories of his touch, worry that she had made a fatal mistake.

She sat up, her hopelessly crumpled riding habit sliding away. She clutched at it, then she let go; there was no one to see. Though the morning was cool, she made her way to the pool and slipped in to bathe. The water was comforting. She glided back and forth, letting it soothe aching muscles. It was quite a while before she climbed out again, refreshed, and stood at the edge.

Waiting a moment to dry before dressing, Emily had the sudden sense that she was being watched. She turned quickly. The hidden glade was empty. The pile of stones at the entrance was undisturbed.

There was nothing, no sound to betray a watcher. Yet the feeling remained, and she was suddenly convinced it was Richard, silently back from wherever he had gone.

Her heartbeat accelerated. A pulse of heat passed

through her body as if she'd been dipped in flame. It was partly embarrassment. But it was also something else that she didn't recognize. That something directed her hands as she slowly picked up her underthings and slid them on. It informed her fingers as she buttoned her blouse languorously, hands lingering on her own skin. It arched her back as she lifted her skirt and dropped it over her head. By the time she was fully dressed, Emily's breath was coming faster, and she was thoroughly astonished at herself.

There was no sign of the audience she had been certain was there, and she was glad now to think that she had been imagining it. What was wrong with her? Events of the last few days seemed to have scrambled her brain.

Memories of Richard's touch rose up in sharp contradiction. Emily went to sit on a rock and catch her breath.

"Good morning."

She jumped and nearly fell off. Richard had materialized out of nowhere and was bending to retrieve his coat from the pile of ferns.

"I've been up above getting bearings." He spoke as if yesterday had never happened, as if they were back in the first hours of their flight together. "If we move quickly, we can reach my cousin's house tonight."

Emily stood, brushing down her skirts to mask her nervousness. "That's good," she managed. He was intimidating this morning. It seemed this couldn't be the man who had come so close to her in the dark.

Richard went to the entrance and began removing the stones they had piled there. She moved to help.

"Quietly," he warned.

Emily reached for a rock, and their hands brushed, making her tremble. She thought his hand jerked a little. He grasped a larger stone and turned to set it aside. When it came time to move the boulder out of the way, and they had to push side by side, he gave no sign that he noticed her nearness. Emily was torn between wanting to put her arms around him and wanting to give him a thundering setdown. She settled for silence.

At the outer end of the entry, they paused for some time while Richard reconnoitered. Finally, he signaled with a gesture, and they started out along the rough ground. It was much more difficult than at the start of their journey together, Emily thought. She was deeply tired and terribly hungry and confused. Her feet kept wanting to stumble.

Richard led them to the end of the valley and then up a tumbled incline to a ridge masked by trees. They followed this north for most of the morning, and when it veered off in another direction, they made their way down into a gully that ran in the right direction.

Clouds began gathering at noon, and it was soon clear that rain was on the way. Emily concentrated on taking one step after another.

"There," Richard said, pointing.

Emily looked, and saw a manor house on the side of a hill beside a stream.

"We'll have to take particular care from now on," he added. "They must have suspected we'd come here."

The shots in the night seemed to have happened ages ago. "That would be sensible of them," she acknowledged.

He gave her a quick glance. Something flickered in his hazel eyes, and it seemed for a moment that he would speak, but he didn't.

It started to rain.

Richard led them behind the crest of the ridge, staying out of sight of the house. As they worked their way along it, rain muffled their footsteps. The skirts of Emily's riding habit dragged at her legs. Cold drops pelted her scalp and shoulders. She trudged along, boots squelching, feeling a kind of misery descend. The strain of being hunted was weighing on her. But as she watched Richard through the rain, she knew it was more than that.

"We'll work our way around to the back, and come down on the house from the heights," Richard said softly. "It's farther. But I don't want to arrive until it's dark anyway. It's our best chance to avoid being seen."

"I know." Water dripped onto her face from the pine boughs above. She wiped it away. Picking up her heavy sodden skirts, she started walking.

"Emily."

She froze in the middle of a step then turned to him. It was the first time he had used her name.

He was looking at her as if he needed to tell her something important. She thought she glimpsed a yearning question in his face. But even as she responded, it vanished. His chest rose and fell in a deep breath. "This way," he said.

The disappointment she felt then was so sharp that she told herself she'd been mistaken. She was probably becoming delirious from hunger. He had only wanted to tell her that she was going the wrong way. He was not going to explain why he scarcely looked at her now, after he had touched her in a way that…

Emily banished these thoughts. She was not going to stumble over this rough country soaking, starving, and weeping like a watering pot. She could do nothing about the first two, but she could…she could damn well control the third, she thought defiantly. "Damn well," she muttered, savoring the phrase.

Richard heard it. She didn't know whether she'd meant him to or not, but the utter astonishment on his face was so satisfying that she was glad. It buoyed her up for some time as they plodded on.

Emily lost all sense of where they were, or how much farther they had to go. Thus when Richard said, "This will do," and stopped, she bumped into him before the words sank in.

He reached out and steadied her. She leaned against

him. After a moment, his arm encircled her waist and remained there.

"The house is below," he whispered close to her ear. He took her hand and led her through the dark, sodden woods. He seemed to know where he was going, and she tried to match his steps and avoid obstacles.

After what seemed hours, Emily made out a light in a window high above their heads. They came to a wall. Richard put a hand on it and moved left until they came to a gate. There, he stopped to listen.

Emily could hear nothing but dripping water. Then there was a soft rattle.

"Bolted," Richard murmured in her ear.

In the light from above, she watched him take hold of the top of the wooden gate, pull himself up, and swing over. A moment later, the bolt slid back and the gate opened for her. Richard left it unlocked behind them.

The windows in this part of the house were dark, and securely locked. Richard moved along the building to another gate and into the kitchen garden. Here, the house showed more signs of life, and a back door.

Richard strode over to it, listened at the panels, then tried the latch. He made a sharp beckoning gesture. When she reached him, he threw the door open and surged inside. On his heels, Emily hurried in, and came face to face with a trio of startled servants sitting around the kitchen fire. "Fetch your mistress at once," Richard said.

The young man jumped to his feet, looking as if he intended to defend the two women servants—one older and one young as himself.

"I am Mrs. Farrell's cousin," Richard told him. "I must see her at once. Privately."

The young man eyed them suspiciously.

They must look like vagabonds, Emily thought, drenched and exhausted and dirty.

"He brought his mum here," said the girl. "That Lady Fielding."

Richard nodded. The young man seemed unconvinced.

"We mean no one any harm. But I must speak to Mrs. Farrell."

"I'll fetch her, Sam," said the girl. She picked up a lighted candlestick and slipped out of the kitchen looking excited.

The other two servants stared at them. Richard offered Emily a chair, and she sank into it gratefully. They had done it, she thought. They had reached safety. Magistrates would be summoned, the countryside scoured. It was over.

A scent, a glorious intoxicating scent captured her attention. Turning, she discovered a loaf of bread on a board and a round of golden cheese on a plate. Beyond politeness, she reached for them.

Seeing her move, Richard turned. He picked up a knife to slice the bread, and Emily nearly snarled at him before realizing that he meant it for her. When he handed her a thick sandwich, she tore into it before he could cut another for himself. Oblivious to the stares of the servants, they ate like the starved creatures they were.

Footsteps approached. The door swung open, and Lydia Farrell entered the kitchen in a rustle of silk. "Richard! Miss Crane!" She looked stunned. "You can't be here. Come with me." Taking the candle from the servant, she gestured urgently for them to follow her. Emily snatched the bread from the table as she obeyed.

"Don't go near a front window," Richard commanded as they moved down a corridor.

Lydia looked upset. "Come," she repeated. Opening a door, she revealed a staircase. "Down here."

They descended quickly into a large brick-walled cellar. The light of a single candle did not reach into its corners. "This way," said Lydia. She strode across the floor. Opening a thick wooden door, she added, "You'll be safe here."

Richard went through it. Emily followed. The door thumped closed behind them, cutting off all light. There was the sound of a key turning in a lock, and then silence.

Emily clutched her loaf of bread to her chest. "What…why did she…?"

Richard cursed.

"I don't understand," said Emily.

"It appears that we have made a mistake."

Richard sat on the stone floor of what he took to be a storage room. He had explored the perimeter, reaching as high as he could, and found only brick walls, without windows. Five paces square, with a sturdy plank door and a lock in sadly good repair. It was pitch black and silent, assuring him that sounds made here were unlikely to carry beyond the basement.

"Couldn't we talk a little?" said Emily. "It's so… oppressive in here."

Her voice wavered a bit, and Richard felt a pang of guilt. He had shouted at her when they were first shut in, furious with himself and the situation. "There doesn't appear to be anything else to do," he acknowledged.

"There's no way out?"

He shook his head, realized she couldn't see it, and said, "Just the door."

Richard listened to the silence. It felt thick, like a blanket draped over him cutting off the air.

"Mrs. Farrell… You don't think she's…?"

"She wants my land," Richard answered. "She tried to buy it from me."

"Because of the coal?"

"I suppose they discovered it some time ago. No doubt the seam runs through the Farrells' estate as well."

"And they want it all for themselves."

"Yes." He felt like a fool for not having seen it.

"So, you think…they hired those men in London?"

Richard sighed. "Hired them, and when they failed, Lydia came up to town herself to see what could be done." His short laugh was humorless. "She settled in my own house, made a friend of my mother, who is now her hostage, and persuaded me to come to Wales where I could be more easily disposed of."

"But if you were dead…"

"The estate would pass to my mother as nearest kin. I never made any other provision. I'm sure Lydia thinks she can bilk her of it." It was almost unbearable—to have been so deceived, to have failed to see any signs of Lydia's true thoughts and purpose. He still couldn't quite believe it. He'd thought he'd developed keener instincts.

"That is…difficult," Emily said in an oddly tentative voice.

"It's damnable."

The silence returned. Richard found that now he couldn't tolerate it. He had a sudden desire to see Emily's face. "Are you all right?" he asked instead.

"You mean, aside from being wet and cold and shut up in the dark? Probably about to be killed?"

Despite their circumstances, Richard smiled. Nothing they had endured, not even imprisonment, had broken her buoyant spirit.

"I stole the loaf of bread," she added.

"Prescient of you."

"You don't think it will attract rats?"

"I don't think we will give them time to notice it."

"Oh." She didn't sound comforted. "Would you like some now?"

He wasn't particularly interested in eating. But he wanted to be closer to her, to feel her as a real presence rather than a voice out of the dark. "Yes," he said, rising.

Emily's skirts rustled.

"Stay where you are. Just say something, and I will come to you."

"Uh…do you think perhaps there are no rats, since this room is empty?"

Following her voice, he found her sitting against the opposite wall. It was a great relief, somehow, to sink down beside her and feel her shoulder warm on his. When she handed him a piece torn from the loaf, he realized that he was still hungry. He ate it, and then they finished off the rest between them.

She shivered, and Richard pulled her close without even thinking. She nestled in the curve of his arm. "It's so dark."

He said nothing. There was no cheering answer to this.

"What will she do with us?"

Richard considered various vague answers. But he knew Emily wouldn't believe them for a moment. "I suppose she is sending for her hirelings, to put us in their hands."

"The ones who shot at us?"

"Yes."

She assimilated this silently. He had never met a woman with such courage, Richard thought. Or a man, for that matter. She took each catastrophe as a new obstacle to be overcome. She would continue fighting right to the end of her strength. A fierce protective anger blew through him. He had to find a way to get her out of this.

"What was your favorite game when you were a child?"

"What?"

"Mine was making villages. I would clear a patch of grass and build houses of twigs, with leaves for the roof."

Her voice was meditative. She was searching for a distraction. It wasn't a bad notion.

"There were streets of pebbles, and usually a little square. A delphinium blossom makes a splendid church steeple."

"Does it?" Richard could see her, suddenly, a small girl with bright hair bent over, placing a blue flower at the peak of her creation. The vision made his throat tight for some reason.

"Of course, in a day or two, it would wilt. But that didn't matter because I wanted to keep working on it, making it better. Once, I dug a whole little river—coming out of a stream—to run through my village, with a bridge and a waterfall. That was the best one."

Her voice was beginning to soften toward sleep.

"What was your favorite game?" she asked again.

Richard considered. "When I was very small, we lived in Somerset. Before my father died."

She made a sympathetic sound.

"I liked the usual sorts of games." Richard suddenly remembered something he hadn't thought of in years. "I liked to build things, too. Not villages."

"What?" she murmured.

Her head had come to rest on his chest, and he felt her voice there. "Machines." A self-deprecating laugh escaped him. "That's how I thought of them. They weren't, really."

"What do you mean?"

"They were mechanisms, made of things I found around the place—bits of wire, gears from a broken clock—but they didn't do anything."

"And a machine must do something."

"Yes. That's the beauty of it."

Emily raised her head as if to look at him. In the thick darkness, she sank back again at once. "Beauty?"

He groped for the thought. "It begins as an idea of how to accomplish some task. And when the machine is manufactured, the idea comes to life. It works. It must be such a thrill when you start up something you have conceived, and it goes, it succeeds."

Emily said nothing. Richard suddenly felt self-conscious. He had never talked to anyone like this.

"Why did you stop?"

"What?"

"Why did you stop building your 'mechanisms'?"

He'd not only stopped, he'd forgotten all about them. "My father got me a pony," he remembered. "And he was teaching me to fish and…other things I was supposed to do. There wasn't time any longer."

"Supposed to," she echoed.

"Yes." Richard grimaced in the darkness. "A country gentleman has no interest in machines. Still less a man of fashion."

"Your father wished you to be a man of fashion?"

"No. That was my mother. He would have settled for a country gentleman, I believe."

"As he was?"

Richard tried to remember his father's face. "I don't really recall. I was very young when he died."

"That must have been hard," said Emily softly.

"I missed him. But I was small. All I knew was that we were moving to London to my grandparents' house. I'm sure it was much harder for my mother." He'd never thought of that before, he realized. She must have been frantic, with the abrupt loss of a young husband, debts left behind, a child.

"Everything suddenly changing," said Emily, echoing his thoughts.

Almost the way his life had shifted when he was shipwrecked, though they hadn't had to eat grubs, he thought with a smile. "You know what that's like," he said, recalling things she had told him about her own childhood.

"But both my parents were always there."

"Very much so," he joked.

She nodded against his chest. Richard felt a kinship vibrate between them. Their lives hadn't been alike in the particulars, yet the end result was similar.

A sudden certainty descended on Richard. She was the only kind of woman he could admire now. He would never tolerate a partner without her unique blend of courage and sensitivity and humor.

Ideas opened out in his mind, one after the other, like curtains parting to reveal a wide vista. Perhaps the things that had pushed them toward an engagement—for he had been pushed—weren't mere convention or accident. Perhaps it was larger, more portentous, than that. "We're meant to be together," he murmured.

She made no reply, and Richard was shaken by a dread that she didn't feel this, that it was a delusion he'd woven of longing and fatigue. The idea was so bleak he couldn't speak for a moment. And then when he could, he didn't know what to say. Why didn't she answer him?

The silence was heavy and lightless. The brick storage room seemed to close around him, the walls drawing in to stifle.

"Emily?" he managed at last.

There was no response but her even breathing, the weight of her head on his chest. It was another few moments before Richard realized that she had fallen asleep.

Relief coursed through him, and he didn't know whether it came from the explanation of her failure to answer, or the knowledge that she hadn't heard his admission in the first place.

She stirred, nestling closer to his side. His body responded with a jolt of desire and a confusion of emotion. He could taste her lips, feel her skin in his fingertips.

Richard closed his eyes and rested his head against the brick wall, fighting the images in his mind and the echo

of sensation demanding repetition. It was far too dangerous, in several senses, to give way.

Twenty

RICHARD WOKE TO A DIM FILTERING OF LIGHT, YELLOW green along the brick of the walls. There were narrow slitted openings near the ceiling of the room, closed with glass and overgrown with vines. They were well out of reach.

Carefully sliding away from the still sleeping Emily, he rose and surveyed their prison. The room was nearly a perfect cube, and it was perfectly empty. There wasn't a scrap of metal or a bit of lumber he might use as a weapon. And the brickwork looked solid. By the time he could pry one loose and break a window, it would certainly be too late. Nonetheless, he took out his penknife and began scratching at a line of mortar.

Emily sat up. Putting her hands to her hair, she pulled out pins and held them in her mouth while she tidied the unruly mass. Richard couldn't take his eyes off her as she pinned it up again. When she smoothed it back and looked up, he looked quickly away.

"I wish we hadn't eaten all the bread," she said.

Richard laughed.

Bracing one hand against the wall, she stood. "At least we're dry." She brushed at her skirts. "Though covered with dust."

Richard watched her examine the room. He could almost hear her coming to the same conclusions he had reached himself. She went over to the door and tried the lock, rattling it quietly.

"Mrs. Farrell keeps her house in annoyingly good order."

"An estimable housekeeper," he replied dryly.

Emily turned to him. "Will they come for us this morning?"

"I imagine so. Lydia probably had to search the hills for her hired killers."

"I hope they were out in the rain all night!"

Another laugh escaped him. Richard felt a kind of irrational joy bubble up. He wished with all his heart that she was safe elsewhere, but if he had to face death, he couldn't think of anyone he would rather face it with.

"When we hear them unlocking the door, we can hide behind it and grab them," she suggested.

"I'm afraid it opens outward."

"Oh." She examined it again. "If we pressed ourselves against the bricks right beside it"—she demonstrated—"they wouldn't see us at first. Perhaps we could surprise them."

"We will certainly try that."

"But you don't believe it will work."

"They'll have guns, I imagine. And Lydia will most likely keep them from rushing in."

"She leaves a great deal to be desired as a family member," declared Emily severely. "It is enough to make one glad not to be well acquainted with one's family."

"I imagine it is. I am scarcely well acquainted with Lydia, however."

Emily stared at him. "You seemed such good friends."

"She took care to make it seem so," he answered ruefully. "I might have suspected something, since I had met her only once before."

"Only once?"

"When I was fifteen," Richard replied, and then wondered why she cared.

Emily turned away from his gaze. "We will escape," she said staunchly. "The men she hired are incredibly inept."

"They haven't been clever." He thought back over the attacks. They would have better direction this time, however.

"We'll outwit them."

He didn't want to discourage her.

"A distraction," added Emily. She nodded. "I will…"

Without any warning sound of footsteps, the key rattled in the lock. Richard quickly joined Emily against the brick wall beside the door, pressing his back against it.

"Watch me," she whispered.

Before he could ask what she meant, the door swung open.

Lydia Farrell walked in. She was alone and unarmed, Richard saw incredulously.

A wail like a steam whistle reverberated through the little room, and Emily flung herself onto Lydia, wailing and pleading like the most volatile of hysterical women. The room was suddenly filled with flailing arms and frothing skirts. Richard, astonished, stood stock-still.

The melee ended with Emily sitting on top of his cousin, pinning her arms to the stone floor with both hands.

"What are you doing?" cried Lydia, "Have you lost your mind?"

"You think I should simply let you kill us?" demanded Emily. She threw Richard a harassed look, as if wondering why he did not help her.

"Kill you?" cried Lydia in horror.

The emotion was so obviously genuine that Emily eased her grip and sat back a little. "So you can get Lord Warrington's land and the coal on it."

Lydia looked ashamed. "You found out about that." She glanced at Richard and away.

"You hired thugs in London to murder him," accused Emily.

"No!" Lydia frowned. "Is that who they are? But…" She looked bewildered.

"I think you had better let her up," commented Richard.

Slowly, Emily released her captive and rose. Lydia sat up, making no move to flee.

"Tell us about the coal first," said Richard.

Again, she looked ashamed. "We discovered it about a year ago. The deposit is very large. I didn't see why you…that is, you had no connection with this place and you never…"

"You didn't think I deserved a share in it," finished Richard.

Lydia looked at him almost fearfully. "You are very different now."

"But what about the attacks, the men who shot at us?" asked Emily.

"There is a madman in the neighborhood," Lydia blurted out. "He's looking for Richard, and he has two very sinister individuals with him."

Richard and Emily stared at her.

"He had just been at the front door when you arrived last night. He threatened my family—my sons!"

Richard and Emily looked at each other.

"You have to go," insisted Lydia. "Your mother too. I'm sorry, but I can't have my boys put in danger."

"A madman?" said Emily. "But who…?"

"Can you describe him?" asked Richard.

Lydia shook her head. "He wore a hooded cloak, and he had a scarf swathed around his face. But his eyes…" She shivered.

"What about the men with him?"

"Large," she answered. "Scarred all about the face and hands. Not countrymen."

"Bob Jones and Ralph the Thumb," cried Emily. "It must be."

Lydia gaped at her. "You can see why you must go?" his cousin added pleadingly. "He said if I tried to help you, he would kill my sons."

"You will have to lend me a horse," responded Richard.

She bit her lower lip and clenched her hands together.

"Can't we just send for help?" objected Emily.

Lydia made a gesture of denial. "I doubt that a messenger would get through," replied Richard before she could protest. "I will draw them off, and then you can get word out."

Emily swung around to stand right in front of him, her hands on her hips. "You cannot mean to leave here alone?"

"It is the only answer. You and my mother will be safe, while I…"

"While you are shot as soon as you ride out of the stable!"

"I can evade…"

"This is not the jungle," she cried. "We are not talking of snakes and panthers. They're lying in wait for you out there."

"There is no other way."

Emily glared at him. "Oh yes, there is."

"You all have to go," interjected Lydia.

When they turned to look at her, she was scrambling up from the floor. Under their eyes, she took a step backward. "I'm sorry. But I will not risk my family."

"If I am gone," began Richard.

Emily turned to Lydia. "They can't be certain we're here. No one saw us come in. Unless your servants…"

"They wouldn't speak of it."

"You must lend us a carriage. Lord Warrington and I will conceal ourselves in the vehicle while it is still in the stables."

Richard started to object, but she waved him to silence.

"When it pulls up at the front door, only his mother will get in. It will appear that she is leaving. They will probably follow, but…"

"No," said Richard.

"It is a much better idea than yours," declared Emily.

"I'll tell Lady Fielding," said Lydia, and slipped out before anyone could speak again.

"This won't do," said Richard.

"It will have to."

The courage and sheer will in her blue gaze reached into the most guarded coverts of his spirit. "I cannot put you in danger," he murmured. "I can't bear it."

"So you ask me to bear it instead?" Emily demanded. "I am to endure what you cannot?"

Richard couldn't speak.

"Well, I won't," she added almost saucily. She smiled, and Richard's throat grew tight with unprecedented tears.

⁂

Emily sat silently in the Farrells' traveling carriage as the stablemen finished harnessing the team. The curtains had been fastened down at the windows, so no one could see inside the vehicle. In the dimness, she clasped her hands and made herself stay still. She was trembling, but it was exultation more than fear that shook her. The way Richard had spoken to her, and looked at her—he had to feel as she did. The emotion in his face had been unmistakable. He cared for her. Even the threat they faced couldn't outweigh that revelation.

The carriage door opened, and Richard joined her on the forward seat. "Ready?" he asked quietly.

"Yes."

The vehicle jerked and rolled out of the stables and around to the front of the house. Emily shrank back as the door was opened and first Lady Fielding, then her maid were handed in. They both looked irritated. "You are here," said the former as she sat. When Richard gestured sharply for silence, she glared at him.

The door was closed, and they started off at a brisk pace. "I do not understand this at all," continued Lady Fielding in a harsh whisper. "Everyone seems to have lost his wits. First Lydia tells me I must go—not very hospitable! And then she gives me some rigamarole about ruffians threatening her family. It made no sense whatsoever. And you!" She fixed Richard with an accusing stare. "Hiding in the stables? Really!"

"I'm afraid it was necessary, Mother. Things are rather serious." Quickly, Richard told her the whole story. When he had finished, Lady Fielding sat back in her seat, white and silent.

The carriage rocked as the team increased its gait. Richard raised a hand to the window, then let it drop, clenching it on his knee. Hoofbeats sounded off to the side. "Mother, would you look out and see what is happening?" he asked in a rigidly controlled voice.

Lady Fielding complied. "There is a rider coming in from the right," she said. "Check the other side, Jevers."

Her maid looked and said there was another horseman on the left.

Richard looked frightening. "If they hurt the coachman, I will…"

"Mrs. Farrell told him not to take any risks," responded Emily.

A shot rang out up ahead. A horse squealed. The carriage rocked on its springs, then started to slow.

"They will have to open the doors to kill us," Emily said. She was pleased to find her voice steady.

"That will be the time to move," agreed Richard.

"They will not expect me to do anything, so I should be first."

"What sort of woman are you?" wondered Richard's mother.

"The sort who does not sit back and let herself be killed," Emily replied.

Surprisingly, Lady Fielding took this in without hysterics. "So I will leap…" she began.

"You will not," Richard interrupted.

"But it makes sense for me to…"

"It's out of the question."

"They will be most wary of you," she argued. "If we are to take them by surprise, we must…"

"I should do it," put in Richard's mother.

Everyone turned to stare at her.

"They won't expect anything from me."

No one disputed this.

"Tell me what to do."

"Mother, I don't think…"

"I'm capable of more than you imagine."

"The danger…"

"You say they intend to kill us. What is more dangerous than that?"

"No," said Richard. "I will take care of the matter."

"So I expect," responded his mother. "But perhaps I can give you the opportunity."

"She should have her chance," said Emily.

"Thank you, dear."

"Perhaps you didn't hear me?" snapped Richard. "I said…"

"They will probably stand back when they open the door," said Emily.

"Emily! Mother!"

"If you stumble out weeping…"

"Stop this at once!"

"You could pretend to be disoriented and hysterical, and start to wander off. Then they would have to…"

"Shoot her?" finished Richard sarcastically.

"Yes, I see. Very clever, dear."

"I forbid it," said Richard.

The silence that followed didn't sound like the silence of obedience, Emily thought. "What is your plan?" she asked him.

"As soon as the door is free, I'll burst through it and overcome them."

"All of them?"

"Yes."

Emily heard the doubt in his voice. "They'll kill you."

"You must sit on him while I get out first," answered his mother. "Jevers can help you."

The maid gave a little squeak.

"All right," said Emily, her voice a bit self-conscious. She was assailed by a vivid picture of her sitting on him to hold him down.

"You'll do nothing of the kind."

"Richard, it is settled," said his mother in the tone that brooked no argument. "Don't be difficult."

"Difficult? You are proposing to put yourself in…"

"I said, it is settled."

The carriage slid to a stop.

"I can defend my family," added his mother with such pride and dignity that no denial was possible.

Footsteps crunched on the road on both sides of the coach. Richard reached for the door handle, and found two small hands gripping his arm and tugging it away. He looked down, and what he saw in Emily's face held him motionless just a moment too long.

"Why have we stopped?" demanded his mother, pushing the door open and surging forward.

She was met by the barrel of a gun and thrust back. At the same moment, the opposite door was flung back and another gun aimed at Richard. "Here they are," called the huge man holding it. "Just like you said."

Another figure joined him, tall and heavily cloaked. Richard stared into the darkness of the hood, but all he could see was the folds of a scarf and the glitter of eyes.

The reflexes honed in the jungle took over, and he launched himself through the air at the man's throat.

He heard Emily scream as he struck. The man went down under him and thudded onto the road. Richard's hands closed on his throat.

Something struck Richard's head with stunning force. He reeled, but didn't let go. Then a voice snarled, "Get out of that or I'll shoot the girl."

Turning, he saw that the gunman had Emily. Red rage and the urge to kill flashed through him. If he dared to hurt her...

Shaking with fury, Richard let his hands ease. The man under him struggled. At least he would know one thing, Richard thought. As he sprang up, he grabbed the scarf that hid his assailant's face and pushed the hood aside. "Taft?"

The old man rose with some difficulty, ignoring Richard's incredulous gaze. "Put her back in the carriage," he said to his henchman. "And secure the other door."

"Taft?" repeated Richard.

"Get the servant and tie her up with the driver," said Elijah Taft, still paying him no heed. Lady Fielding's maid was dragged from the coach and led off.

"Why?" demanded Richard.

Finally, Taft turned to him, contempt clear in his eyes. "You'll not be pulling down the house I've spent my life preserving. It'll go to a man with some money, and some sense. It'll be saved."

"But I didn't..." He had said something about razing the house in Somerset, he remembered, but he hadn't been serious.

"You'd say anything now, to save your worthless skin." Taft turned away. "Why the good Lord didn't drown you, I'll never understand."

"You sent me to that shipping agent," Richard exclaimed. Taft had recommended the firm, said they were friends and would give Richard a good price on passage to the Indies.

Taft merely turned to the gunman. "Take the reins and get rid of them once and for all. This time, make it look like an accident. Drive them over a cliff. No more shooting."

"We was just trying to flush 'im out of the house," the man murmured sullenly.

"Well, now I have handed them over to you. Don't blunder again."

The man glowered at him but turned to climb up on the box. Richard was shoved back inside. When he tried the doors, he found them secured from the outside.

❧

The carriage bounced along a rough lane, throwing its passengers against the seats and one another. Emily fell against Richard. His arm curved warmly around her for a moment, supporting her, then was withdrawn as the vehicle swung back. Emily's throat tightened and her eyes stung. He had gotten her through so much. She wouldn't give up just yet.

The carriage slowed. Emily heard a voice call out. One of the men on the box above them answered. She couldn't tell what he said. The more distant voice replied. The carriage slowed further.

There was a shout. Two shots rang out as their vehicle jerked to a stop.

"You don't suppose it could be highwaymen?" Emily was shaken by a crazed desire to laugh.

"Whatever it is, we'd better try to take advantage of it." Richard shifted in the seat. "Move back."

Richard turned sideways and kicked the door with both feet, hard. It shuddered, and the carriage rocked on its springs.

"Stow that," bellowed one of the men on the box.

Another shot split the night. It seemed to Emily that it had not come from their guards.

Richard kicked the door again. It gave a little. Their captors pounded on the roof. He kicked again with all his strength, and the carriage door sprang open, the latch shattered.

"Stay back," he commanded.

Scrabbling sounds up above warned them.

"Down," said Richard.

They all crouched. The barrel of a gun appeared in the opening, then the distorted face of one of the London ruffians, hanging upside down. With a lunge, Richard took hold of the gun and twisted it. It fired, and the bullet tore through the carriage roof. There was a sharp cry from above.

Richard jerked savagely and the man hurtled off the carriage roof, landing with a thud on the ground. His gun remained with Richard, Emily saw. He tensed to leap. She put a hand on his arm. In that moment there was a roar of rage outside. The carriage dipped as if a great weight had hit it, swayed as it was removed. "I'll put your lights out for good, Bob Jones," roared the voice.

"Is that...?" began Emily.

"If you move, I will shoot you," someone else declared.

"Papa?" she exclaimed.

"If you've harmed one hair on my daughter's head, I'll shoot you anyway," he added.

The man who must be Ralph the Thumb moaned on the ground beneath the door.

"Emily? Are you there?"

"Yes, Papa," she called.

Richard climbed out of the vehicle, looked around, then turned to lift her over the recumbent form of Ralph. Emily's father materialized from the bushes at the side of the road. Simultaneously, the Bruiser appeared, frog-marching Bob Jones to join them.

"Jerry! How did you get here?"

"I brought him," replied Sarah Fitzgibbon, emerging beside Alasdair. "I had a feeling you were going to need some help, so I set him to watch Lord Warrington's house."

Astonished, Emily tried to take it all in. There

was a post chaise blocking the road. Sarah also held a pistol. "Mama didn't come?"

"Of course I came," answered her mother, pushing out from between some branches on the other side of the road. She gestured with her gun. "Don't be ridiculous."

Lady Fielding emerged from the carriage. She surveyed Emily's parents with far more approval than before. "I see what you mean about the pistols," she said to Emily's mother. "Did you really learn to shoot when you were twelve?"

Olivia approached the group around the vehicle. "Oh no. My father would never have allowed such a thing. Alasdair taught me."

Lady Fielding nodded judiciously. "Richard, perhaps you could…"

"Yes, Mother. We can discuss it another time. Where is Taft?"

"Taft?" Alasdair Crane growled.

"A cloaked man rode off that way," said Sarah, pointing back the way they'd come.

Richard strode over and began unharnessing one of the horses.

"What are you doing?" asked Emily.

"I have to go after him." Richard threw off the last of the straps and mounted the restive horse bareback.

"Wait."

"I must find him," was all Richard said. Setting his heels to the horse's flanks, he pounded off.

Emily took two steps after him.

"You, young lady, are by no means out of trouble," declared her father. "How dare you go sneaking off alone from the inn, without a word? And you have spent days—*days*—in the company of…" He broke off as Olivia put a hand on his arm.

"I didn't mean to be gone for days, Papa." She watched Richard disappear around a bend.

"We should go back to the village," put in Olivia.

"He's taken one of the leaders," objected Alasdair. "How are we to drive without a full team?"

Emily's mother quieted him. They deposited Bob Jones and Ralph the Thumb in the carriage with the single horse, with the Bruiser to watch them. The rest of the party took the post chaise, which Emily's father drove. Once they were moving, Olivia took her daughter's hand. "Are you all right?"

Exhaustion was dragging at Emily now that the ordeal seemed over. It felt like a huge effort just to nod. "I'm tired and bruised and filthy. But I'll be fine once I can rest."

"This is all very inconvenient," complained Richard's mother.

"Very unsettling," said Olivia. And Emily acknowledged that Lady Fielding's amazing transformation earlier was not to be lasting.

"I want to go back to Lydia's. And someone must fetch Jevers."

"And the coachman," remembered Emily.

When this was explained, Olivia promised to send someone from the inn to retrieve them both.

"I don't understand how you found us," said Emily then.

"Jerry saw the attack on Lord Warrington's house," Sarah explained. "He tried to follow, but he's not very good in the countryside. So we started watching the Farrell place instead, and when he saw Bob Jones and Ralph call there, he kept an eye on them from then on."

"Sarah explained everything to us, and we were able to set up an ambush," Emily's mother finished. She gave Emily a reproachful look. "You really ought to have confided in us, you know. Your father was very hurt that you did not ask him to shoot those men."

"I'm sorry," Emily mumbled. She laid her head back against the seat and closed her eyes. She and Richard hadn't been separated for days, and now he seemed very far away. Events had been moving so quickly since the moment she found him lying bound in the field behind her house. She had been whirled off to London, made over by her aunt, and then embroiled in a murderous plot. There'd been no time to think.

The mystery was solved, she realized. They had discovered who was behind the attacks on Richard. Their agreement was at an end.

But things had changed since they set those terms. She rubbed her forehead with one hand. What had changed was not circumstances, but herself. She loved him, she admitted. She wanted to spend the rest of her life with him.

And what did he want?

Sometimes, she was certain he shared her attachment. At other times, he looked at her as if she were an irksome problem he had to solve. Was he thinking then of the engagement? Was he wondering whether she would keep her word?

Emily swallowed. He would come and speak to her once things were more settled. She would see in his eyes what he felt, and then she would know what to do.

"Emily."

She started violently.

"We've reached the inn." Her mother sounded quite concerned. "Are you burnt to the socket? Come inside and rest."

Slowly, she climbed down from the chaise. There was no sign of the other carriage, or of Richard. Weariness dragged at her. Nothing more could be done tonight. When she saw Richard again, she would decide what to say.

Twenty-one

THE NEXT FEW DAYS PASSED IN A FLURRY OF ACTIVITY. Messengers came and went from the inn. There were visits to and from a solemn magistrate. Richard appeared at unexpected moments, always preoccupied and hurrying, and left again without saying much of anything. People seemed to swirl around Emily with dizzying speed, but none of them appeared to want her opinion or her help.

Richard certainly made no effort to speak privately to her. He hardly seemed to notice her existence, and Emily grew more apprehensive with each hour. Perhaps she had been mistaken. Perhaps he was waiting for her to fulfill her promise and set him free.

"Warrington knows how to get things done," said her father approvingly at dinner two nights later. "He's even managed to get that poor excuse for a magistrate to move. I daresay he'll have the business wrapped up by the end of the week."

"What will happen to that man Taft?" asked Emily's mother.

Alasdair shook his head. "Warrington didn't want to prosecute. Said it was a misunderstanding. He's pensioning the man off." He seemed torn between outrage and admiration.

"I still don't understand what he thought he was doing," said Emily.

"He's a bit unbalanced," replied her mother. "Apparently he has devoted his life to preserving the

Warrington estates in Somerset, and now that he is getting old, he became obsessed with leaving them in good hands. He seemed to think Lord Warrington's heir was the answer."

"So he decided to get rid of R—Lord Warrington?"

Olivia nodded. "And those close to him. Who might prevent the heir from inheriting."

Alasdair growled.

Emily tried to imagine being so attached to a place that you were willing to kill for it.

"The man's demented," said her father. A thought seemed to strike him. "Still, he'd make a splendid Mephistopheles." His hand moved as if it held a paintbrush.

"Too old," protested Olivia.

"Not necessarily."

Emily's thoughts drifted as they disputed the matter. They would go back to their painting, and Papa's bickering with the neighbors, and the love which sustained them through every difficulty. She had to see Richard. Why didn't he come to her? Just then, his name caught her wandering attention.

"Warrington will be here tomorrow at three," said her father.

Both her parents looked at her.

"It's all arranged," Alasdair added.

Was he coming to say good-bye? "Good. I need to speak to him," she said.

Alasdair raised his dark eyebrows. "You'll have plenty of time for that."

Emily rose from the table. "I'm going to walk a little."

"Emily," began her mother.

"I won't be long. I'll stay near the inn." Emily hurried out before they could object, leaving behind a concerned silence.

"I hope we're doing the right thing," said Olivia after a while.

"No question of that," answered her husband.

"I wish I could be as sure as you."

"How can you think of any other course of action?"

Olivia shook her head. "I don't understand what Emily feels about it."

Alasdair nodded. They contemplated this enigma for a while. "Never have understood her," he ventured finally.

"I know." Olivia sighed. "She's always been so self-contained. It's worrisome."

After another interval, Alasdair brightened. "Been that way since she was a tiny creature," he pointed out.

"That's what I just said."

"No, I mean, perhaps she's very happy. Wouldn't show that either, would she?"

Olivia pondered this.

"Warrington hasn't been about much," he added. "Perhaps she's pining for him."

"Do you think…?"

"Dragged us all down here to save his neck."

"That's true," said Olivia, looking happier.

"Went haring off into the wilderness with him." Alasdair scowled. "Alone. When I think that *my* daughter…"

"Yes, yes. You must be right."

"I dashed well am right. Warrington sees it."

"I know."

"It's all settled. Let us say no more about it."

Setting aside her doubts, Olivia nodded.

❧

Emily rose early the next morning and set off before anyone else was stirring. Finding a secluded spot not too far from the inn, she sat in the summer sunshine and tried to prepare herself for the afternoon. She moved her hand, making the ring glitter and throw rainbow reflections on the stones. It was an exquisite piece. But more than that, it was a symbol of what she wished for more than anything else in the world. Emily slipped it off and put it carefully in her pocket. She wouldn't put it on again until she was certain.

She didn't return to the inn until past noon, and when she got there she found her parents were out. "They said they had some things to do to get ready for this afternoon, miss," the landlady told her. She smiled broadly at Emily as if they shared some secret.

Mildly puzzled, Emily ate the luncheon set before her and then went up to her room and lay down. She hadn't slept well, and the walking had tired her a bit. After a while, she dozed.

It seemed only a moment before someone was shaking her awake again. She blinked sleepily up at her mother's face.

"It's time to dress. How can you be sleeping?"

Emily sat up, surprised by the urgency of her mother's tone.

"I found some flowers. One of the local landowners let me take some from their cutting garden."

Emily rubbed her eyes. "What time is it?"

"Nearly two. We haven't much time."

Her gown was crumpled and her hair in disarray. "I must change."

"Well, of course. I thought the blue sprigged muslin. I had them press it."

Emily looked at the gown hanging on the door of the wardrobe, then at her mother. Why should she take such an interest in what Emily wore for Richard's visit?

Swinging her legs around on the bed, Emily stood. "I'll be down in a few minutes."

"Don't you want me to help you dress?"

Emily stared. Her mother hadn't helped with her clothes since she was four years old. "I can do it."

Olivia looked oddly disappointed. "Are you sure?"

"Yes, Mama."

"Well, all right." With obvious reluctance, she moved toward the door. "Your father and I will be waiting downstairs."

She would have to find a way to get rid of them, Emily thought.

Emily washed her face, dressed, and tidied her hair. She transferred the ring from the pocket of her crumpled gown to the sprigged muslin. All she wanted now was to get this over. She couldn't think clearly, or make any sensible decisions, until it was.

There was a tap on the door. "Emily?"

"Yes, Mama?"

Her mother came in. "I made you this." She held out a garland of summer flowers—blues and yellows with a touch of white. "I thought it would look so lovely with your dress."

She never grew accustomed to her parents' artistic fancies, Emily thought. They would suddenly take it into their heads to decorate all the china with eccentric designs, gather seaweed to make some sort of exotic paint—or to weave circlets of blossoms that their daughter was expected to wear.

"May I put it on?" asked Olivia. Her mother settled the flowers on her head, then stood back. "You look lovely," she said, her voice catching as if she might cry.

That was something. Perhaps Richard would think so too? "Shall we go down?"

"We hadn't so much as a daisy when we married," said Olivia as they walked down the stairs. "Not even a bit of green."

Emily hardly listened. She had heard the details of her parents' runaway match so often that she could have told it herself.

In the private parlor on the ground floor, they found Emily's father talking with Richard. "Warrington

came early," said Alasdair jovially when they walked
in. "Couldn't contain his eagerness."

Emily scarcely heard him. She couldn't attend to anything except Richard, looking very handsome in a dark
blue coat and buff pantaloons. She wondered fleetingly
why he was so dressed up. But the thought evaporated as
soon as she reached him.

"You look splendid," he said with a small bow.

He seemed stiff and strained, Emily thought. Perhaps
he was worrying about what she meant to do. "I must
speak to you," she said quietly.

One corner of his mouth quirked. "We will have
ample time to talk later on."

Emily looked around. Had her parents planned
some event?

"Where is your ring?" asked Richard abruptly.

"In my pocket. I…"

"Put it on at once."

He seemed angry. Meeting his eyes, Emily swallowed.
They were hot with something she didn't understand at
all. He frowned. She slipped the ring back on her finger,
her heart pounding.

"There he is," said her father, who was gazing out the
window. He took a folded sheet of paper from his pocket
and left the room.

"Who?" asked Emily.

"The vicar," answered her mother.

Emily grimaced. Had her father already become
embroiled in some dispute with the local parson? She
wouldn't have thought he had time.

Her father returned, followed by a small, dark-haired
man in clerical bands. Emily was relieved to see that the
latter was smiling. "All in order," said Alasdair, rubbing
his hands together.

To Emily's surprise, Sarah Fitzgibbon and Richard's
mother came in behind them.

"And all present and accounted for," her father added. "We can get started."

Olivia took Emily's hand and squeezed it. Emily gave her a wild look.

Suddenly, Richard was standing beside her. The vicar came over and faced them both. He smiled benignly and opened the small book he was holding. "Dearly beloved…"

Emily's throat closed in astonishment. She gaped at Richard. His attention was on the parson. She stared at her parents. They looked serene. She turned to Sarah, who winked at her.

The vicar was speaking Richard's name, asking if he took this woman for his wife. His face solemn, Richard said, "I do." He looked down at Emily. His hazel eyes were clear, but unreadable. The parson turned to her.

How had this happened? Emily wondered in a panic. Her gaze flew over the faces again. Richard's mother looked resigned. They had all thought the engagement was real, Emily recalled. They would have no reason to question a marriage. But Richard…

She met his eyes again. He didn't look angry. He didn't look anything.

The parson was asking if she would take him for her husband.

Emily's throat was tight with tears. She wanted to, and she was afraid to. Had her father forced him to stand up with her?

"Miss Crane?" said the vicar. He started to frown.

Emily swallowed. "I…"

Richard took her hand and held it. His fingers were warm on her icy ones. He held her eyes—steady, serious. She tried to ask with her expression what he really wanted. But he simply waited.

"Emily?" said her mother.

She couldn't look away from Richard. Her senses

swam a little as she lost herself in his gaze. It felt almost like being in his arms. She could think of nothing else. "I do," she said.

Several breaths sighed out in relief. The vicar eyed her for a moment, then went on with the ceremony. In another few moments, it was complete. Richard's lips brushed hers for an instant, then the others crowded forward with congratulations.

Emily put a hand to the flowers in her hair. Had she actually gotten married?

Her father was opening a bottle of champagne; Richard was opening another. Glasses were poured. Toasts were made. Through her turmoil, Emily gathered that Sarah and Lady Fielding were traveling back to London together the following day. Her parents would be leaving for home soon after. And she would be left here with her new husband, whose only words to her so far had been an apology for the lack of a wedding journey because there was "far too much to do here."

Perhaps she was dreaming, Emily thought as the party went on. Perhaps she was actually still asleep in her room at the inn, having a nightmare in anticipation of breaking things off with Richard forever.

But she didn't wake. The parson took his leave. A carriage with ribbons tied to the traces was brought round, and her trunk—which she had not packed—was fastened to the boot. Before she knew it, Richard was handing her in and the others were waving and tossing blossoms at them. He climbed in after her, and the horses started off. Emily watched out the window as her parents grew smaller and smaller and finally disappeared around a bend in the road.

"I managed to get a few more furnishings for Morne," Richard said. "Lydia was very helpful. And I've engaged some servants. I think you will be tolerably comfortable there."

His tone of voice was perfectly normal. He was looking at her as if there was nothing odd about the sudden change in their situation.

"I have some people coming to talk about development of the coal," he added.

Now he sounded apologetic. Emily couldn't imagine why.

"It's rather important. My other estates are heavily encumbered."

The tension in Emily was rising too high to ignore. "I was going to break the engagement," she blurted out.

Richard's head jerked slightly, as if taking a blow.

"I was going to keep my word."

"That was no longer possible," he replied, his words clipped.

"I meant to tell you today, but there wasn't any time. I didn't know… Everything happened so fast." Emily fell silent. It sounded as unreal as it had felt.

"Your father told you he was sending for a special license."

Richard sounded bewildered, and perhaps something more. Emily couldn't be sure. She remembered her father mentioning a bishop, and thinking it odd. But she hadn't been paying attention. "I didn't want a forced marriage," she murmured.

The carriage bounced in a rut. Emily grabbed one of the leather straps to stay upright, fighting a growing sense of panic. She longed to ask Richard if he had married her against his will, but she was afraid of the answer.

❧

Richard stood on the bit of lawn in front of his house and watched the last streaks of sunset fade in the west. This land that his stepfather had left him, which he had once thought worthless, was going to redeem all the rest. With the funds the coal brought, he would be able to pay off mortgages, improve his estates. He appreciated the irony as much as he regretted the way he had made the discovery.

The sky dimmed. Stars were winking into view, and there was a hum of insects. One of the upstairs windows turned golden with lamplight. Richard stared up at it. His wife was there, in their bedchamber. It was his wedding night.

One corner of his mouth jerked. He had never imagined that Emily would feel forced into the marriage. He had been too occupied with his own struggle over the matter, and with all the business that had to be dealt with. But he shook his head, refusing the easy excuse. He could have found time to talk with her.

When she had said they had to marry, he had resented it. Why should he be so astonished, or angry, if she felt the same? He had known she wasn't like other women. His mouth jerked again. There was no one like her. If he hadn't been such a fool…

Above his head, the casement opened. Looking up, he saw Emily sitting in the window, the lamp throwing a golden aureole around her. Her hair was down, falling over her shoulders like liquid fire. She wore a pale nightdress that left her neck and arms bare. A mixture of desire and tenderness burned in his chest.

She was looking upward. Suddenly, she raised a hand as if startled. Following her gaze, Richard saw a shooting star hurtle across the sky. Turning back, he thought he saw her lips move. What was she wishing for? Was it anything he could give her?

He must have moved, because Emily looked down, putting a hand to the front of her gown. "Who's there?"

"It's all right," he said. "I was getting a breath of air."

"Did you see the shooting star?"

"Yes."

"They're a sign of good luck."

They could use a bit of luck, he thought.

Emily leaned out, a figure of copper and ivory and gold. She seemed to be gazing at him, but he couldn't make out her expression in the shadows.

Silence lengthened between them.

"Are you…coming up?" she said finally.

Richard had to close his eyes at the fierce longing that shot through him with the question. No qualms or doubts were going to keep him from her bed tonight. The feel of her was branded into his nerves; the mere memory could make him shudder with desire. "In a moment," he replied, his voice thick.

Emily hesitated, then withdrew from the window. Richard stared at the empty square of golden light, then turned and strode inside.

She was sitting on the bed, waiting for him, her legs curled under the silky folds of her nightdress. The lamplight was molten after the darkness outdoors, and Richard blinked at it, and at her delicate beauty.

"It's…getting cool," she said.

"I'll close the window." He started toward it.

"No!"

He stopped.

"I like hearing the crickets, and the wind."

He turned away from the casement.

"Unless you want it closed," Emily added hurriedly. "If you would rather…"

"I prefer it open."

"Oh." A smile trembled on her lips. "We…we will have to learn each other's habits."

Richard was finding it difficult to breathe. They had trekked for days in the wilderness without this awkwardness. Did marriage destroy all that? The idea weighed on his spirits intolerably. He stripped off his coat and put it over the back of a chair. Sitting down, he pulled off his boots.

When he looked up, Emily was gazing at him. Her eyes dropped at once, then rose again. A flush spread from her face down her neck and under the scooped neckline of her gown.

Richard felt a thrill of recklessness. Pulling his shirt free of his breeches, he jerked it over his head and let it fall to the floor. Holding Emily's eyes, he stepped closer to the bed. Her gaze strayed downward, then quickly back to his. Richard felt a wild desire to laugh.

He took another step. Putting a hand to the fastening of his breeches, he raised a questioning eyebrow. At first, Emily didn't react. He waited, watching her eyes flicker from his face to his hand and back again. Her cheeks were flaming now, but she was leaning forward with what certainly appeared to be eagerness.

He moved his hand a bit, but continued to wait. Emily's lips parted. Richard cocked his head. She nodded, then looked daunted by her own temerity.

He undid the fastenings and stripped off his final garment, standing before her in the light of the lamp. He had never done such a thing with any other woman. Wild laughter rose in him again, an exultation that he didn't begin to understand. It burned him. He felt as if his eyes were glowing with it.

He reached the bed in two steps, and swept Emily into his arms, molding her against him. Her lips were sweet and pliant, urging him on. Her arms slid around his neck. Richard smoothed the curves of her back. Her body was intoxicating, maddening.

Her knees slipped around him. He ran his hands up her thighs and cupped her hips to press her closer. Their kisses were incendiary now, rising to a pitch beyond anything he had experienced.

The nightdress was becoming a nuisance. He grasped the silky material and tugged it up. Emily released her arms, but not her legs. She leaned back a little and helped him pull the garment free. When he threw it across the room, she laughed.

Richard pushed her back onto the bed. He couldn't take much more. And he wanted to hear her gasp. He dropped kisses across her shoulders and down to tease first one rosy nipple, then the other. His fingertips found the warm liquid spot that brought him the gasps he wanted.

She moaned his name. He ached with wanting her. Her fingers brushing over him were sweet torment.

Feeling her muscles go rigid, he shifted and buried himself in her warmth, moving with her as she pulled him closer. When she cried out, he loosed the iron control that had bound him and let himself rise to ecstasy in her wake. The world fell away. Every secret part of him thundered with release. It left his heart pounding, his breath rasping, and an odd, unexpected ripple of happiness spreading through his chest.

Richard held his wife close as the sensation ebbed. He could feel her heart beating under his hands. He kissed her neck, her shoulder. When he rolled onto his back, he pulled her with him, drawing her close to his side.

The sounds of the night spread around them. A current of cool air from the window caressed their heated skin.

"I should have…" began Richard, then stopped. Emily had said the same words at the same moment.

"Go ahead," they both said.

Emily gave a nervous laugh.

"You…" each of them began.

Richard closed his eyes, shaking his head slightly. "I never meant to force you into this marriage," he blurted out. Then he rose on one elbow. Emily had said almost the same thing once again. "You didn't…" he started to answer. So did she.

"Stop this at once," Richard said.

Emily pressed her lips together. She looked apprehensive and hopeful at the same time. Silently, she waited.

Now that he had the opportunity, Richard couldn't think what to say. She looked so very beautiful, lying there with her hair spread over the pillow.

"*You* didn't force *me* to marry," she said at last. "It was my aunt, and then Papa, who made you…"

"No."

Emily's celestial blue eyes were intent.

"I told your father to send for the special license."

"You did?"

"I've known for some time that you were the only woman for me."

She stared at him. "But you never said…"

"Until our adventure together, I had no right."

The delicate flush that showed her skin's translucence appeared again. "If you mean what happened by the pool…"

"You did say that I was obliged to marry you after that," he pointed out, gaining confidence now.

"It was a joke!"

"Was it?"

"Yes."

"Many women wouldn't think so."

"I am *not* 'many women.'"

Richard let himself smile. "I know. But I wasn't referring to that, er, interlude."

"What then?"

"Perhaps you don't realize that until we discovered that coal deposit, I was nearly penniless?"

She frowned as if he had said something confusing.

"I had no right to marry."

"Because of money?" She looked incredulous.

"Absolutely."

"You mean, if we had not found the coal…"

"I never would have touched you. I would have asked that you honor our bargain and break off our pretended engagement."

Emily shivered. Richard pulled the covers up.

"Even though you cared for me?" she whispered.

"Even though I have known for a long while that I would never love anyone else."

She gave a little gasp at the word *love.* "You would have left me alone—for money?"

"Honor," he corrected this time.

She sat up and glared down at him. "I would never have forgiven you as long as I lived! I don't care anything about money."

He laughed a little. "I know you don't."

"But you still…"

"*I* cared. I wanted to give you the ease and comfort you've never had. I wanted you to have all the luxuries of the duchess's household *and* the passion of your parents'."

Emily gazed at him. Her blue eyes pooled with tears. "How did you…?"

"I know you. How else could I love you?"

She threw herself into his arms. He thought she might weep, but she didn't. She held him fiercely, possessively, for a while. He enjoyed it.

"There's something you haven't said," he pointed out when she relaxed a little. "It's rather important."

She raised her coppery brows. There was a challenging glint in her eyes.

"I have told you that I love you," he pointed out.

She nodded regally, a smile tugging at the corners of her mouth.

"You haven't…reciprocated."

Emily tossed her head. "I don't believe I shall. I think I'll keep you wondering for, oh, a year or two. You'll have to cater to all my little whims and fancies and…"

Richard pulled her down against him and kissed her lingeringly. "I could keep you here until you admit it."

"Mmm," breathed Emily. "Oh," she said as his hand moved. "Yes, why don't you?"

Dizzy, intoxicating minutes passed. Richard was breathing hard, desire driving him further than he had believed possible before this night. It was like a molten wave carrying them both beyond ordinary realms of sensation, into the transcendent. It rose and rose until the demands of passion nearly overwhelmed him.

"Richard," murmured Emily. "Please," she pleaded. "Oh, please."

"Tell me," he demanded through gritted teeth. He resisted the wave with all his strength.

"I love you," Emily breathed. "I'll never love anyone else so much."

Gloriously, the wave broke.

～

Emily nestled closer into the curve of Richard's shoulder, her arm thrown across his muscular chest. They would sleep side by side in the night for the rest of their lives, she thought drowsily. She could hardly believe it even now. "So everything came right in the end," she murmured, mainly to herself.

"Very right," Richard agreed.

"When are they coming about the coal?"

"Tomorrow, I'm afraid."

Emily remembered something else. She rose on one elbow. "What did you mean that night, at the evening party, when you said I had cut through weeks of pondering and confusion?"

Richard looked up at her, his expression tender. "You said someone should make certain that the new inventions were used wisely."

She nodded.

"It was the hint I needed. The purpose I had been looking for in my life," he added simply.

The appreciation and respect in his gaze rendered her speechless for a moment.

"And with this coal deposit, I will have the funds to act as well."

"And you owe it all to me," she teased. "If I had not come down to Wales, you would not have been chased through the countryside and found the coal."

Richard frowned. "A method of discovery not to be repeated."

"I certainly hope not."

A thought struck Emily. "You know, I have a friend who might be very helpful about new inventions…"

Richard's expression stopped her. "Another friend?"

She nodded.

His hazel eyes danced. "A pickpocket? A singing teacher who used to smuggle brandy out of Napoleon's France?"

"No. He is quite respectable. Except…"

"Yes?" He was smiling. "Except?"

Emily gave him a look. "He has a sad habit of designing his own banknotes."

Emily's brand-new husband dissolved in laughter as he pulled her close.

About the Author

Jane Ashford discovered Georgette Heyer in junior high school and was captivated by the glittering world and witty language of Regency England. That delight was part of what led her to study English literature and travel widely in Britain and Europe. She has written historical and contemporary romances, and her books have been published in Sweden, Italy, England, Denmark, France, Russia, Latvia, the Czech Republic, and Spain, as well as the United States. Jane has been nominated for a Career Achievement Award by *RT Book Reviews*. She lives in Los Angeles.

Heir to the Duke

Book 1 in Jane Ashford's brand-new Regency series,
The Duke's Sons, available January 2016 from
Sourcebooks Casablanca.